The Stan Turner Mysteries

Book I - *Undaunted*

White Supremacists, a serial killer, love, murder and the Marines. This is a gripping tale of fate out of control! *Rapport Magazine.*

A sexy, steamy thriller. *Joshua Emmons*

I thoroughly enjoyed *Undaunted* and expect to see your name on a future best seller list. *Parris Afton Bonds, author of 31 romance novels..*

Book II - *Brash Endeavor*

...fabulous-a real page turner. I didn't want it to end!" *Allison Robson, CBS Affiliate, KLBK TV, Ch 13*

***Manchee* spins a good yarn, and Stan Turner is a believable, likable character that I plan to read again and again**. *Chris Rogers, author of Bitch Factor and Rage Factor*

***William Manchee* may be Dallas' answer to John Grisham.** *Dallas Observer*

Visit author **William Manchee** at his website
www.billmanchee.com

SECOND CHAIR

Second Chair

A Stan Turner Mystery

Book III

by

WILLIAM MANCHEE

Top Publications, Ltd. Co.
Dallas, Texas

Second Chair
A Stan Turner Mystery

A Top Publications Paperback

First Edition

Top Publications, Ltd. Co.
12221 Merit Drive, Suite 750
Dallas, Texas 75251

All Rights Reserved
Copyright 2000
William Manchee

ISBN#: 0-9666366-9-4
Library of Congress # 00-130193

No part of this book may be published or utilized in any form or by any means, electronic or mechanical, including photocopying, recording or information storage and retrieval systems without the express written permission of the publisher.

The characters and events in this novel are fictional and created out of the imagination of the author. Certain real locations and institutions are mentioned, but the characters and events depicted are entirely fictional.

Printed in the United States of America

To my son and partner,

James J. Manchee

Contents

Prologue

It was the third time for me. The second time in two months. You'd think I was a hardened criminal, a fugitive from the law or something. As I drove toward Sherman and past McKinney, I daydreamed of just driving right on through—into Oklahoma, through Missouri and all the way to Canada. I chuckled. Wouldn't that give the press something to write about?

Then I took a deep breath trying to muster a little courage. I could get through this. A little jail time is no big deal. No, big deal except everybody would be watching as I was taken into custody. My wife, my children, my parents all of the people I love and care about would be watching my humiliation before the entire nation.

As we approached the Sheriff's office I could see the big crowd of reporters gathered to watch my surrender. Slowing down to a crawl to avoid accidentally killing one of them, I eased into a parking space that had been reserved for me. The Sheriff and two deputies were there to accept my surrender. One of the deputies opened the door. As I got out the cameras started flashing and the questions poured out.

"How do you feel this morning, Mr. Turner?" a reporter asked.

"As well as to be expected," I replied.

"Do you think the judge was too harsh with you?" a second reporter said.

I shrugged. The Sheriff took my arm and pulled me toward the door. He said, "Alright, clear a path. No more questions. He and his deputies pushed the reporters aside as we made our way inside. Once inside the Sheriff said,"Well, Stan before we book you and take you to your cell, there is someone here to see you."

"Really," I said quite surprised I would already have a visitor.

They escorted me into a small interrogation room where a woman was seated. When she turned and smiled at me I immediately recognized her. She got up and came over to me. We embraced.

"Mrs. Stone," I said laughing. "What in the world are you doing here?"

She smiled. "I've been hearing a lot about you Stan. My God, can't you stay out of trouble? My editor wanted to get your story. He figured it was only appropriate that I come."

I shook my head. "Well, I'm afraid you can't bail me out of this one, Mrs. Stone. I went and pissed off the judge and now I'm in here for God knows how long."

She nodded. "Well, I wish I could do something, I really do. But anyway, I talked the Sheriff into this interview. I hope you don't mind."

"No, I'm not anxious to go to my cell."

"Has anyone got your story yet?"

"No, I've been a little too busy to talk to reporters, but now I've got lots of time."

"Good, then I'd really like to get the inside scoop on all the bizarre things that have been going on with you lately. Can I have the story?"

"You don't even have to ask. You know you're the first person I'd give it to."

"Well then, lets get some coffee and you can start by enlightening me as to why the Sheriff has furnished your cell with a refrigerator full of beer, a TV and a Lazyboy recliner!"

A sudden rush of relief came over me. Tears welled up in my eyes. "My God, did he really go and do all that?"

Chapter One
Ice Storm

A wicked howling sound came from the front of the house. An early December Norther had just blown in and the wind blowing underneath the door sounded like a pack of wolves had gathered on the porch. Rebekah looked up and shook her head. She was putting the finishing touches on the dining room table in preparation for an expected throng of a hundred or so clients and friends who had been invited for our first office Christmas Party.

Marketing, I had been told, was the key to a successful law practice. It was important to stay in touch with your clients, to wine and dine them so they wouldn't forget you when they got rear-ended or someone sued them. Rebekah wasn't crazy about the idea of having an annual Christmas party, but I convinced her it was a great way to solidify the client's allegiance to the firm. I even suggested it might be fun. She said it might be fun for me, but not for her since she had to arrange the whole affair. She reminded me it would be particularly difficult for her since we didn't have a large budget to work with and she'd have to do much of the work herself.

At ten minutes to eight I went out on the front porch to see how bad the weather was getting. I shivered as the cold wind pelted my face. A light mist was falling and icicles were forming on the trees and bushes in front of the house. As I proudly gazed at the colorful display of lights that adorned the house, I thought back to when my father used to take the family to Beverly Hills every year to see the elaborate decorations of some of the Hollywood Stars of that era. It was something I looked forward to and how I had become a decoration addict.

The cold wind finally drove me back into the house. I went directly to the fireplace to warm up. Staring into the flickering flames I was in a momentary trance when Rebekah came up from behind and put her arms around me. I turned around and we embraced. She was wearing a red knit Christmas dress that she had painstakingly procured several weeks earlier. Looking as sexy as ever, she looked up at me with her big brown eyes.

"I hope the lights don't go out during our party." she said.

Our home was equipped with the latest safety device to prevent electrocution. I'm not sure exactly how it worked, but whenever it rained and we had the Christmas lights on, the circuit breaker would blow. Needless to say it was very annoying.

"Well, so far so good. Maybe we'll get lucky."

The door bell rang and Rebekah rushed to answer it. It was Tex and his wife, Toni. He was a short, robust man in his late fifties. Tex was one of my most cherished contacts. A fellow agent at Cosmopolitan Life, Tex Weller had referred me dozens of clients over the past two years. He was a rambunctious character who always cheered me up.

"Wonderful night for a party," Tex said as they stepped inside and wiped their feet. "The roads are terrible."

A blast of cold air sent a shiver through me. I quickly closed the door. "No ice, I hope."

"No, not yet, but the bridges and overpasses are supposed to ice over tonight."

"Wouldn't you know this would happen on the night of our party," Rebekah said shaking her head in disgust. She took their coats and went off toward the bedroom. Tex shook his head. "Well...I can't believe you've been practicing law nearly two years now, Stan. It just seems like yesterday you were in the bullpen selling insurance." The mention of selling insurance made me shudder. The "bullpen" was the large room that housed the 24 debit agents who serviced the Dallas region. Each agent had a desk, a chair and a telephone from which to operate. The company didn't want the agents to get too comfortable since they were supposed to be out beating the bushes for new insureds. It was a time in my life I wanted to forget. "It seems like an eternity to me. So much has happened these past two years."

"Yeah, you *have* had your hands full, haven't you?" Tex laughed.

"Just slightly," I said thinking back to how close we had come to losing everything. In fact, it was a miracle that we were having this party at all. A miracle indeed that I was still practicing law after that first tumultuous year. Starting with nothing and barely surviving financially we hadn't had the wherewithal to buy a big fancy house. That was another reason Rebekah was against the party. She was a little embarrassed at our modest abode, but I had assured her people would understand and wouldn't hold it against us.

Rebekah alternated from greeting newly arrived guests to supervising the maid and bartender we had hired for the evening. I was mingling with my clients and friends trying to make sure everyone was having a good time. After awhile I decided it was time to address the gathering and propose a toast. I alerted the bartender to start passing out the champagne.

"Ladies and Gentleman," I said as I began tapping my fork on the champagne glass. "I'd like to say a few words and propose a toast."

It took awhile but the noise from the crowd finally subsided enough for me to speak. "I just wanted to thank all of you for coming tonight. I apologize for the bad weather. This isn't what I ordered."

Somebody said, "You don't have much clout upstairs, do you?"

"I guess not," I laughed. "Anyway, one reason Rebekah and I decided to throw this party was to give us an opportunity to thank each and every one of you for your support over these last two years. As you know we've been through some tough times but with your encouragement and prayers we've managed to survive. In fact, this last year has been great. As you know we moved to a new location on Central Expressway and I was lucky enough to find a wonderful secretary, Jodie Marshall."

Jodie stood up, smiled and nodded to the crowd. "Let me just say it is so great to come to work every morning and smell coffee brewing." We all laughed. "Anyway, I think it's time to propose a toast." I lifted my glass, smiled and said, "To all my wonderful clients and friends, may all of you have a Merry Christmas and a Happy New Year."

"Here, here," someone said.

"Before I let you go, there will be some carolers coming by later on to entertain you, so relax, eat and drink all you want and have a good time. Thanks again for coming."

After consuming the rest of my champagne I went and got a plate full of food. I figured I'd better eat something before all the booze I'd been drinking got the best of me. As I was eating my niece, Alice, approached me. An attractive brunette, sharp as a pick, she was a clone of her mother.

"Hi, Uncle Stan," she said. "Great party."

"I'm glad you could come. Where's your mother?"

"She wasn't feeling well. She said to tell you she was sorry she couldn't make it."

"Oh, that's too bad," I said.

"So where did you hide my cousins tonight?" Alice asked.

"They're with Rebekah's mom. I didn't figure they could sleep with all the noise. Besides, Rebekah didn't need any distractions."

"I guess not."

"So how's school?" I asked. Alice was attending ASU, a small but prestigious liberal arts college in Sherman, Texas. She was majoring in education hoping to become a grammar school teacher.

"Not too bad, I guess. Once I get through finals and have a little time off."

The doorbell interrupted our conversation. Rebekah opened the door and Bobby Wiggins stepped in with his wife, Marleen, at his heals. He let out a big "HO HO HO, it's Santa Claus." Everyone turned and smiled at the two familiar faces. I excused myself to greet them.

Bobby Wiggins, a local CPA, was one of my best friends. Although he was not Santa Claus, he had a heart as big as old St. Nick's and everybody loved him. I had met him at an estate planning seminar a year earlier and was amazed when he told me about all the charitable activities in which he was involved. He put me to shame as I found little time to do anything but work.

"Hi, Bobby. . . . Marleen. Glad you could make it," I said.

"Wouldn't of missed it for the world," he said as he surveyed the crowded room. "Look at all these people. I didn't think you had this many clients."

"Well, they're not all clients. Some are family and friends."

"I just hope they didn't drink up all the good liquor."

I laughed. "No, I don't think so. You know where the bar is. Help yourself."

As Bobby and Marleen headed for the bar, a parade of carolers filed in and formed a half circle in front of the fireplace. They began to sing and before long many in the crowd had joined in. While everyone was being entertained I succumbed to the lure of the luscious deserts Rebekah had prepared. I loaded my plate with Christmas cookies, tarts, strawberry bread and fudge. I heard laughter in the den so I headed that way to see what was happening. Bobby Wiggins was seated in a captain's chair with a mutual client, a stripper named Joanna Winburn, sitting in his lap. He was pretending to be Santa Claus and Joanna was telling him what she wanted for Christmas. It was an amusing sight but not one I thought Marleen would appreciate. I scanned the room and was relieved that she wasn't watching.

Several other women were lined up to tell the would-be Santa what they wanted for Christmas too. I hadn't told Rebekah about Joanna as it would have upset her to no end. I got the feeling Bobby hadn't told Marleen about our mutual client either. Later on, when the women had left, I went to see if Bobby was having a good time.

"You're a popular guy," I said.

"Yes, it seems so. You know woman, they love a man who can make their dreams come true," he said shaking his head. He had that dreamy look in his eyes that women loved. "If only I *were* Santa Claus. Think of the possibilities."

"Think of the mayhem had Marleen seen you with a stripper in your lap. What were you thinking? You better slow down on the booze. It was a good thing she was occupied with the carolers."

Bobby raised his eyebrows. "Ah, yes. Thanks for providing the diversion."

"No problem." I said shaking my head and smiling. "Now behave yourself."

"I will."

As I turned to leave Bobby put his hand on my shoulder. I looked back at him. His demeanor had changed. He looked worried.

"What?" I said.

"I need to talk to you about something."

"Sure, you want to go somewhere private?"

He shook his head. "No. No. Not now. I'll call you Monday and set up an appointment."

"You sure, I don't mind taking a minute now."

"No, you've got guests. We'll do it later."

As we were talking Marleen walked up with a fresh drink for Bobby. We talked a minute longer and then I excused myself to go mingle with the other guests. About twenty minutes later I was talking to Tex when there was a loud crackling sound and the lights on one side of the house went out. The singing came to an abrupt halt and people began talking excitedly.

"Oh, God," I said. "Not again."

"Didn't you pay your light bill?" Tex joked.

I laughed. "I don't know, maybe not."

In the nightstand by my bed I kept a flashlight so I immediately went there to retrieve it. With the flashlight in hand I headed for the garage to check the circuit breakers. Rebekah had already located several candles and was placing them strategically throughout the darkened portion of the house. The garage was pitch black. With the flashlight I found the circuit breaker box. One of the switches had been thrown but not the usual one. That surprised me. I flipped it and the lights came back on to cheers and laughter. Just as I was about to close the box I heard a scream in the house.

Quickly I ran back inside, through the kitchen and into the dining room where I believed the sound had emanated. A crowd of people was standing at the front door which was wide open. After squeezing through to the front of the crowd I was stunned by the sight of Bobby flat on his back in the flowerbed with Marleen slapping his cheeks frantically trying to get him to wake up. He was lying on a string of broken Christmas lights in a puddle of water. The pungent odor of burnt flesh hung in the air.

"Oh my, God!" I said and ran over to her. "What happened?"

"He slipped on the ice and fell into the bushes! You've got to do something, Stan."

Bobby's face was blue and he wasn't breathing. "Rebekah!" I yelled. She was a nurse, she'd know what to do.

Rebekah came running out the door and gasped at the sight of Bobby lying lifeless on the icy ground. Without hesitating she started barking orders. "Stand clear, get some blankets, I'll need a pillow, . . . somebody call an ambulance."

She immediately began trying to revive him, pressing firmly on his chest trying to get his heart to beat, breathing into his mouth to force air into his lungs. But there was no response.

The wailing sound of an ambulance could be heard from the fire station less than a mile away. Rebekah kept pounding on his chest and breathing into his mouth. We all stood by and watched, praying for a miracle. The sirens grew louder and louder and finally an ambulance made its turn into the cul de sac. A fire truck followed closely behind.

The paramedics attempted unsuccessfully to revive Bobby on the spot. Getting no response they loaded him on a stretcher and put him in the ambulance. Marleen climbed in and the ambulance rushed off to the hospital.

Several of the firemen were milling around in front of the house talking to our guests. By this time Rebekah had latched onto my arm and was crying. I put my arm around her and tried to comfort her but there was little I could say. One of the firemen approached us.

"Is this your home?" he said.

"Yes, we were just having a Christmas Party," I said. "I can't believe this happened."

"What exactly *did* happen?"

After telling him everything we knew he went back to his truck and called in on his radio. In a few minutes a police car and a fire investigator arrived. We repeated our story to them and then called the hospital to see if there was any word on Bobby. They didn't have any information but Tex called a few minutes later.

"He didn't make it," Tex said. "I followed the ambulance to the hospital and waited in the emergency room. They tried like hell to revive him but it was no use."

"Oh God, I can't believe this," I said. "Poor Bobby. Why did this have to happen?"

"I don't know, it doesn't make a whole lot of sense, does it?"

"I'll never put up Christmas lights again. I never dreamed something like this could happen."

Rebekah was crying incessantly so I took her into the bedroom where she could lie down. After getting her settled I went back into the den. Most of our guests had left by that time but a few of them had stayed to see if we needed anything. One of them was General Burton.

"Stan, you've got the worst luck of any man I know. This is bizarre."

"I know. I'm just sick. Poor Rebekah worked so hard to make this party a success and look what happened."

The door opened and the fire inspector walked in followed by a police detective named Paul Delacroix. They conferred a few moments and then the investigator approached us. The detective went back outside.

"Mr. Turner," the investigator said.

"Yes."

"The Coroner's office has just completed a preliminary inspection of the body. It appears that Mr. Wiggins died of a massive coronary."

"He wasn't electrocuted?"

"No, the circuit breaker prevented that."

"Huh. . . . A coronary? I didn't know he had heart problems." I said.

"He didn't but apparently the trauma of the fall induced the heart attack."

"Oh Jesus," I said. "What a horrible thing to happen."

"I notice there isn't any sand on the sidewalk?"

"Sand?"

"Yes, sand or rock salt."

"No, I didn't realize it had iced over. It never occurred to me. . . . Oh, God. I feel so terrible."

Terrible wasn't the half of it. My stomach felt like I'd ridden a roller coaster one too many times. The door opened and Detective Delacroix came back in and walked over to us.

"Well, we've done all we can here. We've interviewed most of your guests. You better call your insurance agent tomorrow," he said. "I'm sure they'll be a claim."

"How's that?" General Burton asked.

"Negligence. Mr. Turner had all these guests here and he never even bothered to sand his walkway. Some hot shot attorney's gonna have a field day with this one."

He was right. I hadn't anticipated an ice storm. They were rare in Texas. We had no sand to put down over the ice or salt crystals to melt it off. I just never gave it any thought.

"I just didn't realize the walkway had iced over. Damn it!"

Detective Delacroix shrugged and walked away. Fortunately, I did have insurance. My homeowners policy plus a million dollar general liability policy at the office. So if a judge or jury tried to blame me for Bobby's death the insurance company would have to defend me. Then I wondered, had I paid the premiums? The homeowners policy wasn't a problem. The mortgage company paid that bill every year. The general liability policy was another story. I tried to rack my brain to remember. It seemed eons since I had paid the bill last.

The next morning I went to the office early and pulled the insurance file. The policy in the file was expired but that didn't necessarily mean anything. It should have automatically renewed. Sometimes new policies don't come in for weeks after their issue date. I searched through the checkbook but found nothing to North Texas Insurance Agency within the last year. At 9 o'clock I called their offices. A lady put me on hold as she went to fetch my file.

"I'm sorry Mr. Turner but that policy has lapsed."

"Lapsed! But I don't remember getting a premium statement."

"Well I have a copy of the certified letter advising you of the policy's termination. . . . Oh, my word."

"What?"

"No one picked up the certified mail. You should always pickup your certified mail."

"I always do. . . . Oh, shit. You don't have my new address, do you?"

"Well, not if you didn't give it to us."

Chapter Two
Gut Feeling
Three month later

The law is a jealous mistress. I heard that a lot in law school but I didn't fully appreciate what it meant until I started my own law practice. It seemed every week I was working a little harder and, even though I was getting more efficient all the time, there were never enough hours in the day to get done all that I felt needed to be accomplished.

Even if it were eight or nine o'clock, I never felt good about going home. There was always that nagging feeling that I should complete one more task before I left. Often times the only way I could drag myself away from the office was to fill my briefcase full of files with the intention of working on them at home. I thought by being a sole practitioner I could set my own hours and have a life away from the office. Boy was I wrong about that. Responsibility is a merciless task master.

Rebekah hated me to work at home and would try diligently to keep me from opening my briefcase. Between her and four attention-craving children she was usually successful. As the night wore on I would usually forget about work as I became absorbed in my second job as a husband and a father.

It was nearly eight-thirty when I arrived home from the

office. Rebekah was in the family room watching TV. She had learned to accept the fact that I was a workaholic but she made it abundantly clear she didn't like it.

"Well, who are you? I don't recognize you," she said.

"Very funny."

"What in the hell have you been doing? Do you have a girlfriend or something? I never see you anymore."

"Hey, I had a tough day. Give me a break. I had to get ready for a hearing first thing tomorrow morning. Some asshole attorney served me with a motion to dissolve a writ of garnishment at 4:55 p.m. I've got a hearing on it at 9:00 a.m. tomorrow. Can you believe that shit?"

"Can they do that?"

"They're supposed to give me three days notice, but some attorneys are so damn arrogant they don't give a shit about ethics, let alone common decency."

Marcia came running into the family room. Her big brown eyes lit up when she saw me.

"Daddy!"

"Hi, honey."

She ran over and jumped into my lap. I smiled and gave her a hug. I had always wanted a daughter but after our third son was born in 1975 Rebekah and I almost gave up. As I stroked her long silky black hair, I thanked God we hadn't.

"What did you do today, baby doll?" I asked.

"I colored and played with my dolls."

Rebekah gave Marcia a stern look and said, "What else did you do, little girl?"

Marcia looked at her mother and then lowered her head. "Nothing," she said.

"Uh huh," Rebekah said. "I found her playing with Mark's train set."

"Really. Hmm," I said. "You know you're not supposed to do that. You're too young to be playing with something electrical. It's very dangerous."

The thought of another accident in our home was horrifying. Within days of Bobby's death we had purchased every safety gadget we could find to protect our children from the numerous hazards existing around the house. We spent hours instructing them on each of these perils and how to deal with any emergency that might arise. We weren't about to have another death at the Turner house.

"Not to mention the train doesn't belong to her," Rebekah said.

"I'm sorry," she said as she slid off my lap and ran off. I picked up the newspaper and began reading it. Rebekah looked at me and shook her head.

"Well, do you want to eat or did your girlfriend feed you?"

I dropped the newspaper, smiled and replied, "Yes, I'm starving. My girlfriend doesn't cook."

"Yeah, she doesn't wash clothes either. Too bad, I could use the help," Rebekah said. She got up and walked into the kitchen. I read a few minutes and then joined her. Just as I sat down at the table the telephone rang. Rebekah took a deep breath and then reluctantly got up and answered it. It was for me. She frowned, handed me the phone and then went back to warming up my dinner.

"Mr. Turner. This is Tom Winters. I was referred to you by your niece, Alice. My daughter and her are neighbors up at ASU."

"Oh, really? What can I do for you?"

"It's my daughter, she . . . she . . . well, it's a long story, but she's in serious trouble."

"What happened?"

"I don't know where to start. . . . Oh, God, I can't believe this is happening."

"Just take it slow. Start from the beginning."

"I got a call last night, after midnight. It was my daughter's boyfriend, Greg. He told me Sarah was in the hospital."

"Sarah's your daughter?"

"Right."

"Okay, what happened to her?"

"They say she had a baby. I didn't even know she was pregnant for godsakes."

"Really?"

"But that's not the problem."

"Oh."

"No, they found a baby in a dumpster a mile or so from her apartment. They say it belonged to Sarah. I'm afraid they're going to arrest her."

A chill radiated down my spine. I picked up the base of the phone, put it on the kitchen table and sat down.

"Gee, Mr. Winters, I'm so sorry. What a jolt that must of been."

"You don't know what we've been going through."

"I can imagine. So what does Sarah have to say about this?"

"She doesn't remember anything."

"Really? Huh. Well, who claims she was the mother?"

"Dr. Estaban, the doctor from the emergency room."

"Do you have any reason to doubt him?"

"No. He wouldn't have any reason to lie. But I believe my daughter. I really don't think she remembers what happened. She must have amnesia or something."

"This is pretty bizarre," I said.

"I know it's going to take a while to sort this out, but right now I'm worried about the police trying to talk to her without an attorney. You know how they can intimidate people and get them to admit to just about anything."

"You're right, she does need a good criminal attorney.

Unfortunately, I don't practice criminal law."
"You don't? I don't understand. Alice has told us such wonderful stories about you. She said you've already solved several murders."
"Well, that was an aberration, I'm afraid. I'll be honest with you. I don't like criminal law much and I barely passed the criminal law courses I took in law school. I'm a civil attorney."
"I just don't want my daughter to go to jail."
"I don't either. You need an experienced criminal lawyer. I'd recommend Harry Hertel. He was my criminal procedure professor at SMU. He has a private practice. All he does is criminal cases and he's really good at it, I understand."
"I don't want him, I want you."
"But why? I told you I'm not a criminal attorney. I've never actually tried a criminal case."
"It's just a feeling. It's not easy to explain. You see most of my life I've been a worthless drunk wandering from city to city wallowing in my own self pity. Several years ago I found Christ and my life took a drastic turn for the better. I've learned now to trust God and to look for his guidance. When this nightmare first began your niece suggested I call you. She told me all about you and all the problems you've overcome. You're a street fighter, you don't give up and that's the kind of lawyer I need for Sarah."
"A street fighter?"
"Yeah. You'll do whatever it takes to win. Anyway, the more she talked about you the more I knew you were the attorney Sarah needed. I believe the Lord has guided me to you, Mr. Turner."
"Well, I'm flattered, Mr. Winters, but I'm afraid Alice is prejudiced being my niece and everything. I'm not a miracle worker. Sarah's defense will not be easy. She needs a seasoned criminal attorney if she's to have any chance of getting acquitted."

"Will you at least think about it? I'd really like you to talk to her before you make a definite decision."

I took a deep breath. Why was it so difficult for people to understand English? Obviously I wasn't the right person to handle this case yet there was apparently nothing I could say to convince Tom Winters of that fact. Could it be true that the Lord had directed Mr. Winters to me? Somehow I doubted that, but what if it were true? Perhaps I shouldn't act so hastily. It wouldn't hurt to talk to Sarah.

"Well, I can't promise you anything, but I'll talk to your daughter. If she can convince me she's innocent then I might consider taking the case, if you'll let Snake be second chair."

"Snake?"

"Yeah, that's Harry's nickname, Harry Hertel. Some guys at the DA's office started calling him Snake and after awhile the name stuck. I've never actually seen him try a case but from what I understand, he's the best."

"Okay, that's fine. Can you come up right away? The cops have been trying to get in to question Sarah all day. So far the doctor has protected her but I'm afraid tomorrow she'll have to talk to them."

"What hospital is she in?"

"Bright Methodist in Sherman."

"Just tell her not to say anything to the police. She doesn't have to talk to them. I'll try to get up there tomorrow."

"Oh, thank you Mr. Turner. You don't know how much better I feel. I just know you're the right attorney for Sarah."

"Well, I haven't taken the case yet, but even if I do; it sounds like we've got one hell of a battle on our hands."

"I know, but I still feel better."

"You won't feel so good when we start talking about fees."

"What do you think it will cost?"

"You'd be extremely lucky to walk away for $25,000. It'll

probably cost more than that. How much more depends on how complicated it gets and I have no way of predicting that."

"Jesus, that much," Tom said.

"Yes, I'm afraid so. Your daughter is in very serious trouble and if she's innocent we've got to do everything possible to prove it. Justice doesn't come cheap."

"I don't know exactly where I'll get that kind of money, but somehow I'll raise it. Don't you worry."

"Well think about it. She could get a court appointed attorney for nothing probably, since she's in school."

"I don't want that. I'll get the money."

"Alright, I'll drive up tomorrow afternoon and meet you at the hospital around three."

I hung up the phone, looked at Rebekah and said, "Did you hear that?"

"Well, I heard something about a baby being killed," Rebekah said.

"Yeah, this guy's daughter is suspected of killing her baby."

"Oh my God! Are you're going to defend her?"

"Well, I don't know yet."

"What if she did it?"

"What if she didn't do it?"

"I don't know, I don't like the idea of you representing a murderer."

"Wait a minute, what happened to the presumption of innocence?" I said. "This is America, remember?"

"I know, but she probably did it. Who else would do it?"

"I'm usually pretty good at reading people, so hopefully after I meet her I'll be able to tell if she's telling the truth or not."

"I don't know, honey, what if you're wrong? Can you imagine what people will think of you if it turns out she did it?"

"I don't care what people think. Anyway, I may not take the case. Who knows?"

The next morning I went to work at six since I was going to be in court all morning and had to go to Sherman in the afternoon. There were some things I had to handle that I felt just couldn't wait until the following day. When Jodie arrived fifteen minutes late she was shocked to see me already hard at work.

"Good morning," Jodie said. "I am sorry I'm late but Rodney was almost out of gas. We had to stop off at the filing station."

"Oh, no big deal. So how is Rodney these days?"

"A pain in the ass as usual."

"Typical male, huh?"

Jodie shook her head in disgust. "He just makes me so mad sometimes. I wish he'd grow up and act like a man instead of a teenager."

"He is a teenager," I noted.

"I know, but-"

"If you don't get along why don't you dump him? You're an attractive girl, I am sure you could find someone more mature without much trouble."

"Probably, but I've got this problem."

"What's that?'

"I love him."

"Oh, well then, I guess you better see if you can work out your problems."

"We'll work them out. We always do," Jodie said. "So what are you doing here so early?"

"I've got a nine o'clock hearing. Then I've got to go to Sherman this afternoon to talk to a client. So I thought I better get started early this morning."

"What hearing? There's nothing on your calendar."

"A delivery came in just after you left last night."

"Oh, you're kidding?"

"No, I wish I were."

"Do you need me to do anything for the hearing?"

"No, I stayed late last night to prepare for it. Rebekah wasn't too happy but I didn't have much choice."

"So why do you have to go to Sherman?"

"To talk to a potential client. A young girl who is about to be charged with murdering her baby."

"What?!"

"They found the baby in a dumpster a mile or so from her apartment."

"Oh my God. Why didn't she just get an abortion?"

"I don't know, but that's a good question. I'll ask her that this afternoon."

"Do you need some coffee?"

"Yes, I could use a cup. Thank you."

Jodie nodded and left the room. She was only nineteen years old and I had taken a chance in hiring her without any experience. After practicing law a year without a secretary I finally decided to take the plunge and hire one. Unfortunately experienced legal secretaries were demanding far more than I could afford to pay so I decided to look for talent and potential rather than experience. Jodie was smart, ambitious and wanted someday to be a paralegal. She had a great attitude and didn't cringe at the meager salary I was offering. She had turned out to be an excellent secretary and I felt fortunate to have her around. She soon returned with the coffee and sat down.

"How are you going to defend her?"

"Defend who?"

"The baby killer."

"Oh, Sarah Winters."

"Is that her name?"

"Yeah, I don't know yet. I'm not sure I'll even take the case. I've got to find out more about what happened before I decide. If I do take it, I thought I'd get Snake to help me."

"Snake?"

"Harry Hertel, my criminal law professor. I've told you about him."

She nodded. "Right. Why do you need him?"

"Just an insurance policy in case I get over my head."

"You've never worked with him before, have you?"

"No, not really," I said.

"I don't know if I would want to work with a guy named Snake."

"That's a good point, but as long as he's on my side it should be okay."

"Man who plays with snakes may get bit," Jodie said.

I laughed. "Where did you hear that?"

"I think it was from a fortune cookie I got one time."

I shook my head. "Oh well, thank you for that little bit of wisdom. I'll be careful."

"Have you called him yet?"

Before I could answer her the phone rang. Jodie picked it up and had a brief conversation with the caller.

"That was Rebekah. She said you needed to turn on Channel 12. There's a report on your client coming up."

"Possible client," I said. "Let's go to the conference room and see what Channel 12 has to say about Sarah." Once in the conference room, Jodie turned on the television set and we waited for the commercial to end.

"This is Beverly Blake with a special Channel 12 Report. Everyday we read about atrocities that are occurring all over the globe. Whether it's terrorism in the middle east, religious warfare in Ireland, mass murders in Cambodia or guerilla warfare in Latin America we are often outraged by the heinous acts that are committed by our fellow human beings in distant lands. Well tonight I'm sad to report that right here in Sherman, Texas we have our own local atrocities.

"Police early this morning found a newborn girl in a

grocery store dumpster and the charred remains of a second child in a shallow grave near Baker Road in southeast Sherman. The first baby girl was wrapped in a plastic garbage bag and discarded with common trash. The killer of the other infant apparently tried unsuccessfully to burn the child to get rid of its remains but ended up burying it in a wooded area. The body was found when local dogs were attracted to the scent of the decaying body. There is no apparent connection between the murders other than the common motive behind the killings, the resolution an untimely pregnancy.

"The alleged mother of the first child, Sarah Winters, claims she has no memory of the delivery. Doctors at Bright Methodist Hospital who examined Miss Winters early this morning advised the media today that she had definitely delivered a child within the last 24 hours. Blood tests have been ordered to determine if Sarah Winters is indeed the mother of the child. Doctors at the hospital say that the baby girl was born premature and weighed only about three pounds. They estimate that the mother was about eight months along when she delivered the baby Tuesday night.

"Lt. Bernie Meadows of the Sherman Police, when asked if Sarah Winters was a suspect in the killing, stated that she headed the list of several suspects. He would not comment on when an arrest would be made or if he the DA was planning to take the case to the Grand Jury.

"Police have no suspects in the death of the second baby but are hopeful they will get some clues when the autopsy is finished later today. Anyone who might have seen anything unusual in the last twenty-four hours in the Baker Street area are urged to contact police.

"Lt. Meadows told me privately that he was appalled by these ruthless murders. He vowed not to rest until the killers have been brought to justice.

"We'll have more on these two investigations on the

noon news later today. For Channel 12 News this is Beverly Blake reporting."

Jodie shut off the TV and looked at me. She shuddered. "I can't believe somebody tried to incinerate their child."

"I'm sure glad I'm not defending that mother," I said.

"I can't believe you're considering defending Sarah Winters. Don't you think she must be guilty?"

"Well, she doesn't remember anything. That's not good."

"How could she not remember anything?" Jodie asked.

"Post traumatic amnesia. It's not unusual at all."

Jodie shook her head. "Still, who else could have done it?

"Well, I don't know but the story said there were other suspects, right?"

"Right. I wonder why she didn't call an ambulance and go to the hospital."

"I don't know. She was hiding her pregnancy from her parents apparently. I'm sure that was part of the problem. She hadn't seen a doctor so she may not have known the symptoms of labor."

"I don't buy that," Jodie said.

"I know, but there must be some explanation. I doubt Sarah's a complete idiot. She must of had a plan to deal with the situation. I just hope she'll tell me what it was."

That afternoon I drove up Highway 75 to Sherman. At the information desk at Bright Methodist Hospital I said, "I'm here to see Sarah Winters, I'm supposed to meet with her and her father, Tom Winters."

"Oh yes, he's in the waiting room. Just go down the hall, it's the last door on the right."

I went down the hall and entered the waiting room. A tall, dark headed man got up immediately and extended his hand.

"You must be Stan Turner."

"Yes, and you must be Tom Winters."

"Right, I want to thank you for driving up here to see Sarah."

"No problem."

Tom pointed to Joyce and said, "This is my wife, Joyce, and Sarah's stepmother."

"Nice to meet you. How is Sarah doing today?" I asked.

"She seems fine, however, she won't talk about the baby. She still doesn't remember anything."

"Have the police tried to talk to her?"

"Yes, and we did what you said. We told them she wouldn't talk to them without her attorney present."

"Good, can I go see her now?"

"Yes, I told her you would be in to see her at 1:30," Tom said.

"Okay, I'm ready."

Stan, Joyce and Tom got up and walked down the hallway to Sarah's room. They knocked on the door several times. Getting no response, they entered. Sarah was staring out the window.

"Sarah," Tom said. "Stan Turner, the attorney I told you about, is here to see you."

Sarah looked over at me without changing her somber expression. She had a pretty face with dark brown cautious eyes. Her dirty blond hair had lost most of its curl and a lock hung down partially covering one eye. Her face was a little pudgy like you often see with pregnant women and her stomach was still swollen from the recent childbirth.

"Hi, Miss Winters. How are you feeling?" I asked.

Sarah replied, "Okay."

"I understand you've had a tough couple of days. I'm very sorry to hear about your baby.

She turned toward the window and began to stare again.

"I know it must be very difficult to talk about this, but it's important that I know everything that happened the other night. The District Attorney may try to bring charges against you because of the death of your child. If he does, I need to know what happened so I can defend you.

Sarah continued to stare out the window showing no emotion. I looked at Tom and Joyce and said, "Why don't you let Sarah and me talk alone. Whatever she tells me is protected by the attorney-client privilege but if you're there it might be waived."

"Sure," Tom said. "Come on Joyce, let's go back to the waiting room."

After Tom and Joyce were gone, I tried again to strike up a conversation.

"So what's your major here as ASU?"

Sarah turned and looked at me intently. Then she scanned the room. I guess she wanted to be sure no one was listening.

"Journalism."

"Oh really, that sounds pretty interesting," I said. "Do you want to be a reporter?"

"I'd like to get into television. I'm not sure exactly what I want to do yet, but I think that would a good career."

"How did you get interested in television?"

"My dad took me to the NBC studios in LA one time. It was really a cool place. We got to watch several shows being taped. Ever since that time I've wanted to go into television."

"I see. Well, the way the television industry is growing you shouldn't have any problem finding a job."

"I hope not."

"I understand you have a boyfriend?"

"Yes, Greg Peterson. He lives in Richardson."

"How did you and Greg meet?"

"Mutual friends introduced us."

"Oh, I see. Are you serious?"

"We like each other a lot."

"It must be tough with Greg in Richardson and you up here in Sherman."

"Uh huh, but we call each other almost every day. On the weekend Greg usually comes up and stays with me in my apartment."

"You understand that everything you tell me is confidential, don't you?"

"Uh huh."

"I know you'd rather not talk about it, but I've got to find out what happened Tuesday night. Can we talk about that?"

"You can't tell anyone what I tell you, right, not even my dad and stepmother?"

"No, everything you tell me is strictly confidential."

"Well, I don't remember very much, I wish I did. I'll tell you what I do remember, but I don't think it will help."

"That's okay, just tell me what you know."

"Where should I start?"

"Your Dad tells me you didn't tell them you were pregnant. Is that true?"

"Yes."

"Why didn't you want them to know?"

She sighed. "My stepmother would have gone ballistic. I just didn't want to deal with that. I thought I'd have the baby and then give it up for adoption without anyone knowing that I had even been pregnant."

"That would have been a little difficult to pull off don't you think? Don't your parents come to visit you?"

"No, they're too busy with Nathan."

"Nathan?"

"My step-brother. He's a big football jock at Arizona."

"I see. What about your mother? Do you ever see her?"

"My Mom died when I was a baby. I've had three

stepmothers since then and none of them have cared much about me."

Sarah's motherless life brought back the haunting memory of Rebekah's arrest and how close my own children came to losing their mother. "I'm sorry. . . . How did you find out you were pregnant?"

"I felt the baby kicking."

"You didn't go to a doctor?"

"My Dad is a Christian Scientist now. He doesn't believe in doctors. I'm not allowed to go to them, or learn about health or anything."

I shook my head. "Are you serious?"

"Yes, in high school whenever the class studied health all the Christian Scientists were excused."

"How long have you and Greg been together?"

"Four months now."

"The doctors say you were eight months pregnant when the baby was born, did you know that?"

"No, I wasn't sure when it was due."

"What were you planning to do when the baby came?" I asked.

"Deliver it myself."

"You're kidding?"

"No, women have been doing that for centuries. I have a book."

"You were going to do it by yourself?"

"Greg was gonna help."

"What happened? Why didn't you call him."

"I don't know. I didn't realize I was in labor. It was too early."

"But you said you didn't know when it was due?"

"Well, not exactly, but I had an idea."

I wondered if Sarah was telling me the truth. Her story seemed a little rehearsed. "So what happened?"

"I was feeling horrible. I thought I had eaten something bad. After Michelle left I went to sleep and that's all I remember."

"You don't remember the delivery?"

"No. I was sick, . . . but that's all I remember."

"So if you knew Greg for only four months he couldn't be the father, right?"

"Right."

"So who do you think was the father?"

"Ricky, I guess."

"Who is Ricky?"

"Richard Stein, he was my boyfriend before Greg."

"Is he the only other man you've had sex with in the last year?"

Sarah thought a moment."Uh huh."

"You're sure?" I said.

"Yes, that's all."

By this time an unsettled feeling had come over me. I had so many tough questions to ask Sarah but I knew if I wasn't very delicate and tactful she'd clam up on me.

"What made you end your relationship with Ricky?"

"He was into drugs and had a hot temper. One night he was stoned and beat me up."

"Is that right?"

"Uh huh."

"I don't suppose you reported it to the police, did you?"

"No. I didn't want anyone to know."

"Did you ever do drugs?"

"Once or twice, but nothing heavy."

"When's the last time you've been on any drugs?"

"I haven't taken any since Ricky left. I wouldn't know where to get them."

"Does Greg do drugs?"

"No, he's straight as an arrow. He even goes to church."

"You know, not too many people are going to believe that you can't remember delivering your baby. You understand it's kind of hard to swallow."

Sarah began to choke up. "I'm telling the truth. I don't remember anything! I wish I could remember something, believe me. Michelle shouldn't have taken me to the hospital, damn her! This whole thing has been a nightmare."

Sarah began to cry harder. I looked around awkwardly and then went over to her and put my arm around her.

"Okay, okay. Calm down. I don't think you killed her. I'm not sure why, but I believe you."

"I'm telling the truth, Mr. Turner. I don't remember anything."

"Okay, Don't worry, we'll get you through this somehow. I don't know how exactly, but we'll figure something out. Just don't cry. It will be alright."

Sarah looked up, then she put her arms around me and wept on my shoulder. After she had regained her composure I left and went back to the waiting room. Tom was sitting on the sofa waiting anxiously. Joyce was on the telephone talking to someone.

"Stan, how did it go?" Tom asked.

"Okay, I guess. She says she's sticking to her story that she doesn't remember anything. After talking with her I don't feel like she's the type who would murder her own child. But, I don't know. Just conveniently forgetting what happened is not going to hold water very long. If she does remember but doesn't want to admit it, we're going to have a tough time defending her. She's going to have to level with me. I need to know the truth. If she really doesn't remember, then we may never know what happened."

"She would never kill her own child. She's a wonderful girl, Stan. You've got to believe me," Tom said.

"Did she tell you why she didn't tell us she was

pregnant?" Joyce asked.

"I can't really go into anything she said."

"I understand. Will you take the case?" Tom asked.

I hesitated and then replied. "Well, I do believe she's innocent. I don't have any evidence to prove it, but my gut feeling tells me she is." I looked at Joyce and continued, "Judging from the look on your wife's face, you and I may be the only two people in North Texas who feel that way. Despite what the law says, there's going to be a presumption of guilt here, Mr. Winters. I'm sorry to tell you, but that's the way it's going to be."

"You didn't answer my question. Will you take the case?"

I hesitated again wanting so desperately to say no, no way would I touch this case. The words, however, wouldn't come out. I kept seeing Sarah's sad, desperate face. How could I refuse her pleas for help. A motherless child with a drunk of a father, how she had made it to college was a miracle in itself. She deserved a break.

"I suppose I will, I guess, if you still want me to after what I've told you. I hope she's telling the truth, though." *God, I hope she's telling the truth!*

"I understand you don't have a lot of experience, but you believe Sarah's innocent and that's what's important," Tom said.

"How much will it cost?" Joyce asked.

"A lot," I replied as I began to contemplate what kind of retainer I would need. With Snake involved I knew I'd have to get a substantial retainer or he wouldn't want to get involved. "This is going to be a pretty complicated case and there are a lot of unanswered questions. I'll only take on the case if you all are prepared to do whatever it takes to win. I hate to lose."

"That's what we want," Tom said.

"Good then you'll need to come by my office tomorrow

to sign a fee agreement and bring me a $10,000 retainer."

"You need $10,000 tomorrow?" Tom gasped.

"Yes, because it's easy to say you're committed to the cost of the lawsuit, but I can't pay my bills with commitment, my creditors only take cash."

"Okay, I'll see what I can do," Tom said.

"Good, I'll see you tomorrow then."

"Right."

I got up and walked out of the waiting room. As I started down the long corridor I realized I hadn't given Tom my card so he'd know where my office was located. Quickly I did an about face and walked back to the waiting room. As I approached, I heard voices arguing so I stopped at the door not wanting to intrude. I couldn't help but overhear the heated discussion.

"Where do you think you're going to find $10,000?" Joyce said. "We can't afford that kind of money to defend Sarah. Just let the state appoint her an attorney. We don't have any obligation to pay for one."

"No, the Lord led me to Mr. Turner for a reason. I know he's the right man to protect Sarah."

"I'm sure the attorneys in the public defender's office are quite competent. It's just plain stupid for us to spend our life savings and maybe go into debt to hire an attorney when Sarah could get one free."

"I'm not arguing with you," Tom said. I'm hiring Stan Turner whether you like it or not. Somehow we'll find the money to pay him. I'll go to the bank tomorrow and get a loan. We've just got to know the truth. God will help us through this somehow."

"This is so stupid. We could spend $50,000 on this trial. We're already paying a mint for Sarah to go to college."

"Okay, just shut up! Shut the hell up! I don't want to talk about it anymore. If it was Nate facing a murder charge you wouldn't mind coughing up fifty grand."

"That's different," Joyce replied.
Tom looked at Joyce. "How is it different?"
"Nate's got a future. He's going to the NFL. Someday he'll be a superstar."
"So, Sarah might end up being the damn President."
"Yeah right, Sarah has always been a loser, I mean she's got to be pretty damn sick to kill her own baby!"
Tom glared at Joyce. His face began to turn red with rage. "If you would have been a decent mother, you'd of taught her a few things about sex and being a woman so this wouldn't have happened!"
"Oh. Don't you dare blame this on me!" Joyce said as she began to cry.
Joyce and Tom's argument was becoming so loud the charge nurse had taken notice and was walking toward the waiting room. I decided it was time to make my exit. Jodie could call Tom and give him the office address in the morning.
A sudden rush of guilt overcame me as I walked down the corridor contemplating the argument I had inadvertently overheard. Ten thousand dollars was a lot of money and I knew from experience how difficult it was to fund a murder defense. Perhaps I shouldn't have insisted on such a big retainer. I knew if Snake hadn't of been involved I would have settled for a lot less. Sure, that would have been risky but I wouldn't have felt so much like a vulture feeding on my clients misfortune.

Chapter Three
Engaging Snake

On the way back to Dallas I couldn't help but think about poor Bobby Wiggins. Since the accident we hadn't heard a word from Marleen or anyone else. Rebekah and I had gone to the funeral but very little was said about the circumstances around his death. Maybe there wouldn't be a claim. After all, we hadn't done anything wrong. Then I remembered our last conversation. He told me he had some kind of problem. I made a mental note to talk to Marleen and see if she knew anything about the problem that Bobby was about to discuss with me. Now that Bobby was dead it may not have mattered, but it could still be something that needed attention. The least I could do was help Marleen tie up any loose ends.

It was nearly five o'clock when I pulled into the parking garage adjacent to my office building. When I walked into my office, Jodie was packing up to leave.

"Hey, you made it back," she said.

"Uh huh."

"So how did it go?"

"Pretty good. Sarah seems like a nice girl. She's had a tough life, but remarkably stable under the circumstances. I don't think she killed her baby."

"Really? If she didn't do it, who did?"

"I have no clue, but I intend to find out."

After sitting down at my desk I decided I'd better advise the Sherman police that I was representing Sarah so they wouldn't be harassing her and her parents. Tom had told me that Lt. Bernie Meadows was handling the investigation for the Sherman Police Department. I didn't know the number so I dialed information and got it. The dispatcher put me through to Lt. Meadows.

"Meadows," he said.

"Lt. Meadows, this is Stan Turner, I'm an attorney. I've just been retained by Sarah Winters to represent her in the investigation into the alleged death of her child."

"Oh, okay."

"You needn't bother trying to question her, I've advised her not to talk to anyone about the incident."

"That's okay, we've got all the evidence we need to lock her away for the rest of her life."

"It may appear that way, but she may well be innocent."

"You don't honestly believe that do you?"

"Yes, I believe it. I hope you plan to earn your pay and find the real killer."

Meadows laughed. "Don't you worry about me doing my job, I know who the killer is and she's going to pay for her crime."

"I may be associating Harry Hertel to help with the defense just for your information."

"Snake?"

"Right."

"Splendid," he said. "The District Attorney's office has assigned the case to Howard Hudson. I'll tell him you and Snake are handling the case. It'll make his day."

I didn't know how to take Hudson's remark. Did he know something about me or was the comment directed at Snake. A sinking feeling came over me as I realized I hadn't even

talked to Harry yet about helping me with the case. It was
obviously about time I took care of that minor detail. What if he
refused to help? Oh, God, if that happened I'd be trying a
murder case on my own. After dialing the number I waited. His
secretary answered and put me through.

"Stan, what's going on? I haven't heard from you for a
while."

"Yeah, it's been awhile. . . . Hey, I've been talking to a
potential criminal client about representation. It's a murder
case."

"Oh really, I didn't think you like criminal cases. As I
recall you were going to refer them all to me."

"I don't and I did try to refer it out to you but the client
really wants me to handle it."

"Really, what kind of case is it?"

"You heard of the girl who allegedly killed her baby up
in Sherman."

"Right, I saw something about it in the newspaper this
morning."

"Sarah Winters is her name. I've just been retained to
defend her."

"Hmm. Does she have a defense?"

"Yes, she claims she didn't do it and I believe her."

"Who does she say did it?"

I told him everything I knew.

"A memory loss isn't going to cut it," Snake said. "You
should probably just plead her out. She probably won't get
much jail time."

"No, she's innocent. I couldn't do that."

"What makes you so sure she's innocent?"

"I don't know. She seems to be intelligent, a little naive
perhaps but basically an honest person. I guess it's just a
feeling I have now that I've talked to her."

"From what I hear the DA has a open and shut case."

"It looks that way, I know, but appearances can be deceiving."

"Did it occur to you she may be lying?"

"Of course, but she needs a lawyer whether she's lying or telling the truth, so will you help?"

"Can she afford us?"

"Yeah, her old man's bringing me $10,000 tomorrow morning."

"Is that all?"

"Well, it's just the initial retainer."

"Didn't you pay any attention to me in class, Stan? You always get the entire fee up front in a criminal case. It's nearly impossible to withdraw from a murder case once you make an appearance. And what if the client is convicted? You think the family is going pay you if you lose?"

"I know, I should have insisted on more, but I doubt they could have raised it. I'm sure they'll pay us."

"Ha. Sarah isn't the only naive one."

I chose to ignore that comment. Unlike me, Snake obviously didn't have any trepidations about taking the life savings of his clients. I guessed he had lots of money so ten grand didn't seem like that much to him.

"I'll do most of the work. I just need you for advice and moral support. Will you do it?"

"Okay, I'll help you out, but I have a hunch she's guilty and we'll end up pleading her out."

"I hope you're wrong," I said.

"You better call the detective assigned to the case and tell him to leave her alone. We don't want them beating a confession out of her."

"I already did that."

"Good, well you can buy me lunch tomorrow and we can discuss strategy."

"You're on. How about 11:30 at Carelli's."

"Fine. See you then."

My mind began to race as I contemplated all that needed to be done to prepare to defend Sarah. I'd have to set up interviews with all the potential witnesses and suspects. I'd need some help from a private investigator of course. And, just in case Sarah turned out to be guilty, I decided it would be best to get a psychiatrist to examine her for a possible temporary insanity defense.

Although this appeared to be a hopeless case, I knew from experience that hopeless cases weren't all that bad. If I won, everyone would think I was brilliant, but if I lost no one would think the less of me because it was a hopeless case. I didn't plan to lose this one, though, I really believed Sarah was innocent and wanted her to be vindicated.

As I continued to contemplate Sarah's defense, Jodie walked in to say goodnight.

"I'm going to go. Here's a phone message from some assistant DA up in Sherman. I don't know how they found out already that you're handling the case, but apparently they did."

"I called them. I didn't want them going over to the hospital and bothering Sarah without contacting me first."

She handed me the telephone message. I noted that it was from a Howard Hudson.

"Do you know this Howard Hudson guy?" Jodie asked.

"Yeah, don't you remember, he used to be a football star at Texas A & M."

"Oh really, *that* Howard Hudson. Is he any good?"

"He thinks so, I guess. I've never had to deal with him but Snake tells me he's got quite an ego."

"I bet he doesn't like Snake much either."

"You're pretty perceptive."

"Of course. Well, I'm out of here. Don't work too late tonight. Rebekah already called to see if you were going to be home at a decent hour."

"Poor Rebekah, I don't know why she puts up with me."

"I don't either, I sure wouldn't."

"Thanks a lot."

"No problem." Jodie laughed. Good night."

"Good night."

Howard Hudson was a well known and respected prosecutor. My stomach tightened as I contemplated having to face him in court. Had I gotten in over my head? . . . Yeah, there was little doubt of that, but that's why I had retained Snake to keep me out of trouble. I dialed the number on the message and was quickly connected to Mr. Hudson.

"I heard you're going to defend Sarah Winters," he said.

"That's correct."

"Well it's not looking too good for your client. The citizens are pretty up in arms over what she did. Particularly with two innocent babies murdered in the same night. It looks bad for the community. Swift justice is imperative in this case. Don't expect any leniency from this office."

"We're not looking for leniency. Sarah is innocent and we intend to prove it."

"You haven't tried many murder cases, have you, Mr. Turner?" Hudson said.

"No, that's why Harry Hertel's gonna be second chair."

"That's what I heard. I'm a little surprised. I thought . . . well, Snake was teaching over at SMU these days?"

"He is, but he still practices some."

"Well, I'm glad he's going be on the case. I owe him one. I've been looking forward to facing off with him one more time."

"Oh really?"

"Yes, tell him I haven't forgotten the Miller trial. I'm going to relish the opportunity to pay him back."

"Is that right?. I'll be sure and tell him."

"Good. So anyway, the reason I called was to tell you

that just as soon as your little lady gets released by her doctor you need to bring her in to be booked. We've already made a presentation to the Grand Jury and expect an indictment very soon."

"Already? You guys work fast," I said.

"We protect our children up here in Sherman, Mr. Turner. We don't take kindly to the likes of your client."

"Okay, I'll call her doctor and find out when she's due to be released and then arrange to bring her in."

"Let me know when you're coming," Hudson said."We want to have a cell ready for her."

"Don't bother, I'm sure we'll post her bond immediately," I said.

"If the judge sets a bond. We're going to do everything in our power to keep your client locked up where she belongs."

Chapter Four
Strategy

It was dark outside when I left the house to jog a couple of miles before breakfast. I called my dog, Beauty, and she came bounding down the stairway from Mark's room where she usually slept. She was a year old, an impulse purchase from the local pet store. I hadn't planned on getting a dog but the kids fell in love with her and gave me a hard sell. They promised they'd feed and exercise her every day without fail. Two weeks later when the novelty was over Beauty became my responsibility whether I wanted it or not.

Rebekah wouldn't allow Beauty in the master bedroom. She was not a dog lover, having had some unfortunate experiences with dogs as a child. Being a lawyer's wife was tough enough, she would say, without having to compete with the dog in the bedroom.

There was a cool northerly breeze that almost made me change my mind about running, I knew I needed the exercise or I'd be sluggish all day. Jogging for me was therapy. It was a time that I could be alone and think. When I was at home, I was always conversing with Rebekah or one of the kids. When I got to the office, it would be the phone and the minute by minute pressure to get work done that would occupy my every second.

Beauty ran ahead anxious to see what was around the corner. Periodically she would stop to savor the myriad of smells of the neighborhood and wait for me to catch up. For the first time I began to think about Sarah and whether she was telling the truth. The one thing I couldn't tolerate was a client being less than candid. That could be deadly for both of us. If she were guilty I needed to know it, and the sooner the better. It occurred to me that Sarah may actually believe she was innocent even though she was actually guilty. Her blacking out or lapse of memory could be simply a defense mechanism to protect her from the horrid truth.

When Beauty and I got back to the house we entered through the back gate. I loved the early morning because it was so quiet, so peaceful and uncomplicated. I knew once the sun came up the day would get hectic in a hurry, so I relaxed and enjoyed the simple pleasure of playing with my dog.

"Okay girl, where's the frisbee," I said. Beauty began running around furiously searching for her favorite toy. When she found it she ran back to me and laid it at my feet.

"Good girl," I said and then threw the frisbee the length of the yard. Beauty took off, catching up with it and grabbing it before it hit the ground.

"Nice catch," I yelled.

Beauty ran back and jumped up on me. I took one end of the toy and wrestled her for it until finally she let go. She watched me, waiting impatiently for me to throw it again. As I was about to throw it one more time, I heard the back door open and Rebekah call.

"Honey, breakfast is ready."

"Okay, be right there." I looked at Beauty and shook my head. "Sorry girl, time to go." I went to the faucet, turned on the water and filled Beauty's water bowl. Then I went into the garage, came back with a large bag of Purina dog chow and poured out a day's ration into her bowl.

When I came in Rebekah and the children were already done eating. I sat down and dug into the plate of steaming pancakes and started to read the paper. After Rebekah got Reggie and Mark off to school she came back into the kitchen with Marcia and Peter. I was just getting up to leave.

"I've gotta go, I've got a couple bankruptcy hearings first thing this morning and I need to go see Marleen Wiggins and get started on Bobby's probate."

"Oh, I hope she's doing okay. Say hi to her for me, would you?"

"I will."

Rebekah came over and gave me a kiss goodbye. On the way out I picked up Marcia, hugged her and kissed her on the cheek. Then I gave Peter a squeeze before opening the door to the garage.

"Drive carefully," Rebekah said. "I love you."

"I love you too, bye."

When I got to the office Jodie was anxiously waiting for me. "You've got to leave for bankruptcy court Stan, you only have twenty-five minutes to get to the courthouse. I've got all your files ready."

"Thanks Jodie, I lost track of time this morning."

"Don't forget you've got to be back for your luncheon appointment with Harry at 11:30."

"Yeah, I'm going to try to stop by Marleen Wiggins house if I have time. Then I'll go straight to Carelli's. Give me my phone messages and I'll return them while I'm waiting for the judge to get to my cases."

Jodie quickly walked into my office and pulled the phone messages off the message clip and brought them to me. "Here you go, don't forget you've got Mohammed Barabi coming in to review a construction contract at two."

"I won't, thanks, see you after lunch." Fortunately I got out of bankruptcy court early enough to go by Marleen's house. She answered the door, seemingly pleased to see me, then invited me in. We went into the kitchen and sat down at the kitchen table cluttered with bills and records. She looked pale and rather sickly, not the robust lady I was used to. After forty-five years of marriage I guess it is quite a shock to the system to suddenly be alone.

"How you holding up?" I asked.

"Fair, I guess."

"How is the family taking it? You've got quite a few grandchildren don't you?"

"Seven. It's been hard on them. They were all very close to Bobby. There's a lot of bitterness."

Bitterness. Had she carefully picked that word to let me know trouble was coming? I wondered.

"Have you got a death certificate yet?"

"Yes," she said and then dug through a stack of documents until she found it.

"Good, all I'll need now is a complete list of all your assets and liabilities."

Being in a hurry I suggested she put it together and mail it to me, but she insisted on telling me about everything she had item by item. After we finished the list, I started gathering my things to leave when I remembered the question I had wanted to ask her. "Oh, I was thinking about the last conversation I had with Bobby. He was about to tell me about some sort of problem he was having. Do you know what he was going to tell me?"

Marleen frowned. She lowered her eyes and took a slow deep breath as she contemplated the question. "I don't know. Did he tell you anything at all about it?"

"No. He said he was going to come see me the following Monday."

She shrugged. "Bobby didn't talk much about business. I'm a worrier and he didn't want to burden me with business matters."

"Did you sense there was a problem at work?"

"Yes, it was obvious something was bothering him, but he didn't share it with me."

"Did you ever figure out what it was?"

"Not entirely," she said, "but I have my suspicions."

"Well, tell me what you know."

"I know it involved one of his clients."

"Who?"

"Oscar Valenti."

"The builder?"

"Right."

"What kind of problem?"

"I don't know, but Bobby was upset about it. He had several heated discussions over the phone with him."

"Well, I'll talk to Oscar and see if I can find out what was going on between them. It might be helpful if I had access to your husband's client files."

"Sure, I'll tell his partner to let you look at whatever you want."

After leaving Marleen's, I drove to Carelli's arriving at 11:45. I scanned the room and saw that Snake had already found a table. He waved so that I would see him. I walked over and took a seat.

"Hey, you made it," Snake said. "I thought I might have to eat alone."

"There was a big docket today and the judge was in a horrible mood. I was lucky to get out of there without being sanctioned. Then Marleen Wiggins wouldn't let me leave. She's lonely I guess with Bobby gone."

"She didn't mention whether she'd going to sue you?" Snake asked.

"Hell no, I'm handling Bobby's probate and helping her tie up loose ends. She knows it was a freak accident. It certainly wasn't my fault Bobby fell."

Snake shook his head. "You just better hope she never

gets another lawyer."

"She won't. I'm not worried." It was a lie, of course. I *was* worried about it, but not as much as Rebekah. As much as I tried to forget about the possibility of a multi-million dollar wrongful death suit, Rebekah would invariably bring it up on a daily basis.

"Good, now what's the deal with Sarah-what's her name?"

"Winters," I said.

"Right, Winters."

I told Snake everything I knew about Sarah and the murder. The waiter came over and delivered some garlic bread and two glasses of water. He took our drink order.

"So if Sarah didn't do it, who did?" Snake asked.

"Well, I figure our two most likely suspects are the two boyfriends, Greg Peterson and Richard Stein. Greg is her current flame of about four months. Richard had the honors before that. I don't know much about them yet, but I've heard that Richard is bad news, a drug dealer and addict among other things. Greg, on the other hand, is a good kid, a journalism student like Sarah. He's finished college I understand and is now pursuing an MBA."

"She learned her lesson, huh."

"It seems so," I said.

"Any witnesses?"

"Let's see, there is a roommate named Michelle, my niece who lives next door, but that's about it so far."

"Okay, lets talk to each of them first and then the immediate family to see what they know," Snake said.

"Alright, we're going to need a shrink too."

"I know just the guy, Dr. Gerhardt, Norman S. Gerhardt, PH.D."

"Oh really, is he good?" I asked.

"He's got credentials you wouldn't believe and juries

love him. His PH.D. is from Yale and he even taught a few years at ASU as I recall. Now he has a practice here in Dallas and people come from all of the country just to see him. His specialty is hypnosis."

"Good, after we get Sarah out on bond we'll have to send her to him for an evaluation."

The waiter returned, explained the menu and took our orders. Then he brought us some hot garlic bread layered with melted cheese that totally distracted us from our work. We both took a bite and shook our heads.

"Hmm. I love this stuff," I said. "Okay, what about the bond, do you think we'll have any trouble?"

"I don't think so, she's got a family, she's enrolled in school, no prior arrest I presume, so I don't think the judge could deny us bond," Snake replied.

"Oh I talked to the prosecutor yesterday. Apparently you know him, Howard Hudson."

"I figured they'd put Howie on this one. He's their best prosecutor plus he likes high profile trials. I've been told he's running for District Attorney since the current DA is retiring. I bet he begged the DA to give him this case."

"He was thrilled to hear you were helping me out."

Snake smiled and replied,"Really? I didn't know I had left such a profound impression."

"He wanted you to know he hadn't forgotten the Miller case, whatever that means."

"Oh yeah, the Miller case. I almost forgot about that. He was upset when I called his mother as a character witness for my client."

They laughed. "Did you really?"

"Uh huh, his mother is a high school teacher in McKinney and she actually had Jonathan Miller as a student. Out of ten or fifteen teachers I could have chosen, I thought she'd be the best character witness for him."

I laughed, "Jesus, Howie must have been totally pissed."

"He nearly had a heart attack, the judge had to call a ten minute recess. It was so funny."

"I bet."

When the waiter showed up with our orders, we took a break from our work to enjoy the fine cuisine.

"Mmm. This food is good. We've got to come here more often," Snake said.

"It wouldn't be good for either of our waistlines," I said. "Do you realize how many calories this stuff has?"

"Who cares?"

"What do you think the Judge will do about Sarah's bond?" I asked.

"Well, let me see, who's the judge up there?"

"Albert Brooks."

"Oh yeah, Al Brooks, he's a good judge. Kind of laid back. He'll cut us some slack in order to be sure Sarah gets a fair trial. Just don't get him pissed off though. He's got a temper and can become mean and irritable in a hurry. My guess is he'll set a reasonable bond though. Maybe I can talk to Howie and we can agree on the amount."

"I don't think so. The DA is opposing bond, but since you know him and he has such great admiration for you, maybe you *should* give it a try."

"I will, I'll call him this afternoon," Snake said.

After lunch we parted with the understanding that I would be first chair at Sarah's trial since that's what the client wanted, but that Snake would work very closely with me as second chair to make sure Sarah got the best defense possible. I looked at my watch and saw I had only ten minutes to get to my meeting with Mohammed Barabi.

As I was driving back to the office it occurred to me that Barabi and Valenti probably knew each other. They were both high profile contractors in the North Dallas area and both had attended my party. I decided to ask Mohammed about him. After we had finished our business I brought up the topic.

"So can you believe what happened to Bobby Wiggins?" I said.

"No, what a tragedy. Have the police got any leads yet?"

"I don't think so."

"I must say you throw an exciting party, Stan," Mohammed noted. "I'm not sure I want an invitation next year though."

I laughed. "Yeah, I doubt Rebekah will be up to a party next year. . . . Listen, I've been retained to handle Bobby's probate and I'm trying to wrap-up any business dealings he had in progress on the date of his death."

"Really?"

"Yes, right now I'm just gathering information, in fact, I have a question for you."

"What's that?"

"Did you know an Oscar Valenti."

"Sure, we run into each other a lot being in the same business. We're not close friends or anything like that but we know each other well enough."

"Do you know of anything unusual going on in his life?"

"No, other than a drinking problem since his wife left him. I don't know if it's true, but I heard he was getting professional help."

"Really? . . . Huh. Marleen says Bobby was having some kind of problem with him."

"Right, that would probably be with the IRS."

"What do you mean?"

"Valenti doesn't believe in paying taxes. I don't know how he's got away with it for so long, but I think they were finally coming down on him."

"So Bobby was probably trying to help him negotiate

with IRS?"

"Most likely."

"Bobby wasn't doing any work for you was he?"

"Sure, he was my accountant. Don't you remember, you introduced us."

"Oh, right. . . . So what are you doing about your accounting now?"

"Bobby's partner, Buddy Clark, has jumped right in and taken care of everything. I guess I'll just leave it with him."

After my meeting with Mohammed Barabi I walked over to Jodie's desk and asked, "You haven't heard from Tom Winters have you?"

"No, he hasn't called."

"Damn, he's supposed to come in and sign a retainer agreement and give me $10,000."

"It's only 3:30 he may still make it," Jodie said.

"I hope so, I already called the DA and told him I was representing his daughter."

"What did Snake think about the case?"

"I'm not sure he is as convinced of Sarah's innocence as I am."

"Well, from reading the newspaper accounts I may be in his camp."

"Come on now, I need you on my side. If we don't believe she's innocent how can we expect a jury to believe it?"

"Well, I'll try to keep an open mind. ... Oh, by the way, a couple of newspaper reporters called today while you were at lunch. They wanted to confirm that you were handling Sarah's defense."

"What did you tell them?"

"No comment, of course."

"Good girl. If Tom Winters ever shows up, I'll call them back and confirm the-" Before I could finish my sentence the door opened and Tom Winters appeared.

"Tom, hello," I said.

"Hi, I'm sorry I didn't call and make an appointment but it was getting late so I just took a chance on finding you in."

"No problem, come on in," I said. "This is my secretary, Jodie Marshall."

"Nice to meet you," Jodie said.

"Go on in my office and sit down. Would you like a cold drink, or maybe something more substantial?"

"Yeah, I could use a bourbon, actually," Tom said.

"I bet you could."

I turned to Jodie. She nodded. I said,"How do you like yours, Tom?"

"On the rocks."

"Jodie, you know how I like mine."

She smiled. "Of course, I'll be right back."

"Well, I've got your money," Tom said. "I didn't have time to get a cashier's check. I hope just a company check will be okay."

"Sure, no problem."

Tom handed me the check and took a deep breath. "It wasn't easy getting this money, I had to dig pretty deep."

He told me that he was deeply in debt and cash flow was a major problem. I guess he wanted me to feel sorry for him and take it easy on his bill. Unfortunately my financial situation was not such that I could afford to be so generous. I suddenly wished I had taken Snake's advice and gotten a larger retainer. Jodie came in with our drinks and set them in front of us.

"I know, I'm sorry that we have to do it this way, but with Harry in the case I've got to do everything by the book. If it were-"

"I understand."

"Good. I met with him today," I said. "We've mapped out a preliminary discovery strategy for handling the case. I've already talked to the investigating officer, Bernie Meadows, and the assistant DA assigned to the case, Howard Hudson."

"Already? I didn't figure you'd lift a finger until you had the retainer in hand."

"You have to move quickly in a case like this where the real facts are cloudy. As time goes by memories fade and it gets more and more difficult to find the truth."

"What's your first move?" Tom asked and then took a sip of his drink.

"We've got to deal with your daughter's arrest and then her bond. Snake thinks we'll be able to get a bond set without too much trouble, but we don't know how much it will be. You better start thinking about putting it up. Probably $50,000 or more."

Tom turned kind of pale and shifted around in his seat. He looked at me and frowned.

"I don't know if I can come up with that kind of money."

"Well, you don't actually have to come up with cash, you just need a good bondsman. The premium is usually 10% or so of the actual amount of the bond. Of course, he'll want collateral."

"When do think this will happen?"

"Pretty quick, just as soon as her doctor releases her from the hospital. I've promised Hudson I'll bring her straight in."

"I'm going to see her tonight so I'll ask the doctor when that will be."

"Okay, call me and tell me what you find out. If I'm not here talk to Jodie, okay?"

"Sure."

"Well alright then, Jodie has a legal service contract for you to sign when you leave. You can give her the check. Otherwise, I guess that's all our business today."

Tom and I stood up and shook hands. He was smiling

but it was forced. He was obviously worried, but I guess that was to be expected with a child on trial for murder.

"Thank you Mr. Turner, I'm so glad you're handling this case for me. If you need anything else just let me know."

"Okay, and you let me know what the doctor says."

Tom left my office and was immediately intercepted by Jodie.

"Oh Mr. Winters, I have your contract ready." Jodie escorted Tom over to her desk. He didn't bother to read the contract, just fumbled in his coat pocket for a pen.

"Okay, where do I sign?"

"Look it over and then if it's okay sign it above your name at the bottom," she said as I had taught her. We always encouraged our clients to read everything they signed although few took our advice. Tom signed his name immediately. Jodie rolled her eyes without Tom seeing it. When he looked at her, she smiled and took it from him.

"Thank you, I'll take the check now."

Tom grimaced and then put his hand in his inside jacket pocket and pulled out a check. "Here you go."

"Thank you," Jodie said taking the check.

After Tom left I returned to my office and Jodie followed me inside.

"I got the check and the contract," Jodie said.

"Yeah, I saw that. Now I'll be able to pay you this month and keep a little food in the frig."

"In a few more years you'll have teenagers, then you'll never have anything in the frig no matter how much money you make."

"Please, don't remind me."

"Oh. Snake called and said the DA agreed to a $50,000 bond for Sarah."

"Really, that's a shock. Hudson told me he was going to oppose bond. I wonder how Snake convinced him to change his mind.

"I don't know," Jodie said.

"Well, that's good news, although I don't know if Tom Winters will think so," I said.

"How come?"

"I get the impression he's having to scrape the bottom of the barrel to finance this trial."

"Well, not too many people could afford to fund a murder trial," Jodie said.

"Not too many people have to, luckily."

I was relieved that the DA had agreed to a $50,000 bond. Tom would have difficult enough time coming up with that modest bond. Had it been set at a hundred thousand or more Sarah would most likely have to rot in jail for the duration of her trial."

"Well, it's after five so I think I'm going to call it a day," Jodie said. "Rod's taking me to dinner and a movie tonight."

"Okay, have fun."

After Jodie left, I sat down and gazed at the mass of files and papers that were spread all over my desk and credenza. I wondered how I was ever going to get home that night. I hated to just get up and leave such a mess because when I came to work the next morning the sight of it would depress me for the rest of the day. After a minute I began sorting through the day's work, discarding or filing away the completed items, making a pile of the things that needed work and making notes on my calendar and tickler file.

After about an hour my desk was clear. I felt much better so I started to pack up my briefcase to go home. I looked at my watch and saw that it was 7:18. Just as I was about to depart, the phone rang. It was my private line that I used for Rebekah and my most important clients."

"Stan, I'm glad I caught you," Rebekah said.

"Oh, hi babe."

"Tom Winters just called here to tell you they are releasing Sarah Monday morning at 9:30."

"So soon?" I glanced at my calendar to see what I had scheduled on Monday. "Oh shit, I've got a hearing in Denton, I hope I can find someone to handle it for me."

"Sorry, honey."

"Well, I knew this was going to happen, I just wish I'd got a little more notice."

"Are you coming home tonight, or what?"

"Yes, I was just about to leave, but I'd better call Tom back and give him the name and telephone number of our bondsman so he can arrange for Sarah's bond on Monday."

"Well, hurry up and get home, I'm starving."

On the way home I began to worry again about whether Sarah was telling the truth. A sick feeling overcame me as I realized for the first time that I might go to Hell for defending Sarah. What if it turned out she actually had killed her own flesh and blood? Would God forgive me for defending her? I thought he would, but it was an unsettling thought nonetheless.

On Monday morning I went straight to Sherman from home. I arrived at the hospital at about 9:00 a.m. hoping to have a chance to talk to Sarah before she was released. As I walked down the corridor to her room I noted a uniformed officer standing guard outside her door.

"Good morning officer," I said as I approached Sarah's room.

"Good morning, sir."

"I need to see Sarah Winters."

"May I ask who you are?"

"Stan Turner, her attorney."

"Oh, yes. Lt. Meadows said you'd be coming. Do you have some ID?"

"Sure," I said and then took out my wallet and showed

the officer my State Bar of Texas credentials.

"You're to take Miss Winters straight to the police station once she's discharged."

"Yes, I will certainly do that."

"Then I'm going to leave her in your custody."

"That will be fine."

The officer left and I went inside. Sarah was dressed and had all of her belongings packed up. She smiled when I walked in the room. Joyce was sitting in a chair staring out the window.

"Hi, Mr. Turner," Sarah said.

Joyce turned around and looked at me.

"Good morning Sarah, Mrs. Winters," I replied.

"I'm so glad you're here, I'm getting sick of this place," Sarah said.

"We can go, but before we leave I need to explain what's going to happen."

"Okay," Sarah said.

"I'm taking you to the police station where they're going to book you. That means they are going to fingerprint you, take your picture, ask some questions and advise of your rights. After they have finished all of that, we're going to see the judge. The assistant district attorney and I have already agreed on a bond of $50,000. The judge doesn't have to go along with our agreement but he usually does. I know $50,000 seems like a lot of money, but it's not a high bond for a murder indictment."

"Will I have to go to jail?" Sarah asked.

"It depends on whether your Dad is able to get a bondsman to put up the $50,000 bond or not. I feel certain he will. If he has arranged for the bond then you may not have to go to jail, or if you do go, it would only be for a few hours. If he can't get a bond then you'll have to go to jail until he is able to post one."

"Don't worry Sarah," Joyce said. "Jail isn't so bad, it's just incredibly boring sitting around all day doing nothing. We'll bring you some books and magazines to read."

"You don't you think Daddy will be able to put up the bond?" Sarah asked.

"Well, that's a lot of money."

"He doesn't have to come up with all of it, usually just ten percent is sufficient if you can provide collateral."

"Well, I don't know what collateral he could possible use," Joyce said.

I frowned at Joyce and then turned to Sarah and smiled.

"I talked to your Dad on Friday and he said he thought he could get the bond, but we'll just have to wait and see."

At that moment an orderly entered pushing a wheelchair.

"Ms. Winters, are you ready to go?"

"Yes, I think so."

"If you'll take a seat, I'll escort you out of the hospital."

Sarah walked over to the wheelchair and sat down. The orderly pushed her out of the room with Joyce and I close behind. He took her to admitting, we checked her out and left the hospital. As we were leaving, a half dozen reporters and a camera crew confronted us. I grabbed Sarah's arm and maneuvered her through the group of reporters without stopping. The reporters followed Sarah and I yelling out questions as they walked.

"Ms. Winters, how do you feel about being indicted for the murder of your baby?" the first reporter asked.

"She has no comment," I replied.

"Mr. Turner, will your client plead innocent?" a second reporter asked.

"That's our plan at this time," I said. "Ms. Winters is innocent and we plan to prove it."

"If you didn't do it Miss Winters, who do you think killed

your baby?" a third reporter shouted.

"We don't know the answer to that question, but we intend to find out," I replied.

Finally we made it to my car. After Sarah got in, I looked back to see what had happened to Joyce who wasn't with us. There was a crowd of reporters fifty yards behind us and I saw Joyce in the middle of it. She seemed to be enjoying the attention she was drawing. I got in and looked at Sarah.

"Shall we wait for your stepmother?" I asked.

"No, she's got her own car, let's go," Sarah replied.

"I wonder what she's telling them," I said.

"She's probably telling them how hard she tried to straighten out my sorry ass, but I was a hopeless case."

"Oh, come on, she's not that bad is she?"

She snickered. "Worse than you could possibly imagine. You're lucky you don't have to live with her."

"Do you two fight a lot?"

"No, not really. I just try to stay clear of her as much as possible for Daddy's sake. I don't want to cause him any problems now that he's finally got his life together."

After hearing Tom's confessions about the financial mess he was in, I wasn't so sure how long his life would stay together. But I couldn't share that feeling with Sarah. She had enough to worry about. I looked over at Joyce and saw that she was still talking excitedly to the reporters.

"Well, I guess she'll catch up with us later." I put the key in the ignition, started the engine and eased out of the parking lot. "Listen, Sarah, you've had a little time to think now. Can you remember anything yet about the night of the murder?"

"No, sir. I still don't remember what happened. I've tried to remember, believe me, but there's nothing there."

"That's too bad. It would sure help if you remembered something, anything."

"I'm sorry."

"What were you going to do after you delivered your baby?" I asked with a little annoyance and frustration in my voice. Sarah twisted in her seat nervously. She closed her eyes and took a deep breath. "I've got to know, Sarah," I said. "You must of had a plan."

"Okay, okay. Ricky had a guy, you know, a friend who was going to take the baby and make sure it went to a good family."

"You were going to sell your child?"

"No. No. I wasn't going to get any money. It was just going to be a very quiet adoption. Nobody would know about it except Ricky, Michelle and the lawyer."

"Who was the lawyer?"

"I don't know. Ricky handled that."

"Why didn't you just get an abortion?"

"I don't believe in abortions. I couldn't kill my child."

"Is there anything else you're not telling me, Sarah? If there is anything you're holding back you need to let it out. I can't defend you unless I know the truth."

Sarah glared at me. "I've told you everything I know! Don't you believe me? What do you want me to do, make something up!"

Sarah's sudden outburst surprised me. She had been very calm in our previous conversations. Perhaps the stress was getting to her. Now maybe I'd get the truth. "No! That's not what I want. I'm just trying to understand how you could deliver a baby and not remember anything. It just doesn't make any sense. Everybody's going to think you're a liar."

Sarah wiped her eyes. "I don't remember anything. I'm not lying. It's the truth, I swear to God."

"Well that's a real problem, Sarah. Unless you remember what happened, you may be spending the rest of your life in prison!"

Chapter Five
Dangerous Confinement

We parked in front of the police station. I killed the engine and then looked at Sarah. The memory of my arrest at Quantico came rushing into my mind. I knew how Sarah must be feeling, helpless and alone.

"Are you scared?" I asked.

"Terrified," she said forcing a smile. She was a tough young woman. But I guess that only figured given the life that had been dealt her.

"I am sorry we have to go through this drill," I said, "but unfortunately there's no way around it. Why don't you leave your purse in the car, they'll just take it away from you inside if you take it with you."

"Okay."

"Are you ready?"

"Yes, let's just get it over with."

We got out of the car and walked inside. At the counter I asked for Lt. Meadows. We were told to have a seat. After a short wait Bernie Meadows appeared with an attractive young women in a charcoal striped suit. She was a slender woman with cold grey eyes.

"Mr. Turner?" Lt. Meadows asked.

"Yes, and this is Sarah Winters."

"Hello Miss Winters," he said. Pointing to the grim lady he said, "This is Margie Westcott from the DA's office. She'll be assisting Mr. Hudson in the case."

"Nice to meet you," I replied.

She nodded without smiling.

"I guess we better get this over with," I said.

"Okay, Miss Winters, come this way please," Lt. Meadows said.

Sarah was led down a hallway to the intake room where she was read her rights, photographed, fingerprinted and taken to a holding cell to await her court appearance. While she was being booked Miss Westcott and I talked.

"Can I get a copy of the indictment, Miss Westcott?" I asked.

She shrugged. "Yes, you're entitled to it. I'll give you a copy at the bond hearing."

"Thanks. I'd like to take a look at your evidence as soon as possible too."

She sighed as if annoyed. "We can arrange that with Lt. Meadows after the hearing."

"Fine," I said giving her a smile. She didn't reciprocate. She looked all bottled up as if she was going to explode. There was an uneasy moment of silence and then I found out what was eating at her.

"I've heard you plan to plead Miss Winters innocent," she said.

"That's correct."

"Innocent by reason of temporary insanity?"

"No, just innocent."

She frowned and let out another sigh. "You're joking, right? You'll never convince a jury that she's innocent with the evidence we have."

"Well, after I see your evidence, maybe I'll change my recommendation, but right now our plans are to plead her innocent."

"Do you honestly think she'd tell you if she were guilty?"

"Yes, I'm her attorney. I'm on her side. There's no reason to lie to me."

"Right, and you're going to tell me with a straight face that you think she's innocent?"

"Yes, I do."

She shook her head. "I guess that's what you get paid to say, right?"

"Excuse me."

"You know the people around here don't like baby killers. It takes a pretty sick person to kill an innocent child. The fact we had two killed in one day is disgusting. The jury's not going to have one ounce of mercy for your client."

"If she's guilty I don't expect them to, but I don't think she is."

"Drop the act, Mr. Turner. We both know she's guilty and that you are obligated to recommend she do whatever is in her best interest. Obviously it would be in her best interest to plead guilty with the understanding, of course, that the DA's office would recommend a certain amount of leniency at sentencing."

"I appreciate that, but my client is innocent, so unless your office is prepared to drop the charges entirely then we have no other choice than to try the case."

"This trial is not going to be much fun for you or your client. There's going to be a lot of press coverage and adverse publicity for both of you. We could avoid all of that if your client would just confess to her crime and accept a moderate sentence."

"I'll communicate the offer to her but I wouldn't get your hopes up."

"I'd hate to see such a young girl spend her entire life behind bars. We could live with a plea of manslaughter. That would bring a sentence of twenty years and with good behavior she could be out on the street in six or seven."

I looked intensely at Miss Westcott. She was really giving me the hard press. I wondered why but a different thought popped into my mind. "What do you think it would be like for a confessed baby killer in prison?"

Ms. Westcott turned her head and thought for a moment. I knew I had her on that one. She held back a smile. "Probably not too pleasant but we could arrange special security."

"She wouldn't make it five years, hell, she wouldn't make it one year for that matter, if people think she intentionally killed her child. Her only hope is to be acquitted and that's what I intend to see happen."

"Well I just-"

The door suddenly swung open and Lt. Meadows quickly walked out.

"Okay, they're transporting her over to the courtroom #2 right now so we should go ahead on over."

Miss Westcott and I got up and followed Lt. Meadows down the hall to the connecting hallway between the courthouse and the police station. We went through security and then took the elevator to the second floor. As we entered the courtroom I noticed the reporters that had accosted us at the hospital were seated in the gallery. Joyce Winters was there too, seated in the front row. She waved at me as I walked into the courtroom. I smiled and went over to her.

"I see you were able to extricate yourself from the press finally," I said.

"Well I answered all their questions as best I could. I'm going to be on the six o'clock news, I guess."

"What kind of questions did they ask you?"

"Oh, all about Sarah's childhood, what kind of girl she was, you know."

"I should have warned you not to talk to the press. They have a way of twisting everything you say and taking words out of context."

"Oh, I don't think they'll do that. They were so nice to me."

"I guess we'll see tonight, won't we?"

"I guess we will."

As Stan and Joyce were talking, the side door of the courtroom opened and Sarah emerged with a female bailiff by her side. I got up and joined her at the defense table. Lt. Winters and Miss Westcott stood in front of the prosecution table. After a few seconds the rear door of the courtroom opened, a bailiff walked out and said, "Please stand for the Honorable Albert B. Brooks."

The judge quickly entered the room and sat down on the bench. He motioned for everyone to be seated and then the bailiff announced, "The 877th District Court of Grayson County, Texas is now in session."

"Well, I understand the state and the defense have reached an agreement on the amount of bail. Is that true Miss Westcott?"

"Yes, your honor. We've agreed on $50,000."

"Well, due to the heinous nature of this crime I am not sure that's the figure I would have picked, but I'll respect your agreement and set bail at $50,000. The defendant is remanded into the custody of the county sheriff until the bond has been posted."

The judge got up and left the courtroom. I put my arms around Sarah and gave her a few words of encouragement. The bailiff then led Sarah out of the courtroom. Miss Westcott, agitated by the judge's remarks, complained, "I don't know how Snake talked Howard into a $50,000 bond anyway. I would never have agreed to that."

"It beats me, I guess Snake has a way with people."

"Is your client going to be able to post it?" Miss Westcott asked.

"I think so, I'm expecting the bondsman any minute."

"Well, if you want to see the evidence this afternoon come by my office when you're done and I'll show you what we have. I'll warn you though, I leave promptly at 4:30."

"I'll be over there in a few minutes, thanks," I said.

I went over to where Joyce Winters was waiting and sat down beside her. After a few minutes the courtroom door opened and the bondsman, Bart Colby, walked in and approached us.

"Bart, you made it," I said.

"Yeah, I've got your bond right here."

"Lets get on over to the jail and post it so Sarah won't have to be put in a cell," I said.

"You go on ahead," Joyce said. "I'm going to the ladies room. I'll catch up with you."

Bart and I left the building and headed across the street. Before we got inside my curiosity got the best of me.

"What did he give you as collateral, some cars?"

"No. He gave me two dozen fine black diamonds."

"Black diamonds? You're kidding?"

"No, apparently they belong to his wife and she doesn't know he's using them as collateral."

"Oh God, if Joyce finds out we may have another murder on our hands."

As we got into the reception area of the jail, I noticed Margie Westcott talking to one of the jailers. When she saw me she nodded to the jailer and left. I took the bond up to the counter and waited for someone to help me. There were several clerks working on paperwork but none of them jumped up to help me. Finally I hailed one of them. She reluctantly got up and came over. She looked the bond over and commented, "You'll need to get the prisoner to sign it."

"Yeah, she should still be at intake, they just brought her in here a few minutes ago."

"Okay, I'll go check."

We took a seat while we waited for the clerk to return. A minute later Joyce walked in and we motioned her over. After a few more minutes the clerk came back. I got up and went to the desk. She said, "It's not your lucky day, they just took her back to a cell."

"Damn!" I said. "How could they process her so fast?"

"I don't know, but she's gone."

Seeing me upset, Joyce and Bart got up and joined me at the desk. "What's wrong?" Joyce asked.

I turned around, looked at her and frowned.

"I'm sorry. It's going to take a little longer to get Sarah out than I thought. They've taken her back to a cell. All we can do is go sit down and wait. It could be an hour or two."

We went back to our bench and waited. The seats were hard and I couldn't get comfortable. I crossed my legs one way and then the other. After a minute I began thumping the seat with my fingers. I kept asking myself how they could have processed her so fast. It didn't make sense. I got up and walked over to the window and stared out at the cars traveling down the busy street. Suddenly it occurred to me I could be looking at the evidence instead of sitting there wasting time.

Looking at Joyce, I said, "I think I'll go over to Miss Westcott's office now since we have to wait awhile for Sarah. You two can stay here in case they let Sarah out."

"Okay," Bart said. "I'll stay here with Joyce until Sarah is released."

"Thanks, I'll be back."

I walked across the street to the District Attorney's office, checked the directory and took the stairs to her floor. When I walked inside her office a secretary was busily typing. She ignored me and continued to type. I waited patiently a

awhile until she finally stopped and looked at me.
"Can I help you," she said.

"Yes, I'm here to see Miss Westcott. She's expecting me."

"Your name please?"

"Stan Turner."

"Okay, I'll tell her you're here."

"Thanks."

I sat down and began flipping through some magazines on the coffee table. Since they were all several months old, I didn't bother to pick any of them up. Then I noticed a book of Bible stories like I used to see at my dentist office when I was a kid. Seeing it amused me so I picked it up and looked at it curiously. After a few minutes Miss Westcott emerged from her office and greeted me.

"I've got the evidence in here, come on in."

Miss Westcott turned and walked into her office. I got up and followed her. As I entered I noticed a half dozen or so paper bags lined up neatly against the wall.

"Can I get you some coffee or a cold drink?"

"A Coke would be great."

Ms. Westcott turned to instruct her Secretary to get me a Coke but she had disappeared. She looked around and then went off looking for her. While she was gone I scanned the room for insights into my adversary. Her desk was cluttered, but it was kind of an organized clutter. There appeared to be four or five cases Miss Westcott was working on and the files relating to each were in separate piles. A hand written list of phone numbers was taped to the right side of her desk and she had a "To Do" list taped to each stack of files. She apparently was a well organized and methodical worker.

I looked at the walls and noted her law license and diplomas from St. Mary's Law School and New York University. There were a few plants, a flower arrangement to give the room a feminine touch and on her credenza the Texas Criminal Justice Code, Texas Rules of Criminal Procedure, and the King James Version of the Holy Bible. After a minute Miss Westcott returned with her secretary who had two Cokes and two glasses of ice. The secretary poured us each a glass and then left the room.

Miss Westcott turned to me and said, "Here you go, you may need a shot of Bourbon after you get a look at this stuff."

"That bad, huh?"

"Well, take a look. Here's State's Exhibits 1-6."

"Can I take them out of the sack?"

"Yes, but be careful please."

I walked over and looked into the first bag. It contained a bed sheet stained with blood. I pulled it out and examined it.

"That's the sheet that was taken off her bed," Miss Westcott said.

I nodded, placed it back in the sack and then went to the second bag. It contained some blood soaked towels.

"That's some towels that were found in the dumpster in the same bag as the baby. Exhibit number three contains the yellow bag in which the baby was found."

I looked in the bag and then went to exhibit number four.

"That's a blood stained bathroom rug. It has both the blood of your client and the baby on it."

I closed the bag and went to the fourth one. I was beginning to get a little nauseated from the smell of blood.

"Exhibit number four is a series of pictures of the dead fetus."

I pulled out the photographs and looked at them. They were quite grotesque so I quickly returned them to the bag.

"Have you seen enough?" Miss Westcott said.

"No, I want to see everything," I replied.

"Okay, exhibit number five is the pillow that was used to suffocate the baby."

A chill ran down my back as I pulled the pillow out of the sack. In my mind I tried to picture Sarah suffocating her baby, but I couldn't see it.

"The medical examiner found tiny particles of feathers in the baby's lungs," Miss Westcott said.

I returned the pillow to the bag and went to exhibit number six. Inside were a single pair of rubber gloves. I looked up at Miss Westcott curiously.

"So much for your temporary insanity defense, huh?" Miss Westcott said.

"Do these have Sarah's fingerprints on them?"

She replied, "No, they were washed, but they still have traces of your client's and the baby's blood on them."

"Where did you find them?"

"In a trash can in the laundry room that services your client's apartment. Her roommate, Michelle, has identified them as belonging to Sarah."

"I imagine a lot of people have rubber gloves like these and one size fits all, right?"

"Maybe so, but your client had some in her apartment the day before the murder and they're now missing."

"Hmm, interesting."

"You want to rethink our offer now?"

"No, I don't think any of this is conclusive. It proves somebody killed the baby, but not necessarily my client."

"You must live in a dream world, Mr. Turner. If a jury sees this stuff, they're going to be so outraged, your client won't have a prayer."

"Well, we'll see. Thank you for showing me all of this. You said I could get a copy of the indictment, didn't you?"

"Yes, I've got one for you."

Ms. Westcott went over to her desk and picked up a

single sheet of paper.

"Here it is," she said as she handed it to me.

"Thank you, I think I'll go see if Sarah's been released yet. I've never seen them process a new inmate so quickly, I thought for sure we'd get her bond posted before they took her back into the main population."

Ms. Westcott smiled and replied, "That's too bad, I guess it just wasn't her lucky day."

By the time Sarah was released I had taken a seat next to Joyce in the jail waiting room. Finally the door opened and I saw Sarah standing there. She appeared wobbly. A jailer was partially supporting her.

"What in the hell," I said and rushed over to her. "What happened to you?"

"They tried to kill me!" Sarah yelled and then began crying. "They tried to kill me!"

"What kind of a jail is this!" I screamed to the jailer.

"I am sorry,' the jailer said, "we didn't realize the inmates knew she was a baby killer. I don't know how they found out. We would have put her in an empty cell."

"I want the names of the women who attacked her. We're pressing charges and I'm filing a complaint with the county commissioners, this is inexcusable, this is a disgrace!"

"Honey, are you okay?" Joyce asked.

"I think so," Sarah replied.

"Let's get out of this place," I said. "Come on, let's get the hell out of here."

I escorted Sarah and Joyce out of the building and back to Joyce's car. Sarah was still shaking and crying when they got to the car.

"I'm so sorry, Sarah. This shouldn't have happened. Are you alright? Do you want to go back to the hospital?"

"No, I'm okay," Sarah said.

"I need to know exactly what happened so I can file a

complaint. Do you feel like talking about it now or should we do it later."

"I don't care. I'll tell you now."

"Okay, good."

Sarah explained, "After I left you and Joyce, they took me to a room where they started to do some paperwork. They asked me a bunch of routine questions. I thought they were about to fingerprint me but then Miss Westcott came in and whispered something to one of them. When she left they stopped what they were doing and one of the jailers immediately took me down a long corridor to the main cell block. Once inside, she led me down a hallway until I got to a second door. She took a ring of keys off her belt, unlocked it and motioned for me to enter. I reluctantly walked inside the small cell."

"So Margie wanted you back in the main population," I said. "She must of made sure the inmates knew you had been charged with killing your baby. I can't believe it. The woman tried to have you killed."

"What can we do about it?" Sarah asked.

"I'm not sure. I'll have to give that some thought. Go ahead and finish your story."

"Okay, well the cell had two sets of bunk beds, a sink and toilet. Two young white women were at the far end of the cell talking and a third, black woman in her mid-thirties, was on one of the top bunks reading a magazine. After the jailer slammed the door shut, I got really scared. The three women were glaring at me. They weren't the least bit friendly.

"I said, hello, but they didn't respond. They just stared at me. I figured I needed to keep talking to establish some rapport so I introduced myself.

"Then the black lady asked me if I killed my baby. I told her no, that I was innocent but they didn't seem to hear me. They just kept asking questions like I was on trial. I told them

I didn't remember anything.

"One of the girls said she had two boys and loved them very much. She couldn't understand how anyone could kill their own flesh and blood. I denied killing my child again but they paid no attention. Then the black lady sat up and jumped down from the top bunk. She walked over and stood directly in front of me. The two white women also came over and got up really close.

"They said they heard I had suffocated my baby with a pillow. They wanted to know if it was true. I denied it but they obviously didn't believe me. One of the girls said, 'I think we should give her a taste of her own medicine. Hand me a pillow.'"

The short white girl picked up a pillow and tossed it to the black girl. Then the two white girl's grabbed me by both arms and threw me on one of the lower bunks. The black girl took the pillow and put it over my face and pushed down as hard as she could. I screamed and struggled to get free, but I was no match for them. The other women in cell block began to yell and scream with delight at the altercation. They wanted me to die. But the commotion got the attention of one of the jailers who came running in to see what was happening. She yelled, 'Let her go, get away from her now!'

The black lady didn't respond so the officer pulled her gun, pointed it at her and told her to back off. The rest of the inmates went wild, screaming and throwing things out into the hall. The officer repeated herself, 'Let her up now!' she said. Finally the black lady threw the pillow onto the floor and stepped back. I coughed, gasped for air and then sat up.

"The second jailer escorted me from the cell but was intercepted by the intake clerk. She told us my bond had been posted."

"That's a disgrace," I said. "I can't believe they did this to you. I'm so sorry, Sarah. I'm going-"

"It's not your fault," Sarah said.

"I know, but it just pisses me off. . . . Well, you better go home and rest. You'll feel better tomorrow."

"Okay."

"She'll be fine," Joyce said. "She's just scared, I think."

"I don't blame her," I said shaking my head. We started walking toward the door. Before we parted I said, "Hey, I'm going to need you to come see me in a few days, okay?"

"Why? I've told you everything I know," Sarah asked.

"I've got to really dig into your life and try to make some sense out of what has happened. We've got a tough battle ahead and you and I will need to spend a lot of time together to get ready for it."

"When should I come?"

"Just call my office and talk to Jodie. She'll fit you into my schedule, okay?"

"Alright."

After watching Joyce and Sarah drive off, I went immediately to the Sheriff's office to complain about what happened. Unfortunately the Sheriff was out so I vented my anger at a deputy who was in command while the Sheriff was gone. On my way home I prayed this wasn't a bad omen of things to come.

Chapter Six
Breach of Duty

That night I had a horrible nightmare. One of the most frightening I'd ever experienced. It started with voices in the distance, then loud knocking on my door. I got up but before I made it to the door it came crashing down. Policeman rushed in and grabbed me. They pushed me up against the wall and cuffed me. Then they led me out the front door to an awaiting squad car. The scene suddenly changed. I was in a cemetery now, cuffed and gagged. Several men were digging a grave. When they were done the policemen pushed me into the hole. I turned over and tried to climb out only to be pelted by a shovel full of dirt. Wiping the dirt from my eyes I looked up into the diabolical eyes of Marleen Wiggins who was at the other end of the shovel. She laughed in delight with each shovel full of dirt she threw at me. Somehow I managed to get to my feet again, but when I tried to climb out of the hole Marleen smacked me with the shovel knocking me flat on my back. Then a sudden tranquility overcame me. Now I was looking down at Marleen diligently filling my grave.

The next morning I couldn't get out of bed. Every muscle in my body ached. I felt drained like when you get the flu. When the alarm went off I shut it off and turned over. As much as I tried to muster my strength to get up I couldn't do it. Rebekah took my temperature to see if I was sick but it was normal.

My dream turned out to be a premonition of the misfortune that was about to strike me. Before I had finished my first cup of coffee, Jodie informed me there was a deputy constable in the reception area waiting to see me. My heart sunk as I knew I had been sued. For a moment I thought maybe the citation was for one of my clients but deep down I knew whose name would be on it. Taking a deep breath I ventured into the reception area.

"Hello, can I help you?" I said trying to look surprised to see him. He was a big, muscular man with an unforgiving face. His brown and green uniform fit him like a glove which accentuated the large service revolver attached to his belt. Looking down at his paper he asked, "Stanley Turner?"

"Uh huh," I said meekly.

He handed me the papers and said, "You've been sued. I guess I don't have to tell you but you better get an attorney. You only have a short time to answer this complaint."

"Okay," I said fighting off a sudden nauseous feeling. Not knowing what to say to him, I just turned and went back into my office. A few seconds later I heard the front door close and then Jodie came rushing in.

"What is it?"

"Oh isn't this sweet, Marleen's suing Rebekah and I for two million dollars."

"Two million dollars! I can't believe she would do that. She's always been so nice. It doesn't make sense."

"Yes it does. She figures I have insurance and she might as well tap into it. Besides, I'm sure it's her children who are really behind it. She wouldn't have done it on her own."

"What are you going to do?"

"I have no clue. Call my insurance agent, I guess. My homeowners' insurance carrier will have to defend me."

"Will they pay the claim?"

"They might, but I only have a hundred thousand dollars in coverage."

"Oh God, Stan. I'm so sorry. . . . I guess this means you won't be handling Bobby's probate anymore."

"That's a safe bet. . . . Oh, God. I can't- . .. Oh, shit! I bet the constable is serving Rebekah right now. Get her on the phone so I can warn her."

Jodie called her but it was too late. Rebekah had just been served and she was crying. She handed me the phone. "What are we going to do?" Rebekah moaned. "We'll lose everything."

"No we won't. This is Texas, they can't take shit from us."

"What about your practice?"

I didn't have an answer for that. Even in Texas my accounts receivable, equipment and cash was at risk. The only thing I could claim exempt was my books and they didn't matter much since I owed more on them than they were worth.

"Why did she do this? You've been so good to Bobby and her."

"I know, it's the kids I'm sure."

"It's not fair. We were just trying to have a nice little party," she sobbed. "I hate that bitch!"

"Okay, calm down. We'll get through this. Just relax."

It took me twenty minutes before I had calmed down enough to actually read the lawsuit. It was a typical negligence suit stating that Rebekah and I had a duty to our guest to warn them of any dangerous conditions on our property and to take reasonable precautions to insure their safety. Marleen and her children claimed we had breached that duty by not warning the guests that the sidewalk had frozen over while the party was in progress and in failing to put sand down on the pavement.

It wasn't a slam dunk case for the plaintiffs. We could argue that it was common knowledge that the sidewalk was icy and that warning of the danger wouldn't have mattered. We could also legitimately claim that we had no knowledge of the ice since earlier in the evening when we checked it last there was none. On the other hand Bobby was a prominent CPA invited over for a good time and now he was dead. And, of course, there was the lawyer factor. Everybody loved to kick a lawyer when he was down. Suddenly my optimism faded.

I didn't know exactly how I was going to defend myself. But one thing I did know, if I was to have any chance of coming out of this mess unscathed I would need to know a lot more about Bobby Wiggins and my adversaries, Marleen and her children. At the very least I might be able to tarnish their reputations a little so the jury would at least listen to my side of the story.

When I notified my insurance carrier of the suit they agreed to defend me. I knew it wouldn't be a spirited defense as the insurance company had only a hundred thousand dollars at stake. In fact, I was afraid they might tender the policy limits into the registry of the Court and refuse to defend me. They had that option. Fortunately, they weren't ready to concede liability so they made an appearance on my behalf. I decided to enter an appearance myself as an additional counsel so I could conduct my own discovery and keep on top of the lawsuit. It was highly unusual but I felt it necessary since I couldn't afford independent counsel.

My first order of business was to inspect all of Bobby's business records. I told plaintiff's counsel I wanted to do it to disprove their alleged damages. My real motivation was to look for any exculpatory evidence I could find. The thought occurred to me that Bobby might have had a heart condition all along and had concealed it from his family and friends. If this were the case he may have fallen as a result of the heart attack which made more sense than having a heart attack as the result of a fall.

Chapter Seven
Longing for Love

Going through box after box of Bobby's accounting records wasn't my idea of excitement. I decided the first order of business was to identify all our common clients. Over the years I had referred a lot of business to Bobby. Many of my referrals had come and gone but after careful scrutiny I determined there were eleven active files. Of those, five had been at my party. One of them was Mohammed Barabi and another Oscar Valenti. The other three were Rob Parker, Tom Slater and Joanna Winburn.

Parker owned a printing company that miraculously had survived chapter 11. A year earlier he had called me after the Sheriff had seized all his assets and thrown him out on the street. He was an arrogant client who soon made we wish I had never met him. He was so rude and insolent that he pissed off everyone he met making my job nearly impossible. I had brought Bobby in to do the financial reporting in the bankruptcy before I knew my client's true nature. He gave Bobby equal grief and I felt bad that I had made the referral. Luckily, after about a year, the case was confirmed and my work for Parker was over. Bobby, on the other hand, continued to do Parker's accounting. I often wondered why Bobby hadn't quit, but it wasn't really any of my business so I never asked him.

Tom Slater was a commodities broker who had been sued by a customer who accused him of fraud and defalcation. He had retained me to defend him as he had no errors and omissions coverage when the alleged conversion took place. Slater professed to me his innocence and we hired Bobby to do an audit of the account. The case was pending when Bobby was killed.

Joanna Winburn was an exotic dancer who the IRS was after for failing to file tax returns. When she came to me I told her I could only help her if she would get her tax returns filed. I hired Bobby to actually do the returns. We did it this way to preserve the attorney-client privilege in case the IRS brought criminal charges. If Joanna had hired Bobby herself everything she told him would have been discoverable.

After several hours I was becoming convinced there was nothing in any of the records of any value. But then I started looking through Rob Parker's tax returns. In handling his Chapter 11 I had become well acquainted with his finances. These tax returns didn't make sense. There were assets being depreciated that had never been disclosed on his bankruptcy schedules.

Failing to disclose assets in a bankruptcy proceeding was a federal offense. Surely Bobby wouldn't have been a party to such a thing. He must of discovered it eventually though. That could well be what he wanted to talk to me about the night he was murdered. He wanted me to tell him what to do.

After gathering up all of Rob Parker's records, I left and went back to my office. Sarah was scheduled to come in at 2 p.m. and she was right on time. Jodie was on the phone with a client when she walked in so she motioned for her to sit down. When Jodie hung up she smiled and said, "You must be Sarah?"

"Right."

"How are you feeling? I heard about the little incident at the jail. I can't believe they did that to you."

"I was pretty sick for a couple of days, but I'm feeling better now."

Hearing Jodie and Sarah talking, I came into the reception area. Sarah was wearing jeans, white sneakers and an ASU T-shirt. She looked like a different woman from what I had seen in the hospital. The swelling had left her face and her stomach had flattened considerably. But her eyes still revealed the agony of her life.

"God, you must have been terrified when they held you down and tried to suffocate you"

"I doubt Sarah wants to relive that experience," I said.

"Oh, I'm sorry," Jodie said.

"It's alright."

"Come on in Sarah, have a seat."

I pointed to my office and Sarah smiled at Jodie and then walked in and sat down. I went back to my desk and pulled out a tape recorder.

"I'm going to tape this if you don't mind. I hate to take notes."

"Sure."

"Well, have you remembered anything more about December third?"

"No, it's still a blank."

"Hmm. Well, . . . why don't you tell me about your childhood? I need to know everything about you from the day you were born to December 3, 1981."

"Why?"

"Because your freedom is at stake here. Before we're done I want to know you better than you know yourself. Then maybe I can help salvage the rest of your life."

"Okay, where should I start?"

"At the beginning. Tell me about your childhood."

"Alright," she said taking a deep breath. "My mother died when I was an infant. I don't really remember her. My dad took to drinking after she died. He left me with his mother and disappeared. When he'd get sober enough to remember he had a daughter he'd come visit me. Of course, it usually was only for a few days and then he'd be gone. Before he left he'd always say, "Someday, when I get my life together, I'm gonna come get you, and then we'll be together always."

"My grandmother took care of me until I was eight. We lived in a small house on 64th Avenue in Portland, Oregon. Unfortunately, grandmother was elderly and had a heart condition. Sometimes she would be too sick to take care of me so Uncle Joe and Aunt Martha would come get me and keep me for awhile. If I couldn't stay with them I would live with Uncle Bob and Aunt Thelma. Lucky for me we had a big family."

"So did your daddy ever get his life together and come get you?" I asked.

"Yes, believe it or not, he did. It was on June 10, 1964 that I got a letter from Daddy asking me to come to Alaska to live with him and his wife."

"You remember the exact day?"

"Yes, and time too. It was 9:45 a.m. It was raining and I had just got home from school and I was drenched. I was on my way upstairs to change when Grandma yelled to me that there was a letter. I had never got a letter before so I was very excited but scared at the same time. I ran downstairs and took it from her. For a moment I just stared at it. I mouthed the words, *Tom Winters*, in the return address.

"Grandma couldn't stand the suspense." She said, 'Open it child before I die of curiosity.' Hands shaking, I carefully loosened the flap, removed the letter and began reading. My father was in Alaska. He had just been married and wanted me to come live with him. Joy overwhelmed me. I was so happy I ran outside in the pouring rain dancing and screaming with delight. You just don't know how wonderful it felt after all those lonely years thinking Daddy didn't care about me. Deep down inside there had always lingered a belief that he did love me and would some day come get me. When I got that letter the little seed of optimism that had nearly withered away inside me suddenly exploded. It was the happiest day of my life!

"Everybody was surprised to hear Daddy had gotten married but they were utterly shocked that he had sent for me. They had all written him off figuring it was only a matter of time before he'd be dead or locked away in prison. But they had been wrong, Daddy had finally settled down.

"The letter related how he and Agnus had built a small house on Douglas Island near Juneau. It originally had only one bedroom but they had added on an extra room and they wanted me to come live with them."

"So, weren't you a little upset about leaving your grandmother? After all she had raised you most of your life."

"I loved Grandma Winters and I was sad to leave her, but a girl should be with her father and I wanted so much to have a normal family. I didn't cry when I got on the plane. It was all too exciting. Perhaps it was selfish of me, but I think Grandma was actually glad to see me go. It was hard for her to take care of me at her age."

"So what happened when you got to Alaska?"

"It was foggy in Juneau when the plane landed. I remember looking out the window, hoping to get a glimpse of the city as we landed, but I couldn't see a thing. As I got off the plane I looked around for Daddy but he wasn't there. As you know Daddy is quite tall with dark blue eyes and a handsome face. Even though I hadn't seen him in several years I didn't expect to have any trouble recognizing him. The lady from Alaska Airlines made me wait for him by the gate. I wanted to search the terminal in case he went to the wrong place, but the lady wouldn't let me. It had been a long flight and I was tired so after awhile I stretched out on a bench and fell asleep.

"While I was sleeping I had a dream. *I was playing hopscotch on the sidewalk in front of a big house in the city. I looked toward the house and my mother, my real mother, was sitting in a rocking chair knitting. There was a garden in front of the house and the sweet scent of yellow roses was in the air. As I was playing, a car drove up and parked in front of the house. The door opened and Daddy, dressed in a fine wool suit, jumped out and smiled at me. I dropped my chalk and ran over to him. He picked me up, swung me around and gave me a big hug. After he put me down, my mother walked down the walkway toward us. Mom and dad embraced and kissed passionately. I was the happiest child on earth. Then I was awakened by the sound of laughter.*

"When I opened my eyes my father was smiling down at me. He took my hand and pulled me up. I threw my arms around him."

*****

"I'm sorry I was late honey but we had an emergency at the mine. A couple of the men were overcome by methane gas. We had to take them to the hospital. I hope you weren't scared," he said.

"I was a little bit," I said.

I noticed a pretty lady standing behind Daddy so I smiled at her figuring she was Agnus. Daddy suddenly realized he hadn't introduced his new wife to me so he said,"Sarah, this is your stepmother, Agnus."

"Hi Sarah, I am glad you made it here safely, now come along we've got a long trip back home."

Her abrupt attitude disturbed me. I was expecting a little warmer welcome from my new mother, you know. We went to the baggage claim area, got my luggage and then walked to Daddy's truck. It was cold and rainy when we set out for Juneau.

"Well Sarah, how was your flight?" Agnus asked.

"A little bumpy. The pilot said we flew over a big storm."

"Did they feed you, honey?" Daddy asked.

"No.'

"I bet you're famished," he said. "We'll stop in Juneau and get some pizza."

"Oh, goody. I love pizza."

"I know. I remember. . . . Pepperoni, right?"

"Uh huh, with lotsa cheese."

"No problemo, my little princess," Daddy said in his best Italian accent. Then his eyes lit up. "Oh, and do we have a great surprise for you."

"What is it?" I asked.

"There's going to be a big 4th of July parade in Juneau today. It should be starting about the time we arrive.'

"Oh, neat."

"And after the parade how would you like to go see some eagles?"

"We don't have time to see the eagles today," Agnus complained. "We need to get back to the house and get Sarah situated.'

Daddy sighed. "Agnus is right, we'll do that another time and I'm also going to show you the humpback whales and some grizzly bears, okay?"

"Oh boy! That will be cool," I said excitedly.

"Alaska is full of cool stuff, I know you'll love it here."

"I will, I know I will, Daddy. I'm so glad you sent for me."

"I know. I've been a terrible father, but I'm going to make it up to you. I promise."

"I watched Daddy for a moment trying to determine how he had changed since the last time I saw him. He seemed thinner, a few more gray hairs, but other than that he was just as I had remembered. I laid back against the seat. My mind was racing and I was having trouble relaxing. Suddenly I thought of my room. "Hey Daddy, am I really going to have my own room?"

"Yes ma'am. We built an extra room just for you, didn't we Agnus?"

"Yes, and I hope you appreciate it young lady, it's costing your father forty dollars a month to pay for it," Agnus said.

Daddy frowned at Agnus. He said,"That's nothing she needs to hear about."

"She should know so she'll appreciate what you're doing for her."

"You didn't have to build me a room. I could have slept on the sofa like I did at Grandma's."

"Nonsense, you're getting too old for a sofa," Daddy said. "You need a room of your own where you can have a little privacy."

"Thank you, Daddy . . . and you too, Agnus, for letting me come live with you. I'm so happy."

"We're happy too, honey. Aren't we, Agnus?"

"Sure, but you've got to understand, Sarah, this isn't going to be a picnic. There's going to be lots of work to do and everyone's got to do their share. Your father has a lot of responsibility being a foreman. He works long hours and when he comes home at night he's exhausted."

"I'll do my share, don't worry, and when Daddy comes home at night I'll treat him like a king."

"No you won't. You'll leave him alone so he can rest."

"Agnus, would you relax. You remind me of my drill sergeant at Fort Bragg," Daddy said. "You can treat me like a king, sweetheart and I'll treat you like a princess, okay?'

"Tom, you should be honest with Sarah. She should know that this is just an experiment and-"

"God damn it! Agnus, would you shut up!" Daddy was really angry. His face turned red.

"An experiment? I don't understand," I said. I was crushed to find out my stay may not be permanent. That sick, empty feeling that I thought I'd lost forever came roaring back with a vengeance. I glared at Agnus.

"Damn you, Agnus! . . . I'm sorry, honey. What Agnus is saying is that life up here in Alaska is tough. We have long, hard winters with only three or four hours of sunlight a day. When the summer finally comes it's very short and it's always raining. You may not like it here."

"It rains a lot in Portland too but I don't mind it. I'll love it here, I know I will. I just want to be with you, Daddy. Don't send me back to Grandma's, please."

"Don't worry. You can stay here as long as you like."

After the parade and lunch at the pizza parlor, Daddy took us home. Since there wasn't a bridge we had to take the ferry across to Douglas Island. As we drove up to the house I could hardly contain myself. Daddy parked the car in the driveway and I ran out to see my new home. It was a white frame house, a little small but very neat and cozy. I ran inside and inspected each room.

"This is perfect. I love it!" I said.

Tom laughed. "Well, I'm glad. You're going to be spending a lot of time in here. You better like it."

"I do. It's wonderful."

When I went to bed that night I felt better than I had in years. I knew I would be happy in Alaska. I was a little worried about Agnus but I figured if I worked hard and made myself indispensable to her she would never even think about sending me away.

For the next several weeks Daddy and I did everything together. He showed me Mendenhall Glacier, the humpback whales swimming up Favorite Channel and the bald eagles feeding on young salmon at Shelter Island. He even let me ride a mule around the mining camp and helped me carve a totem pole. But what I liked most of all was just being with him, talking and getting reacquainted. After only a few weeks I felt very close to my father again and the memories of all those rotten years in the past disappeared quickly. Like I said, for the first time in my life, I was happy and was looking forward to each day. Unfortunately it didn't last.

One night, several months after my arrival, Daddy came home very late. Agnus had prepared dinner several hours earlier and she was pissed that Daddy wasn't there to eat it. She glared at him as he stumbled through the front door after ten o'clock. When I saw him I ran over to him because I was afraid he was going to fall.

"Where the hell have you been? It's nearly ten-thirty," Agnus said.

"We had to go into Juneau to pick up some supplies. Two of the loaders at Arrow's Lumber were out sick. There was a line you wouldn't believe."

"And you obviously went to Sollie's Saloon while you waited," she said.

"That's where the guys wanted to go. What was I supposed to do?"

"Damn you, Tom! You've been nine months without a drink. Why didn't you have the sense to stay away from there."

"What makes you think I had a drink?"

"Tell me with a straight face you sat there and watched everyone else drink beer while you sipped a Coke."

Daddy just stared at Agnus without saying a word. I let go of him feeling embarrassed by being in the middle of the argument. So I slowly retreated to my room.

"You think I nursed you back to health because I had nothing better to do! I thought we could build a future together. I even consented to playing mommie to your little princess because I thought you were committed to this relationship."

"I don't have to take this shit from you, Agnus! All I had was a lousy beer."

"Yeah, right. That's why your eyes are bloodshot and you could hardly get through the door."

"I'm not drunk," Tom said.

"I won't put up with this, Tom. I've pulled you out the gutter too many times. I told you this was your last chance."

"So what are you going to do? Leave me because I had a few drinks with the guys. You're making a big deal over nothing. You're acting like I boned your best friend or something, Jesus!"

"You won't think it's nothing when I'm gone and you have to send your precious little daughter back to Oregon!"

I had been listening intently to the argument and had been deeply hurt by what Agnus had said about me. Suddenly I couldn't stand it anymore. I ran out of my room and started screaming at Daddy, "Stop arguing, Daddy! Please stop arguing! You're scaring me."

"Agnus looked at me as I was clinging to Daddy, tears rolling down my eyes. Then she shook her head, walked into the bedroom and slammed the door. I helped Daddy to the sofa where he soon fell asleep. For awhile I sat there and watched him, trembling from a combination of fear of being sent back to Oregon and the cold Alaskan night. The sudden jolt of reality Agnus had provided had been unsettling to say the least. Before I went to sleep I prayed that all would be forgotten by morning.

Unfortunately the fights continued, getting more violent and occurring more frequently as Daddy began to lose control of his life again. I don't know what brought it on. I couldn't understand why he was drinking again. The thought crossed my mind that perhaps he regretted sending for me.

I was cool to Agnus after that night. I knew now that Agnus didn't care about me and that was very painful because I really was starting to like her. After that night everything changed.

It all came to a head one evening a couple of months later. There was a church social scheduled and I had been looking forward to going to it all week. Friday afternoon I had been working on the dress I was going to wear when Agnus walked in.

"I thought I told you to mop the kitchen floor and put out the trash," Agnus said.

"I will in just a minute," I replied.

"Agnus walked over to me and ripped the dress out of my hand causing it to tear down the middle.

"Put that dress down and get in there and do your chores, girl!" she screamed.

"Look what you did! You tore my dress!" I said.

"Too bad! You should have done your chores before you starting working on it. It serves you right."

"I couldn't believe that Angus had ruined my dress. I was really mad so I screamed at her, "You're mean. I hate you."

"Agnus' face got real tight and then she clenched her fist and smacked me across the face. "Don't you talk to me like that little girl! I'll take the belt to you, you spoiled little brat!"

Totally shocked by the sudden violent attack, I stormed out of the house and ran down the snow covered street. I was so mad I could hardly stand it. At first I was going to run away but then I realized how difficult that would be in the snow and besides it would be exactly what Agnus would want. No, I decided I would just hide for awhile, give her a scare and make her miss the social.

I wandered around until I saw the security shack at the entrance to the mine. I decided to sneak inside and hide in the storage room where it would be warm. Once inside I found some blankets, laid down and went to sleep. When Daddy came home he noticed I was missing so he quizzed Agnus about it. She told him what had happened. Daddy got very angry and he almost hit her. When he left to go look for me, Agnus told him that she had had enough and she was leaving.

Daddy was too worried about me to try to stop her. He immediately left the house to search for me. He went to town first searching all around. Not finding me he headed for the mine. As he walked towards it he scanned the surrounding terrain hoping to see me wandering around or playing in the snow. When he reached the security shack he asked the guard if he had seen me. The guard said no but he said he had left for awhile so it was possible I might have come by. When he reached the mine he was worried that he hadn't found me. The temperature was in the low thirties and it was starting to get dark.

Daddy stared down into the mine wondering if I would have ventured down there. He knew I had been in the mine before so it was possible I might have gone in. He hesitated a moment but finally decided to take a look. He grabbed a hard hat and started his descent into the depths of the earth.

"Sarah! Are you down here?!" he yelled.

"When I woke up I went outside to look around. I figured it was time to go home, you know. Agnus had been punished enough. As I was walking away the security guard spotted me.

"Sarah! . . . Your father's been looking for you."

"Oh. Where is he?"

"He was headed down toward the mine. You better go find him before you get in a heap of trouble."

"I will. Thanks, I said."

"I began to wander around the base of the mine looking

for him. After searching everywhere I decided he must have gone in. I grabbed a hard hat with a light and started down into the shaft. The hat was too big for me so I had to hold it with one hand all the time. I was a little scared going down the metal stairs that led into the darkness of the mine, but having been down there before I felt confident enough to continue.

"When I got to the bottom of the stairs I started walking down the short, narrow tunnel towards where I assumed my father would be. It was cold and damp and I could hear water dripping down the walls beside me. I noticed a big puddle that had accumulated behind the staircase. The first time I had been in the mine I had played in the water and got into trouble. Before long I began to smell a strange odor and began to feel sick. Suddenly I heard a noise up ahead. It sounded like someone coughing. I picked up my pace toward the noise. It was very dark so I took it pretty slow. As I moved deeper into the mine, I too began to cough as the gas became stronger and stronger. At times I thought I was going to faint as I breathed in the toxic fumes.

"Finally I saw Daddy in the distance, flat on the ground, straining to get up. I rushed over to him and helped him struggle to his feet. Together we staggered back towards the mouth of the mine. Unfortunately I too was overcome by the poisonous gas and finally we both collapsed and lay silently on the earth near death. Luckily there was a breath of fresh air from the mouth of the mine. I opened my eyes and looked at my father's limp body. "No!" I screamed. "I am not going to let you die!" I grabbed the rock on the wall of the mine shaft and pulled myself up. Then I leaned over Daddy's body and began slapping his face.

"Wake up, Daddy! . . . Wake up!"

"Daddy struggled to open his eyes. He smiled faintly at seeing me. Then he realized what had happened and he tried desperately to get up. Together, somehow, we made our way toward the light at the end of the mine shaft. Luckily for both of us the security guard had come looking for us.

"Sarah, you down there," he yelled.

I perked up at hearing his voice. "Down here! Help us!" The guard came down the metal stairs and carefully made his way toward's us. When he finally made it he began to gag from the stench of the poisonous gas.

"Come on," he said as he extended his hand. "Let's get the hell out of here."

"The three of us picked up our pace and finally reached the metal stairs. By this time I was too weak to make it out so the guard carried me up and then went back down to get Daddy. When he got to the bottom of the mine he leaned over and tried to pull him over his shoulders. This was a real strain for a sixty year old man with a bad knee and lungs full of methane gas. I looked on from above scared to death that I would never see my father again alive.

"As the guard slowly brought him up the stairs he became dizzy and started to stumble. I gripped the rail tightly at seeing his distress and started to go down to help him but it was too late. He fell and he and Daddy tumbled down the stairs. As they fell, the guard lost his hard hat and it crashed against the steel stairwell throwing a spark that ignited the methane gas. Suddenly the gas exploded and I had to quickly retreat to avoid the hot flames.

A massive stream of black smoke began to flood out of the mine. I screamed in terror as Daddy and the guard disappeared behind the wall of smoke. I realized I had to do something fast. Looking around I saw the water tub used for the mules that worked in the mine. I ran over to it, broke the thin layer of ice on the surface and jumped in, drenching my clothes. The frigid water took my breath away. I got out and grabbed two saddle blankets and held them under the water until they were saturated. After that I ran back into the mine, holding one of the wet blankets around my body. I quickly ran down the hot metal staircase. The smoke was so thick I could barely see. When I got to the bottom of the pit I saw the guard and Daddy huddled against the side of the mine shaft in the pool of water I had seen earlier. They were both unconscious, but didn't appear to be burned.

"I shook them and pulled on their arms but I got no response. There was no way I was going to get them out of the mine so I wrapped one of the wet blankets around each of them and then ran back up the stairs to get help. Just as I cleared the mine there was another explosion. Fire shot out of the mouth of the mine high into the air and my heart sank. "No!" I screamed as I fell to my knees and began to cry. "No! Please God, no!"

"Just then I heard excited voices. I looked up and several men were approaching quickly. "Sarah, what happened?" one of the men said.

"They're at the bottom of the stairs! You've got to save them!"

The men began running toward the mine as fast as they could. They ran into the shack and came out with heavy coats and gas masks. Quickly they descended into the fiery pit. I ran back to the mouth of the mine and waited anxiously. I couldn't bear the thought of losing Daddy. He had to be alive. I knelt down, put my face in my hands and prayed. After what seemed an eternity I heard a familiar voice. "Sarah, are you all right?" Daddy said.

I looked up and tears of joy began flowing down my cheeks.

"Daddy, you're alive! Oh Daddy, I was so scared," I said as I stood up and hugged him. "I thought I was going to lose you."

"I know, . . . you're a brave little girl. If you hadn't come looking for me I'd be dead right now. You saved my life."

When Daddy and I got back to the house Agnus was gone.

*****

"Wow, that's quite a story," I said. "So did you ever see Agnus again."

"No, several weeks later Daddy was served with divorce papers. After the divorce we wandered around the country from Bakersfield to LA, to Phoenix and finally ended up in Dallas. Many times my father would come home drunk. I didn't like it when he did that, but at least we were together. When it did happen I'd clean him up, put him to bed and wash the stench of booze and vomit from his clothes."

"Jeeze," I said. "You really had it tough."

"It hasn't been fun. Daddy was married and divorced several times during the time we left Alaska and finally ended up in Dallas. I learned to get along with each of Daddy's companions although I often wondered why he needed them when he had me."

"Well, even if you were taking good care of him, I'm sure he had other needs."

"I know. It's just that none of his wives were worth a damn."

"So did your father ever try to send you away again?" I asked.

"No," Sarah replied. "I guess Daddy and I became pretty close having been through so much together. We had built a strong bond cemented by his guilt and my insecurity, I guess. Our life wasn't great but it was okay until Daddy met Joyce and fell in love."

"Oh, really. She was different than the others?"

"Yes, Joyce was a Christian Scientist and since Daddy had never been religious he agreed to become a Christian Scientist too so he could understand Joyce better and improve his own life."

"How did that work out," I said.

"Well, I will admit this marriage did change Daddy for the better. He dried up and finally gained some control over his life. I was glad he stopped drinking but I couldn't accept the teachings of Mary Baker Eddy. None of it made much sense to me. It was very unrealistic. I tried to learn and understand it for Daddy's sake but I never felt comfortable with it."

"So you didn't convert?"

"Not really. I went through the motions but it never really took."

I looked at my notes and saw that Joyce had a son. "What about Nate?"

"Nate was a few years older than me. I liked Nate okay but it felt a little strange suddenly having a brother. We were never very close. Nate was preoccupied with football and the family and all our friends seemed to be enamored with the idea that someday he would be in the NFL. I don't know much about football. I've never had time for games. To this day I don't understand why everyone, including my own father, seems to revere Nate so."

"Well, athletes are entertainers like movie stars," I said. "Everybody worships them nowadays. If Nate makes it he'll be a millionaire, no doubt."

"I guess," Sarah said.

I looked at my watch. "Well, I guess that's enough for today. That was really fascinating. We'll get together again next week and you can tell me more about the last few years living with your father and Joyce, okay?"

"Sure."

After Sarah had left, I turned and went back into my office to contemplate what Sarah had just told me. She was obviously a strong woman, a survivor who had been through hell. It occurred to me that she would do anything to protect her relationship with her father. But would she kill her own child? I couldn't see it. She would do the opposite. She was a protector. Like a mother bear watching over her cubs, she'd maul anyone who dared touch them. Unless, of course, it was all a facade. I was determined now, more than ever, to find out the truth.

Chapter Eight
Doomsayer

Several weeks went by without much activity on the Sarah Winters case. I used that idle time to continue my investigation of Bobby Wiggins's death. I wanted to question each one of our mutual clients, particularly Rob Parker, to see if they might know something that might help.

Parker, a bald headed man with a redish complexion, didn't look pleased to see me when I showed up at his office. I had decided to come without an appointment so he wouldn't have time to contemplate the purpose of my visit.

"What the hell are you doing here?" he asked.

"Is that any way to greet the man who saved your ass?"

"That was your job and you were well paid."

"True, but why the hostility?"

"Haven't you ever heard of making an appointment?" he said.

"I'm sorry, perhaps I should have, but I was in your neighborhood and thought I'd just stop by. I'm looking into Bobby's death."

"What are you moonlighting as a cop?"

"No, as you might have heard I've been sued for negligence."

He laughed. "How ironic. The lawyer gets a taste of his

own medicine."

"Thanks for your concern," I said.

He took a deep breath. The smile disappeared. "Okay, so how in the hell can I help you?"

"I just need to ask you a few questions."

"Okay, shoot."

"Did Bobby ever mention a medical problem to you?"

"No, we didn't get into personal stuff."

"Did you ever hear that he had a medical condition?"

"No, 'fraid not."

"Okay, on the night of the party, did you see anything unusual?"

"Yeah, I saw my accountant sprawled out on the sidewalk cause his attorney was too lazy to throw a little sand on it. Hell that could'a been me."

"Too bad it wasn't," I said under my breath.

"What did you say?"

"Too bad you didn't see him fall. Nobody actually saw him slip. It's just conjecture that he slipped on the ice."

"Huh. Pretty safe bet I would say."

"So you didn't see anything else unusual before the lights went out?"

"No, nothing."

"Where were you when the . . . when the lights went out?"

"In the dark."

"Seriously, where were you?"

"Shit, I don't know. Talking to someone, I guess."

"Who?"

"How the hell should I know. I talked to a lot of people that night."

"Before the party, how often did you see him?"

"Not too often."

"He's still your accountant, isn't he?"

"So, I sent him my bank statements every month and he sent me a big bill. I hardly ever talked to the man."

"What do you mean? What about your chapter 11?"

"What about it?"

"You must of spent a lot of time with him doing financial projections and monthly operating reports."

"We had a couple meetings."

"Did he ever discuss a discrepancy between your tax returns and your bankruptcy schedules?"

Parker stiffened. "What do you mean, *discrepancy?*"

"The fact that you appear to have suddenly picked up some new assets since your case was confirmed. Did he discuss that with you?"

"No, I don't know what you are talking about."

"I'm talking about filing fraudulent bankruptcy schedules. Where did you get the money to buy all that new equipment?"

Parker looked around and took a deep breath. "Is this confidential?"

"I'm still your attorney."

"Well, you know, I wasn't sure the Chapter 11 would be successful. You told me yourself most of them fail, right?"

"Right."

"So, I put a little something away just in case things didn't go well."

"Did Bobby find out?"

"He never mentioned it."

I shook my head. "I can't believe you did something so stupid."

He shrugged. "So now what?"

"Now, you find yourself another attorney. I can't represent you anymore."

"You gonna tell?"

"No, I can't disclose what I know, but I can't continue to represent you unless you want to come clean."

"Shit!" he said looking away.

"You wanna come clean?"

He laughed. "No way, you think I'm nuts?"

"Okay, I'll close your file and send you a final bill."

"Thanks a lot."

It was 10:45 a.m. when I got back to the office and told Jodie about Parker. She didn't seem surprised. While Jodie went to get me some coffee I flipped open my Day Timer and noted it was Wednesday, April 1. The calendar was clear the rest of the day so I figured I'd get a lot done.

As I was going through my mail I noticed a large envelope addressed with cutout letters from a magazine. How weird I thought. Jodie set a cup of coffee in front of me.

"What is this?" I said as I ripped it open. She shrugged. The message was also written in cutout letters just like the envelope. The message read:

"YE DEFENDERS OF THE DEVIL BEWARE! DEATH WILL BE YOUR ONLY REWARD. REPENT BEFORE YOU FACE ETERNAL DAMNATION. TIME IS SHORT UNTIL THE LIVING WILL AVENGE THE DEAD. DOOMSAYER."

"Look at this," I said.

Jodie walked around my desk and looked at the message.

"What the hell?" she said.

"Maybe its an April Fools joke," I said.

"I don't think so."

"It's a Bible quotation, I guess."

"What do you think it means?" Jodie asked.

"I don't know. It could have something to do with Sarah Winters, I suppose."

"Is it a death threat?" she asked.

I took a deep breath and replied, "No, I don't think so."

"Shouldn't you report it to the police?"

"I don't know, it's probably just some crackpot."

"You better not take any chances," Jodie said.

"What are they going to do?" I laughed. "The guy obviously was very careful not to leave anything that could be traced back to him."

"I don't know, I'm sure they can do something."

"It probably doesn't mean anything. Don't mention this to Rebekah, I don't want her to worry about it."

"Okay, but I think you're making a big mistake," Jodie said. "You can't ignore something like this. There are too many crackpots out there today."

I thought for a moment and then said,"Ah, just forget it."

As we were talking I noticed Jodie looked like she was putting on a little weight. I wasn't going to say anything but she apparently sensed my feelings.

"What?" She said. "Why are you looking at me like that?"

"Oh, nothing. For a minute there I thought you were getting a little belly."

Jodie gave me a cold stare that made me feel quite uncomfortable.

"I'm sorry that wasn't a very nice thing to say, forgive me," I said.

"No, it's true, I'm actually glad you brought it up."

"Huh?"

"I'm not getting fat from eating too much, I'm, . . . well actually, I'm pregnant."

"Really, you and Rodney actually stopped fighting long enough to make love?"

"That's the problem, making love is the only thing we do well. We fight about everything else."

"So is Rodney excited about being a father?"

"I haven't told him, he'd probably leave me if he found out."

"Oh, come on, he loves you, he wouldn't do that," I said.

"You don't know him like I do, he'll croak if I tell him I'm pregnant. He'll blame me for forgetting to take my pills. I'm really scared to tell him."

"So what are you going to do?"

"I don't have any choice."

"What do you mean?"

"I've got to get an abortion."

A chill darted down my spine. I didn't know what to say. I'd never really thought much about abortion. I knew I was against them but I had never had to deal with one before. A sick feeling came over me.

"An abortion! No, . . . you're not going to do that, are you?"

"I have to. This isn't a good time for me to be pregnant. Rodney will leave me and then I'll be a single parent trying to raise a child and work at the same time. What kind of a mother would I be if I left my child at day care all day and then at night was too tired to give it the attention it deserved?"

I got up and walked to the window overlooking downtown Dallas. I thought about Jodie's baby, alive and healthy inside her womb and wondered if it could sense the danger it was facing. Then I thought of Sarah's baby, lying in a coffin six feet under the ground. *What was this world coming to when the life of innocent children meant so little?*

"I know it's none of my business and the Supreme Court says you can have an abortion if you want one, but why not just give the child up to someone who wants it?"

"Rodney would find out I was pregnant if I did that," Jodie said. "I couldn't bear to lose him."

"Is he worth keeping if he couldn't love you and the

baby?"
"It wouldn't work. Anyway, my mind is made up. The only reason I told you about it was that I'll need next week off to have the abortion."
"How far along are you?"
"Twenty-two weeks."
"You kind of waited a long time to do this, haven't you?"
"Don't think this has been easy for me. I've spent many an hour agonizing over this decision. I've felt this life within me and in many ways I want this baby. But it just won't work, I know Rodney too well. We could never have children. Rodney couldn't share me with anyone, even his own child."
I stood silently and stared at Jodie. Tears were running down her cheeks. I went over to my credenza, pulled out a box of Kleenex and handed it to her.
"Okay, take the week off. Do what you think is best."
"Thanks," Jodie said. "I know it's the best thing."
"Since you're going to be gone all week I think I'll spend the time out of the office interviewing witnesses and suspects in the Wiggins and Winter's cases. I shouldn't need much secretarial help for that. I've got to do it sooner or later anyway so it should work out well."
"That's a good idea, but you could get a temporary if you wanted."
"Nah, you've got me spoiled. I'd just waste a bunch of time trying to train her."
"Maybe I won't have to be out an entire week."
"Ah, don't worry about it, I'll be all right. Take whatever time you need."
That night I left early and drove home. It was a long slow ride due to rush hour traffic and a gentle rain that had just rolled in with a cold front. When I arrived home, everyone was sitting down to dinner. It was Rebekah's practice to wait until about six to have supper, but if I wasn't home by then she

would start dinner without me and warm mine up later. She liked it when the family ate together so she was glad to see me home early.

"Well, you just made it in the nick of time," Rebekah noted.

"Yeah, I didn't feel like working late tonight."

"It's a good thing, this weather is miserable. Did you know we're under a flash flood warning?"

"Really?"

"Hi Daddy," Reggie said.

"Hi, bum. How was school today?"

"Okay."

"Don't forget soccer starts next week," I said.

"Oh, yeah. Would you put some air in my soccer ball so I can start practicing?"

"Do we have a needle?"

"Yeah, in the garage."

"Okay, after supper."

As I started to eat I couldn't keep my mind off Jodie. Rebekah watched me twisting my spaghetti around and around and not eating.

"What are you doing Stan? Is something wrong with the spaghetti?"

I looked up at her and tried to smile. "No, I was just thinking about Jodie."

"Jodie?"

"Uh huh, she's getting an abortion. She'll be out all week."

"I didn't even know she was pregnant," Rebekah said.

"What's an abortion?" Reggie asked.

I looked at Rebekah. She shrugged and got up to go to the refrigerator. Thanks a lot I thought to myself.

"Ah. Well, it's when a baby dies before it's born."

"Oh," Reggi said as he picked up a meatball with his

fork and began nibbling on it. He frowned. "Why would it die before it was alive?" I didn't feel comfortable telling a nine year old the truth about abortion so I used my legal skills to dance around the question.

"Ah, . . . sometimes they get sick inside the womb, . . . or they have a defect, you know."

"Oh."

I continued talking to Rebekah. "I keep thinking of poor Sarah who could have had an abortion a few weeks earlier. Jodie's going to be gone a week and then her life will be, more or less, back to normal. Sarah, on the other hand, may well spend a substantial portion of her life in prison. The whole thing stinks."

"I think they both should go to prison," Rebekah said.

"Maybe so, but abortions are legal so you can't send Jodie to prison and I don't see why Sarah should go either, assuming she's guilty, since what she did, in reality, was no worse than Jodie," I said.

The following Monday, I made appointments with Greg Peterson and Richard Stein. I figured both of Sarah's boyfriends had to be my primary suspects. Each had good reason to kill Sarah's baby. The only question was how could I find out if one of them, in fact, was the killer. I figured a low keyed, non-accusatory approach would be best. Perhaps the killer would make a mistake and reveal himself. I met with Richard Stein first on the ASU campus in a library study room. He was sweaty, unshaven and donned a yellowed T-shirt, torn jeans and sandals.

"How's Sarah?" Stein asked.

"Oh, she's fine now, she had a rough time there for a while but now she's doing alright," I replied.

"I'd go visit her but her parents would have a mule if I showed up at their door."

"They don't like you I take it?"

"You got that right," Stein said.

"Why do you think that is?"

"They know how I'm financing my education, you know, and how I make a living."

"How did Sarah feel about your drug dealing?"

"She didn't like it, you know, but she tolerated it. She's had a lot of practice with that kind of thing, you know, cause her old man was a drug addict and a drunk."

"Was she on drugs?"

"Now and then, I made sure she didn't get hooked though. I didn't want no junkie for my woman," Stein said.

"I take it you don't use drugs yourself then?"

"I take a snort once and a while, but I need to stay sober to do my business."

"I see. Did you know Sarah was pregnant?"

He shrugged. "Not really, she was getting a little pudgy but the way she was eating that didn't surprise me."

"That's not what she said."

Stein frowned. "What did she tell you?"

"She said you had arranged for an adoption."

"She's crazy."

"You didn't have an attorney looking for a home for the baby?"

"No. She must be confused. I told her I'd take her to a clinic to have an abortion, but I don't know anything about any adoption."

"But you said you didn't know she was pregnant."

"Not until she told me. . . You know. . . . Then I told her to get an abortion."

"Did you all use birth control?"

"I didn't, I assume she did."

"Do you know for sure?"

"No, I think she was taking the pill, at least that's what she told me."

"I won't beat around the bush about this, weren't you the baby's father?"

"I'd like to deny it, but what's the use. Sarah was a one guy woman, she wouldn't of cheated on me. It's a simple mathematical equation, seven months before she killed her baby, she and I were together."

"You think she killed her baby?"

"Of course, who else would have done it?"

"You think she is capable of murder?"

"Killing a baby is not exactly murder, you know, she had a right to do it. It was her baby."

"Not according to the law. It was too late for an abortion."

"That's just legal mumbo jumbo. What in the hell difference could a few weeks make?"

"Six weeks," I said. Stein shrugged. "Aside from the legalities, you knew her pretty well, was she capable of killing her baby?"

"Listen, she's not as pristine as she pretends to be. She usually has a handle on what's happening and will do what has to be done. She got what she wanted."

"When was the last time you saw her?"

"Oh, a week or two before the murder. We have a class in the same building at the same time so we run into each other from time to time."

"Did you say anything to her then?"

"Yeah, I asked her how she was."

"What did she tell you?"

"Not much, but I could tell she wasn't happy."

"How could you tell that?"

"She had that look in her eyes like she wanted to spill her guts to me, you know, but was afraid. I tried to reassure her, but she wouldn't open up to me. When we were together she would get that look from time to time and after a while she'd unload on me. But not any more."

"What happened to you two?"

"I had a little too much to drink one night and I knocked her around a bit. She never forgave me. I guess I don't blame her."

I sat silently for a moment staring at Richard wondering what next to ask him. Obviously he wasn't going to volunteer anything important. I wondered what I could say to trip him up.

"So, that was it then?" I asked.

"That was it. She didn't speak to me at all for several weeks. When she did finally talk to me it was clear our relationship was over. She said she could put up with about anything but physical abuse."

"It sounds like you still have feelings for her."

"I do, but that's life. Sometimes you got to move on, if you know what I mean."

"When did you hear about the murder?"

"Not 'til the next day when I read about it in the newspaper."

"Where are you living now?"

"I've got an apartment not too far from Sarah's place, about a half mile away."

"Were you home that night?"

"The night of the murder? . . . Ah, well, maybe part of the evening."

"Did you see any of the police cars or the police search parties?"

"No."

"Do you live alone?"

"No, I've got a roommate, she's a senior accounting major."

"Was she with you that night?"

"No, she got home late, after midnight."

"Do you remember when you were home and when you

were out?"

"I was home all night except for a delivery I made about eleven p.m."

"You didn't see anything when you went out at eleven?"

"No, nothing unusual."

"How do you feel about your baby being killed?"

"I feel nothing, I didn't even know she was pregnant. How could I have any feelings for a child I never even saw?"

"What if you had seen it?"

"It wouldn't make any difference. I wouldn't consider it my child."

"But what if the baby had lived and you had to pay child support?"

"That wouldn't be right," he said.

"In your mind, it may not be right, but it's the law isn't it? You were the father."

"I suppose."

"How much do you make as a drug dealer?" I asked.

"Maybe a hundred grand or so but no one could prove it."

"Suppose they did and you had to pay $25,000 a year in child support?"

"No way, it wouldn't happen."

"I don't suppose you pay taxes?"

"Taxes? Are you kidding? What do you think, I'm nuts? I'm not giving my money to those lunatics who run this country."

"If suddenly Sarah got a lawyer and she pressed you for child support and in the process the IRS found out you weren't paying taxes, you could end up losing damn near half of your income; not to mention going to jail for tax evasion."

"They couldn't prove shit."

"I know, but it's an interesting thought," I said.

"A fucking nightmare is more like it!"

"Well, thank you Richard, I appreciate you talking to me, I know you didn't have to."

"No problem man, hope Sarah gets off the hook."

"We'll do all we can."

I got up, shook hands with Richard and left the library. I didn't know what to think of the interview. Somebody was lying obviously. I hoped it was Richard and not Sarah. Richard didn't act guilty, but he certainly had the motive and opportunity to kill Sarah's baby. Before I left town I interviewed Sarah's roommate, Michelle, talked to several of the other tenants in the apartment complex as well as my niece, Alice.

"So you took Sarah's case?" Alice said.

"Yes, I did."

"I told Mr. Winters I wasn't sure if you would but, if not, you would refer him to someone."

"I don't know what you told him, but he was convinced he had to have me and only me on the case. After you graduate how about you come handle my marketing for me?"

Alice laughed. "Okay, I could do that."

"So, how well did you know Sarah?"

"Not that well. We went to a few parties together and I saw her around the apartment complex on occasion. We weren't close friends or anything like that."

"Did you know she was pregnant?"

"We suspected it, but she denied it when we brought it up."

"Did you see her the night of the murder?"

"No, Michelle stopped by to use the phone to call her parents but I never actually saw Sarah that night."

"Did you hear anything?"

"No, not until the police showed up."

"Have you heard anything from your friends about what happened?"

"Just that someone called the police and told them

where to find the dead fetus."

"You're kidding? Where did you hear that?"

"One of the dispatchers is a friend of the leasing agent. She told her that someone called the police that night and told them to look in the dumpster behind Sack'N Save."

"Was it a man or a woman?"

"A man."

"Huh. That means somebody either saw Sarah dump the baby or someone else is involved in the murder," I said.

"I guess,"

"Well, I'm glad I stopped by to see you. If you hear anything else let me know."

"Oh, the District Attorney called me. He said I might have to be a witness."

"Did he say why?"

"Yes, he said he wanted me to testify that I was home all night and if Sarah had wanted any help she could have easily come and got me. He thinks the fact that I didn't hear anything and Sarah delivered her baby without asking for any help is clear evidence that she planned to kill her baby all along."

"That's a good point. I hope there's an explanation for that. Our only hope is that Sarah's memory comes back."

"I sure hope it does."

The following morning I had to go to bankruptcy court for discharge hearings and then I planned to meet with Greg Peterson for lunch. I did a lot of bankruptcies due to the excessive amount of credit that financial institutions were extending to almost anybody who had a pulse. One of these cases this particular morning had boggled my mind. A man of Arab descent had come to my office to file bankruptcy. He had fifteen credit cards, all American Express Cards, two Platinum's, three Golds, eight Greens and two Optimas with a combined balance of nearly $200,000. I warned the client to expect a dischargeability complaint from American Express, however, he never heard from them and the deadline for objecting to the bankruptcy had passed. When I entered the courtroom, I saw Mo sitting quietly in the back of the room. Several other of my clients were scattered around the courtroom. I took them one by and one and explained to them what to expect during the course of the hearings. Finally, the door to the Judge's chamber opened and the Judge appeared. The bailiff commanded everyone to rise.

"Be seated," the Judge said. "Good morning, I'm judge Baldwin. This is your bankruptcy discharge and reaffirmation hearing. Congress has mandated that if a debtor reaffirms any debts that such reaffirmation be approved by the Court. As your attorney no doubt explained to you a reaffirmation is a new promise to pay a debt that has been discharged in bankruptcy. When I call your name please come forward and your attorney will ask the appropriate questions concerning your reaffirmations. We're mainly concerned that these reaffirmations are necessary and that they will not be a hardship on you. Okay, I'm going to call the ten o'clock docket now."

For the next hour I paraded several of my clients before the judge. It was quite monotonous. "Mr. Burns has a Chevrolet Malibu he'd like to reaffirm with GMAC. The payments are $312 a months and he used the Malibu as his primary transportation to and from work," I said to the judge."

"Will this be hardship on you? Mr. Burns," the judge asked.

"No, sir. I can handle it."

The judge nodded and said, "Then the reaffirmation will be approved."

At the end of the docket the clerk passed out everyone's discharge papers. When it was over I shook hands with all of my clients and wished them well. As I was leaving Mo joined me in the elevator.

"Well Mo, you are one lucky guy not to get an objection on all those Amex cards, I still can't believe it."

"You know, I didn't want to tell you this earlier, but I was referred to you by *the Company.*"

"What Company? I thought you were self employed?"

"Well, I haven't been totally honest with you, Stan."

"What do you mean?"

"You're still my attorney, even though the bankruptcy is over, right?"

"Yeah, until your case is closed."

"Everything I tell you is still confidential, isn't it?"

"Yes," I said curious as to what little bombshell he was about to lay on me.

"Actually I work for the CIA."

"Huh, the CIA?"

"They got me all these credit cards and when I was having trouble paying them they said go see Stan Turner and file bankruptcy."

"You've got to be kidding. I don't know anyone at the CIA."

Mo smiled and said, "They know you obviously."

The elevator door opened and Mo stepped out. It all made sense now, somebody intervened to make sure there wouldn't be an objection to Mo's bankruptcy. That made me mad. I hated being someone's pawn, particularly in a game I didn't even know existed. Why did the CIA pick me anyway? Was it because they thought I was a good citizen and would turn my head if I figured out what they were doing? Would this happen again? Was Mo just the first of many to follow? Totally fascinated by Mo's revelation, I couldn't wait to tell Rebekah.

The meeting with Greg Peterson was to be at La Madeline at Forest Lane and Preston Road in Dallas. Greg was a student at the University of Texas also majoring in journalism. I pulled into a parking space across from the restaurant at 11:45. I saw Greg sitting on a chair near the entrance. I got out of my car and walked up to him. We shook hands, entered the restaurant and got in the line that was forming for lunch.

"How's Sarah?" I asked.

"She's doing better. I spent the evening with her last night. She won't talk about the baby though. I was hoping she would open up to me and tell me what really happened."

"So you don't believe her loss of memory story?"

"I'd like to, but how could you forget something like that. She must know what happened. She's just afraid to tell. I think she's afraid that I'll leave her."

I said, "Next week we're going to have Dr. Gerhardt talk to her. He's a good shrink. Maybe she'll open up to him or at least prescribe some sort of treatment for her."

Greg and I finally got to the front of the line and gave the cashier our order, then we took a tray, got something to drink and found a table."Listen Greg, I've got to ask you some questions. Please don't be offended if I ask something indelicate. I don't mean it maliciously, it's just my job to learn all of the facts."

"I understand," Greg replied.

"How long have you and Sarah been going out together?"

"Three or four months."

"I assume your relationship has been intimate."

"Yes, we've talked about getting married someday after we both graduate."

"That's great. Did you know her before you started going out?"

"No, I couldn't have been the father if that's what you are getting at. Lt. Winters asked me the same question."

"Oh, he's already talked to you?"

"Yeah."

"So he must of asked you where you were on the night of the murder, right?"

"Yeah."

"So, what was your answer?"

"I was studying at the UTD library."

"With a study group, I hope," I laughed.

"No, alone."

"Hmm, did anyone see you?"

"No."

"Did you check out a book, make a phone call or do anything that would prove you were in Dallas on the night of the murder?"

"I'm afraid not, but I did get a call on my answering machine from Sarah."

"Is that right?"

"Yes."

"When did you receive it?"

"Well, I got home about 9:45 p.m. and when I checked my recorder there was a message from Sarah. She asked me to call her."

"Did you?"

"Yes, but nobody answered."

"Really?" I said. "Did you know Sarah was pregnant?"

"Of course, she couldn't hide it from me. She was getting fat."

"So what did she say about it?"

"She said she was going to give the baby up for adoption. She couldn't keep a baby right now."

"How did you feel about it?"

"I thought that was the right thing to do."

"That was pretty noble of you to hang in there with her even though she was pregnant by another man?"

"I love her. She got pregnant before she knew me."

"Do you think she killed her baby?" I asked.

"No. She couldn't have done it," Greg said. "She wanted children someday, but later in her life when things were more stable and she was married. She often said when she had kids she'd smother them with love and spoil them rotten. She didn't want them to have a hellish childhood like hers."

"What time was it when you called her back?"

"Probably 9:55 p.m."

"So, she may have had the baby before 9:55 and then passed out. I wonder if there is a telephone record somewhere of your call to her?"

"There should be."

"How long does it take to get to Sarah's apartment?"

"About an hour and fifteen minutes," Greg said.

"So, you're not totally off the hook, you could have driven up there."

"I could have got there by 11:30 probably, had I known Sarah was in trouble."

"When did you first learn she was in the hospital?"

"When Michelle called me about 2:15 a.m."

"2:15 huh?"

"Yeah."

"You had time to go to Sherman, kill the baby and return to your apartment. I'm not saying you did, but just talking possibilities."

"But I didn't know she was in labor."

"To be honest with you, that's hard for me to believe. You'd be the first person she'd call, don't you think."

"Yes, except she didn't want me to be there when she delivered. She told me that. She didn't want me to go through that until we had our own children."

"Do you have any idea who was going to adopt the child?"

"No, I asked her but she wouldn't tell me."

"How about the lawyer. Did she ever talk about a lawyer handling the adoption?"

"No. No lawyers."

"Okay. Just a few more questions and then I'll let you finish your lunch."

"How did you feel when you heard that Sarah had delivered Ricky's baby?"

He grimaced. "Sick . . . but relieved the nightmare was almost over. Ricky was evil personified. The thought of Sarah being with him was appalling to me. How she had been attracted to him was difficult to fathom. Do you know that son of a bitch beat her up! That's why they broke up. Sarah wouldn't put up with that shit. If I'd of seen Ricky that night I might have killed *him*, but not an innocent baby."

"Even for Sarah?"

"I don't know. But luckily she never asked me to do that. Besides, if she hadn't cared about the baby she would have had an abortion a lot earlier."

"It's too bad for her she didn't do that."

"I know, I tried to convince her to have an abortion but she wouldn't hear of it."

Greg's eyes turned red as he struggled to hold back his tears. A couple of the people eating around us looked over and gave Greg a disapproving look.

"I'm sorry Greg, I know all this must be very difficult for you."

"You don't know the half of it. Can I ask *you* some questions?"

"Sure, that's only fair."

"Is Sarah going to go to jail?"

"Realistically, she could be convicted. The DA has a lot of evidence, a lot of it's circumstantial, but it is still enough to convict her unless we can prove someone else actually killed her baby."

"How long will she be in prison if she is convicted?"

"It all depends on the exact charge on which she is convicted. If it's murder it could be 5 years to life in prison. If it's voluntary or involuntary manslaughter it could be six months to twenty years. So, it's premature to really speculate on her punishment right now, assuming she was guilty."

"When is her trial going to be set?"

"I'd imagine it will be in a couple of months. The judge will probably set a date in the next few weeks."

Greg wiped his eyes with the sleeve of his shirt. "You've got to get her off, Mr. Turner, she told me what happened to her when she was in jail for just twenty minutes. She'd never survive any length of time in there. You can't let them convict her!"

When I got back to the office it seemed like a mausoleum it was so quiet without Jodie there. On the way in I had picked up the mail. I dumped the stack of envelopes and advertisements in the middle of my desk. As I was going through it I noticed a letter with my business card used as the address. The sender had cut out my address and telephone number and taped it to an envelope. There was no return address. I opened it cautiously. On a single sheet of typing paper the following message in cutout letters appeared.

"REPENT SINNER, BEFORE THE DEVIL SUCKS YOU INTO THE PITS OF HELL. REBUKE THE KILLER OF THE INNOCENT SO SHE MAY STAND BEFORE GOD AND RECEIVE ETERNAL DAMNATION. JUSTICE IS IMPATIENT! DOOMSAYER."

I studied the message for a few minutes and then decided to call and talk to Snake about it.

"Hi, what's going on?"

I sighed. "You won't believe this. It's so bizarre really, but recently I've been getting some strange letters."

"What kind of letters?"

I described the two messages I had received.

"Damn, apparently someone's trying to scare you. Shake you up to make you less effective or maybe they think you'll just drop the case."

"I just wonder if it's anything to worry about."

"I doubt it, it's probably just a prankster. But you probably should tell Meadows know about it anyway. He may want to do something about it."

"Okay, I'll put a call into him and see what he wants to do."

"It's probably nothing to worry about, but it doesn't hurt to be cautious," Snake said. "So, how did your interviews go?"

I gave Snake a complete rundown on my conversations with Richard Stein and Greg Peterson.

"Unfortunately I wasn't able to eliminate either Ricky or Greg as a suspect. Either one could have done it. They both certainly had a good motive."

"Figures. When do you want me to line up Dr. Gerhardt?"

"Next week I think," I said. "Sarah needs treatment as soon as possible. Her mind is still repressing the whole incident. We've got to find out what really happened."

"Dr. Gerhardt will open her up," Snake said. "He's very good."

"I hope so. If he doesn't we're in deep trouble."

Chapter Nine
A Glimpse of the Truth

It was Friday afternoon and I was rapidly scanning a thirty-seven page lease for one of my corporate clients. My eyes were aching from reading the fine print. It had been a tough week without Jodie around to answer the phone, file, keep up my calendar, handle correspondence and all the other myriads of tasks a legal secretary does. Most of all it had been a lonely week as I had grown accustomed to Jodie's companionship over the eight months that she had been my secretary. As I sat down to review the document the telephone rang. It was Sarah and she was upset.

"Dad and Joyce just had a big fight. Dad didn't come home last night. Joyce is really pissed off. I'm getting the hell out of here."

"Okay, calm down. Tell me exactly what happened.
*****

A little while ago, Nate and I were talking on the phone when I noticed Joyce pulling up in her Lincoln Town Car. She got out of the car, slammed the door and stormed into the house. She gave me an evil glance as she walked by heading toward her bedroom. Then she went inside and slammed the door. I wondered what was wrong so I said goodbye to Nate and went to her bedroom door and knocked.

"Mom, what's wrong?" I said.

She yanked the door open and glared at me.

"Don't call me Mom, I'm not your damn mother. I'm sick and tired of being second fiddle to you around here. Your father better decide pretty damn quick who he's married to or it's going to be all over for us."

"What happened, did you two have a fight?"

"Your father stole my jewels and used them as collateral on your bond. I can't believe he did it!" Joyce collected fine jewels as an investment. Her father was a jeweler so she learned how to pick and grade them. She had acquired quite a collection mainly from estate sales, pawn shops and wholesalers trying to get rid of inventory overstocks. She was very proud of her collection."

"Oh, shit," I said suddenly feeling very guilty.

"Why did you let this happen? Don't you know anything about birth control? What are you some kind of retard? Damn it! You should have got an abortion as soon as you found out you were pregnant."

I looked at her incredulously. "I thought you and Daddy were against abortion?"

Her face turned red with rage. "Don't try to blame this on me young lady."

"I'm not but-"

"You could have given the baby away."

"I was going to but-"

She grabbed my shoulders and began shaking me and screamed, "Then why didn't you? How could you suffocate your own flesh and blood?"

I tried to push her away. "Let me go, you have no right to treat me this way. I didn't kill my baby."

"That no good Jew, what's his name? Steinberg. He was the father, wasn't he?"

I broke away and backed off from Joyce.

"His name is Richard Stein. He was the first man who treated me with a little respect. Hell, he was the first man who gave me the time of day. If it wasn't for his drug problem I'd still be with him. And, for your information, I'm not so absolutely positive he was the father."

I was shocked by my own statement. Why had I said that? An uneasy silence ensued as we stared at one another.

"Oh my God!" Joyce screamed shaking her head. "You're nothing but a whore. If your father only knew the truth about you."

"Ha! If my father only knew the truth about you. You're a pathetic excuse for a mother! I've hated you from the moment I laid eyes on you and if I never saw you again for the rest of my life I'd be ecstatic."

Before she could respond I turned and walked away, not daring to look back.

*****

"You think Richard may not have been the father?" I asked jolted by her statement.

"Like I said, I don't know where that came from. He obviously must be," Sarah said softly. "I want you to know, I don't usually talk like that but Joyce really got me upset when she started shaking me and carrying on the way she did."

"I'm so sorry Sarah. Is there anything I can do?"

"No, I just wanted to tell you that I was leaving home. I'm going to stay with Greg for a while."

"Do you think that's a good idea?"

"I can't stay in the same house with Joyce. I don't have any choice."

"Okay, but stay in touch. I've got to know where you are at all times. Oh, by the way, next week we want you to meet with a psychiatrist, Dr. Gerhardt."

"Why?"

"We need him as an expert witness and he may be able

to help you get over the trauma of the past few weeks. I'll call you when we have a definite time set up."

"Alright."

"Oh, and don't forget you have to appear in Court for a status conference on April 17."

"Right, I'll be there."

I wasn't pleased with the phone call from Sarah. All I needed now was my client floating around between her parents and boyfriend. I was responsible for her appearance in court every two weeks until the trial and I didn't want to have to spend a lot of time trying to track her down. I started to pick up the telephone to call and report to my corporate client about the lease when the telephone rang again. It was Rebekah.

"Stan, something terrible has happened, you've got to come home right now!"

"What is it?"

"It's Reggi, he's in his room crying, some kids were very ugly to him over you defending Sarah Winters."

"You're kidding? What happened?"

"I don't know exactly, but that's not all."

"What else?"

"When Reggie got home, there was a letter. You've got to come home now, he's so upset!"

"Okay, I'm leaving right now."

I got up, grabbed my coat and left. I couldn't believe someone would stoop so low as to threaten my son. It was one thing to attack me, I was a soldier on the front lines, but my family was off limits. I'd knock the crap out of the son of a bitch if I could only find out who it was. When I got home Beauty met me at the door as usual with her tail wagging excitedly.

"Hi, Beauty," I said and then bent down and gave her a hug. "Sorry girl, but I don't have time to play right now."

The mood in Reggie's room was somber. He was lying

on his bed staring at the wall. His eyes were red and swollen from crying. Rebekah was sitting on the chair at his desk holding a newspaper. I rushed over to him.

"Reggie, are you all right?"

He nodded without smiling. "Yes, I'm okay, I guess."

"So, what happened to you?"

"Everybody hates me at school now because I'm your son."

"What? That's ridiculous."

"All I heard about today was how you were defending a witch. Is that true?"

"A witch, where did they get that nonsense?"

"You obviously don't read the tabloids," Rebekah said."

"Tabloids? What are you talking about?"

"Your client is the feature story," Rebekah said as she handed Stan the latest issue of the National Examiner. I took it and looked incredulously at the headline: SARAH WINTERS, A TEXAS WITCH? Investigators Uncover Shocking Evidence of Accused Killer's superhuman abilities, sordid childhood and ties to evil underworld."

"Oh, Jesus," he said "Who told them this?"

"Apparently they talked to her stepmother and she told them about Sarah going into a fiery inferno and saving her father's life."

"Oh God! I can't believe this."

"And, the underworld ties. That's her association with Ricky which is probably a good point."

"And her 'sordid past'"

"A life on the run with a drunken, worthless father."

"Hardly her fault," I said.

Rebekah took the paper and said, "Well, they say she chose that life. She could have stayed with her grandmother and had a quasi-normal life."

I shook my head. "That's ridiculous. She was only eight

years old for godsakes. How a reporter could write something so irresponsible is beyond me. Now we're going to have every crackpot in the country down here wanting to burn Sarah at the stake."

"Do you think she's a witch?" Reggie asked.

"No, this is garbage. Sarah is just an ordinary girl who's had a very tough life."

"There's a big article in the Dallas Morning News today about Sarah Winters too," Rebekah said. "They talk all about you and how you're going to get her off by pleading temporary insanity."

"Who told them that pack of lies? I don't have any idea what my defense is going to be. Sarah hasn't even seen a shrink yet."

"I wish you hadn't taken this case." Rebekah said. "I don't like you defending a murderer?"

"I don't think she did it, but if she did do it she's entitled to the best defense possible."

She took a deep breath, her big brown eyes full of worry. "Oh, I almost forgot. Take a look at this letter."

I walked over to the desk and read the latest ominous message form the coward, Doomsayer.

"THE SONS AND DAUGHTERS SHALL WEEP WHEN THE DEVIL'S DEFENDERS ARE SLAIN IN THE NAME OF GOD AND RIGHTEOUSNESS. TAKE HEED OF THIS WARNING FOR TIME IS FLEETING. DOOMSAYER."

I stared at the message and then shook my head, "Damn it! I can't believe this asshole is doing this again. He must be some kind of wacko."

"What do you mean, *again*?" Rebekah said looking me

expectantly.

"I didn't want to alarm you but this isn't the first message from this Doomsayer lunatic."

"You're kidding?"

"No, I got a couple messages like this at the office. I reported them to the police."

"Daddy, is he going to hurt us?" Reggie asked.

"No, nobody's going to hurt us. They're just trying to scare me so I'll withdraw from the case."

"Maybe you should," Rebekah said.

"No way, I'm not letting some low-life tell me what to do."

"Who do you think it is?" Rebekah asked.

"Probably some religious fanatic who thinks he's omniscient and doesn't need to waste time with a judge and jury."

"What would happen if you withdrew?" Rebekah asked.

"Sarah would either hire a new attorney or the Court would appoint her one."

"You need to call the police and tell them about this, Stan," Rebekah said.

"I know, I will. Maybe this one will have a print on it or some other clue as to who's responsible for it."

"I hope so," Rebekah said. "I'm really worried about the kids getting hurt."

"I know. I'm worried too, but everything's going to be all right. I won't let anyone hurt you or the kids."

The following Monday I was anxious to get to work since I knew Jodie would be back. When the elevator door opened, I was delighted to see the office lit up like a twenty-four hour supermarket. Walking briskly into the waiting room the sweet aroma of fresh coffee uplifted me. I took a deep breath and proceeded into the secretarial area. Jodie was busily working at her desk.

"Hi, Jodie."

"Oh, good morning, Stan."

"So, how do you feel?"

"I've felt better, but I'll live."

"How was it?"

"Not so bad, really."

"I bet you're glad to be done with it?"

"More so than you can imagine."

"Did anyone go with you?"

"My mom was there."

"That's good. Well, I'm glad it's over for you."

"Thanks. So did anything interesting happen while I was gone?"

I told her about the National Examiner story and the messages from Doomsayer.

"Oh, Jesus. Did you call the police?"

"Yes, they've sent the messages to the FBI for analysis."

"Good, maybe they'll catch the bastard."

"I hope so."

"So what's on tap for this week?" Jodie asked.

"Snake has scheduled a session between Sarah and Dr. Gerhardt. He's going to evaluate her mental condition and be one of our expert witnesses. Dr. Gerhardt is an expert in hypnosis so he might take her back to the night of the killing and see if he can find out exactly what happened."

"Does that really work?"

"Come in my office and I'll show you the report I just received on it."

"Okay," Jodie said and then got up and followed me into my office. I sat at my desk and Jodie sat in a side chair directly in front of me. It was so good to have her back.

"Well, I've been researching that question and apparently hypnosis has proven to be very effective at restoring memory," I said and then picked up a report and flipped through it. "For instance, in 1976 in Chowchilla, California 26 children were kidnapped. Shortly after the incident the bus driver was put under hypnosis and was able to remember the license number of the kidnapper's car."

"Wow."

"Then in 1978 a fifteen year old girl was raped, had her arms cut off, and was left wandering along a California highway. Under hypnosis she supplied information that led to the arrest and conviction of her assailant."

"He cut off her arms? My God!"

"You remember the Ted Bundy case don't you?"

"It kind of rings a bell."

"In 1979 two students were killed at Florida State University. Under hypnosis a witness in that case provided police with information that led to Ted Bundy's conviction. There's quite a few more examples in here too."

"Well, good. I hope it works."

Jodie looked at her watch and then said, "You've got a 9:30 docket call, you better get a move on."

"Oh crap, I almost forgot, it's so good to have you back."

"I am glad to be back, believe me."

I packed up the briefcase and left the office. Jodie smiled as I was leaving. I noticed a tear rolling down her cheek as I returned the smile. She quickly wiped it away with the back of her hand and went back to work.

On the way back to the office I stopped by Tom Slater's office. I figured I could tell him about some new developments in his case and then ease into Bobby Wiggins' death. His secretary said he was on the phone so I waited. After a minute he walked in the reception area smiling.

"I didn't know you made house calls?"

"Your office is right on the way back from the courthouse so I thought I'd save you a trip."

"Okay, so what's up."

"I got the interrogatory responses back. It doesn't look like they have much hard evidence to back up their allegations."

"That's because it's all bullshit."

"Maybe so. Anyway, I'm going to set up a deposition just to be sure. Then maybe I'll file a motion for summary judgment."

"Good, I'm sick of this harassment."

"Did Wiggins ever finish your audit?" I asked. "We're going to need it if this thing goes to trial."

"He said it was about finished. I guess I should call his partner and find out."

"Did he ever mention anything to you about a health problem?"

"No, not that I recall."

"Was he ever sick to your knowledge?"

"No, he always seemed pretty healthy."

"So how did the audit go? Any problems?"

Slater hesitated and then replied, "No, not really."

"What do you mean, not really?"

"Oh, you know, just nit picky stuff. Nothing of any consequence."

I gave Slater a hard look trying to ascertain if he was hiding something from me.

"I need to know if there are any problems, Tom. If there are we've got to figure out how to deal with them."

"I know. There weren't any problems."

"Good," I said and then asked him about the night of the murder. Like everyone else he saw nothing so I thanked him and went home.

The next day Sarah came by my office to discuss her case and her meeting with Dr. Gerhardt.

"Have you ever met Dr. Gerhardt?" she asked.

"No, tell me about him?"

"He's a tall, elderly man, in his late 60's, I think. He walks very slowly as if every step was painful for him."

"Really. I wonder what's wrong with him."

"I don't know, maybe arthritis or something. . . . Anyway, he's so nice. I really felt like he cared about me . . . wanted to help, you know?"

"Sure. That's good. . . . So, did he make you lie down on the sofa like in the movies?"

"Yes, and then he asked me if I felt like talking. He was so polite."

"Well hypnosis has to be consensual, I understand. You've got to want to do it for it to work."

"Right, so I told him sure, lets talk. So we talked about school, family, career ambitions, you know . . . all that kind of stuff. He asked about my relationship with Joyce and Nate."

"Right."

"Oh, and I told him about Joyce being a cheerleader in high school and how she worships football players. How she's certain he'll go to the NFL and become a millionaire."

"She was a cheerleader? I didn't know that."

"Then he got to the night of the killing.

****

"I know this is going to be painful for you," Dr. Gerhardt said, "but I need to know what you remember about December third."

"Didn't you read the newspaper?" I said.

"Yes, I did, but I want to hear it from you."

"It's the same story, that's all I know."

"Okay, I'll buy that. Have you ever heard of the subconscious mind?"

"Yeah, a little."

"Well, the subconscious mind often remembers things

that have been purged from the conscious mind. What I'd like to do, with your permission, is hypnotize you and see if your subconscious mind remembers anything that happened the night of December third."

"I don't know, I don't like the idea of someone else controlling me. I guess I've watched too many horror movies."

"I'm not going to control you, all I'm going to do is ask you questions, explore the depths of your subconscious mind to see what's there," Dr. Gerhardt said. "I'm a professional, I would never try to get you to do something against your will."

"Okay, but I would feel better if Greg were in here with us. Is that okay?"

"Sure, Greg can watch if he's quiet."

Dr. Gerhardt buzzed his receptionist and asked that Greg be brought in. A miinute later he walked in looking somewhat perplexed.

"Mr. Peterson, I'm going to hypnotize Miss Winters to try to see if we can find out more about what happened on December third and she'd feel more comfortable if you were present."

"Oh, okay."

"Have a seat, but please be very quiet."

"Yes, sir."

"Okay Sarah, I'm going to shine this little flashlight at you and I want you to focus on it."

Dr. Gerhardt picked up a small flashlight, turned it on and began manipulating it around Sarah's eyes. After a minute the doctor said, "Now Sarah, your eyes are beginning to feel heavy, you're very tired but relaxed. Now I want you to think back to the night of December 3, 1981 and tell me what you see."

Sarah's eyes closed and she began to toss and turn.

"It hurts . . . Oh, my God! . . . It hurts so much. Please make it stop!"

"Where are you?"

"My bed, I think. Yes. . . . . Oh no. . . . Please God I
can't take this pain anymore. Why are you doing this to me?"

"Are you alone?"

Sarah moved her head back and forth as if she were
looking around, but her eyes were closed. "I think so.

She squirmed involuntarily in her chair. "Oh no, this
can't be happening. No, no. Please God. Ah! What am I going
to do?"

"What's happening now?"

Sarah stiffened as if listening intently. "It's a knock. . . .
Someone is knocking at the door. . . . Go away, I'm sick! Oh,
ah! . . . oh shit . . . Oh. . . . it's coming out . . . ahhhhh . . . God!"

"Did you have the baby?"

"Oh God . . . oh God . . . what am I going to do?"

"Is the baby alive?"

"It's crying . . . oh my God, . . . oh God, no . . . what am
I going to do? Please God, help me."

Apparently I began screaming and jerking back and
forth in my chair. Dr. Gerhardt had to hold me down to keep
me from falling out of the chair. "All right, Sarah, calm down,"
he said. "I am going to count to three and then I want you to
wake up. When you awaken you'll feel relaxed and you'll
remember everything you've just been through. Ready . . .
one . . . two . . . three."

I opened my eyes and looked around not knowing
where I was. Then it slowly came back to me. It was then that
the memory of my delivery hit me like an avalanche. I
remembered holding my baby and thinking how beautiful he
was.

"How do you feel?" Dr. Gerhardt asked.

"Tired, very tired."

"I bet. Do you remember what happened to the baby?"

"No. I just remember watching it cry. After that it's a

blank."

"Well, we've made some progress," Dr. Gerhardt said. We also discovered that someone was knocking on your door. Whoever it was may have heard what you were going through. They must have heard you screaming. We need to identify that person. Maybe in our next session we'll be able to do that."

"I hope so, Doctor. Good or bad. I need to know the truth. It's terrible to have lost a part of your life, particularly when people are accusing you of murder and you can't remember anything."

*****

Sarah might have been happy about her breakthrough but I had mixed feelings. If the baby had been a stillborn she would have been off the hook. However, the autopsy report on the baby had already indicated the baby's lungs contained particles of feathers from the pillow. She had breathed and Sarah had now confirmed that. But the fact that someone was at the apartment, knocking on the door, meant there was still a possibility that Sarah was innocent and someone else killed her baby. I immediately picked up the phone to inform Snake.

"Harry, I've got good news!"

"Good, we need some. What you got?"

"I just finished talking to Sarah. Apparently Dr. Gerhardt hypnotized her and found out that someone was at the apartment on the night of the murder."

"Oh really, that *is* good news," Snake said. "What did the crime lab report say about fingerprints?"

"They found a lot of different prints, Sarah, Michelle, Greg, Richard Stein and several unidentified ones."

"Good, I'll check with the lab and see if they've been able to identify any of the other prints yet," Snake said. "You need to check with all the neighbors and see if they saw anybody."

"Okay, so what do you think overall?" I said.

"Well, best case we have the real killer, worst case we have a witness. At least we're better off than we were yesterday."

"True."

"Unfortunately I see the press has already convicted our client," Snake said.

"Yeah, it looks that way," I replied.

"Well, public opinion can change. A high profile case like this is kind of like a football game. The momentum shifts throughout the game. All we need is a fumble or an interception and who knows what might happen," Snake said.

"I suppose, but as I recall when Hudson was at A & M he didn't turn the ball over too often."

"True enough, but this is a different ball game. Hudson may be an All American on the field but in the courtroom he's just another amateur. He'll fumble, I promise you, he'll fumble."

Chapter Ten
Tabloid Trash

When I arrived at the courthouse, I was surprised to see a dozen or so picketers. The message on one sign was, "SEND HER STRAIGHT TO HELL" and another one read "BABY KILLER" on one side and "NO MERCY" on the other. Several of the protestors wore blood spattered T-shirts that read, "Children of Despair." I decided to walk around the back of the Courthouse to avoid a confrontation, but it was too late. One of the newsmen covering the picketing spotted me and started running at me. Before I had time to react, dozens of reporters and picketers had surrounded me.

"Mr. Turner, do you have any comment about allegations that Sarah Winters is a witch?" the first reporter asked.

I laughed. "Yes, the story is ridiculous. Complete and utter nonsense."

"What about her ability to walk through fire?"

I shook my head in disbelief. "There wasn't anything magical about what she did. She just used her head. She saturated her clothing with water and wrapped a wet blanket around herself for protection. It was quick thinking and she was a brave little girl, but it wasn't witchcraft."

"Do you think the Judge will set a trial date today?" the first reporter asked.

"I don't know, he might," I replied.

"Are you going to claim temporary insanity?" a second reporter yelled.

"I can't comment on defense strategy."

"Do you think the DA will seek life imprisonment?"

"I don't know, ask him," I said as I pushed my way through the crowd and up the steps of the courthouse.

"Is it true your client has skipped town?" a TV reporter asked.

I turned around angrily, "Where do you get this stuff? She hasn't skipped town, she'll be in Court this morning. That's all, thank you."

While I was fighting my way through the crowd I saw Tom drive up with Greg and Sarah. They must of seen my plight as they drove around the back. I saw them come in the courtroom a few minutes later while I was talking to the Court Coordinator. They stood by the door and waited for me to finish. When I was done I motioned for them to come forward.

"Good morning, I guess you saw the mess out front," I said.

"Luckily we saw them before they saw us," Greg replied.

"Yeah, I wasn't so lucky."

"Who are they anyway?" Sarah asked.

"I don't know, I suspect they're Hudson campaign supporters trying to create a little free publicity for their candidate."

As we were talking, Howard Hudson entered the courtroom accompanied by Margie Westcott. I excused myself and went over to them.

"Good morning, Mr. Hudson . . . Margie. Looks like you drummed up a good crowd for a political rally."

Hudson smiled at me and replied, "I'd like to take the credit, Stan, but I think it was that wonderful article in the National Examiner that got everybody riled up."

"Of course, you didn't have anything to do with that," I said.

"Again, I'd like to take the credit, but I can't," Hudson said. "That was someone else's genius."

"Seriously, I'm worried about this case getting out of hand. All this publicity is going to make it hard for my client to get a fair trial."

Hudson nodded. "Yes, I'm kind of surprised there is so much interest in this case. We get two or three of these infant murders every year. Usually the press is gone after the first day or two."

"Well, you obviously need to beef up security," I said. "I don't want my client or anyone in my family getting hurt. It's your duty to make sure everyone associated with the trial is protected."

"Yes, I heard about Doomsayer, It's shocking that someone would threaten the life of an officer of the court. I understand the Dallas Police are searching for the person responsible for the threats," Hudson said.

"Yes, they say they are. Who are these picketers anyway? I've never heard of the Children of Despair."

Hudson picked up a piece of paper, stood up tall and read it quite dramatically, 'They're a religious organization devoted to protecting innocent children from our increasingly evil society.' . . . At least that's what the leaflets they are passing around say. . . . 'They demand a return to strong religious values, elimination of sex and violence from TV and movies and a return to prayer in the schools."

"Right wing vigilantes, huh?" I said.

"Not at all," Miss Westcott interjected. "They're patriotic Americans who believe in law and order and old fashioned justice. They're sick and tired of kids getting abandoned, beat up and murdered."

"How do they feel about violence?"

"They are totally nonviolent," Miss Westcott said. "They pretty much play by the rules. They've become powerful in this county because they've worked hard, they're well organized and focused on what they want to accomplish. They already have a majority on the school board."

"Maybe Doomsayer is a renegade," I said.

"Do you have any evidence that one of them is Doomsayer?" Miss Westcott said.

"No, it just seems logical."

"Well Mr. Turner, you're an attorney, you know without evidence you have nothing," Miss Westcott said.

"I know, forget Doomsayer. I'm not going to let him sidetrack me. When do you want to try this case anyway, sixty days?" I asked.

"That's fine, we're nearly ready right now," Hudson said. "You sure your client's not interested in our plea offer? She'd get a maximum of twenty years and probably be back on the street in five."

"It was an exceedingly generous offer and if my client were guilty I would most certainly recommend she take it. However, since she's innocent she'll have to decline and take her chances with the judge and jury."

"Okay, it's her funeral."

As Hudson and I continued to verbally joust, the door to the judge's chamber opened and Judge Brooks entered. The bailiff immediately stood up and said, "All rise!"

"Be seated," the judge said.

The judge sat and began to study Sarah's file. Judge Brooks had been born and raised in Texas but had attended law school at Stanford University. He was a noted scholar, frequently lecturing and writing legal articles. Despite his educational background, he ran his court in the tradition of most rural Texas courts, loose and laid back. After a minute he looked up and addressed the attorneys.

"All right, I'll take announcements."

"Your honor, Howard Hudson and Margie Westcott for the State," Hudson said.

"Stan Turner your honor for the defendant, Sarah Winters."

"I assume you're not ready to try this case today."

"No, Your Honor," Hudson said. "The State is close to being ready, however, we need a little more time to complete some lab work and wrap up our factual investigation."

"Mr. Turner," the Judge said, "when do you think you'll be ready?"

"We'd like about sixty days your honor. Our client is undergoing a psychological evaluation and we've got some additional discovery to complete."

"Very well, I'm going to go ahead and set May 16, 1981 as the trial date. If you're going to plead insanity as a defense I want that disclosed at least fifteen days before trial."

"Yes, Your Honor."

"Due to the gravity of this case, the media interest and the right of the defendant to a speedy trial, I'm going to ask both of you to be ready on May 16. This is a special setting and I won't be granting a continuance absent some major catastrophe."

"Yes, Your Honor," I replied.

"Thank you, Your Honor," Hudson said.

The judge got up and the bailiff yelled, "All rise!"

After the hearing, I slipped out a side entrance to the Courthouse and walked quickly to the parking lot. When I got to my car my heart sunk. All of the tires had been slashed, the windows broken and someone had scratched a message on the hood that read:

"Ye shall not escape the vengeance of the Lord. Doomsayer."

I couldn't believe it, my beautiful Corvette scratched to hell. As I stood by my car in shock, a news team spotted me and came over to see what had happened. They immediately began taking pictures and asking me questions.

"Mr. Turner, who do you think this Doomsayer is?" a reporter asked.

"I don't know but if I find out I'm going to kick his ass," I replied. "He'll wish he hadn't messed with me. Damn him!"

"We understand he's threatened your life, is that true?" he said.

"Yes, I guess he has."

"Are you afraid?"

"Of course I'm afraid, whenever there is a chicken shit lunatic out there lurking about I'm not going to feel very safe. But let me tell you this, nothing will deter me from defending my client. I will not succumb to threats and intimidation."

As my car was being towed off I calculated in my mind what it was going to cost to fix it. I figured it would be at least two grand. Unfortunately I didn't have comprehensive coverage on it so I'd have to foot the bill myself. When we paid the Corvette off we dropped the collision and comprehensive to save money. I figured I was a safe driver and if I got in a wreck it would be the other guys fault. What a mistake.

The next morning I went jogging with Beauty as usual and when I returned the newspaper was sitting on the front porch. I picked it up and went inside to have breakfast. I opened the paper and was startled to see my picture on the front page.

"Rebekah, come look at this!" I yelled.

Rebekah came into the kitchen quickly and asked, "What's wrong?"

"Look at the newspaper."

Rebekah read the headlines out loud, **"WINTER'S DEFENSE COUNSEL'S LIFE THREATENED, CAR**

VANDALIZED."

Rebekah picked up the newspaper and began reading the article. When she was done she handed the newspaper back to me, shook her head and said, "What are we going to do? I'm so worried about you."

"Nothing, he's just trying to scare me. He wouldn't try to hurt me."

"How can you be so sure? Look what he did to your beautiful car."

I shrugged. "Anyway, the police are going to start keeping an eye on all of us. Lt. Winters said he was going to call someone with the Dallas police to arrange it."

"I hope they do it soon."

"They will, I'm sure of it."

As Rebekah and Stan spoke the doorbell rang. Rebekah went to the door and a uniformed police officer was standing on the porch. "Hello, can I help you?"

"Yes ma'am, I'm Harvey Robard with the Dallas Police Department, I've been ordered to provide some protection for your family until the Sarah Winter's trial is over."

"Well, come in Officer Robard," Rebekah said. "I'm very grateful that you're going to be watching out for us. Have you had breakfast?"

"No ma'am, not yet. I was going to grab a donut later."

"Well sit down, I'll get you a cup of coffee and some toast."

"Thank you."

"Well, I'm glad you all are taking these threats seriously," I said. "I'd die if anything happened to my family."

"We'll keep a close eye on them, don't worry."

Chapter Eleven
Every Man's Dream

The next afternoon I decided to go visit my last common client with Bobby Wiggins. Joanna Winburn was every man's dream, slim, sexy and sophisticated. When she walked in a room full of men all conversations ceased. The first time she strolled into my office I nearly fainted. This was the first time I had visited her on the job and I must confess it beat the hell out of an interview in my conference room.

Joanna was happy to see me. It had only been a few months since I had put her into Chapter 13 and got the IRS off her back. With Bobby's help all of her tax returns had been filed and now all she had to do was pay $600 a month for the next 5 years. Considering she was making at least a thousand a week that wasn't going to be a problem for her. She was very relieved to have escaped criminal charges. She took me to a table in the corner. The club wasn't crowded.

"I'm so glad you came by to see me dance," she said. "After my act I'll take you in the back and give you a lap dance on the house."

The idea of a lap dance was very tempting, God was it tempting, but I knew better than to tempt myself with a beautiful woman. I couldn't forget the purpose of my visit.

"Thanks, I'd like that very much. Unfortunately, I'm not

here for pleasure. I need to talk to you about something."

"What?"

"Bobby Wiggins."

"Oh, poor Bobby. Have the police come up with anything yet?"

"No, I haven't heard a word from them."

"So, what do you want to know?"

"You saw Bobby several times during the two weeks before his death, right?"

"Yes, he was so nice to help me get those tax returns filed. I didn't have many records so it was difficult for him. It took us quite a while to reconstruct everything."

"Where did you do this reconstructing?"

"At his office."

"After hours?"

"Sometimes."

"You two didn't-?"

She frowned and said,"No. Give me some credit. He was a nerd." Then she gave me a naughty little smile and said, "You're the only professional I've wanted to fuck."

I didn't know if she was teasing me or she was serious. Either way the thought of us making love was exhilarating. I took a deep breath trying to maintain my concentration.

I laughed. "You're a real tease aren't you?"

"That's my job to get men aroused."

I shook my head, "Well you're doing a hell of job on me. Now cut it out and let's get back to the subject at hand."

"Okay, I'm sorry."

"Bobby never came here did he?" I said.

"No, of course not. It's too noisy around here to work."

"Right. So, did he tell you anything unusual or did he act strange in any way?"

She thought for a moment and then said, "No."

"Did you all talk about anything other than taxes?"

"Sure, he told me about his family and how much he loved his two grand kids. This summer they were planning a road trip to California with them."

"Really? Did he ever mention a medical problem?"

"Nope. His wife was sick a lot. He complained about how much he spent on her medical bills."

"Is that right?"

"Yes, but he was in perfect health. I know that for a fact."

"Why are you so sure about that?"

"We talked about it one time. You know, one of those boring nights when we were going through credit card receipts. He wondered if I was worried about my health cause of all the men I dated. I told him I was very careful, always used protection and had a physical every month. I knew I was in perfect health. He said he just had a physical himself and the doctor had given him a clean bill of health too."

That wasn't what I wanted to hear. Frustrated and depressed, I left the club and headed for the office. When I got to the parking garage I pulled up behind a white Ford Mustang that was waiting for the wooden gate to rise before it could enter. Finally the gate opened and the Mustang went in and parked in the first open spot. I flashed my security card, drove past the Mustang toward the main entrance to the building and parked in my usual spot. I opened the trunk of the rent car I was driving, pulled out my coat and put it on. Then I picked up my briefcase and turned to walk toward my office.

Suddenly the white Mustang pulled out and came barreling straight at me. For a moment I stood there almost paralyzed with fear, but just before the car struck I jerked myself back between two parked cars, barely escaping certain death. As I lay on the ground I could hear the tires screech as the assailant made his escape. The Mustang broke through the wooden exit gate and sped off toward Central Expressway.

Before I could get up, Sam Piper, one of the building security guards came running up.

"Are you all right, Stan?"

"I think so."

"He tried to kill you," Sam said.

"I noticed."

"I'm going to call the police."

"Okay, I'm just going to go up to my office where it's safe. You can send the police up there if they need to talk to me."

"Fine, do you need any help?"

"No, I'll make it."

When I entered my office I was walking kind of awkwardly, breathing heavily and was shaking from all of the adrenalin that had flooded my system. Jodie stood up when she saw me enter the office.

"What in the hell happened to you," she said.

"Some asshole just tried to kill me."

"You're kidding?"

"No, and he was almost successful. I don't know what happened but I just couldn't move. I saw him coming straight at me but I was suddenly paralyzed. It was really weird."

"Did you call the police?"

"Sam saw the whole thing, he's calling the police for me right now."

"This is horrible, I can't believe it," Jodie said.

"I know. This Doomsayer asshole is starting to piss me off."

"Go sit down and relax, I'll get you some coffee."

"Thanks."

I made my way into my office and sat down. Jodie had obviously cleaned it up as everything was in nice, neat stacks. In a minute she brought me my coffee and sat down to chat.

She said, "You've got a busy day today, do you want

me to cancel your morning appointments?"

"No, no. I'm okay, I can't let that bastard slow me down one iota."

"Well you've got a bankruptcy appointment this morning at nine and a man is coming in about a possible will contest at 10:30."

"Huh. What about this afternoon?"

"The Hill depositions remember."

"Oh, right. . . . Oh, call Snake and set up an appointment for a strategy session. The judge set Sarah's case for trial on May 16 so we've got to really get hustling."

"Sure, I'll set it up."

I sat back and sipped my coffee. I was beginning to feel better when Jodie came running in the office.

"Stan, I just got the mail and . . . and Tom Winter's check bounced!"

"What? You've got to be kidding?"

"No, it's been stamped **NSF - PRESENTED TWICE - DO NOT REDEPOSIT**."

"Oh wonderful!" I said falling back limp in my chair. I closed my eyes hoping when I opened them it would turn out to be just a horrible daydream. No such luck. "This is just great, I'm going to have checks bouncing all over town."

"What are you going to do?"Jodie asked.

"Jesus! I don't know. Snake's going to kill me."

I got up, went to the window. "What was the checkbook balance before this fiasco?"

"Eleven hundred twenty-two dollars."

"Oh good, so we're only nine thousand short! Has the bank called?"

"No, not yet."

I got up and started pacing in front of the window. Then I stopped and looked at Jodie.

"Get Tom on the line, maybe he can replace the check

immediately."

"Okay," Jodie said and then turned and went directly back to her office. I followed her anxious to see if she'd get through. She hit the speaker phone button so I could listen in and then she dialed Tom's number. A man answered.

"Winter's Motors," he said.

"This is Jodie at Stan Turner's office, Mr. Turner would like to speak to Tom Winters please."

"I'm sorry ma'am, he's tied up right now, but Stan is his lawyer, right?"

"No, he's Sarah's lawyer, why?"

"Tom really needs a lawyer, the police have just handcuffed him and they're putting him in their squad car as we speak."

"You're joking? What on earth for?"

"I don't know," the policeman said, "something about felony theft."

"Oh my God," she said as she looked at me and frowned.

She hung up the phone shaking her head.

I said, "Well, so much for that fleeting hope." Now what was I going to do? It would be humiliating to have checks bouncing everywhere. Oh, I could explain what happened but people would still wonder if it wasn't just a lame excuse.

"Can you borrow some money from the bank?"

"No, bankers want collateral, something I don't have."

"What about your family?" Jodie asked.

"All poor, I'm afraid. They'd laugh if I asked them for ten grand."

"What about one of your rich clients?"

"No, I can't do that. I'll just have to have faith. Trust God to get me out this jam."

Jodie gave me an inquisitive look. "I didn't know you were religious."

"Well, I don't know how religious I am, but one thing I do know is the good Lord has saved my ass on more than one occasion. I suspect He'll do the same today."

Jodie laughed. "I can't believe you. This just totally blows my mind. . . . I don't think I've ever even heard you mention the word *God* before, and now faced with financial ruin you're just going to throw up your hands and pray for a miracle."

"Not pray, Jodie. . . . Trust," I said. It was true. On so many occasions during my life when all seemed to be lost a miracle would happen which would allow me to survive the ordeal. Maybe once or twice I could have attributed it to good fortune, but as many times as I had seen it I knew it was the hand of God.

"Well whatever miracle He's got in the works, He better do it by two, that's when the bank cuts off its work."

I looked at Jodie and sighed. She smiled sympathetically and then the front door opened. We both looked up. A smiling Korean man walked in and bowed. Several others filed in after him. Jodie motioned for them to take a seat. "It must be your bankruptcy appointment," she said.

"Oh, great. . . . How am I going to deal with this crisis and see clients at the same time."

Jodie shrugged and replied, "I'm sorry."

"Check our accounts receivable and see who's past due. Then call them and see if we can send a runner around to pick up some checks."

"Okay."

"Go ahead and send the bankruptcy case in."

Jodie nodded and left the room. I took a deep breath trying to remain calm. My stomach was in knots. In a minute Jodie brought the group of Korean-Americans. I got up and greeted them barely able to smile.

"You were referred to us by Dong An. He said you do very good job for him," the eldest of them said.

"Oh, well I'm glad he felt that way."

"We got big problem. Not enough people come to our new restaurant. Landlord threatening to lock the doors, you know?"

This was a pretty familiar situation. Foreigners coming to America with dreams of opening a business and being instant millionaires. Unfortunately it wasn't always that easy. "Oh really, how much do you owe him?"

"$7,428 right now, more at first of month."

"Are you a partnership or corporation?"

"Corporation."

"Is the landlord your only problem?"

"No, bank want payment of $18,000 due last month."

"How much do you owe the bank?"

"Quarter million."

"Do you want to stay in business or just get out?"

"Oh no, get the hell out!"

I laughed. At least they were realistic. So many small businessmen didn't know when to quit. They were so sure everything would turn around if they could just hold out a little longer. It suddenly hit me, maybe I was looking in the mirror. "Okay, well then we can just put the corporation in chapter 7 and you guys can just walk away and do something else. Did any of you personally guarantee any of the corporation's liabilities?"

The spokesman for the group smiled proudly. "Oh no, we not dummies."

"Good, then a business chapter seven runs $2,500.00."

"Oh, not too bad. You take cash?"

"Sure."

Several hours later, after the Koreans had left, I called Jodie into my office.

"Well, I raised $2,500, how'd you do?"

"Paul Kelley said he could scrape up $1,500 on his bill if we wanted to send someone over. I tried several others but they were either out or broke."

"Well, we got half what we need. There's not much chance I'll get any money out of the Hill depositions. Is all the mail out yet?"

"The mail man said he had about twenty minutes left."

"Check it in twenty minutes, maybe we'll get that miracle yet. In the mean time I've got to get ready for the Hill deposition."

"Oh, Snake said he'd drop by tonight at 5:30 to take you out to dinner and to discuss Sarah's defense. Don't forget to call Rebekah and tell her you'll be late."

"Right," I said.

As we were talking the phone rang. It was Rebekah telling us to turn on the TV. She said the DA was about to have a news conference. Jodie went over to the cabinet that housed the TV, opened it and turned it on. I advised Rebekah I wouldn't be home for dinner and then hung up.

"This is Beverly Blake of Channel 12 bringing you live coverage of District Attorney, Howard Hudson's news conference. We take you now to the News Conference in progress."

Howard Hudson climbed before a cluster of microphones in front of the Sherman courthouse. A small crowd of about fifty reporters had managed to make it to the hastily called press conference.

"Ladies and gentleman," Miss Westcott said. "If we can have your attention please. We want to thank all of you for coming out here on such short notice. Howard Hudson, the senior assistant DA, would like to make a statement about the attack on Stan Turner, counsel for Sarah Winters."

Howard Hudson came forward and began to speak.

"Ladies and Gentlemen, members of the press. We were shocked today to learn of the attempt on Stan Turner's life. Luckily Mr. Turner is all right and didn't miss even an hour of work. However, the District Attorney's office will not tolerate this type of obstruction of justice. Everyone accused of a crime in this county has a right to legal counsel and a right to formulate a defense without threat or intimidation. We will not tolerate those who abridge that right. They will be brought before the courts, and I promise you justice will be swift and severe.

"I have instructed Lt. Meadows to head this investigation and, accordingly you can be assured that the guilty party will be apprehended."

"Mr. Hudson, are there any leads as to who's responsible for these attacks?" a reporter asked.

"Yes, the FBI is examining some threatening letters for clues to their author and our forensic team has a tire print from the vehicle that tried to run Mr. Turner down earlier today."

"Do you have any idea why Mr. Turner has been targeted?" another reporter asked.

"No, I don't. Anything I said on that point would be pure speculation and of little value."

When Hudson had fielded all the questions he felt like answering, he concluded the press conference. Jodie shut off the TV.

"You think Hudson really cares what happens to you?"

"No, he's worried about his image with an election coming along soon. It would be pretty embarrassing to him if something happened to me or Sarah."

At one-thirty I took a break from my depositions to see how the quest for the funds was coming. Jodie was on the telephone so I motioned for her to come into my office when she was done. After a minute she walked in.

"So, what's the word?"

"You got lucky, two more grand came in the mail so now we're only three thousand short."

"Huh, I wonder if Billie Jo at the bank will cover us tomorrow. It would be nice to have another day to resolve this problem."

"She probably would, she likes you a lot. You run a lot of money through the trust account, she's got to like that."

"I guess it won't hurt to ask," I said. Most bankers I'd run across hadn't liked me much. I don't know why exactly. Rebekah had once said "It's because you have *broke* written all over your face." She was probably right but I liked to attribute it to the fact that I did a lot of bankruptcies and bankers hated bankruptcy attorneys for obvious reasons. Billie Jo had been different, though. She and I had hit it off right from the very beginning.

"No, it won't. I'll get her on the line for you."

Jodie left the office. After a minute she called on the intercom and told me Billie Jo was on the line.

"Billie Jo, how are you?"

"Fine Stan, what's up?"

"Hey I've got a huge favor to ask of you."

"What's that?"

"You know that $10,000 NSF check that hit my account today, well I'm coming up a little short covering it."

"How short?"

"Three grand."

"Hmm."

"Listen, if you could cover me for twenty-four hours I'm sure I can come up with the balance tomorrow."

"I doubt if everything will hit tonight," Billie Jo said. "I'll call you if your account is overdrafted in the morning and, if so, we'll figure out how to deal with it then. If you get it covered tomorrow, I doubt we'll have a problem."

"You're a lifesaver, thanks."

After breathing a big sigh of relief, I left my office to go downstairs and meet Snake. He had said he would pick me up out front at 5:30. I looked at my watch and noted it was 5:27. Snake was not known for promptness so I halfway expected to be waiting around for awhile. Much to my surprise he drove up in his Ford Ranger at precisely 5:30. We exchanged greetings and then Snake eased the pickup out of the busy parking lot and onto the street. Once he'd settled into the flow of traffic he turned to me and said, "So, tell me what happened?"

I shrugged. "I don't know, this white Mustang just came right at me all of a sudden. It took me totally by surprise."

"Did you get a look at the driver?"

"No, I was paralyzed. It was so weird. I almost sat there and let the bastard kill me."

"Did you see the license plate?"

"It was a blur. I remember looking at it but I can't remember what I saw."

"Well, I've got a real treat for you tonight. Something that will take your mind off all your troubles."

"Oh really, where are we going?"

"To the Majestic Mansion. You'll love this place, I guarantee."

"Good, I'm starving and I could use a little diversion."

Snake swung the white Ranger onto LBJ Freeway and headed East. When he got to the Town East Boulevard exit he got off and headed South. He finally turned onto the circular driveway of an old Southern mansion that had been restored and turned into a club. The parking attendant took our car and we opened the big front door of the mansion and stepped inside. A beautiful dark haired woman in a tight fitting evening gown smiled when she saw us. "Hello Harry, who's your good looking friend?" she asked.

Snake looked at me and replied, "Oh, this is Stan Turner. I told you about him."

"Pleasure to meet you Mr. Turner. Welcome to the Majestic Mansion."

"Thank you," I replied.

"Would you like your usual table?" she asked.

"Yes, that would be fine," Snake said.

"Okay, it will just be a minute," she said and then walked away. While we waited to be seated, I inspected the elegant decor of the old mansion that had been made into a restaurant and gentlemen's club. I took a look at the menu that was prominently posted on a easel by the front door. When I saw the prices of the entrees I was glad Snake was footing the bill for the evening. After perusing the menu I looked up and noticed the hostess approaching.

"We have your table ready gentlemen. Please come this way." We followed the young lady through an impressive library, then into a spacious dining room with dozens of tables adorned with fancy white linen. Around the perimeter of the room were beautifully decorated private booths. There was a stage at one end and a small jazz band situated in front of it. The room was crowded with mostly businessmen. The hostess took us to one of the booths.

After a few moments a bar maid came by. My eyes widened as I realized she was topless. "Hi Harry," she said. "You ready for some drinks?"

"Absolutely," he said. "I need a Scotch on the rocks."

She turned to me and asked, "And you, sir?"

"Bourbon and Seven," I said admiring her fine looking breasts.

Snake chuckled. "Aren't you feeling better already, Stan?"

"Yeah, this is quite the place, but do you really expect to get any business done with all these naked women running around."

"Well, actually I find them quite stimulating. I do my best

work here. Later on there will be a show. We can take a break and watch it, okay?"

"Whatever you say."

The barmaid returned with our drinks. She set them down in front of us making sure her tits got right in our face. Snake stuck a fifty in her G-string and then grabbed a handful of ass. She turned and gave him a filthy look. Then they both started laughing. Snake introduced us and they promised to meet later that evening.

Snake looked at me and said,"Don't worry, it will be a productive evening. I promise, no more interruptions."

"Okay," I said skeptically. "But isn't it going to be kind of hard to work here?"

"Oh, we're not going to work here. Let's go back to my office."

Snake led me up some stairs, past several bedrooms and into a small office. There was a cherry desk, a lamp, adding machine and a typewriter. Papers, ledgers, pencils and a red and black silk bra were scattered about on the desk. "This is your office?" I asked.

"Well, not really. It belongs to Priscilla, the manager, but she lets me use it whenever I want."

"You spend a lot of time here I take it?"

"Yes, it's a little too quiet at my office at night. If I have to work after 5 I come here."

Snake sat in the chair behind the desk and motioned for me to sit down. I cleared off part of a small love seat and sat down. Snake opened a drawer, pulled out a couple of legal pads and tossed one to me. He smiled and said, "Now we can get to work. The girls will bring us some dinner later."

"O...kay," I said trying to refocus my mind back on Sarah Winters. . . . So, what do you think our best defense strategy would be?"

"It looks to me like we have five possibilities: (1) Sarah

is innocent; (2) the baby was stillborn; (3) Sarah killed it but she was temporarily insane; (4) Sarah killed it but it was an accident; or (5) Sarah killed it, period," Snake said.

"Stillborn might work," I said.

"I thought Sarah remembered hearing the baby cry?"

"Well, only under hypnosis, and she doesn't have to testify."

"What about the autopsy report showing feathers in the baby's lungs?" Snake said.

"Well, that hurts, but I'm not certain it's conclusive. We might be able to create some reasonable doubt on that issue."

"I think it's weak," Snake said.

"Okay, so we've got temporary insanity, somebody else did it or an accident," I said.

"If it was an accident then why did the baby end up in a dumpster?" Snake said. "And why did the killer wear gloves?"

"Good point. Temporary insanity or somebody else did it, I guess, are our best shots. I wonder if Dr. Gerhardt will back us up on temporary insanity."

"Temporary insanity is hard to prove. You'd have to show at the time Sarah killed her baby that as a result of a mental defect or disease, she did not know her conduct was wrong or was incapable or conforming her conduct to the law. We've got an intelligent girl here, a college student, I don't see us being able to prove temporary insanity," Snake said.

"From talking to Sarah and getting to know her, I don't see how she could have intentionally or knowingly killed her baby. There's got to be some other explanation. She either didn't do it or, if she did do it, she was temporarily insane. Hopefully, Dr. Gerhardt can shed some light on this over the next few weeks," I said.

"What if someone poisoned her?" Snake said. "She said she was violently ill. There are some drugs that induce abortion. Maybe someone slipped her one of those drugs to make her abort. Then they killed the baby and disposed of it while Sarah was unconscious."

"Who do you suspect?" I asked.

"Richard. He's the most likely, but it could have been Greg too. He certainly had a motive."

"I don't know about Richard. He apparently had an adoption all lined up."

"Really? Have you checked that out?" Snake asked.

"No, I need to talk to the attorney who supposedly arranged for it. Sarah didn't know who he was."

During the evening Wendy kept bringing us fresh drinks. Snake said a little liquor helped him think. The booze was having the opposite effect on me. We continued brainstorming, however, for several hours discussing every factual scenario and legal theory we could imagine to use in Sarah's defense. Several hours later I looked at my watch and was alarmed to see it was after midnight.

"I've got to get out of here. Rebekah's probably worried sick about me."

Snake laughed. "She's probably sound asleep by now. . . . Listen I know the girls here pretty well. Why don't I round us up a couple and we can borrow one of Priscilla's guest rooms for a few hours."

I frowned. It was a tempting idea, but obviously not a prudent one. "No, I don't think that would be a good idea. I'm not a good liar. It would take Rebekah about ten minutes to figure out I'd been unfaithful. Then if I was very lucky she'd just divorce me, but more likely she'd kill me in my sleep."

"Damn," Snake said. "I'm glad I'm single."

Chapter Twelve
Flirting With Insanity

Sarah and Greg came by my office after her appointment with Dr. Gerhardt to fill me in on what had happened. She had been very anxious to see him again since her first visit had been so productive. She wanted desperately to fill in the missing hours of December 3, 1981. Arriving early, she and Greg sat impatiently in the waiting until Dr. Gerhardt summoned them into his treatment room. She took a seat in the examination chair and Greg sat in the corner on a stool.

"Well today I feel certain we're going to make some sense out of what happened on the night your baby died," Dr. Gerhardt said. "Would you like that, Sarah?"

"Oh yes, doctor, I really would," Sarah said. "Every night I lie in bed, unable to sleep, desperately trying to remember what happened."

"I understand. Let me warn you though, sometimes the truth is very painful."

"I don't care, whatever happened, I need to know."

"Before I put you into a hypnotic state let's talk a little."

"Okay."

"I understand your father was arrested?"

"Yes, I'm so worried about him. He got in trouble for using some of his customer's money. I'm afraid it's all my fault. If he hadn't of had to pay my attorney's fees and post my bond this wouldn't have happened."

"You shouldn't blame yourself," Dr. Gerhardt said. "Your

father did what any good father would do to protect his child. As I recall you were always there for him when he needed you. I'm sure he doesn't blame you."

"Really?"

"Yes, the only thing I don't understand is exactly how you got into this predicament. Why you didn't use birth control. It's so easy to get nowadays."

Sarah stared at Dr. Gerhardt silently, seemingly deep in thought.

"Sarah," Dr. Gerhardt said.

She blinked. "Yes, I'm sorry. I don't know much about birth control. It's against our religion."

"Really, that's ridiculous."

"I know it may seem that way, but Mary Baker Eddy did save my father."

"I suspect you and your stepmother had more to do with it than Mary Baker Eddy."

Sarah shrugged. "I don't know."

"Is he still in jail?" Dr. Gerhardt said.

"No, Nate got him out on bond," Sarah replied.

"I thought Nate was in school in Arizona?"

"He was, can you believe he cut two days' classes to come home and get Daddy out of jail? And he had to use $2,500 of his scholarship money for the bond since Joyce refused to help."

"Well, that was very good of him," Dr. Gerhardt said. "They must have established a very strong relationship over the years."

"They have. Sometimes I think Daddy loves Nate almost as much as he loves me. Maybe more."

"No, Sarah. He admires Nate as a potential football star, but he loves you."

"You're right, of course," Sarah said. "I guess I'm just feeling sorry for myself."

"That's only normal for someone in your predicament. Anyway, I'm glad he's out of jail, you're going to need his support during the trial."

"I know, I couldn't imagine going through the trial without him."

"Okay, let's go ahead and put you under."

Dr. Gerhardt pulled out his flashlight and began to put Sarah under hypnosis.

"Look at the light. Relax. Okay, I want you to go back to December third of this year. You had just delivered your baby and you heard it cry. What are you doing now?"

Sarah closed her eyes and sank back into her chair. "I feel so weak and tired. The baby's screaming. The apartment is a wreck. I'm picking her up and holding her in my arms trying to quiet her down."

"What are you thinking?"

"I'm scared. She came early, I wasn't prepared to deal with her yet. What am I going to do? She's making so much noise. Someone might hear her."

"Is there anyone in the room?" Dr. Gerhardt asked.

"No, I don't see anyone."

"Is anyone knocking on the door?"

"I don't hear anything."

"What are you doing now?" Dr. Gerhardt asked.

Sarah's body stiffened. Her head rolled back and forth as if in agony. Then she abruptly stopped as if something had captured her attention.

"Someone's here. The door's open. No! What do you want?" she screamed as she felt someone wrap their hands around her from behind. They struggled.

"Who is it?" Dr. Gerhardt asked.

"I don't know," she moaned, gripping the arm of her chair and twisting in pain. "Don't touch me, you bastard. . . . Ouch! That hurts, cut it out. . . . What are you doing? Leave her alone. No. No, you can't have her. Ah! Don't hurt her."

"Who's doing this?" Dr. Gerhardt persisted.

She began to shake and toss and turn uncontrollably in her chair.

"You can't do this!" she screamed.

"Alright Sarah, when I count to three you're going to wake up and remember everything you saw. One . . . two . . . three."

She tried to calm down. She put her hands over her face and tried to breathe, but instead began to convulse. Dr. Gerhardt held her by the shoulders to keep her from hurting herself.

"Who was it?" Dr. Gerhardt said.

"I don't know, I don't know!" Sarah moaned.

Sarah continued to twist and turn in her chair uncontrollably. When she began to choke and gasp for air Dr. Gerhardt stuck his fingers in her mouth to keep her from swallowing her tongue. He yelled for his nurse. After a moment the nurse came running into the room. The doctor said he wanted to give her a sedative. Greg helped hold her down while the doctor gave her an injection. The sedative immediately took effect and she became limp in her chair.

The doctor apologized for what happened. He said Sarah would be okay in a few minutes. "One thing is clear," he said, "We can't probe any deeper into Sarah's subconcious without possibly endangering her health."

"Her health is already endangered," Greg noted.

"I'm sorry but I must look at the immediate health risk of the patient, not her legal predicament."

After Greg and Sarah had left I called Dr. Gerhardt's office to get his opinion as to what had transpired. I wanted to make sure Greg and Sarah's version was accurate.

"You mean you won't be able to find out who killed the baby?" I asked.

"No, I'm afraid not," Dr. Gerhardt replied. "At least not for several weeks, and then I'm not sure her subconscious will reveal the secret. Whatever happened that night must be so frightening that Sarah cannot face it. It would be dangerous to try to force it out of her. We have to wait until she's ready to accept the truth."

"It's going to be dangerous not to try to force it out of her. She's on trial for murder, remember?"

"I know this is difficult. The only thing I can tell you for sure is that Sarah was not alone that night. If she killed her baby someone helped her. You must continue to search for the truth without any further help from her. She's given us all the information her mind will allow us to have right now."

"Doesn't her subconscious mind realize the consequences of hiding the truth?"

"No, the subconscious mind doesn't work that way. It doesn't usually reason or analyze information. It creates, imagines and formulates ideas which the conscious mind must organize, evaluate and structure into useful conscious thoughts."

I sighed. "Dr. Gerhardt, you're familiar with the temporary insanity defense aren't you?"

"Yes, of course."

"I know you think Sarah is innocent, but if it turns out she killed her baby is it possible that she didn't know what she was doing. Could she have been temporarily insane?"

"Well, it is possible. If she was confronted with a situation so unbearable that she couldn't face it she might react without conscious thought or understanding, which if I remember is the standard for a temporary insanity defense."

"Do you think that she would meet the test?"

"It's possible, but I'd have to know what it was that was so unbearable. It would have to be something very extreme."

"What if she were put into a situation where she had to

make a choice between two persons she loved?"

"Yes, if she couldn't bear the consequences of making the choice. That could drive her to a state of insanity."

"Doctor, these hypnotic sessions you're having with Sarah, are they reliable?"

"Reliable? What do you mean?"

"Is it possible that Sarah could be pretending to remember what happened when in actuality she's making it up?"

"Anything's possible, but I'd be quite surprised in this case if Miss Winters were being anything but truthful. The session today seemed quite spontaneous and completely genuine."

"Well, thank you doctor. Call me after your next visit with Sarah, okay?"

"I will, and you be careful. I've been reading about you in the newspaper. Why do think someone is trying to kill you?"

"I haven't figured that out yet."

"Well, be careful. Maybe you should carry a revolver?"

"No, I'd probably end up shooting myself if I did."

Later that afternoon Jodie advised me that Tom was on the line. I was glad to get the call and for a moment fantasized that he had found a way to get me the ten grand he owed me. Unfortunately my hopes were quickly dashed.

"Listen I'm sorry about the check, but you know how those things go."

"Not exactly, what happened? I said. "I heard you were arrested."

"Well, I've been in a little cash crunch lately and I tried to float your retainer check. I had some sales that should have generated the cash to cover it but the bank went berserk on me."

"Well I must tell you, having your $10,000 check bounce caused me considerable grief."

"I can imagine, I'm really sorry."

"Okay. I can forgive and forget, but I need that check replaced immediately. I'm already half way through that retainer."

"I'm working on it, you've just got to give me a little time. Whatever you do, please don't withdraw. I can have $2,500 over to you pretty quick. Nate said he'd loan it to me."

"How does he have that kind of money?"

"It's some scholarship money that he won't need for awhile. I'll have to pay it back before school starts up again in the fall."

"Okay, get that to me and the rest within ten or fifteen days, okay?"

"No problem, I'll do it."

I put down the phone feeling a little better knowing that Tom at least was concerned enough about the check to call. As I was sitting staring out the window, Jodie walked into the room.

"So what did the deadbeat have to say?"

"He said he'd get us $2,500 soon and the rest in a week or two."

"Do you believe him?"

"I don't know, he's kind of flaky, but he does love his daughter so I suspect he'll somehow come up with the money."

"What if he doesn't?"

"Then I'm doing the case pro bono, I guess. Judge Brooks would never let me out now."

"Why not?"

"It would be too prejudicial to Sarah to have to bring in a new attorney at this late date. The judge would just say I should have got a certified check. I took a risk accepting a company check and lost."

"That stinks," Jodie said.

"Well, I can't worry about that right now. Plus, I'm not

sure I would want out anyway. I've become kind of fond of Sarah. I better call Snake and fill him in on what's happened."

When Tom had paid his retainer I had given four thousand of it to Snake. Now since the check had bounced I was out $14,000. I needed Snake to give me back the $4,000 or I'd be sunk. My rent was due soon and bills were stacking up. I didn't relish this conversation.

"I'll get him on the line for you."

"Thanks."

Jodie left the room and I resumed staring out the window contemplating the events of the day. After a minute Jodie's voice could be heard over the intercom, "Snake's on line one."

I picked up the phone. "Hello, Harry."

"Hi, Stan, what's happening?"

"Oh, a few things have come up that I need to talk to you about."

"Don't tell me, let me guess. Tom can't get out of jail so we're doing the rest of the case pro bono."

"No, worse. His check bounced."

"Oh, shit. I knew this was going to happen. Tom is such a flake."

"Anyway, he can only come up with $2,500 right now to apply to the check."

"Great," Snake replied cooly.

"Well anyway, that's not the worst news."

"Oh shit, what else?"

"Sarah's last session didn't go so well. Dr. Gerhardt doesn't think he's going to be able to get much more out of her. He says it would be too dangerous."

"Damn it! How in the hell are we supposed to prove her innocent if she can't even remember what happened?"

"I don't know, I'm starting to get concerned that we won't be able to put together a credible defense. Maybe we ought to consider temporary insanity. Dr. Gerhardt says it might fly if we can come up with some good reasons why Sarah has repressed all memory of the incident."

"Like what?" Snake said.

I filled him in on my conversation with Dr. Gerhard.

"What if she thought the baby would be defective because of Richard Stein's drug habit?" I suggested.

"That's possible, but the autopsy didn't show any abnormalities with the baby."

"Yeah, but she wouldn't have any way of knowing that. She could have just let that fear mushroom in her head until it was too much for her," I said.

"Maybe so, but euthanasia isn't legal either."

"Isn't her father a Christian Scientist?"

"Yeah, I think so."

"They're very strong anti-abortionists. Maybe Sarah was afraid her father would make her have the baby if he found out about it," I said. "And she figured if she had the baby she'd lose Greg and if she had an abortion she'd lose her father. So no matter what she did she would lose one of the two most important persons in her life."

"That may well be her thinking, but it still doesn't justify murdering her baby," Snake said.

"I know, but what if having to deal with those fears made her go out of her mind?" I asked.

"It's not extreme enough, I don't think Dr. Gerhardt would testify to that effect. Even if he did, I'm not sure the jury would buy it."

"Well, I haven't heard you come up with any brilliant ideas. You're the criminal law expert."

"The only way to get Sarah off is to prove she didn't do it or at least prove reasonable doubt," Snake said.

"But what if she did do it?"

"Convince the jury she didn't do it anyway. Juries *ain't*

perfect my friend. She won't be the first killer that beat the system. We've only got a few more weeks before trial, I would suggest you go back and talk to all the witnesses and suspects again. Maybe something new will come up."

"What are you going to do?" I said.

"Oh . . . I don't know, I've got a couple wild ideas I'm going to explore."

"Like what?"

"Well, they're so outlandish I'd be embarrassed to tell you about them."

"I don't care, tell me anyway."

"No, I wouldn't want to bore you."

I paused a moment and then shook my head, "Okay, whatever, I'll talk to you later."

After hanging up the phone I just sat at my desk a moment. What had I got myself into? Sometimes the enormity of my client's problems got to me especially if my own problems were looming in my mind. Snake's attitude didn't help. He seemed distant and unsympathetic to me and Sarah. Maybe I was expecting too much from my Second Chair. Deep down I had hoped he'd just kind of take over but instead he was letting me dangle. Fortunately Jodie walked in and interrupted my self pity.

"So, is he sending a check?"

"No, he didn't offer and I didn't have the guts to ask him directly to return the money."

"Stan, sometimes you let people walk all over you."

"No, that's not it. This just isn't his problem. I took the hot check and now I've got to deal with it. I'll figure out a way out of this mess."

Jodie shook her head."Yeah, I know. I just wish it wasn't so hard for you. I worry about you."

"Don't worry. It's my destiny and I've learned to accept it."

Chapter Thirteen
The Sleep of Death

Snake's refusal to tell me about his wild ideas bothered me. Why was he so secretive? It didn't make any sense. Whatever it was I was too busy to worry about it. So far the Wiggins investigation had gone nowhere. I wondered what to do next. I finally decided to talk to the police detective assigned to the case, Paul Delacroix. Jodie got him on the phone for me.

"I was just wondering if I could take a look at your witness statements and any reports you generated from the investigation of Bobby Wiggins's death. I'd like to look at the autopsy report too."

"There wasn't an autopsy report," he said.

"What? Why not?"

"Mrs. Wiggins was quite emphatic that she didn't want one and technically Mr. Wiggins died of natural causes at a private home so it wasn't required by law."

"Damn, I just assumed there'd be one."

"No. So why do you want to see this stuff anyway?"

"I've been sued by Bobby's widow and I want to see if there is anything in your reports that might help me defend myself."

"Oh. I don't think there is but you're welcome to take a look at them. When would you like to come by?"

"Today if I can. I'm starting a murder trial tomorrow."

"Oh, yeah. We've got a detail protecting your family."

"Right."

"There are a lot of weird-ass people out there these days. Okay, I'll try to get everything together. Come by between four and five."

"Fine, thanks."

The last thing I needed to be doing on the eve of Sara Winter's trial was wading through two dozen witness statements and several police reports. Unfortunately I didn't have the luxury of waiting. The judge in my civil trial had already issued a scheduling order and the discovery deadlines imposed weren't that far off. I knew my insurance defense counsel wouldn't be doing anything anytime soon as he couldn't scratch his ass without permission from his client. If anything was going to happen it was up to me to make it happen and time was of the essence.

Detective Delacroix sat me in an empty office to look through the evidence. I started with the witness statements. The one common thread in the reports was that Bobby had been doing some heavy drinking that night. That interested me since his drinking might have been more responsible for his fall than an icy sidewalk. Of course, I could get blamed for letting him drink too much so I wasn't sure that would help.

Frustrated, I closed my eyes and rubbed my temples. I felt like I was missing something. It was Bobby's tone of voice when he asked if he could see me on Monday that really bothered me. He was worried. And that wasn't like the cool, fun loving Bobby Wiggins I had known and grown to love over the years. He was scared about something, and I sure as hell wanted to find out what it was. In all likelihood it wouldn't be relevant to my defense, but then again it could be my salvation.

After I was satisfied I'd thoroughly reviewed everything the police had in their file, I thanked Detective Delacroix and left. That night I mentioned to Rebekah that there hadn't been an autopsy report.

"I can't believe that," she said. "They're supposed to do an autopsy in all accidental deaths. Marleen must of put up one hell of a stink to prevent them from doing it."

"Yeah, you would think she would want to know for sure what caused Bobby's death," I said.

"Not necessarily, the only thing an autopsy could do is possibly undermine her personal injury claim. Why take a chance on that. She figures you're a rich lawyer with lots of insurance so why not cash in."

I shook my head. "I always liked Marleen. I thought she was a kind and decent person. I just can't believe she'd do this to us."

"She was nice to us just as long as you were sending Bobby business but she really didn't give a shit about us, obviously. You are so good to people and now you see how much it's appreciated."

"A lot of my clients do appreciate what I do for them," I protested.

"Yeah, like Rob Parker."

I laughed. "Yeah, right."

A vision of Joanna Winburn popped into my head. There was one client who appreciated my work. I didn't dare share that bit of information with Rebekah, however. Over the weekend I let Bobby Wiggins go and concentrated on the preparation for trial on Monday.

On Monday morning I was wide awake by 5 a.m. Sarah's trial started at 10 and the adrenalin level in my body was so high my eyes were wide open and my mind was racing over every detail of the case. Rebekah was awakened by my restlessness and rolled over and put her arms around me.

"Hey Honey, relax. The trial is going to go very well. I feel really good about it."

"You're lying. You think she's guilty just like the press and everybody else. You're just trying to make me feel better."

"Okay, maybe so, but I'm sure when they hear your side of the story they'll keep their minds open to the possibility that she's innocent."

"I hope so for Sarah's sake," I said. "I really do think she is innocent."

"As you've said many times, you've just got to trust the jury system. It's not perfect, but it's the best and most reliable legal system in the world."

"Did I say that?"

"I think so."

"Well, I can't sleep, I'm going to go jog."

Beauty, who had been asleep on the floor next to me, got up, stuck her nose in my face and began licking it. I pushed her nose away and gave her a few pats.

"No, you're not." Rebekah said. "There's a maniac out there who's already tried to kill you."

"Oh, he was just trying to scare me. He wouldn't hurt me."

"You don't know that."

"I don't, but if he tries, Beauty here will protect me," I said.

"Yeah, right."

"Well, then I'm going up to the library and work on my voir dire."

Rebekah rolled back over and replied, "Okay, I'll fix breakfast in a few minutes."

I put on a T-shirt and a pair of shorts and Beauty and I went out front to get the newspaper. On the way back in I noticed there was an envelope taped to the front door. I pulled it off and went upstairs to my library, my office away from the office. It was equipped with a typewriter, telephone and all the other items necessary to conduct business. In addition there was a TV, stereo and overstuffed chair to make working at home a little more palatable. I sat down and opened the envelope. The following handwritten message appeared:

"HE THAT IS BLINDED BY THE BEAST AND NURTURED BY THE SERPENT SHALL SLEEP THE SLEEP OF DEATH. IF ANY MAN WORSHIP THE BEAST AND HIS IMAGE, THE SAME SHALL DRINK OF THE WIND OF THE WRATH OF GOD WHICH IS POURED OUT WITHOUT MIXTURE INTO THE CUP OF HIS INDIGNATION; AND HE SHALL BE TORMENTED WITH FIRE AND BRIMSTONE IN THE PRESENCE OF THE HOLY ANGELS. REPENT, FOR HE SHALL COME ON THEE AS A THIEF, AND THOU SHALT NOT KNOW WHAT HOUR HE SHALL COME UPON THEE. AND THE INNOCENT WHO CLING TO HIM SHALL ALSO BE THROWN INTO THE BOTTOMLESS PIT. DOOMSAYER."

I picked up the telephone and dialed a special number given to me by the Dallas Police department and reported the receipt of the message. A Sergeant Clark took the call and said he would be right over to take a look at it.

I put down the phone and examined the message further. The more I starred at it the more outraged I became. I wished I could somehow send a message back to Doomsayer and give him a piece of my mind. As I waited for the call from the police, Beauty got up and began whining.

"Got to do some business, huh? Come on, I'll let you out."

I went downstairs and let Beauty out the back door. Then I walked back into the kitchen and noticed Rebekah in her shear black nightgown making breakfast. She looked so sexy I was drawn to her. I came up from behind and slid my hands underneath her nightgown and began fondling her breasts.

"Hey, if you wanted sex you should have done something about it last night when we went to bed."

"I was too tired to do anything but sleep. Now I'm rested and full of energy. . . . How about a quickie."

"Stan Turner, what am I going to do with you. You got a murder trial in just a few hours and you suddenly get amorous."

"Just seeing your cute little butt when you bent over to get the frying pan out turned me on."

Rebekah turned around and smiled at me. Then she put her arms around me and gave me a passionate kiss. "All right, but you better make it fast."

I pulled Rebekah's lips to mine and began caressing her tongue. Suddenly I heard a horrible whining sound from the backyard.

"What's that!" I said.

"It sounds like Beauty," Rebekah replied.

I rushed outside and saw Beauty lying on the ground shaking violently.

"Beauty, what's wrong? What's wrong with her?" I screamed.

"She's convulsing!" Rebekah replied.

"What should we do?"

"There's a 24 hour emergency animal clinic on Custer Road. I'll drive, you carry Beauty."

"Okay."

I picked up Beauty and started walking toward the garage. She continued to shake and it was all I could do to hold on to her. Suddenly she became limp in my arms.

"Oh no, she's not moving. Come on, hurry Rebekah!"

Rebekah didn't move but just stared at me.

"Come on, let's go."

"She's dead, Stan. Can't you see that, she's dead."

"No, she can't be. She was fine a minute ago."

"Did you give her that piece of meat?"

"What piece of meat?"

Rebekah pointed to a half eaten piece of raw meat on the ground.

"I didn't give her anything."

"Then how did it get here?"

"Oh God, someone poisoned her. What kind of sick person would do something like that?"

Just then Reggie and Mark came rushing out of the house. "What's all the noise. What happened?"

Rebekah intercepted them and gently pushed them back towards the house. "Go back inside, you don't want to see this."

"Why? What's wrong with Beauty?" Reggie persisted.

"Somebody poisoned her! She's dead, honey, I'm sorry. . . . Now get in the house!"

"What? . . . No. . . . Not Beauty. Can't you take her to the vet? Maybe she's just unconscious."

"No honey, she's already dead, it's too late."

Reggie began to cry. Mark, horrified, ran back in the house. Rebekah said. "Who would do such a thing? Was it that Doomsayer bastard?! I hate him!"

"I don't know," I replied, "but if I ever find out who did this I'm going to shove the rest of that steak down his throat!"

"You better call the police, Stan. That maniac may be lurking around the neighborhood. No telling what else he'll do."

"I already called them about the note. They should be on their way. I'll go out front and wait for them."

Before long two police cars turned onto our cul de sac. They pulled up in front of the house and Sgt. Robards got out of one of the cars and walked briskly up to the front door where I was waiting.

"You got another note, huh?"

"Yeah, and someone just killed our dog."

"Oh sweet Jesus! You're kidding?"

"It was Doomsayer, I'm sure."

"What makes you think that?"

I handed Sgt. Robards the threatening letter. "This was taped to the front door. He obviously left the message and then went into the backyard and left the meat. If you read the message carefully I think you'll agree he's threatening my family. Killing Beauty was just a teaser. Next time it will be Rebekah or one of the children."

I noticed the children sitting on the front porch crying. Rebekah was trying to console them. I walked over and sat down.

"I'm so sorry kids, I know you guys loved Beauty. I loved her too."

"Why did you have to take this case?" Rebekah said. "God is punishing you for defending that baby killer."

"That's nonsense. This is the work of a sick person, some kind of mental case who has lost all sense of realty."

Reggie began to cry again so I put my arm around him and held him tightly. Rebekah shook her head.

"I hope you're going to withdraw from this case now."

"What? I can't do that. I can't give in to a maniac whose trying to deny Sarah a fair trial."

"What are you going to do, wait for him to kill you or one of us?"

"I won't let that happen."

"Sure you won't, like you didn't let him kill Beauty."

I shook my head and walked away. Sgt. Robards was writing down a message coming over the radio. When he was done he walked over to us.

"We got a report back on the first message from the FBI."

"What did they find out?"

"Not much. Doomsayer got the letters from Life Magazine. He must of wore gloves while he cut them out as there are no fingerprints on them. The glue was a commonly used one available at almost any grocery or convenience store. The only definitive information gleaned from the message was that Doomsayer is probably a male and he's right handed."

"How did they figure that out?"

"From the way he cut out the letters I guess."

"Hmm. That's interesting but I'm not sure it's much help."

"Well, maybe your luck will change once the trial starts," Sgt. Robards replied.

"I sure hope so."

I looked at Rebekah and said, I've got to get to the office pretty soon."

"You're going to leave us here alone after what happened?" Rebekah said shaking her head in disbelief.

"What choice do I have? I've got a damn murder trial starting at 10 a.m. . . . I'll ask the judge for a continuance, but I'm not sure he'll give it to me. He was pretty adamant that the trial was going to start today."

I swung by the office to pick up my briefcase and files. When I walked in I was surprised to see Jodie sitting at my desk.

"What are you two doing here?"

"Trying to figure out what happened to your trial

notebook."

"What, it was right on my desk last night when I left."

"I know. I was going to work on it some more before you came in but it disappeared. I thought maybe you had it."

"Shit, what else can go wrong?"

"I'm so sorry, Stan. I never dreamed anyone would break into your office and do something so brash."
Damn it! I just can't believe this."

"I'll try to reconstruct it for you, as best I can, this morning. You probably won't need it until tomorrow anyway."

When I pulled into the courthouse parking lot. I could see picketers out front so I parked and entered through a side entrance undetected. As I walked down the hallway to the courtroom I was quickly joined by several reporters.

"Mr. Turner, is your client ready for her day in court?"

"Yes, she's ready to prove her innocence."

"Has she regained her memory?" another reporter asked.

I stopped. "Yes, she has somewhat. She doesn't remember everything but she does remember a lot more than she did."

"Is it true you're going to plead temporary insanity based on the assertion that your client is possessed by demons?"

I smiled at the reporter and shook my head."Give me a break. Okay, gentlemen, that's all. I've got to confer with my co-counsel. Thank you."

I entered the courtroom and was relieved that Snake was already sitting up at the counsel table. Having such an experienced criminal defense attorney on my side felt good. I doubt I'd of been able to get out of bed if I knew I'd be in court all alone.

"I heard about your dog," Snake said.

"Can you believe it? What a chicken-shit thing for someone to do," I said.

"I know."

"He stole my trial notebook too."

"What?"

"After he left a threatening note at the house he went to the office, somehow he gained access and then stole my trial notebook."

"No, you're not serious? Did you lose everything?"

"Pretty much."

"Are Rebekah and the kids okay?"

"Yeah, but they're devastated by losing Beauty."

"I can imagine. . . . Do you want to move for a continuance?"

"I'd like to get a continuance, but then we'd just be playing into Doomsayer's hand. He obviously doesn't want me to try this case. I just need to get this trial over with and then maybe we'll all get some peace."

After a few minutes there was a commotion in the hallway. I looked over at the door to the courtroom and saw Sarah and Tom enter. I motioned for them to come up.

"Good morning Sarah, how are you feeling?" I said.

"Fine, I guess."

"Well, unless the Court grants us a continuance, we'll be starting to pick a jury this morning."

"A continuance?" Tom said.

"Stan's dog was killed today and someone broke into his office, Mr. Winters. He needs some time to regroup," Snake said.

"Oh my God! I am so sorry Stan." Sarah said as tears began welling in her eyes. "What happened?"

"It may have been Doomsayer," I replied. "First he tapes a threatening message to my door and then he drops a poisoned steak in my back yard. When I let Beauty out she obviously smelled it and started eating it."

"Oh, no. I'm so sorry, Stan. You're going through all of

this shit because of me." Sarah closed her eyes and shook her head in despair.

"It's not your fault. It's just some maniac out there. Anyway, at least the kids and Rebekah are okay."

"I feel so terrible," Sarah said.

Another commotion erupted in the hallway and after a minute Howard Hudson and Margie Westcott walked through the door. They made their way up to the prosecutor's table and began setting up. After a minute Snake walked over to them.

"Good morning, Howie," Snake said.

"Mr. Hudson to you, if you don't mind," Hudson said.

"A little touchy aren't we Howie?" Snake replied.

"This is a court of law and I'll appreciate it if you will show me a little respect," Hudson said.

"Margie, is he always this hard to get along with?" Snake asked.

"Listen Mr. Hertel, Judge Brooks isn't going to put up with your little antics during this trial so I suggest you act in a professional manner," Margie replied.

"Oh, don't worry about me and Judge Brooks, we get along just fine."

"Is Stan going to ask for a continuance?" Hudson said. "We heard about his dog. I can't believe someone would do something like that."

"A short one, maybe a day or two. He doesn't want this Doomsayer maniac having any impact on this trial."

"Well, tell him the state won't oppose whatever continuance he needs."

Snake smiled and replied, "I'll do that, thank you."

Snake returned to the defense table where Tom, Sarah and I had been watching and listening.

"What was the point of that?" I asked.

"Oh, I just wanted to get Howie steamed up little bit.

He's more fun when he's irritated."

"Thanks a lot, he'll probably be all over me now that you got him riled up."

"No, on the contrary, he already said you could have your continuance."

"I heard. How considerate."

I looked up at the clock and saw that it was 9:58. I showed Tom where he could sit and asked Sarah to sit at the counsel table with Snake and I. At 10:01 the bailiff stood up and said, "Please rise!"

The door to the judge's chambers opened and Judge Brooks appeared. "Be seated, thank you."

The judge went to the bench and sat down. He looked out at the crowded courtroom and then turned to Hudson and said, "Mr. Hudson, what does the state have to say this morning?"

"Your honor, the state is ready, however we understand that Mr. Turner may have a motion."

"Mr. Turner, how say you?"

"Your honor, this morning my dog was killed and my trial notebook stolen by some maniac who would like to dissuade me from defending Miss Winters. I would respectfully request a continuance for a day or two to calm my family and reconstruct my records."

"You're sure these acts were related to this trial, Mr. Turner?"

"I think so, Sir, but I don't know for sure."

"Your honor," Hudson interrupted. "Mr. Turner may not know it but it definitely was connected to this trial."

I looked over at Hudson curiously. "We've been advised by Beverly Blake, at Channel 2, that she received a message this morning less than two hours after these two incidents."

"What was the message?" Judge Brooks asked.

Hudson pulled out a piece of paper and began to read:

"'The wrath of the Lord has fallen on he who hinders justice; death and mourning are his reward. Doomsayer.'"

"I want a twenty-four hour guard on the defendant, Mr. Turner and Mr. Hertel . . . and their families. I will not tolerate obstruction of justice. Mr. Turner, your continuance is granted for twenty-four hours, however, tomorrow morning at 10 a.m. this trial will start, no matter what."

With that he the got up and left the courtroom. Bedlam immediately erupted in the gallery. Reporters stormed Sarah and I. The bailiffs rushed over to protect us but it was too late, we were surrounded.

"Do you have any idea who Doomsayer might be, Mr. Turner?" a reporter asked.

"No, but I plan to find out," I said.

"Was anyone hurt other than your dog?"

"No, thank God."

"Will this attack on you and your family alter your trial strategy in any way?" a second reported asked.

"No, absolutely not, nobody's going to keep me from providing the best defense possible to my client."

The Channel 2 News team led by Beverly Blake muscled their way into where Sarah was standing. Blake said, "Ms. Winters, are you afraid Doomsayer might try to take the law into his own hands?"

"She has no comment," I said. "Sarah will be well protected so Doomsayer will not be a factor in this trial."

"Ms. Winters," Blake said. "We understand that part of your memory has come back. Do you still maintain your innocence?"

"Yes, she does," I said. "That will be all. Thank you."

I tried to lead Sarah out of the crowd but Blake got in front of her.

"Ms. Winters. If you didn't kill your baby, who did?"

Reinforcements from the sheriff's office downstairs finally arrived and began to flood the courtroom. After a brief scuffle with a reporter and his cameramen they managed to extricate Sarah and I from the melee. I looked around for Snake but he was nowhere to be seen. The sheriff's deputies hustled us out a rear entrance, usually used to escort prisoners out of the courtroom and down to the basement for transport back to the jail. Margie Westcott was waiting there for us. "Are you two alright?" she asked in the most sympathetic voice she could apparently muster.

"I think so," I said. "What a mess."

"I can't believe all these people came to see my trial," Sarah said.

"You're big news," Miss Westcott said. "First the National Examiner article, then the attack on your attorney, the Doomsayer messages and now someone's gone and killed a dog for godsakes. It's a media dream."

"Thank you for your concern, Miss Westcott, but unless you have something to say we'll be going," I said.

"I just wanted to assure you that no matter what kind of a three ringed circus this case turns into, there *will* be justice. Your client will not get away with murder. I promise you."

I stared at Miss Westcott coldly. If it hadn't been for the demonic look in her eye I would have laughed. "So is that supposed to scare me or make me mad?"

"Both, I wanted to be sure you had something to mull over tonight while you're trying to sleep."

I shook my head. "You are a heartless bitch. . . . You were responsible for the attempt on Sarah's life at the jail, weren't you?"

Ms. Westcott smiled, turned and walked back into the tunnel leading to the courtroom.

"That's scary," Sarah said.

"What?" I asked.

"That a deranged woman like her is spending her every waking hour trying to destroy me."

I forced a smile. "Yes, that is scary, but we won't let that happen, okay? Just hang in there."

"Right. . . . I wonder what happened to Daddy?"

"He's probably looking for you out in the hall. I'll get the bailiff to go find him and bring him back in here."

I went over to the bailiff and asked for his assistance. The bailiff nodded and left. After a few minutes he returned with Tom at his side. Tom opened his arms and Sarah rushed over to him and they embraced. Their love seemed quite genuine yet something bothered me about it. Tom stroked Sarah's hair as she clutched him tightly. I felt a little guilty questioning the genuineness of Tom's feelings towards Sarah, but then again, I couldn't afford to be deceived by appearances.

"Baby doll, are you all right? I was so worried about you," he said.

"I'm fine."

He looked at me and smiled. "I can take care of Sarah now, Stan. You go ahead and get back to your family."

"Okay, I think I'll do that. See you in court in the morning."

On the way home I began to wonder what else Doomsayer was capable of doing. As I thought about Beauty and how senseless her death had been, the rage within me grew. I knew I had to find Doomsayer, not only to thwart any future plans he may have, but also to prove Sarah innocent. I knew Doomsayer was the key and I would not rest until his identity was revealed.

That afternoon I went with the family to the pet cemetery where Beauty was laid to rest. After the ceremony we went to the park where we used to bring Beauty to play. We had a picnic and reminisced about the great times we'd had with her. After dinner I went to my office to prepare for trial. Much to my surprise the office was open and Jodie was sitting at her desk up to her elbows in work.

"Jodie, what are you doing here?"

"After the theft this morning I've been doing what I could to reconstruct your files. I knew you'd be coming to the office tonight, so I figured I'd stay to brief you on my progress."

Jodie's devotion to her job moved me. How lucky I had been to find her. "That was very thoughtful of you. I'm glad you're here. I could really use your help tonight. After what's happened the past few days I can hardly think straight, let alone prepare for a murder trial."

"I called and talked to Rebekah today. She told me how devastated she and the kids were. I'm so sorry, Stan."

"Thank you, but I don't have time for self pity right now. Help me figure out who this Doomsayer asshole is."

"How are we going to do that?"

"By the process of elimination. Whoever it is, he's probably right under our noses," I said. . . . "Okay, write down everything we know about him."

"Or her, it could be a woman," Jodie noted.

"Maybe, but the FBI thinks its a man."

"How do they figure?"

"I don't know, let's just assume it could be either for now until we get some clarification of their theory."

"Okay."

"Let's see. . . . The person is religious or has a religious background. He likes to quote the bible," I said.

"Okay."

"The person is intelligent. Everything he has done so far has been carefully planned and orchestrated."

"Intelligent maybe, but deranged for sure."

"Deranged is a given but not something we would likely

see on the surface. . . . Let's go on. . . . The person doesn't want me to defend Sarah. They want her to be convicted."

"Got it."

"The person has no conscience. He or she probably didn't have a normal childhood, perhaps an orphan or someone who was abused in their childhood."

"That would explain why he's so interested in this case. Maybe he was abused as a child," Jodie said.

"Good point. . . . All right, that's four things. . . . Let's start with the last one. Who wants Sarah to be convicted?"

"The killer obviously," Jodie said.

"Yeah, who else?"

"The ones who have been picketing, the Children of God and the other fanatics hanging around the courthouse."

"Right, who else?"

"Joyce Winters?"

"Yeah, I think so, she'd love to get rid of Sarah so she'd have Tom all to her self."

"The DA."

"True, he wants to get elected, but I don't think he would stoop this low. I'm not so sure about Margie Westcott though, she's a nuclear bitch. I think she'd prosecute her own mother if the case were assigned to her," I said.

"No doubt."

It was an amusing idea that the assistant DA would be Doomsayer, but I doubted I could be so lucky. "Yeah, but I seriously doubt if she'd get involved in something like this."

Jodie shrugged. "It wouldn't surprise me," she said and then looked down at her notes. . . . "Okay, so we have the killer, the Children of God, Joyce Winters, Hudson, Miss Westcott. . . . Who else?"

"What about Richard Stein? Since he's a suspect he'd want Sarah to get convicted."

"Okay, that's six."

"What about Tom and Sarah?" I said.

"Huh?" Jodie replied.

"I can't rule out anybody," I said. "Tom's a flake if I've ever seen one. There is no telling what's going on in his mind. He puts on a big show about how much he loves Sarah, but I'm not so sure. He may just want to get her out of his hair."

Jodie frowned. "That's hard to believe. Why did he hire you and why is he spending so much money on Sarah's defense?"

"What money? I've only seen $2,500 and I understand that came from Greg. He may have planned his check to bounce."

"Okay, I can see a possibility there, but surely you don't think Sarah is Doomsayer?"

"Well, look at it this way, if she's guilty she's probably going to get convicted, right?"

"Probably."

"Well, her only hope is to cause confusion and create doubt, right? Doomsayer has certainly done that, besides look at all the money's she's going to make writing a book about all this," I said.

"Jesus, am I a suspect?"

I smiled and replied, "Maybe, where were you this morning?"

"Thanks a lot!"

'Seriously, I'd like to search her apartment to see if we're missing something. I wonder how she'd feel about that?"

"I wouldn't like it," Jodie said.

"Right, but maybe if another woman did it. It wouldn't be so bad."

"I'll do it," Jodie said.

I laughed. "Would you really?"

"Sure, why not. I always wanted to be a PI."

"Good. . . . Okay, who do we eliminate on religion?"

"Maybe Stein, I doubt he knows much about religion," Jodie replied.

"Who do we knock out on intelligence?" Jodie asked.

"Hudson for sure."

"Definitely. Okay, so Doomsayer must be *the killer*, someone with the Children of God, Tom, Miss Westcott or Sarah," Jodie said.

"Throw in Greg, he might be Doomsayer for the same reasons as Sarah. As a matter of fact that makes more sense than Sarah actually doing it."

"So we have five suspects. Now what?"

"Call Sgt. Fields and see if he can do some checking into the Children of God for us. We'll have to check the others ourselves."

"How do we do that?"

"We just find out as much about each of them as we can. Order an investigative report on each of them from Burden Security. We might get lucky."

"Okay, I'll do that first thing in the morning."

"Good, I'm just going to go over my questions for prospective jury members and then go home. I don't think I'll be needing you any more tonight. Why don't you take off, it's getting late."

Jodie didn't respond and made no effort to leave. After a moment I said. "Jodie? You all right?"

Jodie took a deep breath and then looked at me intently.

"No, I'm not alright. I haven't been able to sleep the past few days."

"Why, what's wrong?"

"Stan, I keep thinking about Sarah on trial for murder for the very thing I did?"

"What you did was perfectly legal."

"That doesn't make it right."

"It's over, Jodie. Forget about it."

"I can't. Do you think I'm a murderer, Stan?"

"I think it's none of my business."

"I think about it a lot. Sometimes I dream that I'm holding my baby in my arms. I'm sitting in a rocking chair in front of a fireplace rocking him back and forth and singing a lullaby. Then suddenly I go into a violent rage, grab a pillow and smother it. I scream and cry until I wake up."

"Maybe you should take another week off. Go to one of those support groups or something."

"Do you think I'm going to go to hell?"

"Jodie, come on, this isn't fair. You didn't do anything illegal. I'm not going to pass judgment on you and Rodney. It was your decision, not mine."

"But you wouldn't have done it?"

"I don't think so, but Rebekah and I were never in the same situation as you and Rodney. It doesn't make any difference what I would have done."

Jodie began to cry, "I would have had the baby, but . . . but Rodney wasn't ready to be a father."

"I know. It's too late to change anything now, so just try to forget about it. God will forgive you."

I got up, walked over to where Jodie was sitting and put my hand on her shoulder. She clutched my hand and then pulled herself up to embrace me. I sighed. "It'll be all right. You'll get through this Jodie, don't cry."

Jodie let go of me, wiped the tears from her eyes and said, "I'm sorry I dumped all of this on you. It's just that Rodney won't talk about it and I needed to talk to someone."

"Don't worry about it. You can always talk to me."

After Jodie left I went back to my desk and sat down to work on my jury questions. As I worked I wondered if there was any chance in hell that twelve citizens could be found who didn't already think Sarah was guilty. I had considered filing a motion to transfer venue but quickly dismissed the idea as being futile since the media coverage had gone nationwide. I leaned backed in my chair, took a deep breath and prayed that somehow I'd find twelve unbiased jurors. It was a long shot, but nothing was impossible.

Chapter Fourteen
Voir Dire

The following day as I pulled into the courthouse parking lot behind my police escort, I was shocked to see that the number of reporters and cameramen milling around had increased by tenfold. As soon as I got out of my car the crowd mobbed me. Although I didn't want to spurn the press, it would have been extremely difficult to give an interview under these conditions. Legal ethics wouldn't allow me to say much anyway so I reluctantly responded to each inquiry with a "Sorry, no comment." Luckily my police escort was there to help me through the throng and before long I was in the courthouse.

Snake was busily reviewing the jury questionnaires when I walked in. Hudson and Margie Westcott were also hard at work. I sat down beside Snake. "How do they look?" I asked.

"I don't know, there's an awful lot of young housewives in here," Snake replied.

"Really, what kind of juror do you think we should be trying to get?"

"Young males I think are our best bet. We also don't want anybody who is devoutly religious."

"What about young girls, don't you think they might

sympathize with Sarah?"

"Not necessarily. Frankly there isn't anyone who will be sympathetic to Sarah if she killed her baby, but we need to get a jury panel that will, at least, listen to the evidence and make their decision strictly on the facts."

As we were talking the bailiff stood up and ordered everyone to rise. Then Judge Brooks entered the Courtroom and sat down. "Be seated," he said. After rearranging some items on his desk, he gazed around the courtroom for a minute and then looked at Hudson. "Mr. Hudson, is the State ready to proceed?"

Hudson stood up tall, gave me a glance and replied,"Yes, Your Honor."

The judge looked at me. "Mr. Turner, I trust you've been able to reconstruct your records?"

"Yes, Sir, the defense is prepared to go forward."

"Very well then, bailiff, bring in the jury panel."

The bailiff left the room and after a minute the jury members began entering the Courtroom. The bailiff directed them to take several rows of seats in the spectator's gallery which they did. The judge then introduced himself and advised them how the jury would be selected. He then explained the rules that they would have to follow if they were chosen as jurors. Finally, he said, "Mr. Hudson, you may proceed."

"Thank you, your honor. Ladies and Gentlemen. I want to thank you for coming down here today to serve as jurors. I know you are all very busy and it's a great inconvenience to you, but each of you will be playing a critical role in the judicial process.

"The purpose of the questions which Mr. Turner and I will be asking you today is to determine if each of you would be a fair and impartial jurist. Each of you have different backgrounds and experiences and accordingly different biases and prejudices that could have a bearing on the performance of your duties as members of the jury. We need to find out if any of those biases and prejudices would prevent you from following the Court's instructions and following the law as it should be applied in this case.

"In order for a determination to be made that each of you could be fair and impartial, it is necessary that I explain what this trial will be about. This is a murder trial. The victim was a newborn baby allegedly killed by her mother. The state will attempt to prove that the mother killed her baby. The defense will try to prove she didn't do it or, if she did, that she has some other legal defense to the charge of murder."

"The punishment for killing a baby, depending on the facts and circumstances could be anywhere from six months to life imprisonment. It may even be possible for someone charged with this type of crime to get probation and never see a day in jail. So my first question for all of you is simply this, is there anyone who feels very strongly that they could not consider a short punishment of six months to a year or even probation if it turns out baby was killed by her mother."

Half the members of the jury panel raised their hands. Hudson looked down at his jury diagram and then said, "Mrs. Phillips, I noticed that you raised your hand?"

"Yes,"

"I see you are a waitress."

"Yes, sir."

"Why is it you raised your hand?"

"Well, I think probation would be out of the question for someone who killed her own flesh and blood. I just can't imagine giving her anything less than life in prison. She really ought to be hanged!"

Several spectators applauded the remark. The judge gave them a dirty look and banged his gavel. "Quiet."

Hudson continued,"If the circumstances were such that the law said probation could be considered, could you consider it?"

"I couldn't vote for probation under any circumstances."

"I see," Hudson said.

Hudson went on to question each of the jury panelists who had raised their hands and got varying responses.

"Now, let me reverse the question. Is there anyone who could not consider life imprisonment if it turned out Sarah Winters did kill her baby?

Two men raised their hands. Hudson located them on his seating chart and then asked, "Okay, Mr. Rutledge, you raised your hand. What kind of work do you do?"

"I'm a librarian."

"And where do you work?"

"At the ASU library."

"Why is it you raised your hand?"

"If it's legal for a woman to have an abortion up to a few weeks before the child is born, then I just can't see that killing a baby just a few weeks later would warrant life imprisonment? I think she should be punished, but life imprisonment is too harsh."

"If the Judge explained the law to you and the facts that you found to have occurred clearly showed that the mother should get life imprisonment, could you vote for that?"

"No, I just can't see it."

"All right, thank you."

Hudson questioned the other juror who had raised his hand and he agreed with the first juror.

"Now ladies and gentlemen there has been a lot of publicity in conjunction with this case. You may have read newspaper articles, seen reports on the TV or heard about this case from your friends and neighbors. Is there anyone who has already made up their mind as to Sarah Winter's guilt or innocence based on the publicity this trial has received?"

Several hands went up so Hudson looked down at his

chart and picked out one of the parties to question. "Miss Green, you raised your hand. How are you employed?"

"I'm a secretary at Walters' Electronics."

"How have you heard about this case?"

"I saw some TV reports, you know on channel 2, and I read about it in the paper."

"Based on what you've seen and heard have you made up your mind as to the defendant's guilt or innocence?"

"Yes, I have. She's obviously guilty as sin."

"Now, Mrs. Green, do you believe in the American tradition that a man or woman is innocent until proven guilty?"

"I suppose, but I just can't see how Sarah Winters could conveniently forget what happened to her baby. She must have killed it."

"What if there is evidence that shows she might not have done it. Could you consider that evidence and possibly find her innocent?"

"Yes, perhaps, but I don't think that will happen."

Hudson spent the several hours grilling the prospective jurors. By the time it was my turn to question the jury panel there was considerable question as to whether there was anyone left that wouldn't be disqualified for cause. Judge Brooks called the lawyers up to the bench for a conference. "Listen, I just want to warn all of you right now, I'm not going to let any potential juror off for cause unless it's absolutely clear he or she can't be fair and impartial. With this kind of trial it's not going to be easy to pick a jury so I've got be very restrained here."

Stan and Hudson nodded but Snake commented, "Your honor, there isn't a juror on this panel that shouldn't be stricken for cause."

"I disagree, obviously people are going to be emotional about this type of case, but they still have the capacity to be fair and follow the law," the judge said as he leaned toward us.

"This is precisely my point. Maybe in a DWI trial I would be liberal with my strikes, but we'll never get a jury picked in this case unless I am very careful only to disqualify those that are clearly biased." He sat back in his chair, the implication being that the sidebar was over.

I started to leave but Snake didn't just glared at the judge. He said,"But your honor-"

"Mr. Hertel," the judge said not letting Snake finish his sentence, "your position is duly noted, but I didn't call you up here for a debate, I just wanted to inform you of the Court's intentions as to strikes for cause. Now Mr. Turner, I trust you will finish up questioning the jury panel with some dispatch as it's time to get on with the trial."

"Yes, your honor. I think Mr. Hudson has asked just about every question imaginable. I can only think of a few that he missed."

"Alright, let's get on with it then," the judge said.

"Ladies and gentlemen of the Jury, I know you are all tired and want to either go home or get seated as a juror. I promise you I won't bore you with another day and half of questions."

Hudson turned and glared at me. Snake chuckled. One of the black jurors exclaimed, "Hallelujah! Praise the Lord." The gallery erupted in laughter and the Judge picked up his gavel and slammed it down angrily. "Alright, this is a murder trial not a theatrical performance. I won't tolerate any misbehavior."

I continued. "But if you will indulge me for about ten minutes then we can get on with this trial. There are just two questions I need to discuss with all of you. As I am sure you are all aware, according to the law, the defendant is innocent. Yes, she is innocent because the law presumes her to be innocent. So at this moment you have to consider her to be innocent. It's only if the state is able to prove beyond all reasonable doubt that the defendant is guilty, that you can find her to be guilty. Is there anyone who, right this minute, doesn't think the defendant is innocent?"

Four or five hands immediately went up and several others followed with less alacrity. I looked at one of the jurors whose hand was raised and said, "Mrs. Small, are you unable to consider the defendant innocent right now, before the state has put on its case and presented its evidence?"

"Yes, I just can't see how she could possibly be innocent. I mean she had the baby and according to the paper she doesn't claim anyone else killed it, so- "

"You realize, don't you, that the newspaper is not evidence?"

"Well, yes."

"Can you put whatever you read about it aside and accept the fact that the defendant is innocent until proven guilty?"

"I don't know."

I turned away from Mrs. Small and addressed a male juror who had his hand raised. "Mr. Simonton, do you feel the same way as Mrs. Small?"

"Not exactly, but I can't change how I feel, just because the law says she is innocent that doesn't mean I believe it."

"If Mr. Hudson was unable to meet his burden and prove that Sarah Winters was guilty beyond a reasonable doubt, could you find the defendant innocent?"

"I don't understand."

"Well, right now I get the impression you think Sarah Winters is guilty."

"Yes, I believe she is."

"Then, it doesn't matter in your mind what Mr. Hudson does during the trial, does it? You're going to make me prove she is innocent otherwise you are going to vote that she is guilty. Am I right?"

"I suppose so."

"Well, that's not the way it works in this court. The burden of proof is on the prosecution, not the defense. The Court will instruct you that you must consider Sarah Winters innocent right now. Can you do that Mr. Simonton?"

"I can't change how I feel!"

"Alright. I respect that."

I continued to quiz each juror, who had their hand raised on the issue of the burden of proof, then went on to my next question.

"Yesterday, Mr. Hudson asked you what you had read about Sarah Winters in the newspapers. Do you remember that?" Many of the jury panel shook their heads affirmatively. "Well, Mr. Hudson didn't quite cover that subject as deeply as I would like. How many of you ever read the National Examiner?" About a third of the potential jurist raised their hands."How many of you have read articles about Sarah Winters in the National Examiner?" The same hands went up. "After reading those articles," I said, "how many of you think Sarah Winters is a witch?"

The room went deadly silent. Everyone looked around to see everyone else's reaction. One lady squirmed in her chair. All eyes shifted to her. She looked around at the stares, took a deep breath and then slowly raised her hand. A lady behind her smiled and raised her hand also. I said to the first lady, "Mrs. Mott, do you really believe that or are you just trying to get out of jury duty?"

She replied, "In my heart I believe she is."

I looked at the judge, shrugged then I turned to the second juror and said, "Mrs. Motley, how about you? Do you believe the National Examiner article?"

She took a deep breath and said, "Well, I don't believe all of it but I do think she's possessed."

"What makes you think-" I stopped myself. I wasn't

going to get into this line of questioning. Turning to the judge I said, "Your honor, do I need to question these witnesses further?"

"No," the judge said. "Both of you are excused."

The two women got up and left the courtroom.

"Thank you, Your Honor," I said. "Now I'm almost through. Please bear with me. . . . I would assume most of you have heard about the temporary insanity defense. Raise your hand if you have." Almost everyone raised their hand. "Okay, temporary insanity may be an issue in this case so I want to discuss it briefly. What is temporary insanity? Basically there are two instances under which a person could be relieved of criminal responsibility for his acts. Both require that his or her conduct be as a result of a mental disease or defect. The first instance is that the disease or defect makes the actor unaware that what he is doing is right or wrong. The second instance is that the disease or defect made it impossible for the actor to conform to the law. Now the question I have for each of you is whether you could find a defendant innocent by reason of insanity, if the facts justified it? If anyone would have difficulty finding someone innocent by reason of temporary insanity, even if the facts justified it, please raise your hand."

Five hands went up immediately and two others followed after a few seconds.

"Okay, Mr. Reardon, you would have a problem with finding someone innocent by reason of insanity?"

"Yes, I think if a person's insane he still . . . well . . . he still has to be . . . you know . . . held accountable . . . yeah, held accountable . . . you know . . . for what he did. You know what I mean?"

"I think I understand. You disagree with the law, right?"

"Yeah . . . yeah . . . that's right."

"Could you put aside your disagreement with the law and find a defendant innocent by reason of insanity if the facts justified it?"

"Ah. . . . Well. . . . Yeah. . . . Maybe."

"Are you absolutely sure you could apply the law correctly even if you thought the law stunk?"

"Well, not one hundred percent, you know. . . . I'd try. . . . But, I'm not sure one hundred percent."

I talked with a few more jurors and then said, "That's all I have for now. I want to thank all of you for being candid with me. I know this hasn't been a very pleasant experience for you but I want you to know Sarah Winters, Harry Hertel and I all appreciate the time that each and every one of you has given up in the interest of bringing about justice in this case. Thank you."

"Thank you very much Mr. Turner," Judge Brooks said. "I am going to dismiss the jury panel at this time except for those jurists that counsel desire to question privately before the court. The bailiff will inform you if you need to stay. Tomorrow morning at eight a.m. I want counsel back here to make their strikes and then we'll seat the jury and begin the trial."

When I got back to the office, Jodie was anxiously awaiting my arrival. As soon as I entered the reception area, she intercepted me.

"How did it go?"

"I don't know, there were a lot of prospective jurors who had already made up their mind. I hope we can find twelve who haven't."

"Me too."

I looked at my watch and then remarked, "It's already six o'clock, isn't Rodney going to be missing you?"

"No, we broke up."

"You're not serious?"

"Yes, I'm afraid so. We haven't been doing too well lately."

"I'm sorry to hear that."

"Me too."

"Well, this isn't the first time you two have broke up, maybe you'll get back together."

"I'm not so sure I want to."

How ironic I thought. A few weeks ago a human being lost its life to save this relationship that suddenly had no hope. "You just had an abortion to protect your relationship with him. Don't tell me you're giving up on him that easily."

"You're damn right I am. The bastard. I hate him."

"Well, I'm sorry, Jodie. Maybe it will be for the best then," I said trying to hide my dismay. "Anyway, I'm going to check my mail and phone messages and then get out of here."

"Okay, good luck tomorrow, I'll see you later."

"Good night."

Jodie left and I went over to my desk and started looking through my mail. I was surprised to see a letter from Mo.

"Mr. Turner, I've been reading about you in the newspaper. The trial you have going is very interesting. You're becoming quite the celebrity. I've told everyone that you're my lawyer and they are very much impressed. Listen, if you need any research done or someone checked out I've got the right contacts to do it. Just let me know if I can be of service. Contact me by mail, not by telephone. I don't have a secure line. Keep up the good work. Mo."

I chuckled at the idea of getting help from the CIA. Maybe Mo *could* help me out. The CIA certainly could give me a better report on our five Doomsayer suspects and the Children of God than Burden Security. I decided to take Mo up on his offer. I'd have Jodie type up a memo explaining what we needed and then send it to him at the address in his letter.

After reading the last piece of mail I checked my phone messages. There was a message from Tom. He said it was urgent so I called him back immediately. "Tom, this is Stan. What's up?" I asked.

"I'm so glad you called," he said. "There was a little incident last night at a restaurant I thought you should know about."

"What happened?"

"Sarah, Nate and I were at Steak & Ale in Richardson. A lady said some pretty ugly things to Sarah. She got her pretty upset."

"How did that happen?"

"We were seated at a table waiting for our orders. Sarah had gone to powder her nose and Nate and I were discussing Sarah's defense. Nate was arguing that Sarah ought to plead temporary insanity on account of the fact he thinks she did it. I, of course, disagreed since I'm not so sure she did do it and I didn't want her locked up in a mental institution the rest of her life. Apparently a lady overheard us arguing and realized who we were. When Sarah came back she made sure everyone in the restaurant knew who she was."

"Oh my God," I said imagining the scene in my head.

"She called her a witch and said she should be burned at the stake. Then other people started joining in on the attack. Someone said they ought to string her up right there in the restaurant. Luckily our police escort kept everyone away from her as we made a hasty exit."

"Boy, that is bizarre. It's almost like an episode out of a John Wayne movie. . . . Is Sarah okay?"

"I think so. She cried all the way home though. She's lying down now in her room. Nate's with her."

"Good. . . . I'm curious about one thing you said."

"Yes."

"Why does Nate think Sarah is guilty? Does he know something Sarah hasn't told me?"

"I don't think so, it's just his gut feeling I'm sure. I'm afraid Nate has a rather low opinion of women in general and as much as he loves Sarah, he just doesn't believe her. In his mind pleading temporary insanity is her best shot at staying out of jail."

"Well, it may be too late to plead temporary insanity at this stage of the game, but if you and Nate know Sarah is guilty for a fact you best tell me now so we can rethink our trial strategy."

"No, no. I'm sure she is innocent. Nate's way off base. Forget what he thinks."

"Okay. But I sure hope nobody's holding out on me. I can't tell you how disastrous something like that could be to Sarah."

"I know," Tom said. "Believe me. I know."

Chapter Fifteen
Overwhelming Evidence

It was already eighty-one degrees when I entered the Courthouse at quarter till eight. It was a little early in the year for a heat wave, but after all, this was Texas where temperature extremes were not unusual. Snake was busily at work at the counsel table when I walked into the courtroom. The bailiff was sitting at his desk reading the morning paper.

"You been here long?"

"No, just a few minutes. I was just going over the jury panel one last time. I think I know who we need to strike and who we can leave alone."

"Good, I don't know much about picking juries."

"Don't feel bad, I don't know of anyone who has actually mastered the art. Some lawyers think they have but they're just fooling themselves. We'd probably do just as good if we hung up the jury list on the wall and rented a chimpanzee to throw darts at it."

I laughed. "That's not a bad idea. Do you know where we could rent one?"

"No, but maybe Hudson would volunteer."

I laughed. . . . "So who do you think they'll call as their first witness?"

"Probably Lt. Meadows. They'll want someone who can dwell on the gory details of the murders."

"Did you meet with Greg last night?" I asked.

"Yes, we met at the Majestic Mansion."

I smiled and said, "You didn't?"

"Of course, I told you that's where I have all my important business meetings, at least with men. The decor tends to loosen them up, if you know what I mean."

"Isn't it kind of an expensive place to meet? I saw you hand out several fifty dollar bills the last time I was there with you."

"Yes, but it's money well spent."

I nodded. "So did you learn anything?"

"Not much. I don't think Greg is your guy though."

"You don't?"

"No."

"I don't think so either," I said.

"So what's it going to be? Reasonable doubt or temporary insanity?" Snake asked.

"I don't know yet," I replied. "Nate Winters thinks it should be temporary insanity." I told Snake about the incident at Steak and Ale.

"I think maybe I should have a talk with Nate," Snake said. "He's obviously not telling us something."

"Good idea. I meant to go see him but just haven't found the time."

"No problem. Just leave it to me."

"Thanks," I said, relieved that I could remove one item from my To Do List.

"Anyway, we're getting down to the wire here. You should have already told the judge if you were going to plead temporary insanity. He might still let you do it, but you're going to have to make a decision before your opening statement."

"I know, what do you think?" I said.

"I don't think temporary insanity is going to fly frankly."

"That's my thinking too, reasonable doubt is the only

chance we have. I just hope we can pull it off."

The doors to the courtroom opened and Hudson and Margie Westcott appeared. I nodded at them and then continued with our discussion. After a few minutes the Courtroom began to fill with spectators. A camera crew set up in the back of the courtroom. The judge would not allow the trial to be televised but he did allow the camera crew to film the courtroom before and after the trial each day and during breaks. I smiled as I noticed the big camera pointed toward me.

"Oh, by the way," Snake said. "A messenger just delivered this package for you. He didn't want to leave it with me but I assured him I'd give it to you."

"Who would deliver a package to me at the Courthouse," I asked as I examined the large manila envelope.

"Obviously someone who knows you are in trial today."

"Huh. Do you think it's another note from Doomsayer?" I asked inspecting it warily.

"I don't know. Why don't you open it and find out?"

"You think it's safe?"

"Yeah, I don't hearing anything ticking."

I laughed. "Okay, here goes."

I opened the package carefully and pulled out a half dozen bound reports. The first one I saw was titled, *Margie Westcott.* "Oh, these are from Mo, the CIA guy I told you about." I started reading the report on Margie.

"What's he got to say about our dear Miss Westcott?"

"Well, she's a member of the John Birch Society. That explains why she's so sympathetic to the Children of God."

"Really, somehow that doesn't surprise me," Snake said. "What else?"

"Ah, lets see. She had to take the LSAT twice to get into law school. . . . Her mother divorced her father when she was eleven. She wanted to live with her father but the Court awarded her mother custody."

"Another kid screwed up 'cause mom and pop couldn't get along."

"Oh wait, check this out. She is one of the founding members of the Children of God."

"Really. Wow. That's interesting," Snake said. "Funny she didn't mention that to us."

"It sure is," I said trying to fathom our discovery. "The bitch may well be Doomsayer. . . . God, I can't believe it."

"Well, that doesn't prove she's Doomsayer but it sure puts her at the head of the list of suspects."

"I guess so. I can't believe she'd join a radical organization like that."

"She didn't just join it, my friend," Snake said. "Didn't you say she was one of the founders?"

"That's what the report says. . . . So now what? How can we prove she is Doomsayer?"

"You said you visited her office once, right?"

"Yeah."

"I think it's time you paid her another visit there."

At 8:05 a.m. the door to the judge's chambers opened and the bailiff shouted, "Please rise, the 877th District Court is now in session, the honorable Albert Bryan Brooks presiding."

Judge Brooks took the bench, opened his file and said, "Good morning ladies and gentlemen. After you were excused last night, counsel interviewed a few of the jury panel members privately and then the court dismissed several jurors for cause. What that means is the Court determined that these jurors could not be fair and impartial and therefore were not qualified to be jurors. After that each side got six strikes. That means they got to strike six jurors from the jury panel for any reason that they felt was relevant. From the remaining panel members the jury will be selected. Alright counsel, have you made your strikes?"

Hudson jumped up and replied, "Yes, Your Honor."

I stood and said, "We have, Your Honor."

"Very well, give your lists to the bailiff."

Hudson and I each handed the bailiff a sheet of paper and then sat down. The bailiff took the lists to the judge and they conferred momentarily. When they were done the judge said, "The bailiff will now read off the names of the jury members. If you hear your name please take a seat in the jury box."

One by one the jury members took their seats and when they were all seated the judge said, "All right Mr. Hudson, would you please read the indictment?"

"Of course Your Honor," Hudson replied. *"In the name and by the authority of the State of Texas: The G rand Jury of Grayson County, State of Texas, duly organized at the June Term A.D., 1982 of the 877th Judicial District Court, Grayson County, in said court at said Term, do present that one Sarah Winters, defendant, on or about the third day of December 1981, in the County and said State, did intentionally or knowingly cause the death of her child, a female newborn infant, by placing a pillow over her face and suffocating her until she was dead, such act being against the peace and dignity of the State of Texas."*

The crowd reeled in discomfort over the indictment and then a eerie silence fell over the courtroom. All eyes were focused on Sarah for her reaction. She didn't move, her sad eyes staring straight ahead. The judge made some notations, shuffled some papers and then looked over at Hudson. "Alright Mr. Hudson, would you like to make an opening statement?"

Hudson stood up and replied, "Yes, Your Honor."

"Very well then, you may proceed."

"Thank you," Hudson said. "Your Honor, ladies and gentlemen of the jury. The story I'm about to tell you will not be pleasant, so brace yourself. The state will show beyond any reasonable doubt the following facts: About 7 p.m. on Tuesday, December 3, 1981 Sarah Winters was in her apartment with her roommate Michelle Bowers. Sarah was pregnant, however, she had concealed her condition from everyone but her roommate and a few close friends.

"She began to go into labor and was in intense pain. She wasn't due yet so she told Michelle she had food poisoning and that she shouldn't worry about her. Michelle had planned to go out that evening and Sarah insisted she not cancel her plans. Reluctantly Michelle left, leaving Sarah home alone.

"As the evening progressed, Sarah's labor intensified until she finally delivered between eight and ten p.m. She successfully delivered a baby girl and it, for several brief moments, was alive and well. She cut the umbilical cord and placed the placenta in a garbage bag. Her perinaea, the area of the body between the vagina and the anus, had been badly torn during delivery so Sarah must have been bleeding profusely.

"I can't tell you exactly what happened next. Only Sarah Winters knows for sure. But sometime during the next hour Sarah Jane Winters took her child in her arms and placed it on the bed. Then she picked up a nearby pillow and placed it over her innocent little face, pushed it down with all her might until the baby was dead and lie limp on the bed."

A woman in the audience screamed in horror. A murmur erupted in the gallery. The judge picked up his gavel and banged it on the bench, "I'll have order please!"

"How do I know this happened?" Hudson asked. "The medical examiner will testify that during the autopsy particles of feathers were found in the baby's lungs. Yes, this child was alive until she was brutally and mercilessly murdered by her own mother!"

Several women in the crowd began to wail in disgust.

A man stood up and yelled, "You witch!"

The judge lunged for his gavel and pounded it repeatedly. "I'll have none of this! Bailiff, escort that man out of the courtroom! I will not tolerate any more outbursts."

The audience quieted down and Hudson went on with his account of the night of the murder. "Over the next few hours Sarah cleaned up her apartment, then she threw the baby into an ordinary garbage bag filled with other trash, carried it eight blocks away and threw it callously into a dumpster behind Sac'N Save.

"Now Sarah came very close to committing the perfect crime. The only thing she hadn't counted on was her excessive bleeding. Before long she became weak from a loss of blood and the long journey to Sack'N Save. When Michelle got home after midnight it was obvious to her that Sarah was very sick. So she and her boyfriend took Sarah, against her will, to the hospital. Upon examination by the physician on duty it was discovered that Sarah had delivered a baby that evening and that it was missing.

"Now why would Sarah want to kill her own child? What possible motive would she have for such a heinous crime? Well, the state will show that the father of the child was a ex-boyfriend named Richard Stein. Mr. Stein was also a student at ASU, but more importantly, Mr. Stein was an acknowledged drug dealer as well as an addict. Sarah had finally gotten rid of Richard and taken up with a new boyfriend, Greg Peterson, with whom she planned to be married. Obviously, a child of an ex-boy friend would jeopardize her relationship with Greg and she could not bear that. The only solution in her mind was to kill the child that would most assuredly come between her and Greg.

"But why kill your child when abortions are now legal? This is somewhat perplexing, but the state will show that Sarah's father is a Christian Scientist, and Christian Scientists are well known anti-abortionist. Sarah could not have had an abortion without alienating her father and she could not bear that either. Again, the only viable solution in Sarah's mind was to kill the baby so that no one would ever know she had ever had it.

"Ladies and gentlemen of the jury when the trial has concluded I am certain the facts I have outlined will have been clearly proven beyond all reasonable doubt. It will be your job to see to it that Sarah Winters pays for her crime. It will be your job to see that the murder of this poor, innocent baby is avenged. Thank you," Hudson said.

"All right, thank you Mr. Hudson. Mr. Turner, do you have an opening statement?"

Hudson had delivered a persuasive opening statement. My stomach was in knots. What had I been smoking when I agreed to take on a murder trial? Oh God, what if I botched up her defense and she ended up in jail for the rest of her life. Snake looked at me and smiled. I smiled back and took a deep breath. "Yes, Your Honor," I finally said.

"You may proceed."

"Thank you Your Honor, ladies and gentlemen of the jury. I know you are feeling outrage at this time. I know what you have heard is very painful. I feel that pain and believe me . . . believe me, Sarah Winters feels that same pain more than any of us can imagine. It was her child who was brutally murdered before her own eyes.

"Now Mr. Hudson would have you believe that Sarah Winters killed her own child, but I would caution you not to accept his explanation of the events of December 3, 1981. All of the evidence that Mr. Hudson will present to you is circumstantial and highly speculative. There are no witnesses to what happened to the Winter's baby. The defense will call as an expert Dr. Norman S. Gerhardt, Ph.D., a renown psychologist, who will testify that the events of the evening of

December 3, 1981 were so horrifying to Sarah Winters that she has totally repressed the events of that evening. Sarah Winters has no conscious memory of what happened on that horrid night.

"Ladies and Gentlemen, we will show you that there are several other suspects that are far more likely to have killed Sarah's baby than Sarah herself. These include her boyfriend, Greg Peterson and her ex-boyfriend Richard Stein. Neither of these two witnesses have an alibi. Either of these two suspects could just as easily have killed the Winter's baby. We will show you that the evidence the state will introduce is no more convincing against Sarah Winters as it would be against Greg Peterson or Richard Stein. In short, we will prove that there *is* reasonable doubt as to who killed the Winters' baby. And if there is reasonable doubt, then Sarah Winters is innocent. . . . Thank you."

As I went back to my chair I watched for the jury's reaction to my opening statement. Overall they were stone faced but one of them, an older woman, smiled faintly. Perhaps they all hadn't made up their mind yet, I prayed. The judge told Hudson to call his first witness. He called Bernie Meadows.

"Mr. Meadows. How are you employed?"

"I work for the Sherman police department in the homicide division."

"How long have you been a police officer?"

"Eighteen years."

"And how long have you been with the homicide division?"

"Seven years."

"Were you on duty on the night of December 3, 1981?"

"Yes, I was."

"And did you have an occasion to go to the apartment of Sarah Winters?"

"Yes, I did."

"Why was that?"

"I got a call from the dispatch operator that there had been a call from officials at Bright Methodist Hospital about a missing baby. I was instructed to go to the apartment of Sarah Jane Winters to look for the baby."

Meadows testified how the police searched the apartment and surrounding neighborhood ultimately finding the black plastic bag in which the baby had been left. Several items of demonstrable evidence were admitted into evidence including blood soaked towels and sheets.

"How did you find out about the black plastic bag?" Hudson asked.

"I got a call over my radio about it so I drove right on over," Meadows said.

"And what did you observe?"

"Officer Graves was standing over the black plastic bag which he had removed from the dumpster."

"Was it opened?"

"No, he hadn't opened it. I had instructed him to leave it alone until the boys from the lab arrived."

"What happened next?"

"When the lab team arrived, they opened the bag."

"Did you see them open it?"

"Yes."

"Please describe what you saw."

"The bag was filled with garbage, Coke cans, napkins, tin cans, plastic bottles, Kleenex, you know, miscellaneous garbage."

"Is that all?"

"No, there was another smaller white plastic bag inside the black bag."

"Was that removed?"

"Yes, one of the lab team members pulled it out and

opened it."

"And what was in it?"

"A baby. A newborn female infant."

The court erupted in moans and screams of disgust. A flash went off and the judge grabbed for his gavel and smacked it on the bench. "Order! Bailiff, remove that reporter from the courtroom, confiscate the film in his camera and make sure he doesn't step foot in this courtroom again! I'll have no photographs taken during the trial of this matter! I've already ruled on that issue and I will not tolerate any disobedience of my explicit orders! Anyone who thinks I'm kidding may well find themselves behind bars!"

The judge's harsh attack on the photographer silenced the crowd. All watched intently as the photographer was escorted out of the courtroom. When the reporter was gone Hudson looked over at the judge.

"Now, Mr. Hudson, please continue," the judge said.

"Yes, of course. . . . Now, where was I? Let me see, was the baby alive?"

"No, it was dead. The odor was-" Meadows shook his head. "Quite strong."

Hudson went back to the prosecution counsel table and brought over an evidence bag. He pulled out the black plastic bag, the white bag and various items of garbage.

"Are these the objects you just described Lieutenant?"

"Yes, they are."

"Your Honor, the prosecution requests that Peoples Exhibits 4-7 be admitted."

The judge looked over at me, I looked at the exhibit and said, "No objection."

"Peoples Exhibits 4-7 are admitted," the judge said.

"Did you find any evidence of anyone other than Sarah Winters having been in her apartment that night?"

"No, except Michelle Bowers and her boyfriend."

"Describe what you saw in Sarah's apartment other than what you've already testified."

"Well, it's a two bedroom apartment with a small living room and kitchen. Sarah's room is where we found the blood on the sheets. In her room there was an unmade bed, a night stand with a lamp and clock radio, and a desk with a typewriter on it."

"Were there any signs of a struggle taking place in the apartment?"

"No, not really. The place was a mess but nothing was broken."

"Pass the witness," Hudson said.

Meadows was a seasoned professional. I didn't figure I would be able to discredit his testimony in any way but I thought, with a little luck, I might be able to confuse things a little. I got up and walked toward the witness. "Lt. Meadows, did you see anybody at Sarah's apartment when you went there on December 3, 1981?"

"No."

"Have you found anyone who claims to have been at Sarah's apartment between 7:30 p.m. and midnight?"

"No."

"So you don't know then what happened, do you?"

"I don't personally know. I wasn't a witness if that's what you mean."

"Now you found the baby some eight blocks from the apartment in a garbage bag, right?"

"Yes."

"Did you weigh the bag?"

"No, we didn't have a scale."

"Did you lift the bag?"

"Yes, I wanted to see how heavy it was."

"How heavy was it?"

"Objection, he just testified he didn't have a scale, Your

Honor," Hudson said.

"I just want his opinion." I replied.

"Overruled."

"I would estimate eight to ten pounds."

"Now you've testified that there was a lot of blood in the apartment, and we will concede that the blood was Sarah's blood and it was her baby. So you're suggesting that Sarah killed her baby, began bleeding profusely, cleaned up her apartment, threw the placenta in a garbage bag with a bunch of towels, suffocated her baby, put it in a white bag inside a black trash bag, found a dumpster and threw in one of the bags, then hiked eight blocks carrying a 10-pound trash bag, threw it away in another dumpster, hiked back eight blocks and tried to act like nothing had happened?"

"Well, not precisely. But something like that."

"Let me ask you something, Lieutenant. Did you find any of Sarah's blood along the route to the Sack'N Save?"

"No."

"Did you find any blood anywhere other than in her apartment?"

"Just on the two bags and inside the bags."

"Don't you think your scenario is a little far fetched considering Sarah had just had a baby and was bleeding profusely?"

"Objection!" Hudson yelled. "Argumentative!"

"Withdrawn. No further questions," I said.

After Meadows stepped down the judge dismissed us for lunch. It suddenly occurred to me I hadn't mentioned to Sarah the need to search her apartment.

"Oh Sarah, I want Jodie to stop by your apartment and give it a once over. Do you mind?"

Sarah gave me a puzzled look. "Why?"

"Just routine. There might be something we missed or something you didn't think was important."

Sarah didn't respond so I said, "Is that okay, Sarah?"

Sarah looked at me warily. "Well, I guess, whatever."

It was apparent that Sarah wasn't anxious for us to search her apartment. Was it just the idea of someone invading her privacy or was she hiding something. I watched her a moment trying to figure it out. Finally, she turned away. I got up and looked at Snake. He shrugged.

I said, "I guess I need to figure out how to get into Westcott's office to see if there is any evidence there that might indicate she is Doomsayer. Any ideas how am I might to do that?"

"Tell her you want to review all the evidence again during lunch. Doesn't she have most of it up in her office?"

I nodded. "Okay, good idea."

I walked over to Miss Westcott who was just packing up to leave. "Ms. Westcott, I wonder if I could take one last look at the rest of your evidence before the afternoon session?"

"Right now?"

"Yes, if you don't mind."

"Oh. Gee. I've got a luncheon appointment. . . . Ah . . . Well, I guess I can call my secretary and tell her you're coming by."

"That would be fine. Thanks a lot."

"Okay."

Ms. Westcott left the courtroom and I went back to where Snake and Sarah were still standing.

"Okay, she agreed. I'm going to go over to her office in a few minutes. Her secretary is going to let me in to see it."

"Perfect," Snake said. "She won't even be there to keep an eye on you."

Tom offered to go across the street and get us some sandwiches. I told him to get me a sandwich and I'd eat it when I got back. Tom left with the rest of our orders and then we retreated into the judges conference room to prepare for the afternoon session. The mood was grim. Sarah had little to say and Snake seemed detached and preoccupied. Since no one seemed interested in talking, I left. To avoid the press I took the back entrance and headed across the street to the District Attorney's offices. I remembered where Miss Westcott's office was from my previous visit so I went straight past the main receptionist to where her secretary was stationed.

"Hi, are you Miss Westcott's secretary?"

"Yes, you must be Stan Turner, Mrs. Westcott said you would be coming by. I've moved all of the evidence into the small conference room so it will be easier for you to inspect."

Damn it! I thought to myself. Why did you have to do that?

"You did? Oh, thank you. You're very thoughtful."

I followed the secretary to the small conference room. As we passed Miss Westcott's office I noted much to my dismay that the door was closed.

"Here you are. If you need anything just let me know."

"Thanks," I said.

I started to look at the evidence as if I were interested until Miss Westcott's secretary left. Then I walked over to the door and scanned the hallway to see if anyone else was around. Most everyone had left for lunch it appeared except for Miss Westcott's secretary who was camped out in front of her door.

If there was any chance at getting into her office her secretary would have to leave her desk. As I watched her for awhile my level of frustration grew. After about ten minutes she finally got up and left. I didn't know where she went, or how long she would be gone, but I knew this was my only opportunity to check out Margie Westcott's office. I walked slowly down the hall looking for any sign of life and then I slipped unnoticed into the dark room. I turned on the light and shut the door.

The office was tidy with all of her work neatly stacked up into piles. I went over to her desk but didn't touch anything for fear of leaving fingerprints. I carefully scanned the files on her desk until I came to one entitled Children of Despair. I opened it with the tip of my pen and saw a report entitled, "The failure of the Criminal Justice System - Alternatives."

I was about to read it when I heard a noise outside Margie's office. Quickly moving to the door, I opened it slightly and peaked outside. Margie's secretary had returned and was seated at her desk. *"Damn!"* I whispered. I looked around the room and saw the Bible that sat so prominently on Margie's credenza. I walked over to it and opened it up to where it was marked by a red ribbon. It was opened to Revelations 14. Hearing voices, I closed the Bible and went back to the door to take another look. My heart sunk as I saw Miss Westcott talking to her secretary. I was screwed!

Fear gripped me as I frantically racked my brain for a way out of my predicament. How stupid I had been to go into Margie's office. Oh God, what and idiot! Suddenly the talking stopped and I heard footsteps coming toward me. Then it occurred to me, it would be better to find Miss Westcott than have her find me. I boldly walked out of her office.

"Miss Westcott, I'm glad you're back. There is an evidence bag missing. I thought maybe your secretary left it in your office."

"Ms. Westcott looked at me incredulously and then replied, "What are you talking about and how dare you go into my office alone!"

"Well, there's an evidence bag missing, your secretary was gone and you weren't here. I don't have all day!"

"Which bag is it?"

"Number seven."

"You idiot, number seven was just admitted into evidence!"

"It was? . . . Gee. . . . Oh God, I am so embarrassed. I'm so sorry."

I smiled, raised my hands, shrugged and then made a hasty retreat. As I got into the elevator I wondered what Miss Westcott was thinking. I'd give a penny for her thoughts, hell I'd give her a hundred bucks. When I got back Snake was alone staring off into space. He had a small silver flask in front of him. I didn't say anything, but wasn't pleased to see that he'd been drinking on the job. He sat up and smiled.

"So, how did it go?" he asked.

"Not so good, they moved the evidence out of Margie's office."

"Oh wonderful. Then you wasted your time?"

"Well, not exactly. I slipped into her office anyway."

"Without her permission?"

"Right."

"Are you crazy?"

"Yeah, probably. Anyway, I didn't have time to do much snooping around but I did find a file on Margie's desk about the Children of Despair."

"Children of Despair?"

"Yeah, I wish I would have had more time but Margie's secretary came back and I had to cut my visit short."

"That's all you got?"

"Well, pretty much, I looked in her bible. She had Revelations 14 marked."

"How did you get out of there?"

I told him.

"Do you think she bought your story?"

"I don't know, I hope so."

Snake stared at me with a worried look. "So do I."

When Tom and Sarah returned, the smell of hot barbecue seemed to awaken us from our doldrums. Snake and Tom quickly began eating. I noticed Sarah was not eating.

"You've got to eat. You're going to be under a lot of stress during the trial and you'll need your strength," I told her.

"If I had eaten anything this morning I probably would have puked," she said. "You wouldn't want that would you?'

"No," I said.

"Do you work out or jog, Sarah?" Snake asked.

"Are you kidding?" she replied. "I hate exercise."

"That was a good cross, Stan. The jury's got to be wondering if Sarah's some kind of Wonder Woman."

"Thanks. I hope it gave them pause for reflection."

"What's your strategy with Estaban?"

"Well, I figure since he examined Sarah on the night she delivered I might use him as my unofficial expert witness. What do you think?"

"Good plan, he's independent so it shouldn't matter to him."

"I hope not."

At one-thirty everyone had gathered back in the courtroom for the afternoon session except Miss Westcott who was absent. I was nervous that she had not returned. Was she filling out a complaint against me with the Sheriff or calling the State Bar to file a grievance? At 1:37 p.m. the judge entered the courtroom and the trial resumed. At 1:43 Miss Westcott finally showed up and joined Hudson at the prosecution counsel table.

"Mr. Hudson, call your next witness," the Judge said.

"The prosecution calls Dr. Manuel Esteban."

The bailiff brought in Dr. Esteban and he walked to the witness stand where the court reporter administered the oath.

"Dr. Esteban, how are you employed sir?"

"I work for Bright Methodist Hospital in Sherman as an emergency room physician."

"And were you on duty on the night of December 3, 1981?"

"Yes, I was."

"And did you have the occasion to examine Sarah Winters that night?"

"Actually I didn't see her until after midnight."

"What were her symptoms when she was admitted?"

"She was weak, pale, low blood pressure and running a temperature."

"Did you examine her?"

"Yes, I did?"

"What was her condition?"

"She was bleeding heavily from a large laceration caused from a recent childbirth."

"How did you determine that?"

"I did a pelvic exam and found her uterus to be extended and her stomach to be enlarged as it would be if she were pregnant."

"What did you do then?"

"I asked her where her baby was."

"What was her response?"

"She said she didn't know."

"Did she say anything else?"

"Not really, she was in shock and couldn't really communicate effectively."

"Did you do anything else?"

"I asked Michelle Bowers about the baby, but she hadn't even known Sarah had delivered."

"I see. Is that all?"

"No, then I called the police."

"Thank you, Doctor, pass the witness."

I stood up and looked intently at Dr. Esteban.

"Doctor, you testified that Sarah Winters was weak, pale and had lost a lot of blood, is that right?"

"Yes."

"You said she was in shock, I believe?"

"Yes."

"Would she have been in shock immediately after having her baby in your opinion?"

"It's hard to tell for sure, but that's quite likely."

"Could a woman in Sarah's condition carry two heavy bags several hundred yards, unload one of them and then carry the other one eight blocks, dump it and walk eight blocks back to her apartment?"

"It depends."

"It depends on what?"

"Well, her general physical condition and mental state."

"I see, and could Sarah Winters have done this considering her physical condition and mental state in which you found her on December 4, 1981?"

"No, but several hours earlier she might have been able to do it. You see when a person is in distress the body produces adrenalin which often gives a person abnormal strength and energy."

I didn't figure arguing with the doctor about the effect of adrenalin on the body would do much good. My point had been made and the jury, especially the women, seemed responsive to it. The judge dismissed the witness and Hudson called his next witness, Michelle Bowers. Michelle got up and approached the witness stand. The bailiff gave her the oath and then she sat down.

"Ms. Bowers, you're Sarah Winter's roommate, is that right?"

"Yes, sir."

"So you recall the evening of December 3, 1981?"

"Yes."

"Could you describe what happened, let's say starting at about 7 p.m.?"

"Yes, sir, I had a date but Sarah was so sick I wanted to cancel it. Sarah wouldn't let me do it though. She insisted I go ahead. She said she just got a little food poisoning and she'd be okay."

"What time did you leave?"

"Around 7:30 I think."

"Did you do anything before you left?"

"Yes, I went next door to be sure Alice would be home if Sarah needed her . . . and I called Sarah's parents."

"Did you make contact with Sarah's parents?"

"No, they were out so I left a message with Nate."

"Who's Nate?"

"He's Sarah's step-brother."

"Okay, did you leave then?"

"Yes."

"When did you return?"

"Around twelve-thirty or one."

"When you returned did you see anyone?"

"No, the place was pretty deserted."

"What happened next?"

"We went inside. Sarah was asleep. The light was dim so I didn't look at her too closely, but when I went into the bathroom and saw all that blood, well, I got concerned. I woke her up and saw that she was very pale and looked awful. I knew I had to do something."

"So, what did you do?"

"We took her to the emergency room."

"During the time you came home and took Sarah to the emergency room did she say anything to you about a baby?"

"No."

"Did you ever suspect she had delivered a baby?"

"No."

"Did Sarah ever take drugs?"

Michelle paused a moment and replied, "Not to my knowledge."

"Isn't it true she dated a known drug dealer, Richard

Stein?"

"Yes, it wasn't easy for Sarah to get dates, she was so shy. So when Richard came along it was a new experience and she liked it. But after a while, when she found out Richard was a drug dealer and basically no good, she dumped him."

"How long did they date?"

"Several months."

"Didn't they date over four months?"

"I guess."

"And they were intimate during that time, weren't they?"

"Yes."

"And during that time didn't Sarah take drugs. And I must remind you, you're under oath."

"Maybe. I don't know."

"Did Sarah ever tell you she was worried about the baby being abnormal because its father had been on drugs?"

"The topic came up, but Richard wasn't a big user. He sniffed a little coke once in a while but he knew better than to become dependant. He was a businessman."

"What were Sarah's plans for the baby when it came?"

"She didn't share them with me."

"I find that hard to believe," Hudson said. "You were her best friend. She never told you if she was going to keep the baby?"

"Oh, I knew she wasn't going to keep the baby. That was a given."

"Why is that?"

"She kept the pregnancy from her parents so obviously she couldn't show up at home one day with a baby."

"So you assumed she was going to have an abortion?"

"No, Sarah didn't believe in abortions so I had pretty much come to the conclusion that she had made plans to give the baby away," Michelle said.

"Did you ever observe Sarah make any contact with

anyone about putting the baby up for adoption?"

"No."

"What if I were to tell you that Sarah did not contact one single adoption agency in the city of Sherman prior to the night of the murder?"

"She was a procrastinator."

Hudson shook his head. "I guess so."

"Thank you Miss Bowers, no further questions," Hudson said.

"Mr. Turner, your witness," Judge Brooks said.

Being Sarah's friend, I knew Michelle would try to help Sarah with her testimony any way she could. All I had to do was ask her the right questions so she'd get the opportunity. I walked up to her and smiled.

"Thank you, Your Honor," I said. "Ms. Bowers, you must have gotten to know Sarah pretty well since you were her roommate, right?"

"Sure," she said.

"Is Sarah an intelligent girl?"

"Yes, she's very smart and studies hard."

"Is she religious? Does she go to church?"

"Not really, she's technically a Christian Scientist, but I don't think she's totally committed to it."

"How would you describe her personality?"

"Quiet, reserved. She was kind of a loner."

"How did you two meet?"

"We were assigned dorm rooms together our freshman year and we got along so well we got an apartment together this year."

"So you've known her for several years?"

"Right."

"Would you consider her to have a high moral character?"

"Absolutely!"

"What about Richard Stein?"

"Like I said he was a novelty for Sarah. She had never had a real boyfriend and he was nice to her at first. She didn't know about this drug dealing until later."

"Did she dump him immediately upon hearing of the drug dealing?"

"Not exactly, she ignored it at first, but one day when Richard was stoned out of his mind he beat her up. That was the end. Sarah never spoke to him again."

The gallery erupted in chatter so Judge Brooks picked up his gavel, slammed it a couple of times and said, "Order, I'll have order please."

"Did Sarah use birth control pills?"

"No, she couldn't take the pill, it was against her religion to go to a doctor."

"So did she use any kind of birth control?"

"Objection, calls for speculation."

"Sustained," Judge Brooks said.

"Ms. Bowers, do you know who was the father of Sarah's child?"

"Objection! Calls for speculation," Hudson said.

"Your Honor, she may know," I replied.

"Answer, only if you know from your own personal knowledge."

"It had to be Richard."

"Why is that?"

"Sarah didn't date anyone else, I know she didn't. I was with her every day."

"Did Sarah tell Richard Stein she was pregnant with his child?"

"I think she did."

"You think?" I said.

"Sarah bumped into Richard after she had figured out she was pregnant. He called her several times after that so I assumed it was about the baby."

"Do you know what they talked about?"

"No, Sarah wouldn't tell me. I asked her but she said she didn't want to talk about it."

"Did you ever talk directly with Richard?"

"No, I never liked him much. He'd sell drugs to his own mother if he could. Anything to make a buck," Michelle said.

"Doesn't Sarah have a new boyfriend now?"

"Yes, Greg, but he has only known her for a few months."

"Ms. Bowers, in your opinion could Sarah Winters kill anyone?"

"No, absolutely not! She'd never do that."

"In your opinion could she have killed her own child?"

"No way. Never."

"Thank you, Miss Bowers. No further questions."

"Mr. Hudson, redirect?"

"Yes, Your Honor. Miss Bowers, you say Mr. Stein must have been the father of Miss Winter's baby, right?"

"Yes."

"But you were not with Sarah every minute, were you?"

"Objection," I said. "Counsel is leading the witness."

"Your Honor, it's obvious Miss Bowers is friendly to the defendant and would like to help her any way she can. I ask that she be declared an adverse witness."

The judge nodded. "Request granted."

Hudson turned to the witness, "You may answer."

"What was the question?"

"You were not with Sarah every minute, were you?"

"No, not *every* minute."

"Did you ever go home for the weekend and leave Sarah alone?" Hudson asked.

"Yes," Sarah replied.

"So it's possible Sarah could have had sexual relations

with someone you didn't know about?"

      "I don't think so."

      "But it's possible, right?"

      "I guess."

      "Now you said Sarah couldn't kill anyone, right?"

      "Yes."

      "Particularly her own child, right?"

      "Absolutely."

      "That's your opinion, right?"

      "Uh huh."

      "Did you ever think, in your opinion, that Sarah would date a drug dealer?"

      Michelle didn't respond.

      "Isn't that right, you never dreamed Sarah, innocent little Sarah, would date a drug dealer, did you?"

      Michelle still did not respond.

      "Your Honor, would you instruct the witness to answer the question."

      "Miss Bowers, you must answer the question," Judge Brooks said.

      "No."

      "So you were wrong about Sarah and Richard Stein and you could be wrong about whether Sarah was capable of killing her baby, isn't that right?"

      "No, she wouldn't kill her own flesh and blood. I know she wouldn't."

      Hudson and Michelle's eyes locked. The courtroom became deadly silent as they stared each other down. The judge looked at Hudson and then Stan. "Okay, any more questions gentlemen?," he said.

      Hudson turned to the judge, rubbed his chin as he contemplated the question, and then replied, "No, Your Honor.

      "No further questions, Your Honor," I replied.

      During the balance of the afternoon Hudson brought on

the coroner who testified about the cause of death and specifically that the baby had been suffocated. Then he brought on a forensic expert who testified that Sarah's fingerprints were on each of the plastic bags used in the crime. It was nearly 4:30 p.m. when I took Sgt. Smalley on cross examination.

"Mr. Smalley, now you've established that Sarah's fingerprints were on each of the three trash bags used to dispose of the placenta and the baby, is that right?"

"Yes."

"Did you find any other fingerprints?"

"Yes."

"What other fingerprints did you find?"

"Mr. Peterson's print was on one of the bags."

"Which bag?"

"The big black one used to dispose of the placenta."

"Did you personally inspect the crime scene?"

"Yes."

"Were you able to determine where the bags in question came from?"

"Yes, the bag used to dispose of the placenta had been under the sink lining the trash can there."

"And the others?"

"The small white one had been in the bathroom and the other black one had come directly from the package from which it was purchased."

"So it's possible that Sarah, or for that matter, Greg Peterson could have touched the bag from under the sink or the one in the bathroom before the murder, isn't it?"

"Sure."

"What about the one straight from the package, the one in which the baby was placed. Whose fingerprints were on that one?

"There were two sets of prints, Sarah and an

unidentified person."

"Oh really? You mean there was a set of prints that did not belong to Sarah or, well tell me, . . . who all did you check the prints against?"

"We checked the prints against the defendant, Greg Peterson, Richard Stein, Michelle Bowers and her boyfriend, Henry Hampton and several others that frequented the apartment."

"I see, but none of these matched."

"No, sir."

"So some unidentified person must have been there when the baby was killed."

"Objection, calls for a conclusion, calls for speculation."

"Sustained."

"Where on the bag was the fingerprint found?"

"Near the top where the opening is situated."

"So, is it your opinion the print was from someone holding the bag open?"

"Yes."

"How many prints did you find?"

"Two, a thumb and an index finger."

"Did you find any of these prints in the apartment?"

"No."

"Thank you, no further questions."

"Any redirect," Judge Brooks asked.

"No, Your Honor."

"Very well, it's nearly five o'clock so we'll recess until ten a.m. Monday morning. Court's adjourned."

"All rise!"

I tried to slip out the back door with my police escort but I was spotted leaving the courthouse and a mob of reporters surrounded me.

"Mr. Turner, has the prosecution surprised you with any of it's evidence?" a reporter asked.

"No, not at all."

"How is your client holding up?"

"Very well, she a tough little girl."

"What about the unidentified prints?"

"What about them. Obviously someone else was at the scene of the crime, most likely the real killer."

"Do you know who he is?"

"We've got a good idea."

I was lying, I had no idea, but I figured if I could create a little doubt with the press, it might somehow trickle down to the jury.

I was mentally and physically exhausted but I went straight to my office anyway to see if there were any emergencies. Two weeks out of the office could spell disaster for a solo practitioner and I was painfully aware of that fact. Clients got very restless when they couldn't talk to their attorney and new business usually came to a halt. So I wanted to answer as many phone calls as I could before I called it a night.

It was shortly after six p.m. when I finally walked into my office. It was dark as Jodie had obviously left at five. I turned on the lights, walked over to Jodie's desk and grabbed the large stack of messages that she had left me. I sorted through them and separated out the ones I thought I might reach that evening. I went to my desk, sat down and started calling. I made ten or fifteen phone calls before I came to one from Marleen Wiggins.

It wasn't ethical for me to call her since she had an attorney and we were in the middle of a lawsuit, but my curiosity was so great I dialed her number anyway. She picked up on the second ring.

"This is Stan. You called?"

"I'm so sorry, Stan," she said. Her voice strained like she'd been crying, "to have to do this to you in the middle of your murder trial. I always liked you until you sold out to the devil. I"m curious though, what kind of a retainer did Satan give you?"

"Are you drunk?" I said noticing her slurred speech.

"Yes, of course I'm drunk. I've been drinking a lot since Bobby's death."

I was flabbergasted. Marleen Wiggins was a sweet old grandmother and she had suddenly gone mad. What had happened to her to cause this? I took a deep breath trying to figure out where to go with the conversation.

"How did I sell out to the devil?"

She laughed. "Don't play innocent with me. You know everything. You planned it all."

"What did I plan?"

She began to cry. "To destroy Bobby and me," she said. "To destroy our lives."

"Marleen. I don't know what you're talking about. Maybe we should get together and discuss it."

She suddenly regained her composure. Her voice was now firm and steady. "Yes, I'd like that."

"Okay, after the trial is over. Give me a call. You'll have to get your lawyer's permission though, otherwise I can't talk to you without him present."

"No, we must talk alone. I'll get his permission and call you."

What was that all about, I wondered? I had believed that greed motivated the civil suit against me, but now I wasn't so sure. Marleen was harboring some serious bitterness toward me and not because I hadn't warned them about an icy sidewalk. Something terrible must have happened between her and Bobby and she obviously blamed me. That's why she didn't resist her children's insistence on suing me. Everything was starting to make sense, but what was it that I had done to cause so much bitterness?

Chapter Sixteen
Children of Despair

On the way home I went over everything Bobby and I had been involved in over the past year. Nothing stuck out in my mind that would cause her to be upset. Unless it was a referral. That's one of the dangers of referring business to someone. Either party could hate you for putting them together. But who was it and what had they done? It was a puzzle I wasn't going to solve that night. When I got home it was after 8 p.m. Rebekah was sitting in the kitchen watching her mother, Sylvia, work. She didn't smile, just raised her eyebrows.

"Well, who is that? I don't recognize him, do you ma?" Rebekah said.

"Very funny, where is everybody?"

"The kids went to the movies with their grandfather."

"Oh, lucky kids. What's for dinner?"

"Dinner? That was two hours ago," Rebekah said.

"All right Rebekah, Stan's obviously had a rough day in court," Sylvia said. "I've got your supper all ready Stan." "Come sit down, I'll bring it to you."

I sat down next to Rebekah and grabbed her hand under the table. She turned and looked at me with her big brown eyes and smiled warmly.

"I've missed you. I'll be glad when this damn trial is

over."

"Me too, believe me."

"So how is it looking?"

"Oh, it could be worse. I think we've given the jury a few things to think about. Not a lot, but a few tidbits."

"So, why were you so late tonight?"

"I had to make phone calls, I had a stack of messages you wouldn't believe. Unfortunately I do have other clients. Their problems don't disappear just because I'm in trial."

"They all know you're in a murder trial. I can't believe they still call you."

"They do, believe me. Anyway, we may have figured out who Doomsayer is."

"Really?" Rebekah said.

"Yeah, but you can't mention this to anyone."

"Who is it?"

"Well, we think it's Margie Westcott."

"Who?"

"Margie Westcott, the assistant DA helping Hudson with the prosecution."

"You're kidding? How could that be?" Rebekah said.

"Well, we're not sure, but it seems to be a strong possibility."

"Why would she do something like that?"

"We're not sure yet," I replied. "I think she's mixed up with the Children of Despair. You know, the ones who have been picketing."

"Geese. I can't believe that," Rebekah said. "How could a public official do something like that?"

"I don't know. It's pretty mind boggling."

"Do you think she tried to kill you?" Sylvia said.

"No, probably not. I think she just wanted to cause us a little grief."

"Well, you can't let her get away with something like

that. It's not right. She's put us through hell and she should pay for it," Rebekah said.

"We don't know for sure she is Doomsayer, we're only speculating."

"So how will you find out if she is or isn't?"

"I don't know, but I need to look at a Bible."

"A Bible?"

"Yeah, when I was in Margie's office I looked at her Bible and noticed it was turned to Revelations, 14."

"Well, you know where the Bible is. On my nightstand."

"Would you get it for me?" I asked.

"I will," Sylvia said.

Sylvia finished what she was doing and then went down the hall. After a minute she returned with a Bible in her hand and handed it to me. I turned to Revelations, 14 and began reading aloud. '*If any man worship the beast and his image, the same shall drink of the wine of the wrath of God which is poured out without mixture into the cup of his indignation; and he shall be tormented with fire and brimstone in the presence of the holy angels.*' Doesn't that sound familiar?"

"That was part of the last message you got before Beauty was poisoned," Rebekah replied.

"You're right, that's quite a coincidence that there was a page marker on that citation."

"What are you going to do?"

"I don't know. I'd like to get back into her office when she's not there. We need some hard evidence to connect her to Doomsayer. If we accuse an Assistant District Attorney of obstruction of justice and then we can't prove it, we'd be in deep trouble. The judge would think the whole thing was a ploy to get a mistrial."

"I can't believe you can't do anything. She's obviously a sick person. She needs to be put behind bars. What if she hires someone to kill you?"

"No. She wouldn't do that. Anyway, we've got twenty-four hour police protection. Don't worry, nothing will happen," I said.

"I'm not so sure about that. If she really wants to hurt us she will. One police officer won't stop her."

"I think you're overreacting," I said with more irritation in my voice than I had intended.

"Overreacting? Bullshit!" Rebekah screamed.

"Margie wouldn't try to kill me anyway. That would be stupid."

"Well, somebody has been trying awfully hard to kill you."

"I don't really think so. They're just trying to scare me. They just want to distract me so I won't do a good job defending Sarah."

"If they killed me or the kids that would really be a great distraction."

"What do you want me to do? I can't withdraw. You know that."

"I know," she said. She took a deep breath, her eyes wet with tears. "I'm just so scared, Stan. I'm just so scared."

Rebekah dropped her head and began to sob. I put my arms around her and said, "No one is going to get hurt, I promise you."

*****

On Saturday afternoon I was at the office working on my trial outline, witness list and direct examination questions. I had to be ready to present Sarah's defense on Monday because Hudson could finish up anytime now. I was surprised when I looked up and Jodie was standing there. "What are you doing here?"

She smiled. "Jodie Marshall, Private Eye, reporting in," she said giving me a crisp salute.

I shook my head. "PI's don't salute. They just grab a flask out of their trench coat and pour themselves a shot of whiskey."

"That sounds good. Shall I pour us a round?"

"No, I get sleepy when I drink and I've got several more hours of work to do. . . . Just tell me what happened."

"Okay, you're no fun. . . . . So, anyway my search took place around 10:30 this morning. Michelle was still asleep when I arrived. She was kind of surprised to see me but accepted my explanation for the visit.

"She let me in and made us some coffee while I got started poking around Sarah's room. The room had been cleaned up since the night of the murder. The bed was made and all of Sarah's things were neatly arranged around her room. There were some pictures on the nightstand, one of Greg and Sarah, another of Tom, Joyce, Nate and Sarah at Six Flags. Tom and Joyce seemed so happy in the picture and Nate and Sarah looked to be quite close, almost like a real brother and sister.

"I felt very guilty going through Sarah's things, I must tell you. It didn't seem right, but like a good little PI, I continued to search. First her chester drawers, then the closet and even the pockets of all her coats and jackets. From the pocket of a charcoal coat I pulled out an envelope folded in two. It was an old TU Electric envelope. On the back it had the name *Dusty* and a phone number handwritten in blue ink. I didn't know if it was significant so I took it with me. After finishing the closet I went to the desk. There I found a bundle of letters and a note pad. There were some interesting letters," she said as she pulled one out from its envelope. "Should I read them to you?"

"Sure," I said.

"'Sarah, I got your message about the A on your term paper. This weekend we can

celebrate. Call me if you read this before eleven.
Greg.'

She handed it to me and then said, "Here's another one, it's from Nate."

> *'Sis, about our discussion the other night,*
> *you really should take it slow with Greg. You*
> *don't want to make the same kind of mistake you*
> *made with Richard. I know you think Greg is a*
> *great guy and all, but people are often different*
> *from what they appear. I just don't want you to*
> *get hurt again, I couldn't bear that. You know I*
> *care about you. Love, Nate.'*

Jodie handed the second letter to me. I read it again.

"Michelle caught me reading the letters and seemed upset," Jodie said.

"Really."

"Yes, she came in to tell me the coffee was ready. I explained to her why we had to do it. Then we started talking about Greg and Nate. I had noticed a lot of letters from Nate. She said he was a wonderful stepbrother. She wishes her own brother was as kind and considerate. Apparently he even sent her flowers on her birthday.'

'Wow, that *is* unusual," I said.

'She also thinks Nate's pretty cute too. When he came to visit Sarah during Spring Break she came on to him but much to her sorrow, he ignored her."

"That figures," I said. "A big football star destined to be a millionaire probably has a dozen gorgeous women at his beck and call."

Jodie nodded.

"She asked how the trial was going? She's worried Sarah will be convicted."

"Join the club," I said. "So that's it, huh?"

"Yeah, I'm afraid so."

"Damn, I really thought you might find something more."

"Sorry, Stan."

"It's alright, it was just a long shot."

"Well, I'm going to run. I just wanted to report in."

"Listen, before you go, let me run something else by you."

"What's that," she said.

"I got a strange call from Marleen Wiggins. She was drunk and very angry. She said some pretty ugly things. I'm really at loss to know what I did to warrant such bitterness."

"That is strange. I wonder if her attorney knew she was calling you directly."

"Obviously not," I said.

"What do you think it is?" Jodie asked.

"I don't know. He and I have always been such good friends. We send each other business. Hell, I do all his kids legal work. This is so bizarre."

"Could it be the Parker thing?" Jodie asked.

"Yeah, I've thought of that, but Rob says Bobby never mentioned it. He probably had just discovered it when he was working on his tax return? I doubt this is the source of Marleen's anger."

"What are you going to do?"

"I don't know. If I could just figure out what it was that was eating her, then maybe I'd know how to deal with it."

Jodie looked at me pensively. Then she said, "Maybe you didn't do anything?"

"Huh?"

"Maybe attacking you is a diversion," Jodie said. "Maybe Marleen is trying to hide something either to protect Bobby's reputation or herself."

"From what?"

"From the truth. Did it ever occur to you Bobby's death wasn't an accident after all?"

"You think Marleen killed Bobby?"

"I don't know, but it's a possibility you can't afford to ignore."

Chapter Seventeen
The Deception

    I got up early Monday morning and went jogging. It had been raining and the air was cool. A dense fog hung along the saturated ground. It felt strange and lonely without Beauty at my side. I recalled how playful and energetic she was in the mornings. How she loved to jog with me and would sit by the door each morning waiting impatiently for me to start my run. When I left the office for home each night I looked forward to opening the door and having Beauty jump all over me bubbling with excitement at my arrival.

    Glancing back, I smiled at my police escort following me in a squad car. It would have been more rational to stay in the safe confines of my home, but I was determined not to let Doomsayer alter my normal routine. Jogging cleared my mind and gave me energy which I would need for the grueling week of trial that lay ahead. Doomsayer had miscalculated, rather than being intimidated by his invidious deeds I was outraged and more determined than ever to defend Sarah with all the vigor I could muster.

    After breakfast, I went straight to Sherman. As I

approached the courthouse with my police escort I was amazed at the number of media vehicles lined up along Travis Street which led to the downtown square. It seemed interest in the case was swelling with each day of trial. I was glad the judge had not allowed the case to be televised as it was difficult enough performing before the judge and jury without having a national TV audience. As I got out of the car I was barraged with questions from reporters.

"Mr. Turner, have the police figured out who Doomsayer is yet?" a reporter asked.

"No, I don't think so, but I've got a good idea who it is."

"Who is it?" the reporter pressed.

"I can't say yet. I can't comment on it since I can't prove it a hundred percent yet."

"When do you think you will have the proof you need?"

"I don't know, but as soon as I do I'll turn it over to the police."

"Why did you abandon a temporary insanity defense?" another reporter asked.

"Our client is innocent so a temporary insanity defense would not be appropriate."

"Have there been any more threats on your life?"

"No, I've got to get into the courthouse now, thank you."

I pressed my way through the crowd and, with the help of several sheriff's deputies on duty, managed to make it to the steps of the courthouse. There I met several lines of picketers from the Children of Despair.

I made my way into the courthouse and was escorted through the back entrance up to the courtroom. Snake and Sarah were already seated at the counsel table. Miss Westcott and Hudson were talking with their next witness. I sat down just as the bailiff yelled, "Please rise!"

The judge entered the courtroom and took the bench. He instructed the bailiff to bring the jury in, which he did, and the trial resumed.

"Your Honor, the prosecution calls Greg Peterson."

Greg was brought in and made his way to the witness stand. He was sworn-in and Hudson began his questioning.

"Mr. Peterson, do you know the defendant, Sarah Winters?"

"Yes, I do."

"How do you know her?"

"She's my girlfriend."

"How long have you known her?"

"Four or five months."

"Do you two have any plans for the future?"

"Yes, before all this happened we were seriously considering getting married."

"What are your plans now?"

"I don't know. Everything's so screwed up now I'm not sure."

"You weren't happy about the pregnancy?"

"No, not really."

"You didn't want to raise someone else's child, did you?"

"No."

"You told Sarah that, didn't you," Hudson asked.

"Yes, we talked about it," Greg said.

"She loves you, doesn't she?"

"I think so."

"She didn't want to lose you?"

"No."

"So she had to get rid of the baby?"

"She had to deal with the problem, if that's what you mean."

"How was she going to do that?"

"I assumed she was going to give it away."

"Have you ever seen any evidence of that or is that just speculation?"

"It's just my guess."

Hudson continued to question Greg for nearly an hour about his background, employment and relationship with Sarah and then he finally got to the night of December 3, 1981."

"Did you see Sarah Winters on the night of the murder?"

"No."

"Did you talk to her?"

"No."

"Where were you on that night?"

"At the UTD library."

"What were you doing there?"

"Studying."

"Did you see anyone there you knew who might verify that you were there?"

"I don't remember anyone."

"Did you know Sarah was pregnant?"

"Yes."

"How did you feel about it?"

"I wasn't thrilled since it wasn't my baby."

"Did you tell her you were unhappy?"

"I didn't have to. She knew."

"Now you've talked to Sarah a lot before and after the murder, isn't that right?"

"Yes."

"What were her plans for the baby?"

"She didn't share them with me."

"I find that hard to believe," Hudson said. "You two were in love weren't you?"

"Yes, but Sarah made it quite clear from the beginning that her pregnancy was her problem and she didn't want my help in dealing with it."

"Is it safe to say she had no plans to keep the child?"

"I made that assumption but she never said anything one way or another."

"How did you feel about raising someone else's child?"

"It's not something I'd enjoy doing. I want children, but I want my own."

"Has Sarah said anything to you about what happened the night the baby was killed?"

"Well, she didn't remember much at first, but she's gradually getting her memory back."

"Has she ever told you that she killed her baby?"

"No."

"Has she ever told you that she might have killed her baby?"

"Well, for a while she didn't remember exactly what happened so at one time she was worried that she might have done it."

"So she admitted she might have done it. Alright, do you have any evidence to the contrary?"

"Excuse me?"

"Other than Sarah claiming that she didn't kill her baby, do you have any knowledge, information or proof that she didn't do it?"

"I don't know, I guess not, but I'm sure she didn't do it."

"You testified you were planning to get married, right?"

"Yes."

"And you testified you were concerned about her being pregnant, right?"

"Yes."

"Did you express this concern to Sarah?"

"Yes, she knew I was worried about it."

"Why were you worried about it?"

"Well, we weren't married yet, we were still in school and it wasn't a good time for her to have a baby."

"Couldn't Sarah just get an abortion if she were pregnant?"

"No, she'd never get an abortion, her father wouldn't

allow it."

"Did she tell you that?"

"He told me that."

"Mr. Winters told you that?"

"Absolutely, he warned me not to get her pregnant because no one in the Winters family would ever get an abortion. He said if she got pregnant I'd better be ready to settle down and be a father."

"Were you worried about anything else?"

"No, not that I can think of."

"What about Richard Stein?"

Greg sat back in his chair and replied, "What about him?"

"Did Sarah tell you about him?"

"Yes, she did."

"Weren't you worried that she might be pregnant by him?"

Greg starred at Hudson and did not reply.

"Mr. Peterson, I repeat, weren't you worried about Sarah being pregnant by Ricky Stein?"

"Yes, of course I was, the bastard was a dope dealer, wasn't he?"

"And Sarah knew you were worried about that didn't she?"

"Objection, calls for speculation," I said.

"Your Honor, if he knows, it's not speculation."

"I'll allow it," Judge Brooks said. "You may answer."

"Yes, I think she was worried about it too. She would never admit it, but I can't see how she could ignore that possibility."

"Thank you, Mr. Peterson, pass the witness."

"Mr. Turner, your witness," the judge said.

"Thank you, Your Honor." I replied. "Mr. Peterson. How far is it to Sarah's apartment from the UTD Library?"

"About 60 miles."

"How long does it take you to drive there?"

"A little less than an hour usually."

"When did you leave the library?"

"About eleven p.m."

"When did you get the message from Sarah?"

"Right after I got home."

"But all we have is your word that you were in the library between seven and eleven p.m., isn't that right?"

"I guess."

"You had enough time to go visit Sarah, stay there an hour, and return, didn't you?"

"Objection, argumentative," Hudson said.

"Are you going anywhere with this Mr. Turner, or are we fishing?"

I looked up at the judge, hesitated a moment and then replied, "Withdraw the question."

"Do you love Sarah?"

"Yes."

"You wanted to marry her?"

"Yes."

"Are you still going to marry her?"

"Objection! Irrelevant," Hudson exclaimed.

"Sustained."

"When did you find out that Sarah had been beaten by Ricky Stein?"

"Just recently."

"After the death of Sarah's baby?"

"Yes."

"How did you feel when you heard about it?"

"Objection. Irrelevant," Hudson said.

"Sustained," the judge ruled.

"You said you suspected that Sarah was carrying Ricky Stein's baby, is that right?"

"Yes."

"Prior to the death of Baby Winters did you think about what you would do if it were true?"

Greg paused a moment to reflect and then replied, "Yes, I decided that I would stay with Sarah anyway."

I grimaced in disappointment. Then I asked, "Did you tell Sarah that?"

"No. . . . No, I didn't. I meant to but the right moment never came up."

"Thank you, Mr. Peterson, pass the witness."

"Mr. Hudson, redirect?"

"No, Your Honor."

"Call your next witness then."

"The State calls Ronald Wheatland."

The bailiff went out into the hall and brought in a young, lean, blond headed man. He walked to the witness stand and was sworn in. I looked at my witness list and then conferred briefly with Snake.

"Your Honor, I object, this witness is not on the witness list," I said.

"I can explain Your Honor," Hudson replied. "We just found this witness this morning. We didn't have time to inform Mr. Turner."

"Very well, proceed," the judge said.

"Mr. Wheatland, where do you reside?"

"Fourteen thirty-one Perimeter Trail #1134, Richardson, Texas."

"And what do you do?"

"I am a student at UTD."

"And where were you on the night of December 3, 1981?"

"At the UTD library."

"Do you know a student named Greg Peterson?"

"Yes, not socially, but I know who he is."

"How is that?"

"He's in one of my classes at school."

"At UTD?"

"Yes."

"And how is it that you know him?"

"He's pretty smart and the professor calls on him a lot."

"I see. And did you see Mr. Peterson at the UTD Library on the night of December 3, 1981?"

"Yes, I did."

The gallery erupted in chatter and several reporters began hastily taking notes. I squirmed in my chair. Snake remained poker-faced. The Judge scowled at the crowd and banged his gavel to restore order.

"When did you first see him?" Hudson continued.

"He was there when I got there at 7:30 p.m."

"And when did he leave?"

"He was there when I left at 10:30."

"Could you point Mr. Peterson out to us?"

The witness pointed toward the back of the courtroom where Greg had taken a seat. "Yes, he's sitting in the back row. I saw him when I came in a minute ago."

"Could you go point him out to us so there's no question in the jury's mind that he's the one you saw on the night of December 3, 1981?"

Mr. Wheatland got up and walked slowly to the back of the courtroom. When he got close to Greg he pointed to him and said, "This is Greg Peterson, this is the man I saw in the library that night."

The crowd stirred. I sank back in my chair. Sarah's eyes met Greg's and they smiled at each other.

"Thank you, Mr. Wheatland, pass the witness."

I conferred briefly with Snake then looked up and said, "Your Honor, we don't have any questions at this time, but since this witness was a surprise to us we would like the right to recall him later should we turn up any discrepancies in his story."

"That seems only fair. The witness is excused, subject to recall," the judge ordered. "It's 10:30, let's take a fifteen minute break."

When the trial resumed, Hudson called a noted psychiatrist who had examined Sarah and determined that she was very intelligent, quite sane and knew exactly what happened on the night of the murder. He denied she had post traumatic amnesia. I cross examined him for hours but he was adamant in his position and couldn't be shaken. Then Hudson called Alice who testified that she saw and heard nothing, but would have helped Sarah had she been asked. Then as the prosecution's last witness, Hudson called Richard Stein. The bailiff brought in the witness who was accompanied by his attorney.

"Your Honor, my name is Rocky Valentino. I represent the witness, Richard Stein."

"Very well, Mr. Valentino, you may sit in one of the chairs behind the defense counsel's table during examination."

"Thank you, Your Honor."

"You may proceed Mr. Hudson."

"Please state your name?"

"Richard Stein."

"And how are you employed?"

"I'm a student at ASU."

"Yes, do you know the defendant, Sarah Winters?"

"Sure, absolutely."

"How do you know her?"

"She was my woman for a while."

"When was that?"

"About a year ago we started hanging out and then five or six months ago we split."

"Did you live together?"

"Not exactly, Sarah had her own pad, but like I say, she hung with me a lot."

"Were you lovers?"

"Yeah, we did a little humping, if you know what I mean."

"When you and Sarah broke up was she pregnant?"

"How would I know that? I assume she was using some protection."

"Did she ever tell you she was pregnant?"

"No. It came as a big news flash to me, if you know where I'm coming from."

"Where were you on the night of December 3, 1981?"

"In my pad."

"All night?"

Richard's attorney began to shake his head no.

"Ah I think my lawyer is signaling that I need to take the fifth, if you know what I mean."

"Are you taking the fifth?"

"Yeah, I guess I better, that's what I got a lawyer for, right?"

"Your Honor," Hudson said. "May we have a side bar with counsel for Mr. Stein?"

"Yes, you may approach the bench."

All the attorneys came up to the bench and began to discuss the invocation of the fifth amendment by the witness.

"Your Honor, Mr. Stein is not on trial here, he can't take the fifth amendment."

"I beg to differ counselor," Mr. Valentino replied. "My client may not be on trial for murder but he is under investigation for narcotics trafficking and any testimony about his whereabouts on the night of the murder could be incriminating."

"Your Honor, it would be very misleading for the jury to listen to Mr. Stein take the fifth amendment. They would invariably think he was involved in the murder," Hudson argued.

"Then are you prepared to grant Mr. Stein immunity for anything he did on the night of December 3, 1981?" Judge Brooks asked.

"We'll grant immunity as to any drug related offense, Your Honor, that might have occurred that evening."

"Okay, then I will instruct the witness to answer the question."

"Thank you, Your Honor," Hudson said.

The attorney's returned to their chairs and the judge instructed Mr. Stein to answer the question."

"Where is your ah . . . pad?" Hudson asked.

"Not too far from Sarah's place."

"And were you there the entire evening?"

"No, I went out about eleven to take care of a little business."

"How long were you gone?"

"About forty-five minutes."

"Was anybody back at your place who could corroborate your story?"

He shrugged. "No, my old lady was gone that night."

"What did you do all evening, other than take care of business?"

"I watched a little TV, you know, listened to some music, just messed around, you know."

"Did you see Sarah that night?" Hudson asked.

"No."

"Do you have any knowledge as to what happened to her baby that night?"

"No, other than what I read in the papers, you know."

"Thank you Mr. Stein, pass the witness," Hudson said.

I got up and approached the witness.

"Mr. Stein. Did you ever beat up Sarah Winters?"

"Uh. Well, I wouldn't call it beating her up. She was a bitch sometimes so I had to put her in her place a time or two."

"Isn't it true she left you because you beat her up?"

"It wasn't like that, I was drunk, you know. I didn't know what I was doing. I can barely remember what happened."

"You don't use birth control, do you?"

Richard smiled and replied, "No. I want to feel everything man, if you know what I mean. I figured she would take the pill or something."

"Isn't it true you were the father of Sarah's baby?"

"How should I know?"

"It's just a matter of mathematics isn't it? Isn't that what you told me?"

"Yeah, I might have been the father, you know, but I didn't hang with Sarah every minute. She could have done it with someone else."

"Do you know of her having sex with anyone else at this time?"

"No."

"Are you aware of a father's obligation to support his children?"

"Hey man, you're not going to try to hang this thing on me are you?"

"You had a motive to kill Sarah's child, didn't you."

"I didn't kill anybody. I'm not into that stuff."

"How much did you make last year, a hundred grand?"

"I don't know, I don't keep records."

"Let's see, that's $20 to $30,000 a year child support, right?"

"Objection, the witness testified he didn't keep records, " Hudson said.

"Withdrawn." I said. "Didn't you tell me once you made about a hundred grand last year?"

"Well, I might have."

"Then, I repeat. Conceivably you might have to pay $20 to $30,000 a year in child support had the baby not died?"

"I don't know anything about that, I never even thought of that until you brought it up."

"It'd be very inconvenient to be a father, wouldn't it?"

"Hey, she was supposed to give the kid up for adoption, I thought."

"You thought?" I said.

"Isn't that what you told me?"

"No, I asked you if you had arranged an adoption for Sarah and you denied it."

"Right, I didn't know she was pregnant."

"Come on, Mr. Stein. Sarah's going to testify later on in the trial that she told you about the pregnancy and you suggested a very private adoption. You even hired an attorney to arrange it."

"That's a lie," Stein said.

"Is it?" I said. "Why would Sarah lie about something like that? What would be the point? Besides, Michelle Bowers will corroborate her testimony."

"I don't care how many witnesses you drag up here, it ain't true."

"Do you think anyone's going to believe a drug dealer, Mr. Stein?"

"Objection! Counsel is badgering the witness," Hudson said.

"Sustained, Mr. Turner, this witness is not on trial here."

"Yes, Your Honor. Mr. Stein, have you ever been convicted of a crime?"

"Objection! Irrelevant." Hudson said.

"I concur," Valentino added.

"Your Honor, it goes to credibility."

"Overruled."

"I did a few months for possession and burglary."

"Were you involved in a criminal act on the night of the death of Baby Winters?"

"I take the fifth."

"Objection!" Valentino said.

"Your Honor, he's been given immunity," I replied.

"Answer the question," the judge ordered.

"Well, I provided a customer with a little stuff, you know what I mean."

"So you were engaged in illegal drug dealing, but not murder, is that your story?"

"Yeah, you got it."

"What other illegal activities are you involved in?"

"Objection!" Hudson said.

"Sustained," the Judge said.

"No further questions at this time, Your Honor, but I would request this witness remain available for the duration of the trial."

"Very well," the judge said, "Mr. Stein you are not released. Please advise the bailiff where you can be reached should further testimony be required."

"Okay," Stein said.

"Mr. Hudson, redirect?"

"No, Your Honor, the state calls Willie Nichols."

Stein got up and left the courtroom. I looked down at my witness list again and then conferred with Snake. "Your Honor, we don't have a Willie Nichols on the witness list."

Hudson jumped up and replied, "Your Honor, we just found this witness in the last few hours and we didn't have time to tell the defense about him."

"This is an outrage! I can't believe the State would pull a stunt like this twice in the same trial," I said. "This is unfair and I strongly object to this witness being allowed to testify."

"Your Honor, we've been searching for this man for three weeks and we just found him."

"Mr. Turner, I'm sorry, but if they just found him then I've got to let him testify.   Unless, of course, you've got some evidence that they knew where he was before today."

"But, Your Honor I just now-"

"Do you have any such evidence?"

I shrugged. "No."

"Very well then, Mr. Hudson, you may proceed."

"Mr. Nichols, are you acquainted with Richard Stein."

"Yes, sir."

"Did you see him on the night of December 3, 1981?"

"That's right."

"What time would that have been?"

"Eleven o'clock."

"Where were you?"

"Up at the lake."

"What lake?"

"Lake Texoma."

A commotion broke out in the gallery.   The Judge picked up his gavel and pounded it several times to restore order.

"Whereabouts on the lake?" Hudson asked.

"Little Mineral," Nichols replied.

"What's Little Mineral?"

"It's a campground and boat dock."

"Why were you there?"

"We had a little business to transact with Ricky."

"Ricky being, Richard Stein."

"Yes."

"What time did Mr. Stein leave?"

"About 11:20 as I recall."

"Have you ever been to Ricky's apartment?"

"Sure."

"How long does it take to get to Little Mineral from his apartment?"

"Forty minutes or so."

"So he would have had to leave at 10:20 to get there by eleven and couldn't have gotten back before midnight, is that right?"

"I suppose so."

"Did you notice anything unusual about Mr. Stein that night?" Hudson asked.

"No, not really."

"Was he nervous or preoccupied?"

"No, he was just his normal self, joking and kidding around as usual."

"Did you transact your business?"

"Hey, we did what we came to do."

"Thank you, no further questions," Hudson concluded.

"Mr. Turner, your witness," the Judge said.

"How long have you known Richard Stein?" I asked.

"A couple years," Nichols replied.

"Did you know Sarah Winters?"

"Sure, she used to hang around with Ricky."

"Did you see her the night of December 3, 1981?"

"No."

"Do you know anything about the murder of her child?"

"No."

"Richard never talked to you about Sarah's baby?"

"No, he never mentioned it."

"Has Richard ever got a woman pregnant before?" I asked.

"Objection! Irrelevant," Hudson said.

"Your Honor, we've had no opportunity to question this witness. We request a little latitude here."

"Alright, overruled, I'll allow you a little leeway."

"Thank you, Your Honor. . . . Mr. Nichols, you may answer the question. Has Richard ever got a woman pregnant before to your knowledge?"

"Yes."

"How many girls has he got pregnant to your knowledge?"

"A few."

"A few. Is that more than three?"

Nichols shook his head. "Probably half a dozen or so."

"Objection, Your Honor. Irrelevant," Hudson said.

"Overruled," the Judge said.

"Really? How do you know this?"

"Richard liked to brag about it."

"What happened to the babies?" I asked.

"I don't know."

"He didn't tell you how he got rid of the babies?"

"Objection!" Hudson said.

"Sustained."

"Did you know any of these girls?" I asked.

"No, they were just ASU girls that Richard picked up."

"So you don't know how all these pregnancies were resolved?"

"Huh?"

"You don't know whether these girls had abortions, put the baby up for adoption or what?"

"No, except for a girl named Paula Walsh."

"What do you know about Paula Walsh?"

"Her baby was adopted," Nichols said.

"How do you know that?"

"'Cause she told me."

"When did she tell you?" I asked.

"Richard brought her along one night when he was making a delivery. I got to talking to Paula and she told me she had just had a baby. I asked her what she done with it and she said Richard had arranged an adoption."

"Did she mention an attorney's name or an adoption agency?"

"No, that's all I know." Nichols said.

"Thank you, Mr. Nichols. No further questions."

"Any redirect, Mr. Hudson?" the judge asked.

"No, Your Honor. The prosecution rests."

"Very well, we'll reconvene tomorrow morning at ten a.m."

The judge left the courtroom and immediately the TV camera's came alive to record commentary on the day's testimony. Several correspondents requested an interview, but I declined, being too depressed to face the media. All I wanted to do was get the hell out of the courtroom. Tom came and got Sarah and they both were taken by their police escort out of the building. Snake was stunned. He just sat in his chair and shook his head.

Both Hudson and Margie Westcott quickly found a camera and a microphone and began proclaiming victory. We delayed our departure to listen to them be interviewed.

"Mr. Hudson, you've got to be pleased with how the testimony went today," a reporter commented.

"Yes, we are very pleased. We knew we had a strong case and I think our presentation went very well. I feel certain we'll get a conviction."

"Were you surprised that Mr. Turner didn't plead his client innocent by reason of insanity?" another reporter asked.

"Not really, Sarah Winters is a very intelligent girl. She's not insane nor has she ever been insane, temporary or otherwise. She knew what she was doing on the night of the murder and she must pay for it."

"Do you think the defense will let Sarah testify tomorrow?" another reporter asked.

"I think they almost have to, it's their only hope," Hudson replied.

"What about this last witness. Do you think the fact that Mr. Stein may have got other girls pregnant will have any impact on the case?"

"No, it's totally irrelevant to this case," Hudson said. "Even if Sarah Winters had contemplated an adoption it makes no difference. She still murdered her baby and she must pay for her crime."

Chapter Eighteen
Hypnotic Testimony

That night I took the family out to dinner at Cheddars. I figured we all needed a break from the trauma of the murder trial. I hadn't seen much of Rebekah and the kids over the past few weeks and I wanted to have a little time alone together to reassure them that everything would soon be back to normal. We checked in with the hostess and then took a seat at the bar while we waited for a table.

"How did the trial go today?" Rebekah asked.

"Not so well."

The six o'clock news came on the big TV over the bar. "As a matter of fact, in just a minute or two you can see just how bad it went," I said as I pointed to the TV. "Listen."

"This is Mike Collins with the Channel 12 Metroplex News. Good evening. In the Sarah Winters trial up in Grayson County the prosecution closed their case today with a one two punch that may send Sarah Winters straight to prison. Two unexpected prosecution witnesses may have destroyed Sarah Winter's defense to charges she murdered her baby girl. We have a report from Paul Barnes."

"This is Paul Barnes reporting from Sherman, Texas where prosecutor, Howard Hudson, produced two surprise witnesses that apparently decimated Sarah Winter's defense built around two other possible suspects in the murder of the

Winters baby. Defense attorney, Stan Turner, had hoped to cast doubt about his client's guilt by showing that Sarah Winter's two boyfriends also had motive and opportunity to have committed the murder. Unfortunately for Sarah Winters, the prosecutors at the very last minute found witnesses who provided alibis for both Greg Peterson and Richard Stein," Barnes reported.

"So is it all over for Sarah Winters?" Collins asked.

"It may well be unless Stan Turner and his co-counsel, Harry Hertel, come up with a miracle tomorrow when the court reconvenes at 10:00 a.m. Central Standard Time," Barnes said.

"Thank you Paul. We'll check in on you again tomorrow night. In other news-"

"Gee honey, I'm so sorry. It looks like Sarah is about out of luck," Rebekah said.

"It kind of looks that way, doesn't it?"

"Maybe she actually did it. I know you did the best job you could but if she's guilty, she's guilty."

"If she's guilty then she's one hell of an actress, let me tell you. She certainly made me believe she was innocent," I said.

"Well, if she's such a great actress, why don't you put her on the stand maybe she'll convince the jury she's innocent," Rebekah said.

"That's very dangerous. It's almost a cardinal rule not to let a defendant testify whether or not she's innocent or guilty."

"What does she have to lose?"

"Even if we put her on, she doesn't remember anything except when she's under hypnosis," I said.

"So, have her shrink put her under hypnosis on the stand," Rebekah replied.

I laughed. "The judge would never go for that. Hudson

would have a stroke if I even mentioned that."

"So, you don't care what Hudson thinks, do you?"

"No, obviously not."

"So, if the judge will let you do it, maybe you should."

A voice came over the intercom, "Turner, party of six, your table is ready."

"Okay, lets eat guys," I said.

After dinner I went back to the office to make final preparations to put on my case the following day. Jodie was there like a trooper to help anyway she could. I briefed her on what had happened that day at trial and what I needed to do to prepare for the following day. Before we got started she said she wanted to talk about Bobby Wiggins.

"I've been thinking about Bobby Wiggins like you asked me to."

"Oh, good. I've been too busy with Sarah to give it much thought. So what do you think?"

"I spent a lot of time with Rob Parker helping him get his schedules filled out and filed. I didn't tell you this but he came on to me. He wanted me to go out with him."

"You're kidding? The scumball. He's twice your age."

"I know," Jodie said. "I told him to forget it. But I remember him mentioning something about some cash he had stashed away. He suggested I might want to help him spend it."

"What?"

"I didn't say anything to you because I thought he was just joking. You know how men are."

"Yeah, well that just confirms what Bobby's records show. The man's a crook. Unfortunately that doesn't solve our little mystery."

"Well, I've got another theory about that."

"Boy, you've become quite the PI."

"Actually I'm thinking of changing careers. This PI stuff

is much more fun than typing."

"Don't quit on me yet please. Not in the middle of a murder trial."

"I won't. Anyway, I think the reason Marleen was so pissed off was the fact that you referred Joanna Winburn to Bobby."

"Joanna?"

"Yes, you know how Joanna is always coming on to you even though you're married and have made it clear you have no interest in her?"

"That's her business."

"I know, and I'm sure she did the same thing with Bobby. The difference is Bobby was in his late fifties. He would be very vulnerable to someone seductive like Joanna."

"But what would Joanna want with Bobby?"

"Easy money. Being an exotic dancer is hard work. I'm sure she's getting tired of it. She's been doing it for, what, ten years?"

"I guess."

"I think she wanted a sugar daddy. She knew a couple blow jobs a week would keep him happy, and once he was hooked she could get as much money as she wanted. He'd pay, he'd have to or she'd blow the whistle on him."

"That's an interesting theory, but we don't have any proof."

"Why don't you go see her tonight and ask her," Jodie said. "She likes you. Use that to your advantage. It should be fun."

I laughed. "Yeah, it could be a lot of fun but it could also be dangerous."

"Why? You think she killed, Bobby?"

"No, it's not her I'm worried about, it's me."

Jodie smiled. "Get weak around a pretty face, huh?"

"Yeah, that's always been a problem with me. I can't tell

you how much grief it's caused."

"Well, you'll just have to be strong. Stay in control. You can do it. You're a professional."

I laughed."Okay, but what do I tell Rebekah when I show up at midnight smelling like smoke, or worse yet, perfume."

"I'll stay here and cover for you. If she calls I'll tell her you're on another line or something. When you leave the club go to the men's room and make sure you're presentable to go home."

I shook my head. "You're something else, you know it?"

"Well, since Rodney's gone I don't have anything more exciting to do tonight."

"Okay, This seems a little crazy, but I guess I don't have anything to lose. I'll call you when I leave the club."

"Okay."

As I drove down Northwest Highway toward the Ruby Slipper where Joanna danced, I wondered if I had lost my mind. I looked at my watch and saw that it was about 9:30 p.m. Here I was in the middle of a murder trial and I was off on what would probably turn out to be a grunion hunt. I was tempted to turn around and head home, but Jodie had certainly got me thinking. Now I was curious. Had Joanna lied to me before about her relationship to Bobby and, if so, what did it mean? Obviously, I had to find out. As I neared the club I felt that wonderful tingling sensation that I experienced around Joanna. I couldn't believe it. I hadn't even laid eyes on her and I was already getting a hard-on.

The parking lot of the club was packed. I drove slowly around the lot and finally found an empty space around back. It was dark except for the blinking light emanating from the big red neon slipper on the roof of the club. I got out, locked the car and went inside.

After paying my cover charge I made my way through

the crowd until I had a good view of the stage. Joanna wasn't dancing so I walked around to see if I could find her. It didn't take long. She was in the midst of giving a young executive a lap dance. I stood and watched her, mesmerized.

When she was done he put a twenty in her panties, she kissed his cheek and turned to walk away. She spotted me, smiled wryly and came on over to where I was standing.

"Stan, you're back. You just couldn't stay away, could you?"

"No, I guess not. I decided to take you up on that lap dance."

She smiled. "You little devil. I thought you were the faithful husband and father."

"All I came for was a lap dance, nothing more. I've been a little stressed out lately. You know, with the trial and everything."

"Oh, you poor baby. Come on, let's go in the back room where we can have a little privacy. I'll make everything better."

As she sauntered toward the back room I took a deep breath. Be strong I said to myself. Be strong. In the back room there were several private booths draped in red velvet. In each room there was a padded contour chair without arms and a small lamp on an end table. Joanna told me to sit down and lay back. I obeyed. She hit a button and music began to play.

"Is this where you brought Bobby?" I asked.

"What?"

"Bobby Wiggins. Did he like lap dances?"

Joanna gave me a disappointed look. "Bobby Wiggins? Not tonight. Tonight it's just you and me."

She began to sway her body to the slow rhythm of the music, twisting her arms over her head erotically and smiling down at me. Then she reached behind her back and popped the snap on her bra. It fell to the ground exposing her magnificent breasts. She kept her eyes locked on mine obviously enjoying the control she knew she had over me. Then she leaned over and brushed my face with her breasts. It was all I could do to keep my hands still beside me.

When she stuck her hand down my pants. I stopped her.

I said. "You know there isn't going to be a you and me."

She took a deep breath and pulled her hand away. She folded her arms over her naked breasts. "Then why in the hell did you come here!?"

"I got a belligerent phone call from Marleen. She's real pissed with me because of something I did. The only thing I can figure it could be is you. I introduced you to Bobby."

"I told you our relationship was strictly professional."

"I know what you said but what I want to know is the truth."

"The truth is Bobby Wiggins is a dirty old man like every other man I've ever known. He had one thing on his mind whenever we met and it wasn't Form 1040."

I laughed. "So did he get what was on his mind?"

"He did, but it cost him . . . plenty."

Jodie was right. I couldn't believe it. I got up and looked Joanna in the eye. I took a deep breath wondering where to go from here. I asked her if Marleen ever found out about them. She said she didn't think so. So now where was I, I wondered? Before I left I called Jodie and told her what I had found out. She said she'd call Rebekah and tell her I was on the way home.

The next morning Rebekah was cool to me. I knew she was suspicious about the previous night. I wasn't about to fill her in on what I had been doing.

"I've got to work today, honey, I'm sorry."

"But it's Sunday."

"I know, but I've still got a lot to do before tomorrow. I've got a couple leads to follow-up on."

"Damn it. I'll be so happy when this trial is over. Promise me you won't ever take a murder case again. We don't need all this stress in our lives."

"Okay, I promise. No more murder cases. No more criminal law."

"Good."

When I got to the office I decided to call Detective Delacroix and suggest to him that maybe Bobby Wiggins was murdered. I figured that would make his day. He wasn't on duty so I asked the dispatcher to find him and have him call me. I told her it was urgent. Several minutes later he called.

"So what's so urgent?" he asked.

"I don't have any solid evidence but I'm starting to believe Bobby Wiggins was murdered."

"What? Not a chance."

I told him about Marleen's phone call and Joanna's admission to the affair.

"You're grasping at straws, Mr. Turner. You're just looking for a way out of your lawsuit."

"Maybe so, but the only way to find out is to exhume the body and do an autopsy."

"It's too late. The body was cremated."

"What? Shit, she had this whole thing figured out. She is one smart lady."

"Do yourself a favor, Mr. Turner. Just concentrate on one murder at a time."

"Oh, so you think it *was* a murder?"

"No, but I'll give the file another once over, just to see if we might have missed something. Don't hold your breath."

"Thanks, Detective. You're a good man."

After I hung up I called information and got the number for Paula Walsh. It was early but I had no choice but to call her immediately since time was running out.

"Listen there was some testimony Friday in court about

you and Richard Stein."

"Really?" Paula said.

"Yes, apparently you and he dated for awhile?"

"Right."

"You had his child?"

"He told you that?"

"Well, not exactly but he didn't deny it. Is it true?"

"Well, . . . yes."

"I understand you put the child up for adoption?"

"That's correct."

"Who handled it? Was there an attorney or an adoption agency?"

"There was an attorney. His name was Mike Simpson."

"Did you ever go to his office?"

"No, I met him at Richard's apartment."

"What hospital was the baby delivered at?"

"It wasn't a hospital. It was a doctor's office."

"What? You delivered your baby at a doctor's office?"

"Yes, Richard said all private adoptions were handled that way."

"Didn't you think that was a little strange?" I asked.

"No, it made sense because the adoptive parents wouldn't want me trying to find them later, you know, if I changed my mind."

"Do you know the name of the doctor or where his office is located?"

"No, I was blindfolded."

"What?"

"Richard said I couldn't know who the doctor was or I might come back later and try to find out who had my baby."

"And you went along with that?"

"Yeah. It made sense."

I raised my eyebrows. "What made you decide to give your child up for adoption anyway?"

"I wanted an abortion but Richard was against it. He said that was murder and he wouldn't have any part of it."

"Are you serious? Do you think he was sincere?"

"I was surprised. I thought he'd go for the abortion but he explained how many woman there were who couldn't have children. He said having the baby and giving it away was the decent thing to do."

"Did you get paid anything by the adoptive parents?" I asked.

"Oh no, all I cared about was that my baby was put in a good home."

"Do you know Sarah Winters?"

"No, I've seen her a couple times around campus but I don't know her."

"Did you know about any of the other girls Richard got pregnant?"

"There were others?" Paula asked.

"Apparently, several others."

"No, I don't know anything about them."

I didn't know what to make of the conversation with Paula except that Richard Stein had obviously been lying. Whether or not the truth would help Sarah I didn't know, but I had to search for it. It was my duty. I called Jodie at home and told her to see if she could find any of the other girls who had been knocked up by Richard. She said she'd talk to Michelle and maybe check with the student health office to see if they knew anything.

At 10:00 the next morning the Judge took the bench. Sarah and I were sitting alone at the defense table. Snake had not yet arrived. I called his office and his secretary told me he had called in and they were instructed to tell me that he was following up on a new lead and may not make it to court today. I was flabbergasted.

"Mr. Turner, where is your co-counsel?"

"I don't know Your Honor, I got a message he might not be able to make it in today."

"Really? Is he sick?"

"No, apparently he's following up on a new lead."

"Well, we can't wait for him."

"I know, Your Honor, we can go ahead and get started."

"Very well then, you may proceed."

Hudson sat up, crossed his legs and scanned the courtroom. Then he whispered something to Miss Westcott. I figured he was wondering what Snake was up to, just as I was. Whatever he was doing, it better be important I thought to myself as I picked up my examination outline. I wanted to run the idea of putting Sarah on the stand by Snake, but obviously that wasn't going to happen. It was the moment of decision, what was I to do? Hudson looked at me and then laughed at something Margie told him. I took a deep breath and then made my decision.

I said,"The defense calls Dr. Norman S. Gerhardt."

The bailiff went out into the hall and brought in Dr. Gerhardt. He took the stand and was sworn in.

"Dr. Gerhardt. State your occupation please," I said.

"I am a clinical psychiatrist."

"And how are you employed?"

"I have a clinic in Dallas, I'm also a part time professor at ASU."

"And what is your educational background?"

"I graduated from Duke University with a BS degree in 1965. I received a Master's Degree in Psychology from Yale University in 1967 and graduated from medical school at Tulane University in 1971."

"Are you licensed professionally?"

"Yes, I have a license to practice medicine issued in 1973 and I'm certified in hypno-therapy."

"Do you belong to any professional organizations?"

"Yes, I belong to the AMA, the TMA, the National Society of Clinical Psychologist, the Dallas Chapter of the American Psychologist Union and I'm a fellow in the American Psychological Foundation."

"Have you published any books or papers?"

"Yes, I've published seven books, thirty-five articles in various trade publications and I often lecture at seminars and conventions."

"Have you had an occasion to meet Sarah Winters?"

"Yes, she was referred to me by your office several weeks ago for evaluation and treatment."

"How often did you meet with her?"

"I met with her three or four times."

"And how would you characterize her mental condition?"

"She is a shy, but highly intelligent young woman. Unfortunately she has endured a very unstable childhood which has left her angry, depressed and slightly paranoid. She lacks confidence and has low self esteem."

"Did you undertake any treatment of Miss Winters, Dr. Gerhardt?"

"Yes I conducted two sessions of hypnosis to help her restore her memory of the events of December 3, 1981."

"She has no memory of those events?"

"She didn't before I started the hypno-therapy. But now she can remember parts of it."

"In your opinion what caused this memory loss?"

"Normally post traumatic amnesia is caused by a concussion to the brain or the subconscious mind intentionally repressing events that the conscious mind cannot deal with. This type of memory loss is often the only buffer between sanity and insanity."

"How did you conduct the two hypno-therapy sessions?"

"I placed Sarah under hypnosis and asked her to go back to the events of the night in question."

"And what was the result of that request?"

"She began to relate the events of that evening."

"Your Honor, I object to Mr. Gerhardt testifying for the Defendant. If Mr. Turner wants Sarah Winters to testify he should put her on the stand."

"Your Honor, I was going to call Miss Winters as my next witness, but what I would actually like to do is have them testify together."

"Excuse me," Hudson said.

"Your Honor, Dr. Gerhardt has testified that Sarah's conscious mind cannot remember what happened on the night of the death of her child. However, he has testified that her subconscious mind is fully cognizant of what happened. Therefore, what I would propose to do is have Dr. Gerhardt stay on the stand, but have Sarah Winters join him so that she might be hypnotized. Then her subconscious mind can testify as to what happened on the night in question."

"Objection! This would be highly irregular and potentially prejudicial to the prosecution."

"Objection sustained. Mr. Turner. We are not turnng this trial into a three ring circus."

"But Your Honor, I think the doctor has provided sufficient medical evidence to establish that Sarah's subconscious mind has relevant testimony in this trial."

Hudson shook his head. "Your Honor, there is no legal precedent-"

"I sustained the objection, Mr. Turner," the Judge said. "Now lets move on."

The judge's ruling didn't surprise me and I wasn't one to intentionally disobey the Court's ruling. But Sarah's life was at stake. I finished up with the Doctor and when Hudson was through cross examining him, I asked for a short recess before I called Sarah to the stand. Sarah and Dr. Gerhardt joined me in the library conference room. .

Second Chair

"Dr. Gerhard, can you hypnotize Sarah from the gallery?"

"Well, I suppose but the Judge-"

"Forget the judge. This is the only way we're going to get to the truth."

"But I could get in serious trouble disobeying the Court's ruling."

"I know, but-"

Sarah said. "Why don't you hypnotize me, Mr. Turner."

"What? Me. But I don't-"

"Wait," Dr. Gerhardt said. "What we can do is hypnotize her now and I'll tell her to answer your questions when she is on the stand and to wake up at your commmand."

"Great. That's perfect," I said. "And you don't even have to be in the courtroom."

After the recess I called Sarah to testify. I had told her to dress like she was going to church and she had followed my advise. She stood up and walked mechanically to the stand. She took her seat and then closed her eyes. I looked around for a reaction but apparently no one noticed anything unusual.

In the back of the courtroom I thought I saw a young cameraman filming. He leaned over and looked through the view finder. I squinted to see if I could see the green light that indicated the camera was rolling but he had his hand in the way. I figured he thought this was too good an opportunity to pass up. I looked at the judge to see if he had noticed, but he was focused on me.

"Sarah, I want you to think back to the night of December 3, 1981. Tell us what's happening."

Sarah opened her eyes and gazed at me thoughtfully. Hudson stiffened in his chair. He looked over at me and frowned. Then he looked at Miss Westcott. She shrugged.

"I'm holding my baby," she said almost in a whisper. "It's so small. I can't believe it's mine."

"Now what are you doing?"

"I'm bleeding. I feel so weak. I just want to lie down and go to sleep but I know I can't," Sarah moaned and then put a hand in the air and froze. "Wait. There's someone knocking at the door. I'm in so much pain I can't get up to answer it. Oh God, it hurts!"

Hudson stood up apparently to object but nothing came out of his mouth.

Sarah began to roll her head around and around as she moaned in pain.

"What's happening now?" I said.

"No . . . no!," she screamed. " What are you doing? What are you doing to my baby? Don't take it."

"Who is it Sarah?"

"I don't know, it's so dark. What are you doing with that pillow?! Don't kill my baby! No. No! Stop it. I'm going to call the police."

Hudson finally said, "Objection, Your Honor. This is-"

"Is he talking to you Sarah?" I asked.

"He says it's the best thing for both of us. He says he will take care of everything."

"Who is it Sarah? Who did this?"

"I don't know, it's dark, I don't know. . . . Don't kill it," Sarah sobbed. "You don't have to kill it! Please. No. . . . God. . . . Please, no! Ahh!"

The judge said, "Mr. Turner, what is this? Is she-"

Sarah cried out and began to convulse and gasp for air.

"Sarah, wake up. It's okay," I said.

Sarah didn't respond. Her whole body started shaking. I rushed over to her and put my arms around her.

"Your Honor, I think we should call an ambulance."

"Bailiff, get an ambulance up here now," the Judge said.

Sarah began to turn a pale blue as she slumped in the witness chair. Finally, two paramedics rolled in a stretcher through the front door. Tom ran up from the audience to help. The paramedics gave her oxygen. After a few seconds her eyes opened, she squirmed around a little and then began breathing again. Tom and a crowd of reporters followed them as they took her out of the courtroom and down to a waiting ambulance.   The spectators in the courtroom were out of control. Judge Brooks pounded his gavel, but it was no use. Finally, he told the bailiff to clear the courtroom. Then he dealt with me.

"Was your client under hypnosis, Mr. Turner?"

"Ah . . . well, I'm afraid she was."

"You disobeyed the direct order of this Court?"

"I had to, Your Honor. Otherwise, the truth would never have come out."

Hudson said,"Your Honor, I move for a mistrial."

"Motion denied. . . . You know, Mr. Turner I have a mind to send you straight to jail for contempt."

"I understand, Your Honor."

"But I'm going to wait until the trial is over to do that. But trust me, you will be spending some time behind bars to think about how you've made a mockery of this Court. Do you understand?!"

"Yes, Sir."

"Now, there better not be anymore theatrics in my courtroom or I'll bar you from ever practicing in this Court again. Do you understand?!"

"Yes, Sir," I said. "I understand."

"Now, get out of my sight."

Dispite getting chewed out by the judge, I felt better on my drive home that afternoon. Sarah's performance had been no less than spectacular. Surely the jury would have some doubts now after hearing her pleas to the unidentified assailant to spare her baby. Surely they would recognize the voice of a caring mother, incapable of committing the heinous crime for which she had been charged. Surely she would be acquitted.

When I walked into my house I was immediately met by Rebekah. It was early afternoon so she was surprised to see me.

"That was something else, in court today," she said. "Sarah did good."

"How did you hear about that?"

"It was on the five o'clock news, the whole thing was on TV! I didn't think the judge was allowing the trial to be filmed."

"It was on TV? You've got to be kidding?"

"No, I couldn't believe it."

"Judge Brooks is going to have a stroke. The cameras were not supposed to be on during the trial," I said.

"I don't think the cameraman is going to much care since he's sure to get a Pulitzer Prize for that piece of work."

"Turn on the TV, it's almost time for the six o'clock news. I want to see it."

Rebekah went over to the TV and turned it on.

"What station is it on?"

"Channel 12, it's all anyone can talk about."

The television lit up and a commentator was talking in front of the Grayson County Courthouse."

"I've never seen anything like this Mike, the judge denied Stan Turner's request to have his client put under hypnosis purportedly so her subconscious mind could testify. But Turner disobeyed the Judge and put his client on the stand already hypnotized. Once Sarah Winters got on the stand the fireworks began. She described an unidentified assailant and pleaded with him not to kill her baby. It was very convincing."

"Paul, is there any chance Miss Winters was faking this?"

"If she was this may be the beginning of a new career, Mike."

I turned off the TV and shook my head. "Well, your idea

worked out pretty well."

"Pretty well?" she said. "A stroke of genius, if you ask me."

"I wonder what Snake thinks of all this?"

"Where was he?"

"That's what I'd like to know. I can't believe he didn't show up without even a telephone call to explain his absence."

"Well, you did pretty well without him," Rebekah said with a proud smile.

"Yeah, except I'll be going to jail once the trial is over."

"What? . . . Jail?"

I explained the judge's reaction to our little ploy.

"Oh, Stan. I'm so sorry. I shouldn't have suggested the hypnosis. It's all my fault. Now you're going to have to go to jail. How long do you-"

"It's not your fault. Don't worry about it. I'm sure it will be just a day or two."

Rebekah went back in the kitchen to work on supper. She was upset, so upset she could hardly concentrate on what she was doing. I decided it was time to locate Snake. His secretary told me she hadn't heard from him all day. I wondered what was going on, how could he disappear in the middle of a murder trial? Something was wrong.

After a half dozen phone calls without even a hint at where he might be, I called Jodie at home to see if she had had any luck in finding out any more about Richard Stein and his propensity for knocking up young college girls. Jodie answered on the first ring.

"Stan, I'm glad you called," Jodie said.

"What did you find out?"

"You won't believe this. I called the State Bar and they don't have an attorney named Mike Simpson currently licensed. They said, however, there used to be an attorney named Mike Simpson but he was disbarred in 1979."

"For what?" I asked.

"He was convicted of money laundering. He served two years at Texarkana and got out on parole last year."

"So I wonder what he and Richard Stein were up to?"

"I don't know but I checked birth records for the last few years and Richard Stein's name came up."

"Really, so have you located the mother?"

"Yes, she's going to stop by the courthouse tomorrow about 8:30 a.m. to talk to you. Her name is Bonnie Waits. She wouldn't talk to me over the phone but she said what she had to tell you would be very interesting."

"I bet. I can hardly wait," I said. "Thanks Jodie, you did a great job."

"I get double time for PI work right?" Jodie said.

"Yeah, I'll send Tom a bill."

Jodie shook her head. "Oh, thanks."

That night, after dinner, I went to my office to work on my closing argument. I didn't know what Judge Brooks was going to do after what had happened. I assessed the odds that he would declare a mistrial at fifty-fifty. But I had to be ready for anything so I started to outline my argument. After about an hour the telephone rang. It was my inside line so I figured it was Rebekah. It wasn't, it was Snake.

"Nice job today. You may have hit ole Hudson with a knock out punch," he said.

"Where in hell were you?"

"I've been doing some last minute investigation. I think I'm on to something."

"What is it?"

"Our little jock. He may be the key to all this. What I need you to do is stall tomorrow, try not to close until I get there."

"When will that be?"

"Just as quick as I can, but I don't know exactly when.

Oh, and I need you to subpoena him. I'm going to need some questions answered."

"What do think he knows?"

"It's complicated and I don't have time to explain it. I'll see you tomorrow."

"Snake, wait!" I said and then the phone when dead."Damn it!"

On Tuesday the courthouse square was a mob scene. The drama of the previous day, which had been captured on film and showed to the nation, was the number one news story. I was scared. Never in my life had I been under so much pressure and the object of so much attention. I had associated Snake as a precaution in case I got over my head. Now when I should have been feeling thankful for my foresight, Snake was out chasing windmills. Sarah's life was at stake for godsakes and I had virtually no defense. Sure, Sarah had performed well the day before but without corroborating evidence her testimony was worthless. I felt sick inside, I couldn't stand the thought of losing, even if Sarah were guilty. I prayed my 8:30 meeting with Bonnie Waits would be enlightening.

When I reached the city limits of Sherman my single police escort was joined by three Sherman Police patrol cars. Our small caravan made its way to the town square where the police had cordoned off an area away from the press and picketers to allow access and egress for participants in the trial. I parked my car and then made my way into the building and up to the courtroom.

I was supposed to meet Bonnie in front so I sat on a bench in the hallway. I sat back, closed my eyes and tried to relax. Then I felt the bench move from the weight of someone sitting next to me. I opened my eyes and saw the smiling face of a young redhead.

"Mr. Turner, hi," Bonnie said.

"Good morning," I said.

"Tough trial, huh?"

I nodded. "Yes, it's been a nightmare."

"Well, maybe I can turn it around for you."

"I'm listening."

******

I looked at the clock on the wall and saw it was 9:45. Sarah was at the counsel table with Greg sitting next to her. I scanned the gallery and was surprised to see Tom sitting with Joyce in the front row. I nodded at Tom and smiled. The prosecution table was deserted. I sat down and began to unpack my briefcase when Margie Westcott walked over and stood beside me.

"I want to compliment you on a brilliant piece of work yesterday. I've never seen anything like it since I've been a prosecutor. You must have spent hours practicing with Sarah. Did you hire an acting coach?"

I smiled and shook my head. "Well, I'm sorry to disappoint you but, no, we didn't practice it at all. It was actually spontaneous."

"Well, I expected you to say that. But, anyway we think the jury will believe otherwise which leads me to the reason for this conversation."

"Okay, I'm listening."

"This Doomsayer business. You told someone in the press that you thought you knew who Doomsayer was."

My pulse quickened. "Yeah, I've got my suspicions."

"Well, if you have any information you better cough it up or we'll nail you for obstruction of justice."

"What? You got to be kidding," I said. "I'm supposed to tell you everything I know?"

"Exactly."

I shook my head. "It's inconclusive. That's why I haven't

made it public."

"I don't care. Whatever you got I want to hear it," Miss Westcott said.

"Okay. Okay. You'll be the first to know if I find anything out."

Miss Westcott made no effort to leave. She just stared at me. "Oh, one other thing. I hate to break the news to you, but your second chair, Snake. . . "

"Yeah."

"Don't count on him pulling this case out of the fire. He's probably off drunk somewhere with one of his whores. It's happened before."

"You're wrong," I said. "He called me last night. He's following up on some leads."

Margie laughed. "Is that what he told you. You are so gullible, Stan Turner. Trust me, he's off with a bottle and a piece of ass."

My stomach twisted into a knot. Could she be right? Had my second chair deserted me in the heat of battle. Snake did like the Majestic Mansion a lot. He did try to set me up with one of his barmaid friends. He did drink a lot. What if he didn't show up today. Oh God, I'd be screwed.

When the Judge took the bench his mood was solemn. He sat down and said, "All right, now the first item of business is the unauthorized filming of yesterday's court session. I understand it was a Channel 12 camera that was the source of the tape. Is the Channel 12 cameraman in the courtroom?"

All eyes turned to the rear of the courtroom where the Channel 12 camera was set up. A thin, dark haired man of about thirty reluctantly raised his hand.

"Come forward young man," the judge ordered.

The man slowly walked up to the courtroom. A man in a suit quickly joined him.

"Your Honor," the man in the suit said.

"And who are you?" the judge asked.

"I am Thomas Kingsley, attorney for Channel 12 news. Now the camera was turned on yesterday by mistake."

"All I asked was your identity! I didn't ask for any argument at this time. What is your name sir?"

"Jim Robb."

"Were you here when I ruled that there would be no TV coverage of this trial?"

"Yes, sir."

"And were you responsible for the camera that took the footage of yesterday's trial?"

"Yes, sir."

"Was it a mistake as your counsel suggests?"

"Oh, yes sir, I just accidentally hit the power button."

"And I suppose it was a mistake that it was played nationwide on the evening news?"

"Well, I don't know about that. . . . I just gave it to my boss."

"Who's your boss?"

"Arnold Vick."

"Mr. Robb, I find you in contempt of this court. Bailiff, take Mr. Robb to a jail cell and confiscate his camera. I'll deal with you and Mr. Vick after this trial is over."

The bailiff escorted Mr. Robb out of the courtroom. Several deputies began disassembling his camera. The judge then turned his attention to the gallery.

"Now if anyone so much as sneezes in my court today I'll have them removed. And if we have any kind of disorder like we did yesterday I'll clear the courtroom. Is that understood?"

There was silence as the judge glared at the spectators.

"All right, where were we?"

"Your Honor," Hudson said. "I would respectfully request a mistrial. Yesterday's events plus the illegal taping of portions of the trial have caused irreparable damage to the state's case."

"Motion denied, now where were we?"

I stood up. "I believe, Your Honor, Sarah Winters was on the stand testifying on direct examination."

"Oh yes, has she recovered from yesterday, is she prepared to continue?"

"Yes, Your Honor, I believe she has."

"She's not under hypnosis is she?"

"No, Your Honor."

"Do you have any more questions for Miss Winters?"

"Yes, Your Honor."

"Continue then," the judge said.

"Ms. Winters, do you remember what happened the night of December 3rd?"

"Somewhat. I remember delivering my baby and wondering what to do with it."

"You must of had some plans for the baby, didn't you?"

"Yes, Richard Stein had arranged for it to be adopted."

"So, when you finally realized you were in labor did you call him and tell him what was happening?"

"Yes, I remember now I called his beeper but he didn't call back."

"Did you call anyone else?"

"No."

"Did anyone come by the apartment after you delivered?"

"Yes, I remember a man but I can't identify him. He has no face in my memory."

"Was there just one man?"

"I only saw one, but there might have been more."

"Was it someone you knew?"

"I think so, the voice was familiar."

"What happened?"

"The man took the baby away from me. I tried to stop him but he was too strong. He pushed me against the wall and that's all I remember."

"Did you kill your baby, Sarah?"

"No, absolutely not."

"Thank you, Miss Winters. No further questions."

"Mr. Hudson, since Miss Winters has testified under hypnosis do you want to cross examine her under hypnosis?"

"No Your Honor, we've seen enough theatrics for one trial. We'd just like to cross-examine her in her conscious state."

"Very well, proceed."

Hudson slowly walked toward Sarah and stopped directly in front of her.

"Ms. Winters, are you feeling better today?"

"A little," Sarah said.

"Have you ever taken acting lessons?"

"Objection!" I yelled. "That is irrelevant and argumentative."

"Sustained, Mr. Hudson, please," Judge Brooks said.

"Okay, Miss Winters let's go to the night of December 3, 1981. Is it true you weren't feeling too well that evening?"

"That's right, I thought I had gotten food poisoning from the school cafeteria. It's not unusual you know."

"What time had you eaten?"

"About 5:30."

"So when did you first realize you were going to deliver?"

"I don't know, an hour or so after Michelle left."

"What made you realize it?"

"When I started feeling my insides move."

"When the baby started coming out?"

Sarah dropped her head. "Yes, then I knew I was about to deliver."

"How did you feel?"

"Huh?"

"How did you feel about being pregnant?"

"I was sick, I was in pain . . . I didn't have time to think."

"Come on, it doesn't take long to think. You must have had some thoughts."

"I couldn't think, I was in too much pain."

"Didn't you think about the father? Didn't you wonder who the father was?"

"Well-"

"Was it Richard Stein?"

"I think so."

"Were you worried the baby would be defective?"

"No, that never occurred to me."

"Were you worried about Greg's reaction when he found out you were having Ricky's baby?"

"No. No . . . I didn't have time to think about that."

"Did you think about killing your baby?"

"No. Absolutely not. I couldn't do that."

"Did you love Greg?"

"Yes, of course."

"Did you want to marry him?"

"Yes, he's a wonderful person."

"How did you think he would like raising a drug addict's baby?"

"Objection! Calls for speculation. Counsel is badgering the witness."

"Sustained."

"Do you recall delivering your baby?"

"Yes."

"What was its sex?"

"It was a girl."

"Was it breathing?"

"Yes."

"Did it cry?"

"Yes."

"Did you hold it in your arms?"

"Yes."

"Did you hug it?"

"Yes."

"Did you put a pillow over its face and smother it to death?!"

"Y-no!"

"How did it feel to see your baby die?"

"Objection! Counsel is badgering the witness again!"

"Sustained."

"Okay, how did your baby die?"

"I remember now, someone turned out the lights. It was a man's voice. He said it was the best thing for both of us. He grabbed my baby out of my arms. I screamed at him to give her back. He said he would take care of everything. No one would ever know I had delivered a child that night. Then he put her on the bed and picked up a pillow. I got up screaming at him. I ran over and fought with him. I was weak so he easily tossed me aside. He picked up a pillow. I pleaded for my baby's life, but he didn't listen."

Tears flowed from Sarah's eyes as the memory of the evening came flooding into her conscious mind. A dead silence overcame the courtroom. Margie Westcott squirmed uncomfortably in her chair.

"Then he put the pillow over her face. I got up and struggled with him again. He shoved me against the wall and I fell to the floor."

"What happened next?" Hudson asked.

"I don't remember anything else."

"You must of recognized who this alleged killer was?"

"No, it was dark."

"You didn't recognize the voice?"

"No, no I didn't."

"Come on Miss Winters, do you expect the jury to believe that? There wasn't a man, was there?"

"Yes there was!"

"You made the whole thing up, didn't you?"

"No, no there was a man."

He shook his head. "You are a pathetic excuse for a human being!"

"Objection! Argumentative," I screamed.

"No further questions."

I took Sarah briefly on redirect, but Hudson had drained her spirit. She seemed resigned to her defeat and I knew the jury would take that as a sign of guilt. After Sarah stepped down from the witness stand the judge ordered a ten minute recess. I looked at the door to the courtroom praying Snake would show up and give me some advice, but all I saw were reporters and cameramen waiting to record Sarah's fate.

My mouth was dry so I drank some water. Watching Sarah as I drank, I wondered if she was really innocent or had she been lying to me all along. If she were convicted, I might never know the answer to that question and that would haunt me for years to come. I prayed for a miracle, I prayed for the truth and I prayed that my feeling that Sarah was innocent was correct.

It was almost fifteen minutes before the judge returned. I looked at my watch and saw it was 10:45. I had no more witnesses except for Nate, who I had subpoenaed as Snake had instructed, and I could recall Richard. I had no idea how Nate could help, so I didn't plan to call him. The judge took the bench and quieted the crowd by banging his gavel.

"All right, Mr. Turner . . . call your next witness."

I looked toward the courtroom doors but saw nothing but people staring at me, wondering what my next move would be. Sarah looked at me and gave me a sympathetic smile. She looked as if she had resigned herself to a dismal fate. I took her hand and gave her a reassuring squeeze.

"Mr. Turner, call your next witness!"

"Yes, sir. I'd like to recall Richard Stein."

"Very well, bailiff, find Mr. Stein and send him in here."

The bailiff went out the front door and soon returned with Richard Stein. He walked slowly up to the witness chair staring at me as he moved.

"Mr. Stein. You've testified that you did not arrange an adoption for Miss Winters."

"That's right, you got it," Stein said.

"Well, that's kind of hard to believe Mr. Stein since you're so good at setting up adoptions."

Stein glared at me but didn't respond.

I continued, "How many children have you fathered in the last three years?"

Stein looked over at his attorney who was signaling to him.

I looked at Stein's attorney. "You know the state has not granted you immunity from perjury," he said.

Stein took out a piece of paper and began to read it. "I refuse to answer the question on the grounds it may tend to incriminate me as is my right under the Fifth Amendment to the Constitution of the United States and the State of Texas."

"You don't have to tell us Mr. Stein, I've got two witnesses outside ready to explain how you got them pregnant and then convinced them to give the baby up for adoption. . . . What I don't understand is why you killed the Winter's baby rather than just go through with the adoption?"

"Objection," Mr. Stein has an airtight alibi," Hudson said.

"I didn't kill anybody," Stein protested.

"Did you have someone do it for you?"

"No, I don't know who killed her. I assumed it was Sarah."

"Were you mad when you found out the baby was dead?"

Stein just stared at me obviously fuming. His attorney was signaling him to take the fifth again but he was wavering. He finally shook his head and said, "Okay, okay. Yes, as a matter of fact I did have a nice family lined up to take the baby. I couldn't believe it when I found out it was dead. What a waste."

"So you lied to the jury before?"

Richard shrugged. "Our plan for the baby was not relevant to this trial. We never talked about killing it."

"You never considered an abortion?" I asked.

"No, neither of us believed in abortions. An adoption was the only alternative," Stein said.

"How much were you getting paid for the Winter's baby, Mr. Stein?"

"Objection!" Hudson said. "Assumes facts not in evidence."

"Overruled," the judge said.

Stein's attorney began waiving at him furiously. He looked down at his paper. He took the Fifth Amendment.

I continued. "Isn't it true you were on the ASU campus for one purpose and one purpose only? In addition to selling drugs you preyed on young girls, getting them pregnant and then convincing them to put the babies up for adoption."

Stein took the fifth.

"How many babies have you sold in the past year? Two or three? A half dozen?"

Stein took the fifth again.

"What's a newborn baby going for these days? $10,000, $20,000."

Stein refused to answer.

"Do you know a ex-lawyer named Michael Simpson?"

Stein closed his eyes and then read his script one more

time.

"Your Honor," Hudson said. "I object to Mr. Turner testifying for Mr. Stein. He's misleading the jury. Obviously Mr. Stein is through testifying."

"Sustained. Mr. Turner, I think you've got all the mileage out of this witness you're going to get. Let's move on."

"No further questions then," I said.

"Cross, Mr. Hudson?" the judge said.

"No, Your Honor."

Alright, then please call your next witness," Mr. Turner."

I called Paula Walsh and questioned her about her relationship with Richard Stein. Hudson objected on relevancy grounds but the judge overruled the objection. She explained how Stein had got her pregnant and then insisted on giving the baby up for a private adoption. She told the bizarre story of how she went to the doctor's office blindfolded, was put under a general anesthetic and never allowed to see her child. Then I called Bonnie Waits.

"Objection, Your Honor," Hudson said. "This witness was not on the witness list."

"Your Honor," I said. "I just met Miss Waits for the first time this morning. I only learned about her last night."

"Objection overruled," the Judge said.

"How did you meet Richard Stein?" I asked.

"He used to hang around my dorm. I thought he was a student. He was kind of cute, so when he asked me out I was delighted."

"How long did you go out before you became intimate?"

"Not long. A couple weeks."

"Again, Your Honor, I must object to this line of questioning as being totally irrelevant to this lawsuit."

"Your Honor, if my client was a victim of an illegal baby-selling operation that certainly would have a bearing on her culpability," I said.

"Overruled, I want to hear this," the judge said.

I nodded. "Thank you, Your Honor. Did you spend a lot of time with Mr. Stein?"

"No, he said he was taking 18 hours and working part time to make ends meet. That didn't leave much time for dating."

"When did you find out you were pregnant?"

"When I was about four months along," Bonnie said.

"How did Richard take the news?"

"He was upset at first, he said there was no way he could support me and a baby. I suggested an abortion but he said it was against his religion. He couldn't be a party to it."

"What religion was he?"

"He said he was a Baptist."

"Did he ever go to church?"

"No, I don't think so."

"So what was his plan?"

"To give the baby up for adoption. He had a lawyer friend who he said could make all the arrangements."

"Did you meet the lawyer?"

"Yes, at Richard's place. He explained how the adoption would take place and the need for secrecy. I was to call a number at the first sign of going into labor."

"So did you?"

"Yes. It was late one Sunday night when my water broke. I knew labor would start soon so I called the number. It wasn't ten minutes before two men dressed like paramedics showed up."

"Where did they take you?" I asked.

"They put me in the back of a closed van that had two banks of seats for transporting passengers. I couldn't see where they were taking me. Before we got to our destination we got into a traffic accident. I was thrown to the ground. I screamed for help but nobody came for the longest time.

Finally the police arrived and rescued me. I was rushed to the hospital where, thank God, I had a normal childbirth"

"Did the police find the men who were driving the van?"

"No, they ran off immediately after the accident and were never apprehended."

"Did you see Richard after all this happened?"

"Yes, he came to the hospital immediately. He said not to tell anyone about the adoption. It was illegal and if anyone found out we'd both go to jail."

"Did the police question you?"

"Yes, but I told them I had hitched a ride to the hospital because I couldn't locate my boyfriend to take me. Since the baby and I were okay they didn't pursue the incident any further."

"When Richard told you the adoption was illegal what did you do?"

"I was pissed. I asked him how much he was going to get for my baby on the open market?"

"Did he tell you?"

"Yes, he said he could get $25,000. He offered me $10,000 to keep my mouth shut."

"Did you take it?"

Bonnie began to weep. "Yes, I was certain that if I didn't Richard would kill me. I didn't think I had a choice."

"So why did you come to me and tell me all this?" I asked.

"I couldn't live with myself. When I read about this trial I knew I couldn't be silent. I couldn't let Sarah be convicted when what happened to her was not her fault."

"Thank you, Bonnie, you did the right thing," I said. "No further questions."

"Mr. Hudson, cross?" the judge said.

"No, Your Honor, this testimony is totally irrelevant to this case. Mr. Stein has an alibi and this witness has no clue who picked her up in the van. It may be that Mr. Stein is involved in some kind of illegal activity but it has nothing to do with the facts of this case," Hudson said.

"Objection, Your Honor," I said. "I don't think the court has asked for closing arguments yet."

"Sustained. Do you have any more witnesses Mr. Turner?" the Judge asked.

"I don't have any more witnesses right this minute Your Honor."

"Then do you rest?"

"Ah. . . . well . . . I am expecting Mr. Hertel to be here momentarily to examine our last witness."

"Where is he?"

"I don't know, Your Honor. He should be here."

"Well, I'm sorry Mr. Turner, but unless you-"

The door to the courtroom suddenly swung open and Snake appeared with a his usual poker faced expression. A sudden wave of relief washed over me. All eyes turned toward Snake as he briskly walked to the defense table. Hudson's mouth fell open and Margie threw her legal pad down on the table and put her hands on her hips.

"Well, Mr. Hertel we're so glad you could make it," the Judge said. "Now, do you have another witness or are you prepared to rest?"

"Yes, Your Honor, we have one more witness."

"And who might that be?"

"The defense calls Nate Winters."

I sat down and fell back into my chair. The bailiff went out in the hall and returned with Nate at his side. Nate walked up to the witness stand and took a seat.

"Mr. Winters, do you swear to tell the truth, the whole truth and nothing but the truth?" the judge said.

"I do."

"Proceed Mr. Hertel."

"Please state your name for the court?"

"Nathan Alan Winters."

"And Mr. Winters, how are you related to the defendant?"

"She's my stepsister."

"How long has she been your stepsister?"

"About five years, she was thirteen and I was sixteen when our parents got married."

"What do you do for a living?"

"I'm a student at the University of Arizona."

"Are you on a scholarship?"

"Yes, a football scholarship."

"Do you come home very often during the year?"

"Well, usually just at Christmas and spring break, but this year I've come back quite a lot."

"Why is that?"

"Well, first Sarah got into this trouble and I came back to give her support. Then my Dad got arrested and I had to bail him out of jail."

"I understand you had to dip into your scholarship money to fund his bail, is that right?"

"Yeah, but it was no big deal, I've always considered him my real dad, you know. I haven't seen my natural father for years."

"Sarah tells me you are a model brother. She says you always are there when she needs you. Is that right?"

"Well, I try to be."

"You're a regular Boy Scout, aren't you?" Snake said.

"Excuse me?" Nate replied.

"What kind of a car do you drive?"

"At school I have a Chrysler Le Baron convertible."

"What about when you're home?"

"Well, I drive my Dad's pickup or Sarah lets me use her car."

"Do you have a friend who owns a Mustang?"

Nate didn't answer.

"It's a white Mustang isn't it?"

"Objection! Assumes facts not in evidence." Hudson said.

"Sustained."

"Do you have a friend who owns a white Mustang?"

"Yes."

"Who is this friend?"

"John Smith, he's my roommate at college."

"So if John is not home using his car then he lets you use it."

"That's right. That way the battery stays charged up."

"I see. When you came home to bail your father out of jail did you drive the white Mustang?"

"Yes, yes I did."

"Do you recall while you were home someone tried to run down Stan Turner with a white Mustang?"

The courtroom erupted in commotion. I sat up straight in my chair intrigued by this line of questioning. Sarah's face turned pale. The judge banged his gavel and demanded order.

"Please answer the question?" Snake said.

"Ah. Well I remember reading something about that."

"Were you driving that white Mustang?"

"No. Absolutely not."

"Where were you on March 9, 1982 at 8:27 a.m.?"

"I have no idea, that was a long time ago?"

"Have you noticed that I have not been in attendance during the last couple of days of this trial?"

"Yes, I have."

"Well, I bet you're curious where I've been."

"A little."

"Let me tell you. I've been running around all over the

country learning everything there is to know about you. Now, I have a forensic expert outside ready to walk through that door and testify that the tire marks left in the parking garage by the Mustang that nearly killed Stan Turner, belong to the Mustang you're driving. As a matter of fact, that Mustang is sitting out in the parking lot of this courthouse right now, isn't it?"

Nate slumped back in his seat and said nothing.

"Now I will ask you again, were you driving the Mustang that nearly killed Stan Turner?"

"Okay, I wanted to scare him."

"Why?"

"I thought by scaring him he might drop the case."

"Why would you want him to drop the case?"

"He was too expensive, Mom and Dad were fighting all the time. I just wanted them to stop fighting. Sarah didn't need such a high powered attorney. A public defender would have been fine."

"Of course. And when the assault with the Mustang didn't work you killed his dog."

"No, I didn't have anything to do with that."

"Come on Nate, the game is over. Nobody else had any motive to kill his dog. The assault with the Mustang hadn't worked so you decided to try something stronger, something Stan couldn't ignore."

"No, I wouldn't do that."

"You wouldn't? You were in town on the day Beauty died, weren't you?"

"I don't know, I might have been."

"How could you murder an innocent dog?" Snake asked.

"I didn't kill the dog!" Nate said.

"Did you know that it's very common for a criminal to go back to the scene of his crime?"

"Is it?"

"Yes, and one of things I did in the last few days was to show a picture of you and your Mustang to all of Stan's neighbors. It's funny but several of them saw you drive by Stan's house several times the day Beauty was poisoned. Do I need to bring one of those neighbors in to testify?"

"Okay, okay. . . . I didn't plan on killing the dog, I only wanted to make her sick so Mr. Turner would get the message and drop the case. I was worried that I had given the dog too much poison so I drove by a couple times hoping to see the dog alive or to hear her bark. I didn't mean to hurt the dog."

Nate hung his head and starred at the floor.

"One thing I'm curious about though. Why did you want to kill Stan?"

"I told you, I wasn't trying to kill him. I just wanted to scare him."

"And I suppose you didn't mean to kill Sarah's baby either?"

Several women in the courtroom cried out. Nate squirmed in his seat, cleared his throat and wiped the tears from his eyes.

"You were the father weren't you?"

The courtroom was deadly silent.

"Your Honor, would you direct the witness to answer the question?"

"Mr. Wilson, answer the question."

"No, everybody knows Richard Stein was the father."

"Come on Nate, you didn't try to run down Stan Turner and then kill his dog just because he was a high priced lawyer. You wanted Sarah to be convicted, didn't you? You thought if he withdrew she'd be forced to plea bargain and you'd be off the hook."

Nate became pale, closed his eyes and exhaled.

"No. . . . You've got it all wrong. I just wanted my mom

and stepfather to stop arguing. They were driving me crazy."

"You raped Sarah the night before you left for school last fall, didn't you, Nate?"

"What! No way. That's a lie."

"Isn't it true you bragged to your roommate you could get all the pussy you wanted right at home?"

"No, it's not true."

Nate put his hands over his face again trying desperately to maintain his composure.

"When I visited Mr. Smith in Arizona last night, he tried to protect you but he wasn't a good liar. After I threatened to subpoena him and put him under oath, he told me everything. Do I need to bring him in here to testify?"

"Okay. Okay. . . . So what if I *was* the father?"

"That night wasn't the first time you raped Sarah, was it? How many times have you had your way with her? Five . . . ten . . . twenty . . . how many times?"

"I don't know what the big deal is, this wasn't the first time I've got a girl pregnant. We're not actually related."

"No, not by blood?" I said.

"So what if I killed a baby, millions of babies are killed every year and nobody gives a rat's ass. Why is this any different?"

Snake shook his head and then turned and looked at Sarah and me. I had my arm around Sarah to console her as she was crying.

"Oh my God!" Sarah screamed as she turned very pale. I looked down at her.

"Do you remember now?" I asked.

She nodded slowly as a look of horror came over her face. "Yes, I remember the delivery now, both of them."

"Both of them?" I said incredulous. I sat up in my chair, my mouth opened looking at Sarah. "You had twins?"

"Oh God, Mr. Turner. I had twins!".

The gallery erupted into chaos. Sarah was crying hysterically and I put my arm around her to try to comfort her. Hudson stared at Sarah in disbelief. Cameras began flashing in disregard of the judge's orders. Judge Brooks picked up his gavel and began banging it, but no one paid any attention. Finally, he ordered the courtroom cleared and the Sheriff's deputies began removing the spectators one by one. When order had been restored, the judge addressed the parties.

"Do you have any further questions, Mr. Hertel?"

"Just a couple, Your Honor."

"Proceed."

"Did you see another child when you visited Sarah that night?"

"No, there was just one child lying on the bed. I don't know anything about a second child."

"Why did you kill Sarah's baby? Was it the humiliation you'd face if the truth came out or was it because you would have lost your chance to play in the NFL?"

"I busted my butt for fifteen years to make it to the NFL. Do you think I'd let anything stop me?"

"No, I guess not. Did Sarah have anything to do with the murder?"

"No, she tried to stop me but she was too weak to put up much of a fight and then she passed out."

"No further questions."

"Mr. Hudson, cross?"

"Yes, Your Honor, one question. Mr. Wilson, just to clear up a loose end, are you Doomsayer?"

"No."

"You didn't send any messages to Mr. Turner?"

"No."

"I see. No further questions," Hudson said.

When Hudson sat down Snake got up to address the Court. "The defense moves for a dismissal of all charges against Miss Winters."

"Mr. Hudson?"

"Your Honor, until we figure out what happened to the second child I must oppose the motion."

"I would tend to agree," the judge said. "I'm going to recess this case for a couple days to give both of you time to investigate the possibility that Sarah Winters had twins. I'm going to issue an order for the arrest of Nathan Winters for the murder he confessed to here today. I'm also ordering the detention of Richard Stein for questioning as to the allegations of the two young ladies who just testified. This has been a very disturbing day for me as I'm sure it has been for both of you. I think we all could use a break to contemplate what has happened here today and try to make some sense of it."

After the judge left, Richard Stein was escorted away by the bailiff and two policemen arrested Nathan Winters and took him to jail. Tom and Joyce followed Nate to the police station. Snake and I were alone with Sarah in the courtroom huddled around the counsel table. I took a deep breath and looked at her.

"Where's Greg?"

"I don't know. He got up and left during Nate's testimony."

"Oh," I said. "Well, he just probably went for some air."

Sarah shrugged.

"Anyway. Now that your memory has come back tell us what happened that night," I said.

Sarah shifted in her chair. "I remember now, after Michelle left, I realized I was in labor so I called the number that Richard had given me. The person who answered asked me who it was. I told him and he said lie down and relax and they'd be there in just a few minutes. The next thing I remember the doorbell was ringing. I looked down and there was a precious little baby on the bed. The pain I was feeling was horrible. Somehow I managed to go the door and let them in."

"Who did you let in?" I asked.

"Two men in white uniforms. They came in and straightened up the place. They took all the bloody towels and sheets and put them in a garbage bag. Then they wrapped the baby in a blanket and they were gone. I saw them throw the garbage bag in the dumpster as they were leaving."

"Did they say anything to you?" I said.

"Just that I should relax and get a good nights sleep. They had me drink something before they left."

"What was it?"

"I don't know but just as soon as they were gone I started getting horrible cramps again. It was terrible. I thought I was going to die. Then I realized I was delivering another baby."

"Oh Jesus," Greg said burying his face in his hands.

I shook my head and looked at Snake who was emotionless.

"Somehow I delivered the baby and put her on my bed. I don't know if it was just such a relief to get her out of me or the drugs the men had given me were beginning to affect me. Whatever it was caused my vision to blur and the room to spin.

"There was a voice, a familiar voice I'd come to dread. I'd hear it at night when I was at home asleep in my bed. 'Everything will be all right.' Then I'd feel Nate's cold clammy hands slide across my bosom. I let out a silent scream and then pretended I was comatose hoping he wouldn't want to screw a corpse. He didn't care. I was just a warm mindless body for practicing his mating ritual.

"By this time I was nearly unconscious. It was like I was in a cloud. He picked up the baby. He kept saying 'It will be alright. I'll take care of everything.' Then he picked up the pillow. I knew what he was going to do but I was so weak.

Somehow I struggled to my feet and ran over to him but he just pushed me hard against the wall. From the floor I saw him take the pillow and press it hard against the baby's face. I screamed and that's all I remember."

There was a moment of silence and then Snake said, "Well I guess there's just one piece of the puzzle missing. Where did the two men take your other baby."

"That could be difficult to figure out," I said.

"I'm not so sure," Snake said. "Do you remember the night of Sarah's baby was murdered there was another baby discovered. A baby burnt beyond recognition."

"Oh, shit. You don't think?" I said.

"Ah!" Sarah screamed "No, it can't be true. She has to be with a family by now. They both can't be dead."

I looked into Sarah's terror stricken eyes. For the first time I realized the incredible pain she was feeling.

"I hope so, Sarah," I said, "but we've got to check out all the possibilities."

"Find my baby, Mr. Turner. Please find my baby!"

"If she's alive, I'll find her, Sarah. I promise."

"You take Sarah home," Snake said. "I'll go visit the coroner."

"Okay, but you're wrong," I said turning to Snake.

"Wrong about what?" Snake asked.

"There are two pieces of the puzzle missing, not one. We still haven't identified Doomsayer."

"I wouldn't worry about him anymore, I am sure he's history," Snake said.

"He won't be history until I find out who he is and why he threatened me and my family. Until I find that out, I won't sleep."

Chapter Nineteen
The Devil's Den

To say I was depressed would be an understatement. When Snake finished with Nate I was sure it was all over. I was already starting to feel that incredible high that always follows a stunning courtroom victory. Then Sarah jolted everyone with the revelation of a second childbirth. Now we had to start all over again, almost from scratch to solve a even more perplexing murder. It wasn't a certainty that the burnt fetus, found the same night as the Winter's child, was her twin but it was too coincidental to disregard. We knew we must solve that murder to find the truth or to get closer to the truth about the fate of the Winter's twin.

The coroner wasn't thrilled about coming back to work after he'd just got home, but Snake was adamant he had to see everything on the child immediately. He was pacing at the front door of the morgue when the Coroner, Dr. Walter Herman, drove up.

"What was most shocking about this murder was the manner of death," Dr. Herman said. "The child was murdered and then incinerated."

"How was he killed?" Snake asked.

"A knife through the heart."

"Really?"

"My guess it was some kind of Satanic ritual. The child was probably a human sacrifice to Lucifer or some pagan god."

"I've seen that in the movies and read about it in the newspaper but I never suspected anything like that happened around here," Snake said.

Herman shook his head. "I wish it weren't true but how else do you explain something like this? Babies are almost always suffocated when they are murdered. It's the simplest and cleanest way to kill them. It doesn't make any sense to use a dagger."

"Have the police done anything about this?" Snake asked.

"Not really. No one reported a missing baby. There was nothing at the scene to indicate where the baby came from. They just blew it off."

"What about the sacrificial manner of death? Didn't anyone care that a Satanic cult was preying on innocent children?"

"They didn't want to cause a panic in the community. Without proof of what happened, they figured it was a puzzle that was better left unsolved."

Snake told Herman what happened at the Winters trial and then asked him, "Can you determine whether this is Sarah Winter's baby?"

"Maybe, we can compare blood and tissue samples from both children and, if they are twins, they should be identical."

"How long will it take to do that?" Snake asked.

"A couple days maybe."

He handed Herman his card. "Let us know just as soon as you make that determination," he said.

"I will."

*****

After dropping off Sarah at her apartment where she

had been staying the last few days of the trial, I got in my car and headed home. Exhausted both physically and mentally by the vicious emotional swings of the day, I began lamenting my career choice. Why in the hell I ever wanted to be an attorney. What I hated most was the constant fear and worry. I could never rest because there was always some pressing problem, some client who was depending on me to complete an impossible task or the lurking thought that I hadn't adequately prepared for one thing or another. Tonight, just when I thought I could go home and enjoy a peaceful evening with Rebekah and the kids, Sarah had dropped her bombshell.

Okay, I said to myself, calm down. I began to analyze the problem. How could I find Sarah's baby, assuming she's alive and had been given to an adoptive family. Richard Stein must know where she is. I needed to talk to him, but not today, I was exhausted. Then I realized the police would be interrogating him right at that moment. I pulled off the freeway and looped back toward Sherman. I headed to the sheriff's office where I knew they had taken him. I went inside and spotted Lt. Meadows.

"What are you doing here?" Meadows asked.

"I want to talk to Richard Stein."

"Well, I can't let you do that, . . . but I will let you watch us interrogate him."

I nodded. "Okay, I'd like that. Thanks."

"Listen," Lt. Winter's said. "I wanted to congratulate you and Snake. That was some performance today. I'm curious though, do you guys ever talk or do you work independently?"

I laughed. "We haven't talked much the last few days."

"I didn't think so. You were both running down completely opposite trails. I didn't think either one of you would find anything."

"We got lucky, I guess."

"I don't think luck had much to do with it."

"Thank you, Lieutenant. I appreciate the compliment coming from a fine detective like yourself."

"You know," Lt. Meadows said. "I envy you defense attorneys sometimes. You get to search for the good in people whereas I'm always forced to focus on their inherent evil nature."

"Well, I guess it takes both approaches to find the truth sometimes."

Lt. Meadows nodded. "Let's go see what Mr. Stein has to say."

"I'm ready," I said.

We walked down a corridor to a small observation station adjacent to the interrogation room. Lt. Meadows, myself and Margie Westcott watched as one of the homicide detectives interrogated Richard Stein with his attorney, Rocky Valentino, present.

"Mr. Stein, there's a lot I need to talk to you about but the most pressing issue right now is the whereabouts of the other Winter's baby. You heard Sarah Winter's state in court that two men came and picked up her child, right?"

"Yeah, I heard what she said," Stein said.

"Who were you selling the babies to?" the detective asked.

"I'm going to have to advise my client not to answer any question that might tend to incriminate him," Valentino said.

"Listen, we've got three woman just dying to testify against your client. That'll be plenty to put him behind bars for the rest of his life. But, if he cooperates and helps us shut down this baby-selling operation that would be significant. The judge would definitely take that into consideration at sentencing."

"What are you offering?" Valentino asked.

"Nothing but a statement to the Court that Mr. Stein was very cooperative and instrumental in shutting down this contemptible baby-selling operation. It can't hurt you and it's bound to cut your jail time."

Valentino and Stein conferred a moment and then Valentino responded to the proposal. "Alright, my client will accept your offer. What do you want to know?"

"Who have you been selling your babies to?"

"I don't know exactly who gets them, but I deal with an ex-attorney named Michael Simpson."

"Where can we find Mr. Simpson?" the detective asked.

"He doesn't have an office, you know. We always dealt by telephone or we'd meet at a mutually convenient public location."

"Do you know the men who picked up Sarah's baby?"

"Not personally, you know, but I know how we can find them," Stein said.

"How's that?"

"I've got their phone number."

"Will they talk to you?" the detective asked.

Stein smiled. "No, but if the right young lady says she's in labor they'll come a running, if you know what I mean."

It was about eight-thirty when Lt. Meadows and I pulled up across the street from a small duplex on the east side of Sherman not too far from the ASU campus. Margie Westcott had declined Lt. Meadow's invitation to come along claiming she had a pressing engagement. After a minute Richard Stein pulled up into the driveway, got out and walked to the front door. He knocked and a young lady opened the door and let him in. She looked as if she was due any day. Stein was wired so I could listen in to what was transpiring.

"Hi, Veronica. How do you feel?"

"Like a moose," she said. "I can't wait to shed all this extra weight. I get tired so easy and-"

"Listen, Veronica, honey. We've got a little problem. You know the adoption agency we signed up with, well it turns out they're not legit."

"What? How could that be?" Veronica said.

"The police contacted me and told me they weren't properly licensed. They want us to help shut them down."

"Oh, my God," Veronica said. "What do they want us to do?"

"You need to call them. Tell them you're in labor so they'll come to get you."

"But-"

"Just call them, the police will take care of everything else."

"What about the adoption?"

"The police have promised to arrange for a legal adoption. You have nothing to worry about."

"Are you sure?" Veronica said.

"Yes, just make the call."

Stein led Veronica over to the phone and handed it to her. She gave him a skeptical look and then dialed the number.

"Yeah," a man said.

"Hi, this is Veronica."

"Oh, hi. What's wrong?"

"I think it's time."

"What? You're not due for another month," the man said.

"I've got terrible contractions, it must be time."

"Are you sure, did your water break?"

"Yes, an hour ago."

"Oh, Jesus. We'll be right over."

Veronica handed Richard the phone. He took it from her and hung it up. She walked over to the sofa and sat down. Richard walked to the front window, pulled aside the shade and looked out. He took a deep breath.

"Isn't this the shits?" Richard said. "You trust people and

this is what happens to you."

Veronica didn't respond. The squealing of brakes could be heard in the driveway. Veronica got up and went to the front door. There was a knock so she opened it. Lt. Meadows started his car, shifted into drive and moved quickly in behind the van to block its exit. Two unmarked police cars pulled behind the duplex. One officer went to the back door while another came around the side. The two men turned, looked at Lt. Meadows and realized what was happening. They glanced at each other and then took off in opposite directions.

The shorter of the two men collided with the officer coming around the side of the house knocking his gun from his hand. He got up quickly and started running again. The officer behind the house suddenly appeared and said. "Freeze!"

The man stopped and put his hands in the air. Down the street Lt. Meadows finally tackled the taller man about a block from the duplex. He rolled him over, pulled the man's hands behind his back and cuffed him. Lt. Meadows got up and escorted the man back to his car.

It was nearly ten when I got back to the station. While I was waiting for the interrogation of the two drivers I called Rebekah.

"Where have you been?" Rebekah said.

"I'm sorry, honey. I'm at the police station. It's been an unbelievable day."

"On TV they said the court recessed at 3 p.m. What have you been doing? I've been so worried."

"I know, I should have called. I've been trying to track down Sarah's twin."

"Tonight?"

I explained what happened.

"Why don't you just let the police handle it?" Rebekah asked.

"I can't. The momentum has shifted our way. I've got to

push as hard as I can to find the truth."

"They said on TV you've proved Sarah innocent."

"Innocent of killing one of her babies but not both."

"Shit. Do you plan on coming home tonight?" Rebekah asked.

"I don't know. It depends on what we learn from the two drivers."

"Damn it! Stan. I'm worried about you. Please come home."

"I will pretty soon, tell the kids I'm okay."

After I hung up the phone I got a call from Snake. He said he was close to locating some of the satanic cult members. He gave me an address and said to meet him there.

As I approached the ASU campus I wondered who we were meeting. Snake, as usual, didn't tell me much about what he was thinking, just that we needed to talk to someone. I parked in the parking lot adjacent to the library and waited. Soon Snake came out of the library and motioned for me to follow him. I did as I was told and in less than ten minutes we were in front of a big white frame house in a middle class neighborhood. As we walked up to the front door Snake advised me were meeting a man named Martin Wolf.

He was a tall stout man in his mid-forties. I figured he was an ex-marine who probably saw time in Vietnam. Snake explained who we were and the man anxiously let us in.

"That was quite an amazing day in trial," Martin said.

"Yes, were you there?" Snake asked.

"You're damn right I was. I'm sorry to say I wanted your client to spend the rest of her life in jail. Anger has a way of clouding good judgment. So why did you come to see me?"

"Your organization, the Children of Despair. What are you an anti-abortion group?"

"No, abortion is only one of the threats against children that concern us. We also focus of infant murder, gang violence, child abuse, drugs, cults and anything else that threatens our children today."

"That's quite an agenda," Snake said. "Is picketing a common tactic of your organization?"

"Sometimes, where we want to draw public attention to an issue. We decided to use the Sarah Winters case because of the National Examiner witchcraft article. It wasn't that we believed any of the garbage in the article, it was just a great opportunity to focus the country's attention on the astounding number of infant murders in this county."

I nodded. "I see."

"Did you know in the Dallas Metroplex area there were eight known infant murders this year. The sad thing is the actual number is probably double or triple that. A lot of people get away with this particular crime because no one knows the child ever lived."

"That is pretty disturbing. Listen, the reason for my visit is to find out if you know anything about a satanic cult in this area. Do you remember the child that was found incinerated the same night Sarah Winters had her twins?"

"Yes, a sad night it was," Wolf said.

"Well, I just visited the coroner and he speculates that some kind of satanic cult may have used the baby as a sacrifice. The child was killed with a dagger before she was burned."

"A Black Mass."

"What?" Snake said.

"A Black Mass is a mockery of the catholic mass. The murder of an innocent child as the offering would be the ultimate insult to God."

"Do you know of that ever happening here?"

"There was a rumor of that a branch of the Church of Satan had been formed in this county last year. Malcolm Vector is the suspected leader of the group. They usually don't have to buy babies though, they normally have breeders."

"Breeders?" I said.

"Yes, some of the women in the cult do nothing but get pregnant so their babies can be sacrificed at birth."

"Oh my God," I said. "You can't be serious?"

"It's true. I swear to God it's true. That's one of many reason we formed the Children of Despair."

"Where can we find this Malcolm Vector?" Snake asked.

"He lives in a trailer park about 10 miles south of here on Highway 5."

"What does he look like?"

"He's in his late twenties, tall, dark hair and rides a motorcycle with the license number MAL 666."

I laughed. "Really, that'll make it easy."

"Thanks for your help," Snake said and then we left.

We decided it wasn't our place to be talking to Malcolm Vector so we went back to the police station to tell Meadows what we had found out. It was nearly 11:30 p.m. when we arrived. When Lt. Meadows saw us he invited us into the interrogation observation room to watch and listen to one of the drivers being interrogated. I was exhausted and wanted to go home. I knew Rebekah was worried about me and she would be pissed if I didn't get home soon. As much as I wanted to, I couldn't leave, something told me we were close to finding the truth and I wanted to be there when it was revealed.

"If you guys want to watch this you better get in here," Lt. Meadows said.

I looked at Snake and said, "Be right there."

We finished our discussion and then entered the observation room. A detective was in the process of interrogating the taller of the two drivers. After being arrested he had been identified as one Ivan Fielding. He was about six feet tall, muscular, blue eyes with dirty blond hair. The detective and the driver sat across from each other at a small table.

"So, you ever watch the news, Mr. Fielding?" the detective said.

"Sometimes," Ivan said.

"You been watching the Winter's murder trial?"

"Yeah, I saw some it."

"Sarah Winters, she was a client of yours wasn't she?"

The man stared at Detective Marsh but didn't respond.

"Listen, we talked at length with Veronica and Richard Stein. Plus we've got two other witnesses who can identify you as being part of this baby selling organization. You might as well cooperate. We've already got your ass nailed."

"I don't know nothing about it. I'm just a driver."

"I believe you. We're not after you. We're after whoever is the brains of this operation. Just tell us what you know and we'll ask the judge to go easy on you."

"I want it in writing and I want a member of the DA's staff to sign it," Ivan said.

"It's nearly midnight for christsakes. There's nobody around from the DA's office now. You can trust us."

"Ha!", Ivan said. "Do I look that stupid? What's the big rush anyway?"

"Okay, just tell us one thing and then we'll reconvene this session tomorrow with a rep' from the DA's offices present."

"What's that?"

"Where did you deliver Sarah Winter's baby after you picked her up that night?"

Ivan thought for a moment."That's easy. Back to the clinic."

"Where is the clinic?"

"You said one question?"

"I lied. Now where's the frickin' clinic!"

"Okay, it's in a little office warehouse building on the

south side of town."

"Who was there when you brought the Winter's baby in?"

"Michael and some woman."

"Michael Simpson?"

"Yes."

"Who was the woman?" Detective Marsh asked.

"His girlfriend, I think," Ivan replied.

"Did he take the baby?"

"Yes. He took two actually."

Detective Marsh frowned. "How many babies did you keep there?"

"We usually had five or six a week."

"Jesus!" Detective Marsh said. "Did he say where he was taking them."

"No."

"Do you have any idea where he was taking them?"

"No."

Detective Marsh gave Ivan a cold stare and abruptly got up and left the room. Lt. Meadows shook his head and looked at Snake and Stan. "What is happening to this country? I've lived in this community all my life and I would have never dreamed people were buying and selling children right under our noses."

"It's pretty sad," I said.

"I think I know where Michael Simpson went with at least one of the babies," Snake said.

Lt. Meadows looked at Snake. "Where?"

It was a little after midnight when Lt. Meadows, Detective Walsh and someone from the Sheriff's office arrived in front of Malcolm Vector's mobile home on the outskirts of town. It was dark but a full moon provided sufficient light to make out the silhouette of the big doublewide ahead of us. Meadows told us to stay in the car and watch, which didn't upset me in the least. He and the other officer went to the front door as Detective Walsh went around back. Lt. Meadows knocked on the door. A light came on and voices could be heard inside.

"This is Lt. Meadows of the Sherman Police Department. Please step outside a moment. I'd like to talk to Malcolm Vector."

The door opened and a tall blond man stepped out wearing a pair of jeans and a T-shirt. He scanned the area and then looked at Lt. Meadows.

"What do want? It's after midnight."

"Are you Mr. Vector?" Lt. Meadows asked.

"Yes, couldn't we do this during regular business hours?"

"I apologize for the late hour Mr. Vector but we're investigating some missing babies. Do you mind if we come inside and look around?"

"Do you have a warrant?"

"No."

"Then I mind," Malcolm said.

Lt. Meadows took a deep breath. "Is there anyone here with you tonight?"

"Just my girlfriend."

"Has she had a child recently?"

Malcolm hesitated. "No. It's just her and me."

"Have you ever heard of the Church of Satan?"

Malcolm frowned and shook his head from side to side.

"Listen, I don't have to take this crap. Come back during the day," Malcolm said and then turned to go back inside. Before he could shut the door the piercing cry of a baby could be heard from inside. Lt. Meadows pulled his gun and pointed it at the man.

"Step outside, sir!" he said.

Malcolm looked at Lt. Meadows and then jumped inside

and slammed the door shut. Meadows went to the door and turned the handle to try to get it opened. From inside Malcolm picked up a rifle, pointed it at the glass window of the front door and pulled the trigger. The bullet pierced the glass and hit Lt. Meadows in the shoulder. He fell to the ground grasping his gushing wound and reeling from the pain. Detective Walsh took a shot through the window but missed Malcolm as he had ducked down behind a sofa.

Snake got on the police radio and called for backup. I got out of the car and ran over to Lt. Meadows to see how badly he had been hurt. He was bleeding profusely so I applied pressure to the wound while I got him up to move him out of the line of fire. A shot rang out and I heard the bullet pass just to my left. We quickened the pace and took refuge behind a riding lawn mower. The Sheriff's deputy ran over and kneeled down next to me.

"Is he alright?"

"He's alive," I said. "Cover me while I get him back to the squad car."

I helped Lt. Meadows up again and we started back toward the car. Snake ran over to help. The sheriff's deputy opened fire on the mobile home. When we had made it to the car, he stopped shooting.

Inside I could see Malcolm was running around in panic. His Chevy pickup was parked about thirty yards from the door of the trailer. He looked out at the deputy sheriff who had been firing and then picked up a grenade. He pulled the pin then ran to the front door and threw it at him. The grenade exploded instantly killing the deputy and Detective Walsh. Malcolm grabbed his girlfriend's hand and they made a run for the truck. They got in, started the engine and took off kicking up a cloud of dirt and scattering gravel behind them.

I looked over at the slain lawmen, took a deep breath and grabbed Lt. Meadow's gun. I looked at Snake and said,

"Stay here with Meadows, I can't let that asshole get away." Before Snake could protest I ran to the Sheriff deputy's car and took off.

Malcolm headed out into the country down an old county road. It was paved but poorly maintained. I pressed the accelerator hard trying to catch up with him as he was already a half a mile ahead. As I sped along the bumpy road I wondered what in the hell I was doing. I hadn't fired a gun since I was a teenager. Even in the Marine Corps I hadn't made it far enough into training to fire a weapon. Malcolm was obviously a trained soldier and I realized I was no match for him. I looked down at the dashboard of the Sheriff's vehicle. I grabbed the radio microphone and held it to my mouth.

"Hello, this is Stan Turner. Is anybody there."

"Yes, I read you Mr. Turner. Who the hell are you?"

"I don't have time to explain. I'm chasing the man who just murdered one of your Sheriff's deputies and a Sherman police officer. I'm traveling south on FM 697. We just passed Choctaw Creek."

"Do you know who you are chasing?" the dispatcher asked.

"Malcolm Vector and his girlfriend. They're traveling in a blue late model Chevy pickup."

"Alright, we'll set up a road block at Ida. Just keep the suspect in sight. Don't try to apprehend him."

"You got it," I said focusing on the tail lights a hundred yards ahead of him.

Malcolm came to a fork in the road. First he went left staying on FM 687 but then suddenly he veered to the right. As I went through the intersection I saw why Malcolm had changed his course, the flashing lights of police cars could be seen in the distance on FM 687.

"Damn it!" I screamed. I couldn't believe they hadn't shut off their lights until Malcolm got close. Fatigue was starting to set in as I tried desperately to keep up with the Chevy. I got on the radio and advised the dispatcher of his new position. I watched the two taillights jumping up and down, twisting and turning as Malcolm navigated the narrow county road. Then Malcolm came to a place where the road descended down into a flood plain. When he hit the crest of the road he suddenly saw four police squad cars blocking both lanes of traffic. Upon hearing his approach they turned on their lights.

Malcolm hit his brakes and came to a screeching halt two hundred yards from the blockade. He looked at the blazing lights for a second and then made a quick u-turn. As I hit the crest I saw the Chevy coming straight at me. I swerved to the right to avoid him but we collided anyway. My car was knocked into a ditch and Malcolm's Chevy rolled three times and came to a stop upside down in the middle of the roadway. Smoke began pouring out from under the hood. I shook my head trying to clear my vision. I looked over at Malcolm's car and saw him wiggle out and run into the woods. I looked around for the gun. Seeing it on the floor I picked it up and tried to get out of the car. The door was stuck so I had to roll down the window and slide through it.

After I was back on my feet, I looked back at the police cars rapidly approaching and decided to let them chase Malcolm. Then I remembered Malcolm's girlfriend. Where was she? Suddenly Malcolm's truck caught on fire. I ran up as close to it as I dared to see if she was still inside. Her arm was dangling out the window. I knew unless I pulled her out she'd die when the truck exploded.

I ran over, opened the door and felt for a pulse. She was alive so I pushed her forward and then grabbed her from behind and pulled her out of the truck. Then I carried her into the drainage ditch where she'd be sheltered if the car exploded.

When I turned back toward the truck Malcolm was there

pointing his rifle at me. Instinctively I dropped to the ground. I felt the trail of a bullet fly over my head. Malcolm darted to the left to get a better shot but I rolled down into the ditch next to his girlfriend.

I checked my gun, took a deep breath and then waited for Malcolm to move. If he came at me I'd kill him. The police cars came to a stop a hundred yards away. Malcolm turned and started to run into the woods. I heard an officer yell, "Halt!" but Malcolm continued to run. There was gun fire and then silence. I dropped my gun and then the lights went out.

When I opened my eyes again Rebekah was sitting next to me reading a book. I looked around the hospital room trying to remember how I had gotten there. Rebekah smiled when she saw my eyes opened. She put down her book and came over and sat on the edge of my bed.

"How do you feel, honey?" she said.

"Groggy. What did they give me?"

"Pain medication. You were hurting pretty bad after your accident. The doctor says you dislocated your shoulder and cracked a few ribs, not to mention the concussion."

I closed my eyes and winced in pain. "I'm glad I didn't become a cop. Last night was not much fun."

"I bet. I've been so worried about you."

The door opened and Reggie and Mark walked in.

"Daddy, you're awake," Mark said. "Are you okay?"

"Yeah, I think I'll live."

"Dad, I can't believe you chased down that Devil worshiper. That is so cool," Reggie said.

I frowned as the memory of the previous night came rushing back to me. "How did you know he was a devil worshiper?" I asked.

"Dad, it's been on TV all day," he said.

"That's right," Rebekah said. "After you chased Vector down and saved his girlfriend, the police killed him. Then they went back to his place and found an old bomb shelter that had been built back in the sixties. He had converted it into a Satanic Church. Apparently they started out sacrificing animals and birds as part of their rituals and ceremonies but Malcolm wanted something better. He wanted human sacrifices. He recruited some girls to be breeders but they couldn't produce babies quick enough to suit him. That's where Michael Simpson came in."

"Was Simpson supplying Malcolm exclusively?"

"No, he would sell to the highest bidder," Rebekah said.

"Huh, so is Lt. Meadows okay?"

"Yes, he's down the hall. He's going to be fine."

"What about Walsh and the Deputy?"

Rebekah closed her eyes and took a deep breath. "They're dead."

I shook my head. "I figured. What about the baby?"

"The baby's fine," Rebekah said. "She's down in the nursery. We saw her a few minutes ago."

"Is it Sarah's baby?"

"No, it was a newborn."

"Oh, I never saw it actually," I said. "I can't believe Simpson was buying and selling children like they were cattle."

"I wish they'd of killed him too," Rebekah said."Someone like that deserves to die."

"He will, it'll just take ten or fifteen years and a couple million dollars of the taxpayer's money to get it accomplished."

"That is so ridiculous."

"I know," I said. "Did Snake say when the tests results will be back on the burnt baby?"

"They're supposed to be done this afternoon."

I nodded. "Good, Sarah needs to know one way or the other."

"Yeah, I guess you didn't hear."

"What?"

"Snake said Sarah told him if they found her baby she wanted to keep it."

"How does Greg feel about that?"

"He made it clear he wouldn't bring up someone else's child."

"Really, that's too bad. Sarah needs somebody."

"She'll have her baby."

"So this nightmare's almost over."

Rebekah smiled. "That's right and now we're taking a vacation."

I laughed. "You won't get any argument from me."

It was after four when Snake came by my room. Rebekah was sitting in a chair watching TV. I was reading a magazine Rebekah had brought me. He was carrying a manila file in one hand and some flowers in the other.

"Flowers?" I said.

Snake frowned. "They're not from me. The girls from the Majestic Mansion sent them. I promised I'd deliver them."

"What's the Majestic Mansion?" Rebekah asked.

"Oh," I said. "Ah. . . . It's a little restaurant that Harry enjoys a lot."

"Why are they sending *you* flowers?" she asked.

"I don't know. Ask Harry," I said.

"What?"

"Ask Harry. They're his friends."

Rebekah looked at Snake. He laughed. "Well, they really admire what Stan's been doing for Sarah and . . . they realize how difficult this trial has been on you so they sent these for you."

Rebekah's eyes lit up. "These are for me?"

"Yeah, you don't think a guy would appreciate flowers, do you?"

Rebekah took the flowers from Snake. "Oh, that is so nice. You'll have to take me to dinner there some night so I can thank them."

"Not anytime soon," I said grinning at Snake.

Rebekah frowned. "Why not?"

I shrugged. "We're going on vacation."

"Oh, right."

"So, did you get the report, Snake?" Rebekah asked.

"Yes, it's negative. The burnt baby was not Sarah's twin,"

"Oh, thank God," Rebekah said."Have you told Sarah?"

"Yes, I called her as soon as I knew."

"So, now what?" I said. "Have the police found Simpson?"

"No, apparently he left town when his name kept coming up at the trial."

"That figures," I said. "Now there's no way to find the adoptive parents."

"They have to get birth certificates, right?" Snake said.

"Yeah, that's right I wonder how they do that?"

"I don't know, but if we can figure it out that might be the way to find the adoptive parents."

I pondered the question a moment and then said, "I doubt they'd chance a formal legal proceeding. That'd be too risky."

"Right, I bet they just get a fake birth certificate, Snake said. "Rarely does anyone verify a birth certificate anyway."

"If I were paying twenty-five thousand dollars for a child, I'm not sure I'd be satisfied with a fake birth certificate. I wouldn't want to have to worry about someone finding out that there was no legitimate adoption."

"True, maybe he paid somebody at vital records to slip in a few bogus birth certificates."

"Maybe we should go talk to somebody over there. It couldn't hurt," I said.

"Hey, our client's off the hook. Our job is done. Let the

police find Sarah's baby," Snake said.

"Yeah, I guess you're right. Besides, I've promised Rebekah a vacation."

Rebekah gave me a disgusted look. "I know you, Stan. We'll be cruising the Caribbean and you'll be two thousand miles away wondering where Sarah's baby is. I'll give you a couple days to find her. That will give me time to plan the trip."

I smiled. "Did I ever tell you how much I love you?"

"You used to before you got too busy for me," Rebekah said.

I held out my hands and said,"Come here. I'm not too busy for you right now."

Snake started to back up toward the door. "Listen, I've got to run. I'll see you two love birds later."

Rebekah laughed."Bye, Harry."

Snake opened the door to leave as we began kissing passionately. He smiled, closed the door and left.

Chapter Twenty
Bitter Revenge

With the help of the Sherman Police Department I found the city employee who Simpson had paid off to manufacture fake birth certificates. It took several weeks to audit the records and identify the bogus certificates. The audit showed that seventy-two illegal adoptions had taken place. Since the birth certificates clearly identified the adoptive parents it wasn't long before Sarah was united with her baby. Rebekah and I had just returned from a cruise to the Caymen Islands when we were summoned to the baptism of Kristina Kay Winters.

The group assembled that night at St. Andrew's Catholic Church. Tom and Joyce weren't thrilled when Sarah announced her plans for the baptism of her baby as a Roman Catholic but, after everything she had been through, they decided not to make it an issue. At Sarah's request, Nate signed papers relinquishing all parental rights to Kristina. Sarah was determined to raise Kristina as a single mother. She didn't think she could ever get over the grief that Nate had caused her if he were a part of Kristina's life.

In one last attempt to get Greg to reconsider the termination of their relationship, Sarah sent him an invitation to the

Baptism. She hoped and prayed he would show up. As the ceremony began, however, he was not there. After the Baptism, Tom threw a small baptismal celebration at his country club. Everyone was in a great mood, eating, drinking and laughing. It was a great moment.

When I got home Rebekah advised me that Jodie had called with a message. It read: Please call Marleen Wiggins immediately. I figured she wanted to get together and talk settlement now that the trial was over. After pondering whether meeting with her was such a good idea, I finally decided it couldn't hurt and might be enlightening.

"Thank you for returning my call," she said. "I'd like to have lunch with you if you have the time."

"Okay, did you talk to your attorney about us meeting?"

"Yes, he said it would be okay if we met as long as we just talked and didn't make any commitments."

"Good, I think we ought to be able to straighten this whole thing out. There obviously has been some kind of misunderstanding."

"I hope you're right, Stan. Where shall we meet?"

"How about tomorrow, noon at Denny's on Preston and LBJ."

She agreed to the place and time. I noted it in my calendar and then sat down for dinner. Rebekah was putting mashed potatoes on the kids plate. The smell of homemade meat loaf was making me very hungry. I winked at Marcia on her booster chair and with the help of her left hand she winked back.

I laughed. "You been a good girl today, chickipoo?"

She nodded. "I got two smiley faces."

"Oh, wow! That's nice."

"I signed her up for co-ed soccer today at the Y," Rebekah said.

"Oh, good. Did you tell them I'd be happy to help out

with the team?"

"Yeah, they made you the coach."

"What? I didn't want to be coach. I don't have that kind of time."

"You'll make time. You did it for the boys so you've got to do it for your daughter. Besides it will be so much fun teaching 15 little five year olds how to play soccer."

"Fun? A nightmare is more like it."

"Can I play goalie, daddy?"

"Sure, why not?"

"She will not play goalie! I don't want all those kids kicking the ball at her. She might get hurt."

"She won't. She's tough. Aren't ya, chickipoo?"

"Uh huh," Marcia said.

"So, are you actually going to have lunch with Marleen?" Rebekah asked.

"Yes, tomorrow."

"What do you hope to accomplish by meeting her?"

"Well, for one thing I'll find out what horrible thing she thinks I did to her and Bobby. I'd also like to find out if she knew about Bobby and Joanna's affair. If she did, I'd like to find out what she did about it, if anything.

"Do you think she killed Bobby?"

"I don't know. That would be hard to believe, but I never in a million years expected her to call me up ranting and raving the way she did the other day. Who can predict what a jealous woman will do."

"True. Remember that the next time you meet with Joanna Winburn."

I looked and Rebekah and frowned. "Where did that come from?"

"Nowhere. But I know you went to see her the other day."

"Okay," I said curious how I'd been discovered. "How

did you know that?"

"Jodie's not a good liar. I knew she was covering for you. Why did you go see her? I assume it was business. I don't think Jodie would be an accomplice to your infidelity."

"I was looking to see if she had a motive for killing Bobby. I know its a terrible thought, but not so far-fetched. But how did you know it was Joanna I had gone to see?"

"If it had been anybody else you would have told me."

"Oh. . . . I guess you're right."

"Did she come on to you?"

"Shit! Rebekah. Give me a break. Nothing happened."

"I know. If you had been unfaithful I'd of known it. But I was just curious. It was obvious she wanted you. I could see it in her eyes. . . . The bitch! I'd like to- . . . You are not inviting her to our next party."

"Okay, okay, she's off the invitation list."

The next morning I called my legal counsel in the civil suit and advised him of the meeting with Marleen. Then I reviewed the file I had been keeping on the Bobby Wiggins civil suit and possible homicide. At 11:45 I got in my newly repaired Corvette and drove over to Dennys. Marleen was waiting for me when I arrived. The hostess took us to a booth and took our orders. After a little chit chat we got to the heart of the matter.

"So, what is it that you're so upset about?"

"Bobby and I have been your friends for God knows how many years. Why in earth would you unleash a whore like Joanna on us?"

"It was a business referral. I thought I was doing Bobby a favor. She needed a lot of accounting work done."

"But didn't you realize how dangerous that would be?"

"How would it be dangerous?"

"Didn't you worry that a woman like that might corrupt Bobby?"

"No, it never occurred to me. Bobby was so religious and your marriage was so strong I didn't think it would be a problem for him. I'm really sorry, Marleen. If I'd of known-"

"The little hussy lured him into an affair and made him think she loved him. From the first day they met I knew something was wrong. Bobby became very distant, he didn't have time for me anymore. He often worked late but when I called the office no one answered. When I asked him about it he said his secretary always answered the phone during the day so he never paid any attention to it at night. Just to see if such an explanation were true, I went to his office a few times after hours. His car was never there. The very last time I went I saw them together. She got in his car and they took off. I followed them to a motel."

The waitress brought our orders and set them on the table. Marleen asked for cream for her coffee. The waitress left to go get it. After putting some sugar in my tea and stirring it, I took a drink. She watched me intently, then she continued.

"It was the Howard Johnson down the road on Central in North Dallas. They registered and then got a room. I couldn't believe after 32 years he would do something so wretched. I blame you, Stan. How could you be so thoughtless?"

"I am so sorry. I swear I never dreamed something like that would happen."

"That's just it. You are such a pathetic human being you didn't even stop to consider what you were doing. I can't let you get away with such reckless conduct, Stan. You've got to be punished."

She was scaring me now. I didn't know how to respond to her. How did she plan to punish me. Fear suddenly gripped me. Did she have a gun. Was she about to shoot me right here at Dennys?

"Don't you think Bobby is the one at fault here. He didn't have to sleep with Joanna. I knew nothing about it."

"You'd have to be pretty stupid not to figure out what would happen."

"I beg to differ. I never slept with her."

"I bet you thought about it."

She had me there. I shook my head and decided I needed a minute to think about how to handle this situation.

"Excuse me a minute, I need to go to the restroom."

She smiled and nodded. I got up and left. What a bizarre situation. She was so bitter and nothing I had said so far had softened her feelings toward me. I wondered what I could do to convince her I wasn't the culprit here. She obviously needed some psychological counseling but I didn't think that suggestion would be well received. The thought occurred to me that perhaps I shouldn't return to the table. What kind of punishment did she have in mind for me? Finally I decided whatever it was she wasn't likely to do it here with so many people around.

"So, where were we," I asked.

She took a drink of her coffee and then said very slowly, "I'm sorry, Stan. Like I said you've got to pay for what you did."

She closed her eyes and began to sway back and forth. I frowned. What was wrong with her. She opened her eyes and smiled.

"It won't be so bad, not nearly as bad as it was for Bobby. . . . for Bobby and me."

"Are you alright?" I said. "Are you sick?"

She smiled. "No, I feel fine. . . . Are you ready, Stan?"

"Ready for what?"

"Your punishment."

"You lost me. . . . I'm sorry."

"It's okay," she said as she struggled to her feet. Suddenly her legs gave way and she started to fall. She caught herself on the table. I got up quickly and put my arm around her to support her. Several people noticed what was happening and rushed over to help.

With her audience now watching the drama unfolding in front of them, she started to cough and convulse. Then with the look of horror in her eyes she uttered her last words, "Oh my God! You've poisoned me!"

Chaos ensued. Several men attacked me and wrestled me to the floor. Marleen kept coughing and wheezing while several people tried to give her first aid. Then there were sirens in the distance, police cars and the ambulance. With my face pinned to the ground I couldn't see what was happening but I heard the paramedics say Marleen was dead.

Soon the police came, cuffed me and took me to the police station. They left me in a small dark room while they figured out what to do. I was in shock. Marleen had really done a number on me and I was scared. Finally the door opened and Detective Delocroix walked in.

"Congratulations on your verdict in the Winter's case. What a bizarre situation."

"Tell me about it."

"Now, what's this about poisoning that poor little old lady."

"It's bullshit. You think I'd do something that stupid. I'd have to be a lunatic to poison someone in a public place and then hang around to watch them die."

"How did you know she was dead?"

"I heard a paramedic say she didn't have a pulse."

"I'll admit, it doesn't seem logical, but why would she say you poisoned her if it weren't true?"

"She was trying to punish me. She blamed her husband's death on me. This was her way of getting revenge."

"This is the icy sidewalk case, right?"

"Right, but the icy sidewalk had nothing to do with Bobby Wiggins's death."

"Okay, you lost me."

"It's a long story."

"Well, I'm not in a hurry."

I told him the whole story. He shook his head and then left the room. My head was pounding, my body ached all over from the little wrestling match I'd had. I couldn't believe what was happening to me. Surely Detective Delacroix couldn't believe for a moment that I killed Marleen Wiggins. It's true I had a motive and I was there when she died, but it was clearly a setup. The door opened again and Detective Delocroix walked in with another officer.

"I'm afraid I've got bad news for you Stan."

"What?"

"The medical examiner has determined that Marlene Wiggins died of congestive heart failure as the result of an overdose of Percodin."

"Really," I said. "So how is that bad news for me."

"Well, in all the ruckus you left your coat at Dennys. One of my men brought it in. Guess what they found in your side pocket."

"What?"

"An empty bottle of percodin."

I stiffened up, "This is bullshit! The percodin is my pain medication. I had a broken rib recently. She must of taken it from my pocket when I went to the restroom. Don't you see, it was a suicide."

"It gets worse," Detective Delocroix said.

I put my hand over my face not wanting to face the next blow that Marleen was about to deliver from the grave.

"A couple weeks ago Mrs. Wiggins filed a complaint with the telephone company. She told them you had called her, were abusive and threatened to kill her. I've talked to her attorney and he confirms the story. He says she called him to complain about it."

"I give up. Jesus! This woman's a maniac. God, she

must of really hated me to go to all this trouble to ruin me. I can't believe it."

"So, you want to tell us why you did it?"

"Excuse me, you're buying this crap? I'm not saying another God damn word until I've talked to my lawyer. I need a phone. I need a phone, now!"

Detective Delocroix nodded to the other man and he grabbed my arm and escorted me to a telephone. I called Snake. He was incredulous that I was in jail and agreed to come down to the station immediately. After I hung up the officer took me to the jail where I was booked and taken to a holding cell. I was sick. The press was going to have an orgasm with this story. All my clients were going to read about it. My parents and Rebekah's parents were going to be humiliated when they saw the story. My children would be terrified by it. Because of the Sarah Winters trial, it would be national news. Shit, half the world would be reading about it by morning.

I felt like taking a gun and blowing my brains out rather than even contemplate my future. In five minutes Marleen Wiggins had managed to decimate my life. In my mind, it was all over. My only hope was Snake. He'd figure out some way to save me. When he showed up I explained what had happened.

"I'd like to tell you everything will be okay, but frankly I'm worried, Stan. It doesn't make sense that you would kill Marleen and I know you didn't do it, but she's done such a great job of framing you. It's going to be tough defending you."

"No joke. So, what are we going to do?"

"What we do in every criminal case. Work like hell to prove you're innocent."

"Yeah, and in the meantime my career is in the dumpster."

Snake shrugged. "I wish there was an easy solution, but

I'm afraid-"

The door to the visitor's room opened and Detective Delocroix entered holding a piece of beige stationery. He smiled and said, "Sorry to interrupt but I've got some good news for you. Marleen Wiggins left a suicide note. We found it in her desk at her home just a few minutes ago.

A sudden rush of relief overcame me. I said,"Oh, thank God. What did it say?"

"It said you're a son of a bitch for ruining her marriage and she'd see you in hell," Detective Delacroix said. "It also said you didn't kill her, so you're free to go."

"Really? Did she confess to killing Bobby?"

"Yes, but she said it was an accident. She just wanted him to break a few bones so he'd suffer for his betrayal. Then she was gonna sue you for all you were worth."

"Damn, she was one pissed off lady," Snake said.

"Yeah, and the plan would have probably worked had Wiggins not had a heart attack," Detective Delacroix noted.

"Lucky for me," I said once again feeling guilty about the whole Wiggins mess. As I drove home I thanked God for saving me one more time and prayed Marleen was wrong about seeing me in Hell.

Chapter Twenty-One
Snake Bit

Although Sarah was free and I had been cleared of any involvement in Marleen Wiggins' death, I was still bothered by the thought of Doomsayer lurking about. I couldn't stand knowing that someone out there hated me enough to threaten me and my family. I felt reasonably sure that, now that the trial was over, I'd hear nothing further from Doomsayer. But what if I was wrong? I knew I couldn't sleep until Doomsayer had been caught. I wondered how I could find him. The police had been trying for months, but with no success. Then I thought, perhaps Mo could help. The next day I dug Mo's file out of storage and found his home phone number. I dialed it and Mo's wife answered. She explained he was at work but that she would have him call me. I waited. Several minutes later the phone rang.

"Hi Stan, how have you been?"

"Fine. Hey. I wanted to thank you for all your help in solving the Sarah Winter's case."

"What help?"

"You know, the reports you sent me on some of my suspects."

"I'm afraid I don't know what you're talking about."

"Oh. . . . That's right. . . . It's a secret. . . . you can't talk about it."

"No, seriously Stan, there's some mistake here. I didn't give you any help. I mean, I would have had you asked, but you didn't."

"Oh. . . . Okay, I guess I was a little confused, the concussion and everything. I'm sorry I bothered you."

I hung up the phone puzzled by Mo's response. About that time Jodie walked in with some papers for me to sign.

"What's wrong? You don't look so good."

"Mo didn't send me a letter offering to help. The reports from him were bogus. What in the hell is going on? Someone has been manipulating me. Damn it!"

"Who would do something like that?"

"I don't know," I said.

"Who did you tell about Mo?" Jodie asked.

"Well, just you, Rebekah and Harry."

"I didn't send them, I promise you."

"And Rebekah obviously didn't."

"You don't think-?"

"Get Snake on the phone!"

"Right away."

Jodie left and, after a minute, announced over the intercom that Snake was on the line.

"Harry, you son of a bitch!"

"What? What are you so upset about?"

"I finally figured out who Doomsayer is."

"You're still worried about that? I told you to forget about Doomsayer. Doomsayer's history."

"You were Doomsayer, weren't you? You sleazy bastard!"

"Are you crazy? You must be smokin' dope."

"Don't lie to me. It had to have been you. Mo didn't do those reports, it was all just a charade, wasn't it?"

"Hey, I don't know what you're complaining about.

Doomsayer did you a lot of good. You're a celebrity now. Look at all the criminal defense business you're going to be getting. I bet you get ten calls this week."

"How could you do that? My family was terrorized."

"Hey, nobody got hurt. Doomsayer just got you a little press."

"Oh my God. You were behind the National Examiner article too, weren't you."

He laughed. "It is one of my favorite newspapers. They'll believe any garbage you feed them."

"I should report you to the State Bar."

"I wouldn't do that, Stan. They'd never believe you knew nothing about it."

"You little shit! I can't believe this, I can't believe I've been a pawn in your little game!"

"Everybody's a pawn in somebody's game," Snake replied.

"What made you even conceive of something like this?"

"Everyone hated our client and they hated us for defending her. I thought she was guilty. There was no way Sarah could win unless we developed a little sympathy. Doomsayer was perfect, it created not only the sympathy we needed but also some doubt as to whether she was actually guilty. All the publicity that was generated was a bonus that didn't hurt anybody."

"What about the National Examiner article. That didn't get us any sympathy."

"Nobody believed the article. It just made a very dull local story into an exciting national news event."

"Why did you let me try to pin Doomsayer on Margie Westcott?"

"I had to, you were digging too deep and I was afraid you'd figure out what I had done. When you said you thought Margie was Doomsayer it was a perfect way to divert your attention away from the truth."

I shook my head. "I can't believe you would do something so low."

He laughed. "I really don't know why you are so surprised, Stan. You should have expected it. After all, why in the hell do you think they call me *Snake*?"

Epilogue

Mrs. Stone leaned back in her chair and gave me a wry smile. "Okay, you dodged another cluster bomb. You're even a hero for godsakes. So tell me why are you here?"

"Well, there was one little matter yet to be dealt with."

"What was that?"

"My contempt hearing."

"Oh, right. Didn't Judge Brooks drop that considering how everything worked out?"

"Im afraid not. At my contempt hearing he wasn't the least bit forgiving. He said I showed disrespect for his court and contempt for the law. He explained that results don't always justify the means and if he let me get away with what I had done, the entire judicial process would be weakened.

"In retrospect I guess he was probably right although at the time I was angry. After all if the goal of our legal process is to find the truth and to render justice then why should I be punished for my success? What if I hadn't bent the rules and Sarah had ended up in prison for the rest of her life?"

"I agree. So how long is your sentence?"

"Thirty days."

"Well, it's not the exactly the Hilton but the Sheriff is sure going out of his way to make your stay feel like a vacation."

"Yeah, he testified for me at the contempt hearing. He was pretty upset when the judge sentenced me to jail. He said it was an outrage considering what I had done for his men."

"So, are you ready to go to your cell?"

"Yeah, now I'm kind of anxious to see it actually."

"Well, I've got my story so I guess I better go and let you settle in."

"Thanks for coming by," I said. "You definitely made my day."

Mrs. Stone smiled as she got up to leave. We embraced and then she left. The jailer walked in and motioned for me to follow him. He led me down a long corridor to a big metal door. He pushed a button and the door mechanism disengaged. The jailer pushed the door open and entered the cell block. Taking a deep breath I followed him inside.

Much to my shock the corridor to my cell was filled with Sheriff's deputies and police officers. As I entered they all began to scream and yell, they threw confetti, slapped me on the back and shook my hand. Someone handed me a glass of champagne and then I noticed Rebekah sitting in my cell in the Lazyboy. I laughed and shook my head, incredulous at the spectacle before me. The Sheriff then began to speak.

"Alright, settle down men. I have something to say. . . . Stan, it's unfortunate that you have to be a guest here with us these next thirty days. You know how I feel about the judge's decision. It was wrong and . . . well, anyway, since you're gonna be with us for awhile we thought the least we could do was make your stay as pleasant as possible."

"Thank you, Sheriff," I said. "I don't know what to say. This is all so overwhelming."

The Sheriff put his arm around me and replied, "You don't have to say a damn thing, Stan. You saved the life of one of our men and helped us catch a cop killer. Your acts speak for themselves. The Sheriff motioned to Rebekah. "Come here Rebekah. You must be proud of this boy."

Rebekah came over and we embraced. She smiled, looked into my eyes and said, "I am very proud."

The Sheriff raised his glass and said, "Here's to Stan Turner, may his courage be an inspiration to us all."

I laughed thinking back to how scared I was when bullets were flying around me back at the doublewide. Courage? Well, I wasn't so sure about that, more like reckless abandon. But I did know one thing as I sipped my champagne and mingled with my new found friends. The Sheriff sure knew how to make an inmate feel at home.

Other Stan Turner Mysteries

by William Manchee

Undaunted
A Stan Turner Mystery, Book I

Trade Paperback List Price $14.95 ISBN #0-9666366-0-0

As a youngster Stan Turner is determined to become an attorney. He is mysteriously forewarned that the path to his dream will be difficult and fraught with danger. At every turn Stan is confronted with seemingly insurmountable obstacles, yet he pushes forward, undaunted by the unknown forces that seek to derail him.

Forced into the U.S. Marines by a vicious twist of fate, he leaves his family and reports for duty. On his first day he unwittingly befriends a serial killer and soon finds himself charged with the murder of his drill sergeant.

Brash Endeavor
A Stan Turner Mystery, Book II

Trade Paperback, $12.95 ISBN #1-884570-89-5

Step into the shoes of Dallas attorney, Stan Turner as he begins the practice of law in Dallas in the late 70's. Broke but determined to start practice he begins with a two thousand dollars cash advance on his credit card. Then hang on for the ride of your life as Stan immediately steps into a rattlesnake's nest and has to do some fancy two-steppin' to avoid a lethal strike from his own clients.

When Stan's wife, Rebekah, is arrested for murder and a client turns out to be a ghost, Stan turns in his legal pad for a detective's notebook and goes to work to solve these most perplexing mysteries.

Sex, greed and a lust for power drive this most extraordinary novel to a stunning conclusion.

About the Author

William Manchee grew up during the 50's and 60's in the seacoast town of Ventura, California. At an early age he became interested in politics and was a congressional intern for his local congressman. He loved nature and the outdoors and traveled extensively in the western United States with his family.

At age fifteen he met his wife, the then Janet Mello. He was married in 1969 while at UCLA getting his undergraduate degree in political science. He and his wife both worked to support themselves and their four children, James, Jeffrey, Michael and Maryanna, while Manchee went to SMU Law School in Dallas in the early 70's. He received his Juris Doctor in 1975 and immediately started his own practice. Recently his son, James, and daughter, Maryanna, have joined the firm.

Manchee first began writing part time in 1995 after the last of his four children went off to college. With time on his hands, for the first time in twenty years, he began to look for something to do at night and on the weekends. Writing had always interested him and once he got serious about it, he was hooked. *Second Chair* is his fifth novel.